Tyler was gasping, coughing, his hands on the pavement.

"Come on," said Nick, letting Quinn go but taking her hand to drag her with him. Probably making sure she didn't lay into Tyler again.

"Don't be stupid," Tyler choked from behind them. "I only came here to talk."

"Sure you did." Nick dragged her up the steps to the front door, then jammed his key in the lock.

"What really happened at the carnival last week?" Tyler yelled. "I heard the news about pentagrams. Another Guide came here, didn't he?"

Nick ignored him and hauled her through the door, then slammed it, throwing the dead bolt for good measure.

Then he put his head against the door and unclenched his fists.

Quinn stared at him. Their breath still fogged in the air as if the heat in the house wasn't working. Gooseflesh had sprung up along her forearms, and she shivered. "You want to tell me what just happened there?"

"Yeah." Nick turned his head to look at her. "That's the rest of my secret."

Have you read all the Elemental books?

Elemental (novella)

Storm

Fearless (novella)

Spark

Breathless (novella)

Spirit

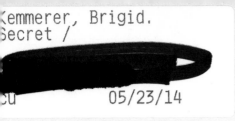

SECRET ✳ *The Elemental Series*

BRIGID KEMMERER

KENSINGTON PUBLISHING CORP.
www.kensingtonbooks.com

KTEEN BOOKS are published by

Kensington Publishing Corp.
119 West 40th Street
New York, NY 10018

ISBN-13: 978-0-7582-9437-1
ISBN-10: 0-7582-9437-9

First KTeen trade paperback printing: February 2014

10 9 8 7 6 5 4 3 2

Printed in the United States of America

First electronic edition: February 2014

ISBN-13: 978-0-7582-9438-8
ISBN-10: 0-7582-9438-7

For my mother,
who has always been there for me.

Always.

ACKNOWLEDGMENTS

If you've read my books for any length of time, you know I always thank my mother first. This time is no different. She's my constant inspiration. You wouldn't be holding this book in your hands if not for her support and influence in my life. Thank you, Mom, for everything.

My husband, Michael, is my sounding board, my confidant, and my best friend. I can't imagine spending a day without him. (Unfortunately, he spends many days without me, while I'm eating cake pops with the Starbucks baristas, *ahem* I mean, when I'm writing.) Thank you, honey, for always being there. And for suggesting Adam's name. And for supporting me even when you weren't sure about the topic of this book. It means so, so much. I hope you know that.

I have a close circle of critique partners. Bobbie Goettler and Alison Kemper Beard, you've been with me every step of the way, and I can't thank you enough for your guidance, support, and friendship. I seriously could not do this without you guys. Could. Not.

My fearless agent, Mandy Hubbard, is beyond compare. Thank you for your support in this book and in my career. And thanks for not minding when I fling the F word into our e-mail correspondence. My editor at Kensington, Alicia Condon, is amazing to work with, and she had no idea that Nick Merrick was interested in boys until I sent her *Breathless*, Nick's novella. It was a risk, and I'm lucky she and Mandy have supported me every step of the way.

Eternal gratitude to the wonderful people at Kensington books who work so hard to make my book a success, especially Vida Engstrand, Alex Nicolajsen, and Mel Saccone. Many, many thanks to the fine people at Allen & Unwin, my publisher in

Australia, especially Jodie Webster and Lara Wallace. I'm so lucky and excited to work with all of you.

This book took a lot of research, in many forms. I am deeply indebted to Danny Rome, Jason Deem, Jim Hilderbrandt, H. Duncan Moseley III, Tradd Sanderson, and Wes Parker for sharing their life experiences and helping me to build well-rounded characters. Many thanks to Jim Kalinosky of the Baltimore County Police Department for being a continued resource about the world of law enforcement. Huge thanks to the brilliant Jonah Kanner for teaching me more than I ever thought I wanted to know about air pressure and physics. Many thanks to Sebastian Serra of the Orlando Ballet as well as Dena Stoll for their insight into the world of dance. Finally, special thanks and big hugs to my sister-in-law, Tina Kasten, and her talented daughters, Jenna and Lexi, for letting me shadow them at dance competitions and workshops so I could get an insider's view. If I got anything wrong, it's entirely my fault.

If it takes a village to raise a child, it takes a community to write a book. Many, many people read early drafts or offered thoughts and insights or just kept me going while this book was in process. Extra special thanks to Jim Hilderbrandt, Sarah Gonder, Brenda Freeman, Joy Hensley George, Nicole Kalinosky, Becky Hutchinson, David James, Erin Kanner, Sarah Fine, and Nicole Choiniere-Kroeker. Additional thanks to Wendy Darling of The Midnight Garden and the many fine bloggers who participated in the Spirit Blog Tour in April. You guys are amazing.

This might sound ridiculous, but I owe many thanks to the fine people of Starbucks in Severna Park, Maryland. You put up with me for twelve-hour writing sprints, even though you have no idea who I am or what I'm doing there. Keep those cake pops coming.

Finally, the biggest thanks go to you guys, my readers. You all make this possible, and I can't tell you how much I appreciate it. Thank you. For everything. I'll try to sneak more pics of hot guys at Starbucks, 'kay?

PROLOGUE

Gareth Brody sat in a chipped plastic chair in the prison waiting room, listening for the guard to call his name. He drummed his fingers on his briefcase, casting a dark look at the guard booth every so often, playing the role of an impatient young attorney.

In truth, the cinder block walls and barred doorways left him feeling claustrophobic. The air felt stale, the lighting artificial and too bright. Outdoors, the prison yard was barely more than a lengthy stretch of concrete, broken only by steel poles supporting basketball nets, all enclosed by chain-link fencing and barbed wire.

Silver must be going *nuts* in here.

Gareth would remedy that soon enough.

A loud buzz echoed in the small room, and the barred door swung open. "Mr. Brody? Your client is available now."

Gareth followed the guard through the doorway, mentally calculating how quickly he could disable the man. Three seconds? Maybe four? This wasn't a high-security facility, and this officer barely looked capable of guarding a box of donuts.

Two hallways, four turns, and three locked doors brought them into a small chamber. Gareth memorized the path, remembering which doors required a slide from the guard's key, and which required a pin code on a pad mounted on the wall.

This would almost be too easy. Perhaps he could ask Officer Incompetent to leave the key on the table.

"Have a seat here," said the guard.

Gareth dropped into the plastic chair—which sported a cracked seat—and plopped his briefcase on the table. The locks snapped open with a loud *click*.

Usually, he did this without files. But today he had several.

He and Silver had things to discuss.

He pulled a pen out of the briefcase and spun it through his fingers. He could eviscerate two people in less than five minutes with nothing more than this pen. Idiots hadn't even checked his belongings. Typical. Flash a business card and a little hair gel, and they assume you're legit. He should have just walked in here with a gun.

It was a miracle they'd been able to keep Silver here this long, honestly.

But then the opposite door clicked open, and another guard led Gareth's *client* into the room.

The last time he'd seen Silver, the younger Guide had been in his late teens. Blond hair, too-dark-to-be-tan skin, slightly slanted eyes all topped off with a British accent and a talent for being ruthless. Silver had achieved control of the elements far younger than any other Guide—including Gareth himself.

Silver had no family, no attachments. He'd been given assignments early. Some had said he was too young, that he'd fail or crumble in the line of duty. That he'd abandon his task of killing pure Elementals.

Silver proved them all wrong. He'd killed without mercy, completing each mission without complaint or unnecessary mess.

He'd done well.

But now he was in an orange jumpsuit, wrists and ankles shackled to a chain that trailed from his waist. His right hand was mangled and scarred, but whatever injury had caused it had left enough wrist to keep him restrained. He was thin, too thin, and Gareth almost wished he'd thought to bring a sandwich.

If Silver was surprised to see Gareth, he didn't let it show. He dropped into the chair when the guard gave him a shove.

Gareth glanced up, realizing he needed to keep up appearances, at least for a little while longer. He half rose from his seat, smoothing his tie as he addressed the officers. "Thank you, gentlemen. We won't be too long."

One of the guards gave him a mocking courtly bow on his way out. "By all means, take your time, your highness." The other laughed.

Then the door slammed.

Silver's eyes lifted from the table. He cut a glance at the door and kept his voice down. "Gareth. It's been a long time. You're looking well."

"I wish I could say the same."

Silver glanced at his wrist, his eyes darkening. The chains jingled as he moved. "I let them get too close. It won't happen again." He paused. "I began to wonder whether they'd send someone."

"Of course." Gareth smiled. "We would never leave one of our own sitting in a cell."

"Do we have a plan?"

So very like Silver. Right down to business.

Gareth opened one of his file folders. "We have to keep up appearances, if only for a little while." He tapped his pen against the table. "I thought maybe we could review what you know of your last assignment."

Silver's eyes narrowed. "Why?"

"If I'm going to help you, I'd rather not go in blind."

Gareth watched the emotion in Silver's eyes: wounded pride warring with resignation over the fact that he was sitting here with barely more dignity than a caged animal. Proof of his failure.

Gareth waited. He would not rub salt in the wound, but he wouldn't coddle the man, either.

Silver gritted his teeth. "I know there are pure Elementals in town, enough to form a full circle. Proven dangers."

Gareth raised his eyebrows. "All proven?"

Silver nodded. "All." He paused. "We can proceed with eliminating them immediately."

"I think I'd still like to observe, to be certain."

Silver's expression tightened. He was insulted.

Gareth didn't care. He would not destroy children based on hearsay.

The Guides had few rules, but this one separated them from the Elementals who were driven by nothing but power.

Observe first. Then destroy.

Silver cleared his throat. "There are numerous young Elementals as well, though few have demonstrated the level of their power yet." He nodded at the papers in front of Gareth. "Show me what you have. I'll fill in your blanks."

Gareth slid a piece of paper off the top of the stack. "Michael Merrick?"

"Earth Elemental. Twenty-three. Runs a landscaping business out of his garage. The legal guardian of his younger brothers. He's known in the community, but there are reports of his involvement with a young girl's death years ago." He paused. "He's romantically involved with the daughter of the county fire marshal. A Hannah Faulkner. No Elemental connection that I could discern."

Gareth nodded and slid the paper to the side. A connection to law enforcement could be troublesome. "Christopher Merrick?"

"Water Elemental. Sixteen. A bit of a loner at school, from what I could see. I thought perhaps he was our weak link, but then I discovered he was romantically linked to a Becca Chandler."

Gareth looked up. "Chandler. As in *Bill* Chandler?"

"The very same. You should see her. She's a dead ringer for Bill. I think he's her father." Silver leaned forward. "I also think she's a rogue Fifth."

A rogue Fifth would be an Elemental who could control all the elements of Earth, Air, Fire, and Water—but who had never been trained to fulfill his or her duty. Silver and Gareth had been trained to destroy pure Elementals who only controlled one element. A rogue Fifth would not only be dangerous because of her ability to focus and intensify the powers of a pure Elemental, but because her connection to the human spirit would make her more willing to side with them.

Gareth tapped his pen again. "Bill never claimed to have any children. Have you spoken with him?"

"Bill Chandler hasn't checked in with anyone since August."

Gareth raised his eyebrows and made a note on the paper. "Interesting."

"What's more interesting is that this Becca Chandler is not the only rogue Fifth in town. I also identified a Hunter Garrity."

Gareth's eyebrows went way up. He wrote the name on the cover of his folder. "As in John Garrity? The Guide who died in the car wreck?"

"Indeed. And to complicate matters, young Master Garrity is living with the Merricks."

Gareth let out a low whistle. No wonder Silver had ended up in over his head. He went back to the original papers. "So I also have Gabriel and Nicholas Merrick."

"Identical twins. Seventeen years old. Fire and Air Elementals, respectively."

"So you're telling me that with Hunter Garrity living in the home, there's a perfect circle of Elemental power just outside of Annapolis."

"And there are more, younger children who may or may not develop into their full Elemental power."

For the first time, Gareth allowed an edge to enter his voice. "I'm more concerned with the immediate threat of a house full of pure Elementals."

Silver wasn't easily intimidated. He held Gareth's gaze. "I will not underestimate them again."

Gareth sighed. "We'll have to lure them apart. I don't like this law enforcement connection. Or the rogue Fifths. What about the twins? Any vulnerabilities there?"

"Gabriel is a noted danger. He was accused of the recent arson attacks in town, though later cleared. It's been widely reported that he assisted in rescuing numerous students from a fire in the school library." A pause. "If you read his file, there are notes that he caused the fire that destroyed his parents."

Gareth glanced up. "Interesting. Was he responsible for the recent fire at the school carnival?"

"No. That was caused by Calla Dean. I have very little information on her."

Gareth flipped through the papers, remembering the name. "She's listed as one of the missing students."

"She's dead."

Gareth stopped riffling through the pages and looked at him. "No body?"

"I shot her in the middle of the carnival. I had no way to remove her body." Silver must have seen the judgment in Gareth's expression, because he quickly added, "It was a clean shot."

"But she isn't listed among the dead."

Silver had nothing to say to that.

Gareth shifted back to the Merricks' file. "What else can you tell me about Gabriel?"

"He's involved with a girl, a Layne Forrest. He spends a great deal of time with her and her younger brother. Their father is a defense attorney—an influential member of the community."

Meaning they would need to be careful not to let these Forrest children be injured in any crossfire. The last thing anyone wanted was a lengthy investigation driven by a distraught parent. That was almost worse than the attachment to law enforcement.

"And Nicholas?"

"Some involvement with a girl named Quinn Briscoe. No Elemental connection I could detect."

Gareth studied the paper. Nicholas Merrick. *Hello, weak link.*

But an Air Elemental. That begged caution. An Air Elemental wouldn't have the flash and drama of the others. An Air's power was far more subtle—and far more subversive. At seventeen, this boy might not have the more nuanced abilities of sensing emotion or detecting an enemy from a great distance, but he'd surely feel any breath of power in the atmosphere.

This assignment would take patience.

Gareth pulled a few more pages from his stack. "And these young men?"

Silver glanced at them. "I know nothing more than you see there. Seth Ramsey isn't a pure Elemental—and he's on some kind of probation or house arrest due to an incident with Becca Chandler. He's a minor, so the records were sealed. Tyler Morgan isn't a pure Elemental, either. His sister died five years ago—and it's rumored that Michael Merrick had a hand in it."

"I know Tyler Morgan."

Silver's eyebrows went up.

Gareth shrugged. "His family was quite vocal about the Merricks at one point. I assume that hasn't changed?"

Silver shook his head. "I had no time to observe him."

"And the only Elemental to be destroyed so far was Kate Sullivan." Gareth glanced up. "Your trainee."

"Collateral damage. Kate lost sight of our goal here."

Gareth nodded. "It happens."

And it did. Not often, luckily, but their connection to humanity sometimes left them vulnerable to the weaknesses of others.

Silver had been doing this long enough to have lost any empathy for humans.

So had Gareth.

He gathered his papers and slipped them back into his briefcase. "Are you ready to get out of here?"

Silver nodded. "What is our plan?"

Gareth stood. "Close your eyes and take a deep breath. Make it look like you're having trouble breathing."

One thing Silver had always been good at—following orders. He pressed a panicked hand to his throat and sucked in a long rush of air.

Gareth's power latched on to that air, feeling it move into Silver's lungs, making them expand, exchanging oxygen for carbon dioxide.

Silver felt that power. His eyes snapped open.

"Again," Gareth said, keeping his voice even, reassuring. His power filled the air in the room. This was all part of his plan. "I'm going to call for help in a moment."

Another breath.

"One more," said Gareth. He moved toward the door. "Hold it. Pretend you can't breathe."

Silver inhaled, a breath full of Gareth's power. He held it.

Gareth gave the element a little *push*, quadrupling the pressure inside Silver's chest. He felt the other man's shock. His sudden fear. His pain.

But his death was silent. Air rushed out of his mouth, but it was too late.

Once his lungs burst, he couldn't make a sound. He collapsed forward onto the table.

"Forgive me," said Gareth. "A dirty trick, I know. Thank you for your years of service."

Silver was drooling on the table. He wasn't dead yet, but it wouldn't be long.

"What did you call Kate's death?" said Gareth. "Collateral damage?" He leaned close. "Funny. I call it failure."

CHAPTER 1

Nick Merrick set a wide piece of flagstone into the sand, shifting it back and forth to lock it in place. Despite the late October chill in the air, the sun beat down on his back, making him regret his long-sleeved black T-shirt. He pulled the red *Merrick Landscaping* cap off his head to wipe sweat away with his forearm. His hair was already damp, and he still had half a path to finish.

He yanked the hat back on and fed some power into the air, asking for a breeze.

The wind was overly happy to accommodate, sending a gust through the trees to scatter leaves and blow sand into the grass. Nick swore.

Quinn shivered and huddled down in her fleece pullover. "Frigging wind."

Nick glanced at her. She was sitting on the slate stone bench his older brother had installed yesterday. "Cold? Go sit in the truck."

"But I'm helping you."

Nick smiled. She hadn't left the bench since they'd gotten here. "Oh. Okay. I didn't realize you were *helping*."

"Not with the landscaping. I can barely pick those rocks up." She turned to lie flat on the bench, letting long blond hair fall almost to the grass. She stretched one leg up to the sky. Next she'd be pulling it back toward her chest and putting her ankle next to her ear. Crazy dancer. "I'm helping you keep up illusions."

Illusions. Nick lost the smile and flung another stone into place. "Are you sure you're not avoiding going home?"

"Okay, so maybe we're helping each other."

He made a noncommittal noise and reached for another stone.

"Seriously," said Quinn. "Your brother gave you crap for bringing me along, didn't he?"

"Not really." And Michael hadn't. If Gabriel or Chris had tried to drag a girl along on a job, Michael would have pitched a fit. But Nick was the dependable one. When he'd mentioned that Quinn was riding along, his older brother hadn't batted an eye.

Then again, Nick had told Michael a little about Quinn's epic fights with her mom, which seemed to have gotten worse since her family's home was destroyed in a fire. Maybe Michael was cutting her some slack, too.

"Huh," said Quinn. "Maybe I should accidentally leave panties in your room or something."

"You don't need to do that."

"You sound pissed."

Nick put another rock into place and rolled the tension from his shoulders. "I'm not. I'm just . . . you don't need to go over the top."

"Panties are over the top?"

He didn't even bother answering that.

"Come on," she said. "If you don't want your brothers to know you're into guys, a little lingerie left in your bedroom might be just the ticket."

Nick slammed another rock into the sand and didn't bother answering that, either.

Quinn was relentless. "Have you seen Adam since that night I caught you kissing?"

"No." At least not in reality. But Quinn's dance partner had occupied nearly every waking moment of Nick's thoughts. And a lot of the sleeping moments, too.

Adam was the first—the *only*—boy he'd ever kissed.

Nick's brothers had no idea. They still thought he was infatuated with Quinn. And Quinn was all too happy to keep up the "illusion," as she put it.

"Have you *talked* to him?" Quinn pressed.

"No." But he read over Adam's last text message about twenty times a day.

When you know what you want, I'll be right here.

Nick knew what he wanted, all right. He just wasn't sure he wanted to want it. His life was already complicated enough. He reached for another stone.

"He asked about you," said Quinn.

Nick dropped the stone on his fingers. He swore again and flexed them to ease the pain. "Yeah?"

"He asked how you were doing."

Nick didn't say anything, just rocked the stone into place.

"Hmm," said Quinn. "What *did* I tell him about you . . . ?"

Nick's heart tripped and stumbled along. He waited.

And waited.

Finally, he looked up. "There's a pool around back. Don't think I won't drop you in it."

Quinn smiled, but it was a little cautious, a little sad. "He asked if you'd be coming with me to the studio anytime soon."

She meant the dance studio at the Y, where he'd first met Adam. Nick enjoyed watching Quinn dance, and he loved the way music coursed through the air to seep into his skin. Then he'd seen Adam, and it was like a missing puzzle piece finally snapped into place.

He'd loved watching Adam dance, too.

Nick grabbed a hand roller and flattened the next expanse of sand. "I don't want to be a distraction."

"I think you *need* a little distraction."

"What does that mean?"

"It means you're completely stressed out." Quinn rolled off

the bench and walked behind him, putting her hands on his shoulders. She dug her thumbs into the muscles there. It almost hurt, but it felt good, too, so he didn't stop her.

"Quinn, it's fine. I have a lot on my mind."

Like the fact that he and his brothers were still marked for death for the Elemental abilities they struggled to control.

Or the fact that a bunch of younger Elementals had nearly destroyed the town a week ago.

Or maybe that the Guide who'd come to town to kill them all was sitting in a jail cell, and could be released at any time.

Not to mention the stack of college responses hidden in his desk at home. Or his family's struggling landscaping business, which was barely turning a profit now, to say nothing of getting through the winter.

Oh, and the fact that he was gay, and one of the only two people who *knew* was sitting right here ragging on him about it.

"Why don't you come to the studio tonight?" she said.

"I have a physics test tomorrow. I need to study."

"Please. Like you couldn't pass that in your sleep. And if you really needed to study, why aren't your brothers doing this job?"

Nick shook her hands off and reached for another stone. "Hannah was off tonight, and Mike needed a break. I offered."

"Of course you did." She paused. "And Gabriel? Chris?"

"Busy, and busy." His youngest brother, Chris, had plans with his girlfriend. And Gabriel, his twin, was trying to catch up on math so he could apply for firefighter school in the spring.

"Come on," said Quinn. "You know you want to."

He did want to. A lot.

A lot more than he wanted to admit.

Too complicated. He shook his head.

"Come *on*," said Quinn. "You could bring your textbook. Wear some glasses. He'd probably think it was sexy."

Nick told himself to stop imagining it.

Quinn grinned. "Nicholas Merrick. You are *blushing*."

"Seriously. Pool. Out back. Get ready to be all wet."

"If you don't come with me, I'm going to tell him to stop pining, because you're not interested."

"You are not going to tell him that."

"Yes. I am. In fact—" She pulled out her cell phone. "I'm going to tell him right now."

Her hands were flying across the keys. Nick was on his feet yanking it out of her hands before he even knew he was moving. She didn't fight him.

Then he looked down at what she'd typed. Not a message to Adam. A message to *him*.

You deserve a break, too, Nick.

He sighed. "I don't know."

Her voice gentled. "I know you still like him." She paused. "It's not a date. It's an hour in the studio."

An hour watching Adam dance. He'd almost come undone the first time. But eager butterflies were hanging streamers for a party in his stomach. "All right. I'll come with you."

"Yay!" She clapped.

"You seem overly enthusiastic. Like you said, it's an hour in the studio. Nothing might happen."

"Oh, it's not that." She smiled sweetly. "Really, I needed a ride."

Nick grabbed her and flung her over his shoulder. "That's it. Pool."

She laughed. "You're excited. Come on. Admit it."

He set her on her feet, but didn't let her go. Up close, he could look into the blue of her eyes. She was very pretty, with enough curves to draw attention. She whined about being fat all the time, but dance kept her body toned and muscled.

After catching him with Adam, she'd offered to continue playing the role of his girlfriend. It let him keep his secret from his brothers, but it also kept her from going out and meeting a guy who *would* care about what she had to offer.

This whole setup was so wrong. "I hate using you," he said.

"Do you want to have an epic breakup?"

"You deserve to date a guy who *likes* you."

"So do you."

Nick clamped his mouth shut and turned back to the path, slapping the next stone into place.

"We can stop if you want," said Quinn. "I'll go back to nightly screaming matches with my mother, you go back to screwing easy girls so you look like a total player."

"Quinn. I was not—"

"Maybe you weren't sleeping with them, but you were using them just the same." At his fierce look, she gave him one right back. "They might not have known the truth about you, but it doesn't make it any different."

"I wasn't using them."

"Yes. You were."

Yes. He was. Nick looked at the rock in his hands, then shoved it into line with the others.

"It's not going to go away, Nick!" cried Quinn. "If you don't want to pretend with me, that's fine. But it's not fair to pretend with anyone else, either."

She was right. It wasn't fair. None of it was fair.

"What are you thinking?" said Quinn. "That you'll break up with me and find some new skank who'll keep your cover more effectively?"

"Stop it."

"Fine. Go ahead. I'll go find my own ride." She stood and stormed toward the road.

Nick caught her before she could get too far. Quinn had a history of making poor decisions. Ending up unconscious on the beach with a few drunken bikers was only the most recent. She was lucky he'd found her before anything else could happen.

"Stop," he said. "Stop."

He expected to find her expression distraught, but instead she looked challenging. "Why are you stopping me?"

"Because you're my friend."

"You're mine, too." She reached up to give the brim of his hat a yank. "Have you ever thought about just . . . *telling* your brothers?"

He sighed and looked away. He thought about it all the time. Then he'd remember the thousand-and-one locker room gay jokes he'd heard from his twin. He'd remember Gabriel's swift and brutal judgment of anything new. Gabriel knew how to cut right to the quick, and this felt so fragile and untested that Nick was afraid to bare skin in the face of that blade.

Then there was Michael, overworked and overwrought, who'd said last week that he couldn't handle one more complication in their lives. Nick did the bookkeeping for their landscaping business—they could practically reach out and touch their bottom line.

That left Chris, brooding and distant, who might be okay with it—or he might not.

They couldn't afford discord right now.

"Things at home—they're complicated . . ." he started. Then he caught her eyes. His *things at home* had nothing on hers. "I don't want to rock the boat," he finally said.

"What about Hunter?" she said. "Are you guys still sharing a room?"

"Yeah, until we figure out a new sleeping arrangement. And seriously, you think I should start with my *roommate*, who, gee, happens to be my twin brother's best friend? You're right, Quinn. That's a *great* idea." He left her and went back to the path. At least slinging flagstone gave him a way to work off frustration.

Quinn came back to the bench and resumed stretching. "Is that weird for you? Sharing a room with a guy?"

"I shared a room with Gabriel for the first twelve years of my life."

"That's not what I mean, and you know it."

Nick rolled more sand flat. "No," he said, his tone resigned. "It's not weird. At least not for me."

"You think it would be for him?"

Nick had no idea. He didn't say anything.

"Tell me," said Quinn. "Does he have tattoos and piercings all over his body, or what? Though I can't decide whether that would be hot or disgusting—"

Nick threw a handful of sand at her.

But really, he had no answer. He was so well practiced in the art of *Do Not Look at Other Guys* that he kept his head in a book anytime Hunter was even in the room.

And Hunter totally wasn't his type anyway.

"I'll stop pushing," said Quinn.

"Thank you."

"But you're definitely coming tonight."

He sighed.

"Oh, you can't back out now. I already texted Adam that you'll be there."

His head swung around. "You *what*?"

"He's looking forward to it. See?" She held up her phone.

A smiley face.

A *smiley* face? Nick had no idea what that meant. Was that casual happy? Excited happy? An obligatory response that didn't mean anything? It wasn't even a D smiley. It was one of the parenthesis ones.

God, he was trying to puzzle out the hidden meaning of the punctuation in a frigging *emoticon*.

"You look nervous," said Quinn.

He shrugged.

She got down on her knees next to him in the grass. "Don't be nervous," she said quietly. "He really likes you, Nick."

Nick knew that.

And that was the problem. He really liked him back.

Quinn thought Nick Merrick was the best boyfriend in the world.

He'd been pretty sweet before she found out he was gay, but now . . . now she knew he liked her for *her*, when all the other guys she'd ever dated took every opportunity to get into her pants.

It seemed fitting that the best relationship in her life would be just as dysfunctional as all her other ones. Her alcoholic mother. Her more-absent-than-not father. Her stoner older brother and her video game–obsessed younger brother. The cheerleaders who hated her, the dance team that didn't want her—if a gay boyfriend was the best she could do, she'd take it.

He worried he was using her—well, she worried she was using *him*. Hanging out with Nick gave her an opportunity to avoid her own family. And Becca, too, if you got right down to it.

Quinn didn't resent losing her best friend to Chris Merrick. Much.

"You're quiet," said Nick.

Quinn glanced over. He was driving the landscaping truck with one hand on the wheel, the other arm across the seat backs.

For one second, she regretted the whole gay thing and wished she could curl up against him, let his arm wrap around her shoulder and make her feel wanted.

Then she told that moment of longing to shove it.

"I was thinking about Becca," she said.

"She and Chris seem to be getting pretty serious." He seemed amused.

She snorted. "Like a heart attack."

He was silent for a moment. "You guys aren't hanging out much lately?"

Nick could always see right through her. Quinn shrugged. "It's fine. I'm glad she's happy."

"And you sound so sincere about it."

Quinn hit him on the arm. "No. I am. I just . . . miss her, you know? And I'm . . ."

Jealous. She was jealous.

But she couldn't say that.

"It's fine," she said. "I shouldn't have brought up Becca. She's just spending all this time with Chris, and I get it, but she doesn't talk to me anymore. I don't think she's hiding something, but it's almost like she's got this new life that I'm not a part of. If that makes any sense."

Nick sighed. "Yeah, Quinn, it actually makes a lot of sense." He hit the turn signal for their street. "Did you tell Becca about me?"

"Of course not! God, what kind of friend do you think I am?"

He held up a hand. "I'm just saying—maybe you both have secrets."

"Maybe."

He dropped his arm to give her half a hug—totally platonic,

and nothing she really wanted. But she took the comfort all the same.

"You're a *good* friend," he said. "That's the kind I think you are."

Quinn straightened and studied him. Nick really was a looker—all dark hair and blue eyes and broad shoulders. Muscled arms from all the landscaping. Just enough freckles sprinkled across those high cheekbones to make him look boyish and charming.

Then again, his twin brother had those same freckles, and there was nothing boyish and charming about *him*.

"Actually," Nick said slowly, "it's probably time I should tell you another secret—" He broke off, his voice hardening to steel. "*Damn it.*"

Quinn followed his gaze. They were turning up his driveway, and a blond guy was making his way down the walk from their house. The guy looked pissed.

"Who's that?" she said.

"Tyler Morgan. He's an asshole." Nick threw the truck into park and hesitated there, glaring at the guy as he walked toward them.

Tyler's expression was full of fury. He said something, but Quinn couldn't hear him over the diesel engine with the windows closed.

Then Nick killed the engine just as Tyler turned his gaze on Quinn.

"—with your stupid, white trash girlfriend," he finished.

Quinn froze. Oh no, he did not.

"Wait here," said Nick.

No way was she *waiting here*. Quinn threw herself out of the truck. This Tyler guy was a lot bigger than he'd looked when she was sitting in the cab of the pickup, but he could be fifty feet tall and she wouldn't give a crap.

"What did you just call me?" she demanded.

Nick appeared at her side. "Quinn, go in the house."

Tyler sneered down at her—a shame, because he might be

kind of attractive if he weren't trying so hard to look like a prick. "You heard me. I called you a *stupid*—"

Quinn punched him.

She shocked the hell out of him, too. He was probably one of those jerks who thought girls roamed the earth for nothing more than his pleasure. But she'd been holding her own for years, and the punch knocked him back. She knew how to swing, and she sure as hell wasn't holding back with this tool.

"At least trashy girls know how to hit." She drew back a fist to hit him again.

Nick got hold of her. "Jesus, Quinn. Stop it."

"That's right," said Tyler, his voice a little nasal. "I forgot you Merrick douche bags like to let your girls fight for you."

"Get the hell out of here," said Nick. He had a death grip on her arms, his hands full of tension. The air was suddenly ice cold.

"Let me go," she said. "I want to make sure he can't pass on his genes."

"No worries, blondie. Seeing you is enough to turn me off forever."

"Right back atcha, dickhead," Quinn snapped.

Then Tyler stepped toward her, drawing back a fist. She sucked back into Nick.

But Tyler stopped there. He smirked. "Yeah, all you girls think you're so tough, but then you can't take—"

His words cut short like he ran out of breath. No puffs of steam escaped from his mouth, though hers and Nick's were going a mile a minute. Tyler shook his head fiercely, and then put a hand to his throat.

His eyes started to bug out, and he dropped to a knee.

Had he inhaled a fly? Was he choking? What was happening?

"Get out of here, Tyler." Nick's voice was quiet, low and full of intensity. "No deal, nothing to stop me. Understand?"

Quinn had no idea what that meant, but Tyler was on his knees, suffocating on nothing. Nick's hands were gripping her arms so tightly she could feel faint tremors, belying the strength in his voice.

Was Nick *afraid* of this guy?

She kicked Tyler. "Yeah, asshole. Get out of here."

He nodded hard, his hand pulling at his throat now.

And then he was gasping, coughing, his hands on the pavement.

"Come on," said Nick, letting her go but taking her hand to drag her with him. Probably making sure she didn't lay into Tyler again.

"Don't be stupid," Tyler choked from behind them. "I only came here to talk."

"Sure you did." Nick dragged her up the steps to the front door, then jammed his key in the lock.

"What really happened at the carnival last week?" Tyler yelled. "I heard the news about pentagrams. Another Guide came here, didn't he?"

Nick ignored him and hauled her through the door, then slammed it, throwing the deadbolt for good measure.

Then he put his head against the door and unclenched his fists.

Quinn stared at him. Their breath still fogged in the air as if the heat in the house wasn't working. Gooseflesh had sprung up along her forearms, and she shivered. "You want to tell me what just happened there?"

"Yeah." Nick turned his head to look at her. "That's the rest of my secret."

CHAPTER 2

Quinn sat backward on Nick's desk chair and watched him fidget. He was sitting on the end of his bed, twisting his ball cap between his hands. A sudden noise would probably send him sky high.

No one else saw this side of Nicholas Merrick. She'd always thought he had his life perfectly in order, with a college plan and a handle on everything. When they'd first started dating, she'd thought she'd finally found the perfect boy to latch on to.

Then she'd caught him kissing Adam, and there went that.

"I'm still waiting for your secret," she whispered mockingly.

His eyes flicked up to meet hers. "I know." He paused, running a hand through his hair. "I've never told anyone, and I'm not sure where to start."

"Wait. Don't tell me. You're gay."

He flung the hat at her. Quinn uncurled it and pulled it on her head backward. "Why don't you tell me about the idiot in your driveway. His name is Tyler?"

"Tyler Morgan." He hesitated. "His parents hated my parents. So much that Tyler grew up hating us. He used to go to school with Michael, but he's a few years younger." Another pause. "Tyler used to have a sister named Emily. She was in Michael's class. She died in the old rock quarry south of Severna Park. There was a rock slide and she drowned."

"When?"

"Five years ago. I don't know a lot of the details, but Tyler thinks Michael had something to do with it."

Quinn sat up straight. "Holy shit. Like . . . how? Like he built a bomb or something?"

Nick shook his head quickly. "No—nothing like that. Michael has . . . he has . . . we have this affinity for the—" He cut himself off and rolled his eyes. "Jesus, this is impossible. Everything sounds ridiculous, and I want you to *believe* me."

She studied him, trying to puzzle this out for herself.

She was coming up with nothing.

Abruptly Nick stood and seized her by the hand. "Come on. We need to go outside. This will work better with show-and-tell."

He trudged through the woods, dragging her behind him. She could feel the tension in his grip. Whatever his *secret* was, it had him keyed up. The sun had already begun to dip behind the horizon, letting a chill seep into the air.

"Keep walking," he said. "I need some distance from the neighborhood."

"Your secret is in the woods?" said Quinn, shivering. "Dude, if you turn into a werewolf, I am *outta here*."

He smiled, then stopped and turned to face her. "I'm not a werewolf."

"Vampire? Alien?" She snapped her fingers. "Harry Potter. Or wait, you'd be one of the Weasley twins . . ."

"If you could shut up a second, I'd tell you."

"Should I hold your hands? Are we going to phase out and appear in Narnia?"

"No." He glanced around. "If any trees fall, I don't want them to hit a house."

Trees falling? What? "So you're secretly Paul Bunyan?"

"Quinn."

She shivered again. "What? Seriously, Nick, what's out here?"

"Air." As he said the word, the breeze kicked up, finding a

true wind that ruffled his hair and swirled between them. Leaves shifted and rustled along the ground.

Quinn frowned. "Air?"

Nick nodded. His expression said that she was missing something important.

But . . . air? Air was *everywhere*.

Leaves lifted from the ground and began to spiral around their feet. She started to shiver again—but then the leaves swirled off the ground, forming a moving wall to enclose them. First two feet high, then three, then eye level.

Quinn felt the first lick of fear. She moved closer to him—then wondered if that was worse than moving away. "You're freaking me out a little, Nick. Is the mother ship landing?"

"Relax." He spoke gently, confidently. "It's just wind."

She stepped away from him, but not too far. The swirling leaves remained out of her reach, and the wind caught her blond hair and tossed it across her face. "Are you doing this?"

"Yes."

"How?"

"I'm feeding it energy."

She looked at him again. "I don't understand."

"I can control air. Wind. Atmosphere. Whatever you want to call it." He paused. "That's how I choked Tyler."

Quinn put a hand out. Leaves caught against her palm immediately, crumbling before getting swept into the maelstrom again. It wasn't enough to disturb this mini-tornado. A bare path appeared on the ground where the wind continued to whip in a circle.

"You're telling me you're doing this all by yourself?" said Quinn. "No machine? No—"

"All me," he said. "But the wind is willing."

She turned to look at him again. "Okay. Make it stop."

He didn't move, but she felt the change. The wind in the clearing died. Leaves spun wildly and fluttered to the ground.

Quinn jammed her hands in her pockets and stood a few feet back from him. Her brain couldn't wrap itself around this quickly enough. She wasn't sure she wanted to believe him yet. This was a little too . . . weird. "So . . . what? Your brother blew that girl off a cliff?"

Nick's eyes widened. "What? No. He's not—Michael's not an Air. He's an Earth."

Quinn licked her lips. "Do I need a twenty-sided die here, Nick?"

"Would you stop making jokes? I'm trying to explain this to you, and you're—"

"Freaked out." She took another step back from him, looking at the leaves that had fluttered to the ground. Nothing abnormal, no sign of any device that could have done . . . that.

Nick studied her. "Do you have your iPod?"

That was like asking if she'd brought her boobs along. Quinn fished it out of her pocket and held it out.

Nick shook his head. "You listen. Dance. Do that one you were doing the night I picked you up at the Y."

When the hell had Nick Merrick gone insane? "You want me to *dance* right now?"

He nodded, looking perfectly serious.

"But you won't hear the music."

"I want to show you something."

Quinn hesitated, figured she had nothing to lose, and plugged the buds into her ears. She had to close her eyes to shut out Nick's searching face, but once the music caught her, he could have *been* an alien and she wouldn't have cared.

She didn't remember all the details of this routine, but Nick wouldn't know the difference, and she was good at improvisation. Her weeks of studying with Adam had made her stronger, more balanced, and she could feel the difference even in something unpracticed. Her legs carried her through spins and leaps more effortlessly. She spun and dropped and flung her body into the rhythm, every movement punctuated perfectly.

Then she felt it. The air changed, as if the music could suddenly seep into her skin. Her movements had more energy, more control, and each time her feet left the ground, she felt vaguely like a marionette, suspended for just a fraction of a second too long—but *effortlessly*.

The dance changed against her will, turning from something she was doing with the music into something she was doing *because of* the music, as if the very song animated her body. Her next leap left her in the air for a moment too long. She almost lost the beat, and spun to find it. One foot, pivot, step, *leap*.

This time her height, her suspension in the air, was downright inhuman.

She stumbled on the landing, from shock more than anything. Nick caught her, his hands warm and steadying on her elbows. Quinn braced her hands on his chest, unsure whether she should shove him away or not. Her breaths came quick.

Frightened. She was frightened. She'd *felt* his power in the air. Exactly how high had she gotten?

She yanked the earbuds free. "Did you do that?" she demanded.

His expression was guarded, but he nodded. "Yes."

She didn't say anything for the longest moment, letting her breathing settle.

She could still hear the song, tinny and distant from the headphones. Music was in the air, drawing at her limbs. Not frightening. Exhilarating.

Quinn grinned. "Can you do it again?"

An hour later, Quinn was sprawled on his bed, watching Nick rifle through a dresser drawer. She'd learned about his brothers, how they were marked for death because of their abilities. She'd learned about their deal with Tyler's family to keep the Merricks hidden from discovery—a deal that created a rift in the Elemental community, putting the Merricks on one side, and the Morgans on the other. She'd learned about the rockslide that had killed Tyler Morgan's sister, right in front of Michael Merrick.

She knew about the Guides who'd tried to kill him and his

brothers more than once—and who would try again, when they had the chance.

The front door slammed downstairs, and Quinn sat up on the bed. One or more of his brothers were home. She slid her phone out of her pocket and wanted to tell Nick to get the lead out.

But he was so adorably anxious about seeing Adam that she didn't want to rush him. "I think I always knew there was something about you," she said.

He didn't glance up. "Yeah?"

"That suffocation thing—you did that to Gabriel once, didn't you? That day I made you dinner and he came home acting like a real shit?"

Nick's hands went still. "Yeah."

He sounded ashamed. Quinn snorted. "Too bad you didn't follow through."

He turned to look at her. "It's not a game, Quinn. I could have lost control."

"Well, you sure didn't seem to mind using it on Tyler."

Nick turned away and shoved the drawer closed with a *bang*, moving on to the next one.

Quinn came and crouched next to him. His hair was still slightly damp from a shower—which he'd taken alone, despite her offer to *keep up appearances*—and he smelled slightly sweet and musky at the same time, like one of those guy-brand body washes.

"What's up?" she said. "You okay?"

He turned his head to look at her. "I hate that guy."

"Really? I didn't get that from the warm welcome you gave him in the driveway."

"I don't want to talk about Tyler." He slammed another drawer and moved on to the bottom one.

"What are you looking for?" she asked quietly.

"Something that doesn't make me look like I spent twenty minutes doing exactly this."

"Are you sure you don't have a spandex suit under those clothes?"

"I do, in fact. Little surprise for later."

Quinn snorted. "What you're wearing is fine." And it was: a soft blue T-shirt that clung to his body and made his eyes almost vibrant.

"Are you nervous about what you told me? You said you were in danger."

He gave up on rummaging through the drawer. "We are. We're always at risk of someone coming to town to kill us all."

"The Guides, right?"

"Yeah. But we try to keep our heads down and not reveal our talents. That's one of the rules: we have to demonstrate our abilities to earn a death sentence. When we were younger, Tyler and Seth used to beat the shit out of us to try to force us to use our powers, but we're stronger now and they mostly stay away."

Until this afternoon, she thought. But then she picked up on what Nick had said, that Tyler and Seth used to beat the shit out of them. Like his twin brother, Nick was tall, and landscaping gave his body some solid definition. She couldn't imagine *anyone* beating the shit out of him—but then again, if everything he'd told her was true, maybe he'd been afraid to fight back.

"I just don't understand *why*," said Quinn. "What do they care?"

Nick glanced over. "We scare them."

"They're scared of a little breeze?"

"Remember Homecoming? Remember the tornado that formed over the soccer field? Ripped out a few trees?"

"Yeah?"

Nick gave her a significant look.

"No way," she said.

"Way." He grimaced. "I lost control of it. Ended up breaking my leg in three places."

More events were clicking into place. "You said you threw out your knee playing soccer."

"It made for a good cover story." He looked away from her eyes. "Air is everywhere. I heal fast."

"Can you fly?"

She couldn't keep the hushed wonder from her voice, and Nick smiled. "No. Too much weight. I can't focus the air pressure enough for that."

"What does air pressure have to do with anything?"

"Are you kidding? Air pressure is awesome."

She rolled her eyes. "You are such a nerd sometimes. You're lucky you're hot or you couldn't get away with saying things like *air pressure is awesome.*"

"Seriously. Air pressure affects everything. Haven't you ever heard the expression *nature abhors a vacuum*?" He grinned. "Actually, we were doing this experiment in class once where Dr. Cutter was trying to prove a point with a balloon, but I kept making it pop—"

"You are the only person alive who would use superpowers to be *more* dorky."

"They're not superpowers."

That sounded a lot like the difference between to-MAY-to and to-MAH-to to Quinn. "Would it be okay if I told Becca?"

Nick hesitated. He lost the smile.

She rushed on. "I know it's your secret. I don't have to tell her. I—well, she's dating Chris, too, so maybe he could tell her . . ." She stopped. "What? What's that expression?"

"Becca knows," Nick said gently.

"Becca *knows*," said Quinn. "Like . . . how long?"

"Since that party at Drew McKay's house. Tyler and Seth came after Chris, and chased him and Becca into the water." He hesitated. "According to Chris, he lost control of the current. She almost drowned. He dragged her out."

Quinn sat up straight, rotating to face him from the bench seat. "Becca almost *drowned* and she didn't tell me?"

"Quinn—she *couldn't* tell you. Knowing our secret—it's not a good thing. It makes you a target. It puts you in danger."

That sounded like a whole lot of bullshit. Quinn used to tell Becca everything. *Everything.* "Then why did *you* tell me?"

"Because you're my friend. I wanted you to know." He paused. "And you kept my other secret."

Quinn felt herself softening.

The floor creaked in the hallway.

Quinn shoved Nick in the shoulder. He was off balance and rocked back, sitting down *hard* on the carpet.

Quinn was in his lap before he could move, her hand pulling at the hem of his shirt and her mouth latched on to his neck.

Nick sucked in a breath and grabbed her waist, but then Gabriel spoke from the doorway.

"I'd tell you two to get a room, but at least close the door."

Nick froze. Quinn lifted a hand to give his twin the finger. She didn't take her mouth off Nick's neck.

God, he smelled good.

"Classy," said Gabriel. He was already moving down the hallway.

Quinn straightened and let go of Nick's shirt. "You're welcome."

He gave her a look. "If there's a hickey on my neck, I'm going to *kill* you."

She patted him on the cheek. "Come on, Romeo. Maybe you'll get a chance to get one from Adam."

CHAPTER 3

Nick studied the sign over the door to the dance studio. The last time he'd seen Adam and Quinn dance, they'd been using the back room of the relatively deserted local YMCA. Now it was a real dance studio, with real dancers, and a parking lot full of real cars.

Meaning real people. Real people who might know him.

His head had been full of all the family secrets he'd revealed to Quinn, but in an instant, he forgot about Tyler and anything remotely Elemental.

"I don't think I can do this," said Nick.

"Whatever." Quinn didn't indulge him for one second. She was out of the truck and through the door to the studio before he got the key out of the ignition.

He sat in the silent vehicle, listening to the engine ticking.

Deliberating.

If a girl was waiting in there, he wouldn't hesitate. He could flirt with girls without thinking about it, and they'd be lining up to follow him home. He'd learned the opposite sex with the same efficiency he learned physics or trigonometry: a system of functions and formulas leading to a calculated result.

He had no idea what the result of this evening would be. Worse, he didn't know what he *wanted* the result to be.

Quinn stuck her head back out the door. Her expression
spoke volumes.

Well. Really, just one sentence.

WTF are you doing?

Nick slung his messenger bag over his shoulder and dropped
out of the truck.

"I wish I could get this on video," Quinn said when he
stepped into the tiny lobby.

"What?" he asked.

"Nick Merrick, insecure. No wonder you're such a player."

"What does that mean?" he demanded.

"With girls, there are no stakes." She grabbed his hand.
"Come on. Adam's still teaching. You can catch the end of his
lesson."

"Wait—teaching?"

"He works here. How do you think we get to use this swank
studio?"

"But—"

She shushed him with a glare, dragging him down a narrow
hallway that opened into a huge studio. Parents were crowded
onto a few wooden risers along the back wall. Nick's gaze fell
on everything except the people in the center of the room.

Mirrors lined the longest wall, stretching from floor to ceiling
to make the room look twice as large as it was already. The opposite wall was all windows blocked by sheer screens, letting the
last of the daylight in. A grand piano sat in the corner, next to a
massive stereo.

A dozen kids stood spaced across the hardwood floor, mostly
dressed in loose pants or stretchy shorts. Nine girls, three boys.
None was older than twelve or thirteen.

Adam stood in front of the mirror, facing the group.

Now that Nick's eyes had found him, they didn't want to
look away.

He'd worried that his imagination had built Adam into someone who didn't exist, a memory of perfection that the real deal
couldn't match. But Adam's flawless skin still carried that warm

caramel hue. His hair was still pitch dark. His eyes were still brown and sparkling, his cheekbones still high. The same sinewy muscles traced the lengths of his arms. He moved with the same rhythm, as if a song played in his head.

He didn't notice Nick.

Well, he was occupied. Teaching. Even now, he was talking about lines and balance and something about a firebird leap combination.

But the room wasn't *that* big. His eyes had flicked in their direction when Quinn climbed onto the back row of the risers—but his gaze passed over Nick without recognition.

And now Nick was sitting here staring at him.

God, this was awkward.

In a flash, he understood the smiley in that text message. Maybe Adam was okay with Nick coming along because he didn't care anymore. And honestly, Nick couldn't blame him. Adam was *out*. He was comfortable in his skin. He had an apartment and a job and a life.

He wasn't hiding from his family and ignoring a stack of college correspondence because he didn't want to deal with reality.

At least this was easier. Bringing the physics textbook had been a good call. Nick slid his notebook out of the bag.

He wasn't fooling himself.

His chest felt tight. Breath fought its way into his lungs. Adam might not have been watching him, but Nick felt like the center of attention anyway, like everyone in this room could feel his agitation, his insecurity, his disappointment.

He kept his head down over his notebook, but the rich timbre of Adam's voice kept poking at the edges of his awareness. Adam was a good teacher. Friendly. Engaging, making the kids laugh as he counted off a routine and pointed out their errors.

His bare feet crossed the studio to stop in front of the stereo, drawing Nick's eyes. He hit a button, and music swelled through the room. Country, to Nick's surprise, lively guitar chords backed by a strong bass line and a driving beat.

Then Adam returned to his spot in front of the mirror and counted off the same beat, leading his students into a routine.

Nick's breath caught. Music always rode the air until he felt each beat through his whole body. But the air here was full of energy that sparked and rejoiced with the melody. Nick could practically thread his fingers through the notes. He fed a bit of power to the air, getting it back in spades. The students leapt higher, their movements matching the beat perfectly, invisible streamers of sound-fed power weaving among them.

And Adam—he was magnificent. He moved like the music lived inside him, as if Nick's power choreographed each motion.

When the last chord hit and they went still, the air in the room waited, too, charged with potential.

Then the parents clapped.

Nick felt Quinn breathing beside him. "You did something," she whispered. "Didn't you?"

"I didn't mean to." And that was true. But facing Tyler in the driveway, telling Quinn his secret, the wonder and fear and uncertainty of coming here—all his emotions had rallied.

Adam was looking now. His chest rose and fell quickly.

All this power, and Nick had no idea what Adam was thinking.

Then Adam broke the eye contact and called his class to order, dismissing them for the night.

Nick let go of a breath he didn't know he'd been holding. He rubbed a hand across the back of his neck. He'd left a sweaty handprint along the spine of his physics book.

"Try not to do that while I'm dancing, okay?" said Quinn. Before he could answer, she was climbing down from the risers, stripping out of her sweatshirt, pushing through the crowd of parents fighting for the exit.

Adam had disappeared into the hallway, too.

Damn.

Nick flung the textbook open on the bench and told himself to get excited about mass and acceleration and inclined planes. The room emptied, and when Quinn flicked on the stereo to start warming up, Nick tried to convince himself he would've been better off staying in the car.

His brain wasn't convinced. He didn't move.

The air told him when Adam walked into the room. Nick ignored the swirl in the currents, the minute temperature change as his element reacted to his tension.

Study.

He tried. He read the same equation sixteen times. It could have been written in crayon by a dyslexic toddler for all the sense it made.

Adam walked over to the risers.

Nick's eyes froze on his textbook. Now he couldn't remember what subject he was studying.

Adam put his hand on one of the wooden benches and leapt to the upper level.

Nick had forgotten how he moved, like a jungle cat crossed with an acrobat. Powerful yet agile. Instead of sitting beside him, Adam sat cross-legged on the riser in front of him.

It left Nick looking down at him. The position was casual and nonthreatening.

And kind of hot.

Nick told his eyes to stay on his frigging notebook, but they found Adam's feet, following the line of his calves to his knees and thighs and—

Up. Up. Look up, before you get yourself in trouble.

Nick looked at his face. The darkness of Adam's eyes, the barely-there start of shadow across his jaw. The crooked scar that dragged his lip away from perfection.

Nick flashed on what it had felt like to kiss him. He jerked his gaze back to his book. "Hey."

Hey. Wow. Suave. Maybe Quinn *should* be videotaping this.

"What are you studying?" said Adam, his voice gently teasing, almost provocative. It made him sound like he wasn't talking about studying at all.

If it had been a girl, Nick could have flirted back. *You,* he would have said.

Say it. Say it, say it, say it.

"Physics," he said instead.

Ugh. Suddenly he felt like such a *dork.* Next he'd say he needed to get home to his bug collection.

He cleared his throat. "I enjoyed your class."

"Thanks. They're good kids." Adam paused. "Did you come to watch Quinn?"

No, I came to watch you.

But he couldn't say it.

"Come on," Quinn called from the floor. "You guys can make out later. Let's get this done."

Nick slammed his textbook closed. "Damn, Quinn."

Adam uncurled from the bench. He was smiling. "I forgot you were such an easy blush."

"Yeah, yeah."

Adam started to move away, but then he paused and leaned back to whisper. "It'll make for interesting conversation later."

Nick studied the whole time Adam and Quinn rehearsed.

No. That wasn't true.

He pretended to stare at his textbook the whole time. In reality, he never turned a page, he never took a note, and he didn't take his eyes off Adam.

This was ridiculous. Any minute now, he'd be doodling hearts down the margin of his notebook.

An easy blush. He wasn't usually. But he could feel his cheeks warming just thinking of Adam's last comment.

He wasn't the only one blushing, either. Some younger girls were clustered and giggling in the doorway, whispering about Adam.

Nick couldn't blame them. Adam and Quinn made an eye-catching pair as they spun across the floor. His dark hair and olive skin seemed to shadow her blue-eyed-blond-peaches-and-cream complexion. Nick wondered if Adam played to that, if he'd choreographed the dance to highlight their differences.

The routine was powerful, putting Quinn in the air as often as she was on the ground. She'd told Nick she was trying to live on lettuce and saltines to spare Adam's biceps.

From where Nick was sitting, said biceps did not need sparing.

He forced his attention on Quinn. He'd seen the first incarnations of this dance a few weeks ago, when Quinn and Adam had scraped it together in the back room of the Y. Quinn had been awkward, trying to keep up with Adam's polished movements. But she'd been working hard—now her motions looked like a perfect extension of his.

The air liked their partnership. He could feel their energy in the atmosphere like an electric current through water.

It was good to see Quinn focused on something positive.

By the time they killed the lights in the studio and Adam was locking up, it was after ten. Nick told himself he could force physics lessons into his brain when he got home. It wasn't that late yet.

Then Adam said, "Want to grab a cup of coffee?"

He should refuse. It was late *enough*, and he had Mike's truck.

Then again, Michael would never give him a hard time about staying out. He probably wasn't even concerned. Nick never did anything wrong.

But coffee would be public. Would Quinn come? Did he want her to?

"Don't worry about it," said Adam, his voice easy. "I didn't mean to throw you into an existential crisis. It's all right."

"No! I want to. It's—yeah. Coffee. Yes."

"Maybe decaf," said Quinn. Nick shot her a look.

She yawned. "What? Drop me at home first. I need to crash."

So he'd be alone with Adam.

Normally it took fifteen minutes to get Quinn across town. Tonight it seemed to take three-point-two seconds. Nick was very aware of his fake-girlfriend sitting between him and Adam, providing a buffer of estrogen and snark and pretend heterosexuality. When he couldn't seem to generate any better than one-word answers, she turned her attention to Adam, prattling about the routine and Adam's audition and their practice schedule for the rest of the week.

In her parking lot, Nick hoped she'd want a walk up to her apartment, if only to give him another minute for his nerves to settle.

But she didn't ask and didn't linger, and before he knew it, she was gone, climbing the stairs and disappearing through her door. The air in the cab was chilled from Nick's anxiety, but not enough to make his breath fog—yet. He kicked the heat up a notch and backed out of the parking place. Once they were moving again, Nick focused on the road more closely than he had in driver's ed. They drove in silence for a minute.

That left too much time for thinking, and really, he wanted to turn his brain *off*.

He cleared his throat. "Starbucks?"

"Your call."

Adam's voice was so calm, so sure. Nick glanced over at the next stoplight. While he felt like the slightest noise would send him shooting out of his skin, Adam looked relaxed, loosely coiled in the passenger seat. Streetlights reflected off his hair and eyes, sparking with gold.

"Relax," he said softly.

Nick let out a breath. "Sorry."

Adam's smile turned a little wicked. "We're having coffee there, not getting naked."

Nick nearly jumped the curb pulling into the parking lot. Adam laughed.

Even this late at night, the Starbucks was packed, and they moved to the back of the line. Nick worried that Adam would hang close or drop quasi-sexual banter, but he kept his distance, and his conversation barely strayed from the mundane. Questions about school, about Quinn, about the weather they were having.

Worse, now that Adam was doing what Nick thought he wanted—what he thought he *needed*, this safe distance—Nick found himself missing the charged teasing, the blushing, the warmth of Adam's breath on his neck when he whispered things about *later*.

The air in the restaurant changed, enough that Nick froze. It didn't feel *threatening*, just watchful. He looked around, shuffling forward when the person in front of him moved ahead to order.

Danger? he thought, seeking answers from the air.

But the air only carried the scents of ground coffee. Nick took a second look, trying to be discreet about it.

Silver was in prison. The middle school Elementals had been convinced to lie low. Calla was missing, but this didn't *feel* like a Fire Elemental.

Then the sensation was gone, so subtly that Nick wondered if he'd really felt it at all.

The barista gave him a bright smile when they made it to the counter. "One of the Merrick twins," she said. "Which one are you?"

Nick blinked, surprised, then realized he knew her from school. Cute, with almond-shaped eyes, carefully highlighted hair, and clothes just tight enough to get a second glance from most guys. Courtney or Carrie or something.

Nick felt himself sliding into the familiar, doing what was expected. He *had* to, or people might talk. He returned her flirtatious smile and gave her their typical twin line. "Does it matter?"

She gave him a mock pout and probably thought she looked sexy. It did absolutely nothing for him. "What's going in your cup?" she said.

He met her eyes and gave it right back. "Surprise me."

"Something hot and sweet coming right up."

"Make the same for me, sugar," said Adam.

While she smiled and grabbed a second cup, Adam leaned close enough to whisper to Nick. "I can play this game, too."

He was teasing, but Nick felt the undercurrent of . . . something else. Admonishment? Sadness? Disappointment? All three? Before he could puzzle it out, Adam drew back and pulled out his wallet.

"I've got it," said Nick.

"No way. You're doing me a favor. I got it."

"A favor?"

"Giving me a ride home."

Oh.

Nick felt like he was stumbling through his evening, and every step was wrong. When Courtney-Carrie-Whatever handed them their cups, he could barely get it together to thank her.

She'd written her number on the cardboard sleeve. Along with her name—Courtnie—with a big heart over the I.

"Ready to go?" said Adam.

"Yeah. I—" Nick hesitated, not even sure what he was going to say. "Yeah. I'm ready."

Their breaths fogged when they stepped outside. After the warmth and bustle of the Starbucks, the sudden silence closed in around Nick.

"I'm not chasing you off," said Adam. "I just knew we couldn't talk in there."

"Okay." Nick thought he should apologize, but he couldn't quite nail down *why*. The truck rumbled to life, and he reached out to twirl the dials to get the heat going again. Cinnamon and vanilla wafted from the paper cups to filter through the cab, warm scents that pulled some of the tension from his shoulders.

"So what's it feel like?" said Adam.

"What's what feel like?"

"The back wall of that closet you've buried yourself inside."

His voice wasn't unkind, but Nick heard an echo of what he'd felt inside the coffee shop. Not quite judgment. But almost.

Nick wrapped his hands around his cup and inhaled the steam. "It sucks." He paused. "Sorry—in there—"

"It's all right. You don't have to apologize." A hesitation. "Your family still doesn't know?"

Nick shook his head.

"But you came to the studio."

"Yeah."

Adam took a drink of his coffee and stared out the windshield, a musing smile on his face. "When I saw you walk in with Quinn, I almost forgot what I was teaching."

"I didn't think you noticed."

As soon as he said the words, Nick wished he could kick himself. He sounded sulky, for god's sake. *Sulky.*

Adam didn't let it go, either. His smile widened. "Don't you worry. I noticed."

Nick busied himself with backing out of the parking space, grateful for the darkness, because he was sure heat sat on his cheeks again. But then he got to the edge of the lot and sat there, wondering where to go.

If Adam invited him back to his apartment, he had no idea what he'd say. An invitation equaled an opportunity to say no. A *choice*. Making one decision led to more complicated ones. Worse, he felt Adam watching him, probably deliberating over the same thing.

But Adam didn't offer an invitation. "My place," he said firmly. "Drive."

CHAPTER 4

Adam's place looked exactly like Nick remembered. A simple one-bedroom walkout in the basement of an apartment building. No television, but three packed bookcases and an impressive stereo took up the main wall. Nothing else was noteworthy: a small kitchen with a two-seater table tucked in the corner, a tiny bathroom, and a bedroom dwarfed by the queen bed crammed in there. But the living room was huge and open, especially with the wide sliding door leading to the outside.

Nick had gone to friends' houses before. Parents would either be home, or there'd be plenty of evidence they existed. Parental involvement was a reality. Even his own house had Gabriel's sports equipment stacked in a corner of the garage, or Michael's bills and papers always left on the kitchen counter, or Chris's laundry flung at the bottom of the basement stairs. Always a reminder that no matter what, being alone was practically impossible.

Here, this space was very much Adam's.

And they were very much alone.

"How long are you planning to hang in the doorway?" said Adam. He shrugged out of a fleece pullover and tossed it through the bedroom door. It left him in a loose T-shirt, cords of muscle trailing down his arms. The air carried his scent to Nick, oranges and cloves.

The truth was that he liked watching Adam move, all rhythmic and lyrical as if the music never stopped.

He could hardly say that. He leaned back against the front door and took a sip of coffee. He meant it to look casual. It probably looked like he was eager to escape. His heart was already working double time. He lived his life doing what others expected of him. Being here with Adam had no place in that. And worse, he had no idea what Adam expected.

Except maybe an answer to his question. Nick shrugged a little, feeling the hardness of the door at his back. "I was wondering what you had in mind."

Then he mentally kicked himself again. He shouldn't have said that, either.

Adam didn't tease him this time. He stopped in front of Nick. "You're safe here," he said quietly. "Okay?"

Nick nodded and looked away. His jaw felt tight.

"Seriously. You don't have to watch your words or your thoughts or whatever has you so wound up." Adam put his hands on Nick's shoulders, not letting go even when Nick stiffened. "I only brought you here so we could talk. You just looked like you needed a breather. You can leave any time you want."

A breather. Nick needed a whole oxygen tank. He swallowed and made himself meet Adam's eyes. "I don't want to leave."

"I don't want you to leave." Adam took Nick's free hand and tugged. "Come on."

Nick hadn't held hands with another guy since it was mandated on field trips in kindergarten. It should have felt foreign, uncomfortable. He should have been pulling away.

But it didn't feel foreign. Adam's grip felt warm and secure. He could have led Nick straight off a cliff and Nick would have followed. At the bedroom door, Nick's heart staggered and scrambled to maintain a rhythm, but Adam led him past that, to the couch.

Not like it mattered. They were alone.

Comforting and terrifying at the same time.

Adam sat close, curling into the cushions to face Nick. Their fingers were still loosely twined, and Nick knew Adam was giving him space to pull away. He didn't.

Nick waited, testing the air. He'd always been able to sense changes in air patterns, from a door opening, from someone coming close. But lately he'd also been able to sense emotion indirectly, from the rate and quality of someone's breathing.

The air always talked to him, and now, it echoed Adam's promise. *You're safe here.*

He looked at their fingers latticed together. Adam's thumb brushed against his own, very slowly, very gently, a tentative touch as if he knew that too much would send Nick reeling.

But firm enough that Nick knew he could grab on and cling for dear life.

"I never kissed a guy before you," Nick said, flat out, no preamble. "My brothers have no idea." He winced, remembering Quinn's comments during the landscaping job. "They probably think I'm a total player. Even my twin brother—"

"Gabriel, right?"

"Yeah." Nick glanced up, surprised that Adam had remembered. "He says I'm the good twin, and that's why I get more girls."

"That would make him the evil twin?"

Nick frowned. "If you ask Quinn, she'd say yes. But he's not. He has a good heart. He's very loyal. We got picked on when we were younger, and he always took a beating so I could get away. He's the kind of guy to punch first and ask questions later. Quinn hates him, and I wish I could fix it. But he can be sharp—cruel. He speaks without thinking, and it gets him into trouble."

"You're close?"

"Yeah." Nick hesitated. "I think we're growing apart this year. A little."

"And he has no clue you're into guys?"

Despite the fact that he was sitting here holding hands with Adam, the instinct to reject the notion was so strong that Nick almost denied it. He had to clear his throat. "No. No idea."

"Do you think he'd hurt you if he knew?"

Nick blinked in surprise. "What, you mean physically?"

"Yeah, I mean physically."

Nick had never worried about his brothers beating the shit out of him over something like this. Anger, isolation—those he expected. Not violence.

His eyes zoomed in on the scar pulling at the edge of Adam's lip. Years ago, someone had slammed Adam's face into a locker at school, causing enough damage that he'd needed plastic surgery to put his face back together.

But Nick couldn't imagine Gabriel hurting him. Not with his fists, anyway. Disappointment and rejection were another story.

Nick shook his head. "I don't think he would. But he might not take it well. Gabriel is very . . ."

Adam waited.

Nick ran a hand through his hair, feeling it stand up in tufts. How could he explain Gabriel? "He plays on four varsity teams at school. I think he knows most of the cheerleaders intimately, if you catch my drift. He's got a girlfriend now, but if anyone's a player, it's him. He's brave—I mean, he's trying to get into fire-fighter school. Just very . . . I don't know."

"Alpha?"

"Yes. Perfect word."

"You admire him."

Nick shrugged.

Adam smiled. "You do. I can hear it in your voice." He paused. "How old are you?"

"Seventeen. How old are you?"

"Nineteen."

Two years. It felt like twenty. Nick didn't know how to explain that it wasn't just his brothers, that school would take on an entirely different feel if he had to walk down the halls with all his classmates knowing the truth. Adam could be himself, and he had a safe place to go if the world started to crumble around him.

Nick wasn't sure he had anything. He didn't think his brothers would throw him out of the house, but he didn't want to live there feeling their resentment, their unease. Their judgment.

And he couldn't stop going to high school. Education was his only way out of this town.

But he still couldn't bring himself to tear open those college letters hidden in his desk. What if they didn't want him, either?

"Do your parents know about you?" Nick asked.

"Yes." Adam smiled. "I was obsessed with dance from day one. I used to make up routines to show tunes in my living room. I asked my parents for hot pink legwarmers for my ninth birthday. I'm a walking cliché. I think they knew before I did."

"And they were all right?"

"They were all right until I got hurt. They wanted to send me back to school, but they wanted me to pretend to be straight—like anyone would believe that, right? I mean, I get it, they were worried. I spent two weeks in the hospital. They'd seen what those idiots had written all over my Facebook page. But I couldn't do it. I couldn't pretend, and I didn't think it'd do any good. So I got my GED, I got a job, and I moved out." He paused. "We're all right. They help me with rent sometimes, since I'm going to school part-time."

But Nick heard it in Adam's voice. His parents had asked him to pretend, and that had created a gap that time wasn't fixing.

Nick spent so much of his life pretending not to be an Elemental, risking persecution for something he couldn't control. What if he came out and his brothers told him to keep pretending? This felt like a double whammy.

Nick looked into the warm depths of Adam's eyes. "You spent two weeks in the hospital?"

"I might have played the patient a *little* more than necessary. I had a hot male nurse."

Nick smiled and found himself reaching to trace the line on Adam's face, before realizing what he was doing. He started to pull away.

Adam caught his wrist. "You can touch me."

But Nick didn't move. His pulse was choking him. This was so different from the first night they'd come here. Then, he'd been so confused and desperate that he hadn't even admitted his feelings to Adam until he leapt out of his chair and kissed him.

Now there were too many thoughts in the way. Too many fears. No Quinn to break them up if things went too far. He felt like he was falling, scrambling to find purchase, and the only rope he had was fraying strand by strand.

"What do you want?" said Adam, his voice a bit lower, the sound curling through Nick's thoughts. "Something like this?" He traced a finger over Nick's lip, slow and deliberate.

Every nerve ending in Nick's body responded to that touch. His breath shuddered before he could stop it.

Adam smiled. He shifted closer, putting his palm against the side of Nick's face, sliding fingers through his hair. He leaned in to breathe along Nick's jaw. "Or something like this?"

If Nick turned his head, their lips would meet. Adam's weight pressed into his side, warm and solid and masculine. Just from those simple touches, Nick's body was responding more forcefully than it ever had with any girl. Heck, once Quinn had climbed in his lap and unbuttoned his pants, and his body hadn't stood at attention the way it did for Adam's palm on his cheek.

His brain might have been a hot mess, but his body was definitely not confused.

Adam moved closer still, pressing his lips to the hollow below Nick's jaw, sliding his hand out of Nick's hair and down his neck. His movements were strong, confident, nothing like the feather-soft touches of a girl. Adam's hand slid lower, squeezing Nick's chest through the T-shirt.

Nick swore and grabbed his face, bringing their lips together because he couldn't take it. Adam kissed him back with equal force. Nothing hesitant, tongues and heat and strength. Nick's hands found Adam's neck, his shoulders, the muscled planes of his chest. Tugging at his shirt yielded the smooth skin of Adam's waist, the curve of his rib cage.

Adam grabbed the waistband of Nick's jeans and jerked him closer. Nick's breath caught. His brain stopped working. He wanted to throw Adam down on the couch.

So he did just that.

But when he followed him down, Adam put a hand against his chest. "Easy," he said between breaths.

"The hell with easy." Nick knocked his hand away and kissed him again, pinning his wrist against the cushion.

Adam smiled and yielded, kissing him back before putting his free hand against Nick's shoulder.

Nick grabbed his hand and pinned that one, too. But then he realized Adam had tried to stop him twice. He broke the kiss. Their breathing turned loud in the space between them.

The tiniest bit of tension hung around Adam's eyes, but his voice was teasing. "The hell with easy, huh?"

Nick blushed fiercely. He actually *felt* the heat crawl up his neck.

Adam laughed, but quickly sobered. He flexed his wrists. "You're strong."

"Sorry." Nick let him go. But he didn't draw back.

"I wasn't complaining."

Nick wasn't sure how to read this, and it wasn't like he had a ton of experience to draw from. "You stopped me."

"I stopped *us*." Adam paused and put his hand against Nick's face, almost a caress. Nick closed his eyes and inhaled.

Then Adam's voice lost the softness. "Let me up."

What could he do? Nick shifted back, sitting on the edge of the couch. This felt like a prelude to rejection.

You're safe here.

No. He wasn't. He didn't feel safe anywhere. Emotion clawed at his throat. He'd let a wall down, and now he was furiously trying to put the bricks back together.

Were they going too fast? Had he done that, or had Adam?

The hell with easy.

For a breathless instant, it had been amazing to let go of thought, to let instinct rule his motions. But now he was paying for it, and he couldn't analyze everything fast enough.

"Look." Adam drew a hand down his face. "I don't want you—"

"Forget it." Nick shoved off the couch. The path to the door seemed a mile long.

"Hey." Adam came after him. "*Hey.*"

Nick's hand closed on the doorknob. Adam grabbed his arm. He was stronger than Nick was ready for, and he spun him around.

Most girls couldn't do that, either.

"What?" Nick demanded. The air had dropped ten degrees.

"Well, you're definitely gay. A straight guy wouldn't be such a drama queen."

Nick set his jaw. "Let me go."

"Can I finish what I was going to say?"

Nick stared back at him. For all his gentle grace, Adam had a core of strength. Nick had seen it once before, and he was seeing it now.

"Fine," he said. "*You don't want me . . . ?*"

"I don't want you to rush into something you're not ready for."

Oh.

Adam's hand loosened on his bicep, but he didn't let go. "I've dated guys before who don't want to be *out*. It's a personal decision, and I get it, but . . ."

Nick swallowed. "But what?"

Adam looked at him, hard. "But if you wake up hating yourself, I don't want you taking it out on me."

Nick studied him, allowing some of the earlier moments to click into place. Adam asking if Gabriel would hurt Nick. The tension in his eyes when he said, "You're strong."

Even now, he was holding himself at a slight distance.

There was more to Adam's story, hiding behind this easy self-confidence.

Nick shifted his weight, and Adam almost flinched. Without the air to reinforce his impression, Nick might have missed it altogether.

Slowly, carefully, Nick reached his hands out and put them on Adam's shoulders. "You're safe here," he said softly. "Okay?"

Adam's eyes widened as Nick fed his words back to him.

Nick smiled, just a little. "You don't have to watch your words or your thoughts or whatever has you so wound up."

Now Adam was blushing. "Okay, okay—"

Nick kissed him. Not with the feverish intensity of a few moments ago, but a bare brush of lips.

When he tried to pull away, Adam caught his face and held him there, putting his forehead against his. "You're going to break my heart. I can feel it."

"Not if I can help it." He put a hand over Adam's, holding it to his cheek. "Slow?"

Adam nodded, turning his head to kiss Nick's palm.

Then he grinned. "Well," Adam said. "*Slower.*"

CHAPTER 5

Quinn pulled the hood of her sweatshirt up and shivered. She still had her dance shorts on, but there hadn't been time to change. Her jaw hurt like a bitch, and she knew there'd be a bruise there tomorrow.

Her older brother had welcomed her home by slamming her face into the wall and demanding to know where his money was.

Like she had a clue. Quinn would be so happy when Jake went back to college. Her little brother Jordan had already taken to crashing at friends' houses every night, rotating through his circle of gamer buddies so no one's parents got suspicious.

Quinn had been sitting on the curb out in front of the 7-Eleven, but the old Korean woman who worked there had come out shrieking about teenagers loitering, so now Quinn was sitting on a milk crate out back, clinging to the darkness.

She was *this close* to stealing food from the Dumpster.

When she'd lived within walking distance of Becca's house, Becca's mom had always left her a plate of food. She'd known about Quinn's disagreements with her mom. Quinn still had a key to their house on her key ring.

But now that Becca and Chris were an item, Quinn increasingly felt like a third wheel.

Especially now that she knew the truth about Becca and the Merricks.

A truth she'd learned from *Nick*, not Becca.

Some best friend.

Hunger clawed at Quinn's insides and she wished she'd gone with Nick and Adam for coffee. But she didn't have any money and she didn't want to be a mooch *and* a third wheel.

But now that she had nowhere to sleep . . . Her fingers traced over the face of her cell phone, and she considered texting Nick.

A metal door slammed, a little distance down the back wall. Quinn saw a flare of light, then a cigarette glowed red. The light over the door was out, but from the person's size, it looked like a guy. Dark clothes.

She pulled her hood down, tucking her blond hair more tightly under the covering.

It didn't help. "Hey!" The sharp male voice made her head snap up. The musty scent of cigarettes burned her nostrils. He was coming toward her. "You can't be out here."

Quinn didn't move. "Says who?"

"Says me."

"And who are you, the owner of the parking lot?"

"No. The whole strip mall."

Well, she hadn't expected that answer. She still didn't move. "Prove it."

"What, you want to see the deed?" He moved like he was going to grab her, and she scrambled off the crate, dusting grit from her clothes.

"Fine, fine. I'm going."

He followed her, taking a draw from his cigarette, clearly planning to make sure she exited his property. When she reached the sidewalk running beside the 7-Eleven, she whirled, ready to lay into him for being an asshole.

But here the light found his features. It was Tyler, the guy from Nick's driveway. She thought of Nick's revelations and knew she should be afraid of Tyler, but her life was overflowing with cruel people, and she didn't carry that much adrenaline around with her.

"It's you," she spat.

"It's you." He put the cigarette to his lips and inhaled again. "Where's your boyfriend?"

"He's picking me up. He'll be here any minute." Just because she wasn't afraid didn't mean she was stupid.

"He was picking you up *behind* the 7-Eleven?"

Okay, maybe she *was* stupid. She gestured at the darkened storefronts lining the rest of the strip mall. "Why don't you go back where you came from?"

"What are you doing out here, really?"

"None of your business."

His eyes narrowed. "What happened to your face? Did that Merrick prick knock you around?"

He didn't sound concerned, but he didn't sound like an affirmative answer would surprise him, either. "No. And don't call him that."

He huffed, blowing smoke through his nose. "You girls are all the same. You think those idiots are amazing and perfect and special. Well, you know what? They're *not.*"

"I'm sorry, Prince Charming. Clearly not everyone is up to your standards." She stepped up and ripped the cigarette out of his mouth, intending to break it in half.

But it flared and burned to ash in her hand. Quinn shrieked and dropped it.

Tyler smirked. "You don't know what you're messing with, baby girl. With me *or* them."

"Don't call me that."

"I just wanted to talk to them, and you saw how that jerkoff treated me."

"Yeah, and you were such a gentleman." She swung a hand to shove him away.

He was too quick and grabbed her wrist. "Trust me, they've pushed me way past being a gentleman. Maybe I should get some answers from you."

God, he was strong. She regretted trying to hit him. Her arm burned like he was pressing the cigarette between his hand and her skin. Quinn was gasping before she could stop it. Part of her wished she'd stayed in the apartment and tried her odds against her brother.

"Go ahead," Tyler said. "Scream. I'll tell them I caught you trying to break in."

"Let me go," she whimpered. The pain was immobilizing. He was pulling tears out of her, and she wanted to *kill* him for that. "Let me go."

"You think this is bad?" he said. "This is *nothing*. Just wait until you spend more time with *them*. Wait until you see what they do to you. They are *killers*."

Sweat bloomed on her forehead. "Okay. I get it. Lemme go. Please."

"I want to know what's going on. You hear me? I want to know what really happened at that carnival, and I want to know what happened to the Guide that came to town to take care of it. You tell them I want answers. Got it?"

"Got it," she whispered. The grip on her arm was the only thing holding her on her feet. She was going to pee her pants in a second.

"Good." He let her go. Shoved her, really. She hit the ground, the impact jarring. She was lying where concrete met a bed of large, smooth stones surrounding the streetlamp. She'd probably have sixteen bruises tomorrow, just from this landing.

"Idiot," he sneered.

She seized a rock and punched him in the side of the knee with it, throwing every ounce of strength into the motion. He swore as his leg gave out. He dropped like—well, like a *rock*. Quinn swung her elbow around to jab him in the face.

His hand shot out to grab her, but Quinn was already running. Full out, as fast as her feet would go. Trees stretched along Ritchie Highway up ahead, a gaping pit of darkness full of unseen dangers. Quinn scrambled through the underbrush, not caring about staying silent. She just *ran*.

Branches whipped her legs, but she didn't slow. She stumbled twice. Then a third time, almost falling. Another branch whipped across her face, followed by a cloud of spiderwebs. Quinn screamed and beat at her face.

Then she shut up. Oxygen whistled into her chest, and she told her lungs to knock it off so she could hear.

Silence.

Darkness swelled around her, and she couldn't see anything. Quinn yanked her phone out of her pocket and dialed. Third wheel or not, she didn't know if Tyler would come after her out here.

"Come on," she muttered, bouncing from one foot to another while it rang.

"Hello?"

"Nick," she said as quietly as she could muster. "I need you."

At first Nick saw nothing along the stretch of Ritchie Highway. He peered into the darkness, looking for Quinn, finding only trees. Down the road a bit, the Jiffy Lube sign threw light into space, but here it was pitch-black. He rolled down the window to listen, but the diesel engine made that impossible.

Worry danced with exasperation in his head. It had taken him only ten minutes to get here from Adam's apartment, but that felt like a long time when you were hiding from Tyler Morgan. He knew from experience.

What had she been doing with Tyler, anyway? He'd just seen her two hours ago! Safe at home!

Just when he was about to turn off the truck to go looking, Quinn burst through the trees into the path of his headlights, lit up like a beacon.

Her legs were scratched to hell, long stripes of red crisscrossing her thighs. But more concerning was the bruise on her jaw, cut through by one long scratch that was still bleeding. Her eyes were red and tear-filled.

Then she was out of the light and climbing into the truck.

Fury stole Nick's exasperation. "Jesus, Quinn, are you okay?"

"Do I look okay?"

"No! Did Tyler hit you? I'm taking you to the cops—"

"I'm not going to the cops." Quinn flung her tangled blond

hair back from her face. "Drive, Nick, all right? Drive the fuck-ing truck."

He took a long breath and blew it out through his teeth.

She punched him in the arm. Hard. "Drive!"

He shifted into gear. "You want to tell me what happened?"

"No."

Nick listened to the air threading through the cab, cataloging her injuries as his element fed information to him. Mostly cuts and bruises, nothing more serious than that.

As he thought it, his senses picked up on something else, an unnatural heat making the air jitter around her.

She was cradling her arm.

"He burned you?" Nick asked.

"How did you know that?"

"It's his MO. He's a Fire Elemental. I've felt the effects be-fore." More than once, too. Tyler and his best friend Seth used to wait to trap Nick alone. They'd pin him down and threaten to burn his skin off, knowing Nick wouldn't use his abilities to stop them.

Only they didn't always stop at threats.

Nick should have let him suffocate in the driveway.

"Fire, like Gabriel?" Quinn snorted. "Why is that not sur-prising? They should just burn the crap out of each other."

"Not like Gabriel. Nowhere near as strong. Give me your hand."

"He seemed plenty strong to me." But she held out her hand, snatching it back at the last moment when he went to take it. "Don't touch it, okay? It hurts like a bitch."

He glanced away from the road for a sec. Lights from the roadway reflected off the drying tears on her cheeks. He caught sight of that bruise again and wanted to kill Tyler.

"I won't hurt you," he said. "Come closer."

She unsnapped her seat belt and scooted to the middle of the bench, until her shoulder was against his side and their thighs were touching.

Her face pressed into his shoulder. She smelled like the woods, pine and dirt and nighttime.

Nick sighed and put an arm around her, stroking her hair back from her face. "Quinn. Do you want me to take you home?"

"To your house?" her muffled voice asked hopefully.

He hadn't meant his house, but he felt the pain and fear in every breath she took.

"Please?" she whispered.

"Okay," he said, hitting the turn signal to make a U-turn at the next intersection. "You have to be absolutely quiet. Mike will kill me if he finds you there."

"Are you sure you don't want me to be loud?" she said suggestively.

Nick made a disgusted noise. "You can't be too hurt if you're making jokes."

She raised her head and sniffled. "You smell like Adam."

Nick couldn't figure out the note in her voice, but warmth snuck across his cheeks as he remembered the exotic scent of oranges and cloves. Of course she'd know what Adam smelled like—she'd spent an hour with her hands all over him during rehearsal.

"Your bag is still here, too," Quinn continued, kicking at his messenger bag on the floor of the truck. "Nick Merrick, you dirty dog. It's after midnight."

"We just talked."

"Is that what the kids are calling it these days?"

"Quinn. Shut up and give me your arm."

When she did, he glanced between her wrist and the road. He could feel the heat coming off her skin from here. No wonder he'd found her crying.

He definitely should've killed Tyler in the driveway.

Nick blew air along the burn, feeding power into it.

Quinn sucked in a breath. "What are you doing?"

"Healing it." He had to be careful, though. Too much power could hurt. He knew that from experience, too.

She relaxed against him, resting her head against his shoulder again. "That feels amazing."

"I'll send you a bill."

"Can you fix my face, too?"

"Yes." Another breath, another flare of power. She was relaxed, so he tried for information. "Why did he hit you?"

"I don't want to talk about it. Did you sleep with Adam?"

"Of course not." The thought was terrifying and intriguing all at once, and he told his imagination to knock it off.

"Don't get all indignant about it. Two virile guys? Isn't that like twice the recommended daily dose of testosterone?"

"*Quinn.*"

"Did you make out at least?"

He sighed along her skin.

Quinn made a low sound and snuggled closer. "You really like him, don't you?"

He didn't answer. Honestly, he still didn't know if he'd been relieved to get Quinn's call, putting an end to the night, or disappointed that it had cut their time short. He felt so unprepared to be with a guy, like he only knew the choreography for one dance step, and this was a completely different type of music.

God, he couldn't even fool himself. Disappointed. He'd been disappointed.

He'd never lost control like that before. His life was always about fulfilling expectations. Spending a few minutes acting on instinct—he'd never felt anything like it. He couldn't wait to feel like that again.

Quinn lifted her head and looked up at him. "You *do* really like him. I know you do. I could tell the instant you saw him at the studio."

"I'm glad I'm so transparent."

"You're not transparent. He's just like that. Magnetic. *Everyone* likes Adam."

Nick blew another line of breath along her arm, drawing the burn out, feeling the skin rebuild. *Everyone likes Adam.* Quinn's voice had changed when she'd dropped the words.

Nick realigned what he'd learned from the evening, Adam's gentle teasing, his easy comfort with who he was. They'd shared a moment. More than a moment—Nick had trusted him with the biggest secret of his life. *You're safe here.*

With a start, he realized that Adam's one-liners could have been the same kind of practiced words that Nick dropped on unsuspecting girls.

He'd rushed into this with his emotions exposed and bare. He'd fallen for Adam's quiet confidence, his dedication to dance and school, and his singular focus on what he wanted. Nick had been all instinct and feeling and passion. Adam had been controlled. *In* control.

You're going to break my heart. I can feel it.

God, repeating it to himself now, it felt like such a line.

"Yowch!" Quinn said, sitting up straight and yanking her arm away. "Holy crap, Nick!"

"Sorry," he muttered. "Here. I'll be more careful."

"No—actually—I think it's fine." She held her wrist out, running a finger along the smooth skin. "You're amazing."

"Amazing," he echoed. "Yeah. Right."

"What's wrong?"

"Am I being an idiot, Quinn?"

He could feel her studying him in the darkness. "I think I need more information."

"With Adam."

She was quiet for a minute. He pulled up the driveway to his house and killed the engine. They couldn't sit here too long, but they could never finish this conversation in the house, so he waited with the keys in his hand, his eyes on the darkened dash.

Quinn let out a slow breath. "You *really* like him," she said softly. "Like, full on hearts in your eyes, doodling your last name with his, making up—"

"Quinn."

She pulled her legs up on the bench to sit cross-legged. "Did you go back to his place?"

He winced, feeling like he was admitting something he shouldn't. "Yes."

"Was there more kissing or more talking?"

His face felt warm again, and he fiddled with the keys in his lap. Was this how girls felt? He didn't like it. "Dead even."

"Did anyone's clothes come off?"

"No!" Thank god. But now he was imagining it.

God, this was so confusing. He shouldn't have thrown away the cup sleeve with Courtnie's number. *That* he knew how to handle.

But another part of him railed against the idea, like he'd cracked a door and his subconscious had wedged an arm into the opening.

Quinn was quiet for a while. "I've known Adam for a long time," she finally said. "But that doesn't mean I know him well. He doesn't bring a lot of guys around the studio or anything— but he never seems lonely, either. Are you going to see him again?"

"I don't know. You called, and I left in a hurry. He said he'd text me later." Nick checked his phone. No new messages from Adam. Not even to ask how Quinn was.

"Sucks being the girl, doesn't it?" said Quinn.

"Shut up." But yes. It did.

Nick tried to be quiet when he snuck Quinn into the house, but Hunter stirred and ran a hand across his face when they crept into the bedroom.

His eyes widened fractionally when he saw Quinn, but he took it in stride. "You guys want me to crash on the couch?"

"She's sleeping here, that's all," said Nick.

Hunter yawned and rolled over, turning his back on them. "Yeah, okay. Let me know if you change your mind."

Nick usually slept in a T-shirt and boxers, but out of deference to Quinn's presence in his bed, he pulled on a pair of threadbare sweatpants. They changed in the dark, and then he drew back the blankets.

Quinn slid in beside him. She offered his modesty no deference. His hand brushed bare thigh, but before he could react to that, she was pressed up against him, her leg slung over his.

"What are you *doing*?" he whispered, controlling the air so the sound waves of their conversation wouldn't carry to Hunter.

"Come on," she breathed. "If I'm caught here, it should at least *look* like we're sleeping together."

Nick didn't say anything, torn between protesting and thinking she had a pretty good point.

Quinn snuggled more closely, resting her head on his shoulder. "It's not like you care, right? If you want me to move, I will."

"No." He hesitated. "I guess it's okay."

"Can you still fix my face?" Her voice was sleepy.

"Sure," he murmured. At least her sleeping position made that easy. He turned his head and eased a breath along her cheek.

She relaxed into him, so he fished for information. "You never told me how you ended up with Tyler."

"I walked to the 7-Eleven. He was there."

"You walked there *alone?*"

"I walk there all the time. Stop being such a mother hen."

"Why did Tyler start hassling you?" For an instant, he wondered if Quinn had walked up and started hassling *Tyler*. She wasn't exactly subtle.

"He wants to know what happened at the carnival. He said something about the Guides." She paused. "The news said those explosions at the carnival were due to poor wiring."

"No. That was Calla Dean. She started those."

"Calla Dean!"

"Shh. Yeah. She was behind the arson attacks, too."

Quinn's house had burned down in one of those arson attacks—it was the whole reason they were living in that damned apartment. "I thought that was Rick Stacey!"

"He helped, but she was the mastermind."

Quinn was silent for a minute. She knew Calla Dean from school—but she didn't know her well. Calla had been one of the students who'd disappeared after the carnival, and everyone thought she was dead. There was still a memorial of notes and pictures taped all over her locker.

It seemed ridiculous, but all Quinn could think was, *I always liked her highlights.* "I thought she was one of the students who died in the carnival explosions."

"We don't know what happened to her. When Silver came after us, we found the middle school Elementals, but not her." He shrugged. "Maybe she ran."

"And Silver is one of the Guides that are trying to kill you guys, right?"

"Right. But he's in prison."

"When will they send a new one?"

"Eventually." He brushed a finger across her cheek. "How's that feel?"

Her eyes, normally so bright, were shadowed in the darkness. "Much better," she whispered. "Thanks."

Then, without warning, she shifted up and pressed her lips to his.

For a second, Nick didn't resist. He'd kissed girls—lots of them—and he knew how to respond. If that girl Courtnie had ambushed him with her lips, he probably would have kissed her back without thinking about it.

But this—this was different. Quinn *knew.* And this wasn't like earlier, when she'd been giving him a cover.

He'd never shove her away, but he stiffened and drew back.

"I'm sorry," she whispered.

"It's okay," he said automatically.

But it wasn't okay. He felt like he was hurting her, when he hadn't done anything.

And this would be easier if she weren't still attached to his side like a leech.

"I'm sorry," she said again. "I forgot—what you were doing—it felt—it felt—"

"Shh," he whispered. "It's okay."

"Are you mad?"

He shook his head. "I'm not mad, Quinn." But he kind of was, and he couldn't put it all together. He paused and touched her face again. "I'm so sorry. You shouldn't have to keep doing this."

She caught his hand and held it there. "It's my fault."

He frowned. "I don't mean to hurt you."

"Sometimes I wish you weren't . . ." Her voice dropped even further, and her eyes flicked toward the end of the room where Hunter slept. "You know."

"I know." Truth was, sometimes he wished that, too.

"Do you want me to sleep somewhere else?"

Nick shook his head and kissed her on the forehead. "No. It's okay. Don't worry about it."

She took him at his word. She snuggled back into him, and after a few minutes, her breathing told him she was asleep.

It wouldn't come so easily to Nick.

Sucks being the girl, doesn't it?

But he *wasn't* a girl. And he sure as hell wasn't going to play one. Slowly, carefully, so as not to wake her or Hunter, he slid the phone off his nightstand and unlocked the screen.

Did he want to do this? What message would he send?

Then his message icon lit up.

Adam. Words appeared on the screen.

You free tomorrow? Have class til 8 but free after.

Nick's heart skipped ahead of him, dancing in circles. But he'd already blown off physics tonight, and he had a paper due in two days.

He probably shouldn't seem too eager, either.

God, he couldn't believe he was even having this conversation with himself. He typed back quickly.

Have to study.

As soon as he pressed SEND, he wanted to punch the phone. He had to *study*? Seriously? What the hell was wrong with him? He so couldn't play this from the other side. How would Adam read that? As rejection? More likely, that Nick was the biggest

nerd to walk the earth. The phone silently mocked him, not offering any further messages.

Then, just as he was about to set it on his side table, the display lit again.

Study here?

Nick smiled.

You're on.

CHAPTER 6

Nick rubbed at his eyes and told himself to *focus*. He was usually the first one to hand in a completed test, but more than half the class had walked their papers up to the front of the room. Even Gustav Asciak, the foreign exchange student who barely spoke a lick of English, had turned in his paper.

Nick still had half the test to complete. He never should have blown off studying. He kept mixing up the formulas, and the more he told his brain to spit out the information, the more it supplied him with thoughts of what he *had* been doing last night.

Adam's eyes.

Adam's hands.

Adam's—

Focus.

This wasn't the end of the world. He had an A average in every single class, including this one. Getting a less than perfect score on one test wasn't going to kill him.

But it was definitely going to piss him off. His GPA was everything. He wasn't rolling in money, so he needed scholarships if he wanted to go away to school.

He could imagine the college rejection letters now. *After learning that one kiss and a sleepless night led you to fail a test, we have decided you are no longer a fit for our institution . . .*

The bell rang, and Nick snapped his head up. Students started shoving books into backpacks and pushing for the exit.

Holy shit. He still had seven questions left.

He kept writing, scribbling fast. The room cleared before he was halfway through the next problem. His thoughts were so scattered that he wasn't sure he was tackling the question correctly.

"Nick." Dr. Cutter appeared beside his desk, tapping a finger on the plastic surface. His voice was gentle but carried an air of finality. "Time is up, I'm afraid."

Nick didn't stop writing. "One minute?"

Dr. Cutter didn't say anything for a long moment, but Nick felt his concern in the air.

Finally, he put a hand on Nick's wrist, stilling his writing. "Did you not understand the material?" he said. "I wish you had come to me earlier this week—"

"No." This was pointless. Nick put his pencil down and rubbed at his eyes. "I understood it."

The teacher picked up the test and flipped through the pages. "You've missed the entire last section."

Like he didn't know that. Nick focused on the pencil, wishing he could stab it straight through his hand. "I'm sorry. I didn't have time to study. I kept mixing up the formulas."

Dr. Cutter sat down at the desk beside him. "Is something going on at home?"

Nick knew this voice. He'd heard it twelve dozen times since his parents died. While teachers and counselors had learned to steer clear of Gabriel's temper, they knew they could seek answers from Nick. *Are you okay? Are you getting enough to eat? Is your brother doing enough to take care of you?*

But he was seventeen now, and way too old to get a pass for something like that.

Especially when failing this test had nothing to do with problems at home, and everything to do with one dark-haired dancer.

God, you're obsessed.

"No," he said. "Home's fine. Really."

Dr. Cutter wasn't convinced. "Girlfriend?"

Nick looked at him. "I'm okay. Just tired."

"This is a unit test. If you fail, you'll have to get someone from home to sign it."

Michael probably wouldn't be angry, but he'd definitely want an explanation. That was almost worse.

So, Michael, there's this guy . . .

Nick cleared his throat. "I know. I'm sorry. I'll catch up."

His teacher studied him, and Nick told himself not to look away. Finally, Dr. Cutter clapped him on the shoulder. "I'll let you do a retake. Friday?"

This was a pity move. Nick knew it, and pride was pricking at him to refuse. Like with his brothers, Dr. Cutter was judging him on what he expected from Nick. But this was an AP class, and his performance here might carry a lot of weight when colleges started dishing out funds.

He told his pride to stick it. "That would be great. Thank you."

AP Calculus wasn't much better. Nick had completely forgotten to do the homework. Three questions—three stupid questions!—but he'd never gotten around to opening his assignment book last night, so he hadn't bothered to do them.

He mentally added another zero to his imaginary grade sheet. At least this was only homework.

By the time he sat at a table at lunch, he was ready for some cutlery, just so he could stab something.

Lunch was pizza. Figured. Not even so much as a plastic fork.

A tray dropped onto the table beside him. Four slices of pizza and a coke. The air told him it was Gabriel before his eyes did. His twin dropped onto the bench. "What's with you?"

They hadn't seen each other all morning, but Gabriel could always read his moods like Nick had a news crawl embedded in his forehead.

"Failed a physics test," Nick said.

"You know how I solve that problem?" said his twin. "I don't take physics."

"Hilarious. Where's Hunter?"

"Working on a research project. I was starving." He popped the cap on the soda. "You look like shit."

"Wow, I'm glad you sat down."

"Hunter said you snuck Quinn in last night. I'm guessing you didn't get much sleep."

Nick shrugged, keeping his eyes on his food, torn between defending Quinn's honor and keeping his own secrets. Then again, she wasn't exactly making a strong case for her own chastity.

"She needed a place to crash." Nick hesitated. "Tyler's hassling her." He repeated everything that Quinn had told him last night.

Gabriel listened, stacking two slices of pizza to eat them at the same time. "What was she doing behind the 7-Eleven?"

"She won't tell me." Nick kept rolling it around in his head. Had she been so upset over Tyler? Or had something happened at home?

"Nicky, you need to ditch this girl."

"Why?"

"Because she's nothing but drama. You don't need that."

Nick glared at him. "I think I can manage."

"Jesus, don't bite my head off. I'm just trying to save you the trouble. We have enough drama."

He didn't need a reminder of that. Nick picked up his slice of pizza to spare himself the need to say anything.

"Where is the old ball and chain, anyway?" said Gabriel.

"She had some kind of group project for French."

They sat in silence for a long moment. Nick knew he should say something—*anything*—but he was so worried he'd open his mouth and tell Gabriel everything.

"It's not just your test," said Gabriel. "What else is up?"

I spent half the night with a boy and I can't stop thinking about him. "I'm just tired."

Gabriel didn't respond, but Nick could feel the weight of his eyes.

"You guys are getting serious, huh?" Gabriel said.

"Maybe." Nick chewed his pizza and fought with his brain

as it helpfully supplied him with thoughts of Adam. Adam's apartment. Adam dancing, driving his body into a powerful routine. Adam touching him, first the light brush of his fingers, then stronger. *Adam, Adam, Adam.*

"Who are you doing tonight?" said Gabriel.

Nick choked on his pizza. He coughed hard and needed a drink of soda to get it together. "What did you just say?"

"I said, what are you doing tonight? You're so frigging keyed up. You have plans with Quinn? Want to go out?"

Nick shook his head. "Yes. No. I mean—I don't want to go out. I've got to study."

Gabriel's hand closed over his forearm. "Seriously," he said, his voice a touch lower. "You all right?"

Nick looked at him. For an instant, he felt like six-year-old Nicky, wanting to cry and hide and let his brother fix everything. What had Adam said last night? *You admire him. I can hear it in your voice.*

He was right. Gabriel had always been the fighter. The defender. Nick could see it now: if he told his twin something was wrong, Gabriel would be on his feet, ready to knock heads.

It made Nick feel immeasurably weak sometimes. Like when Gabriel was sneaking around, rescuing people from burning buildings. Or like last night, when Tyler had gone after Quinn. Gabriel wouldn't have picked her up and driven her home. Gabriel would have tracked down Tyler and beaten the shit out of him.

When Nick thought about telling Gabriel the truth about himself, it felt like admitting one more way he didn't live up to his identical twin brother.

His appetite vanished. He flung his pizza down and shoved the tray away. "Yeah. Fine. You want that? I'm not hungry."

Before Gabriel could stop him, he shouldered his bag and walked away from the table.

"Hey!" Gabriel called.

Nick called back over his shoulder. "I'll see you at home later."

Almost immediately, his cell phone chimed. Nick grabbed it from his pocket, hoping for a message from Adam.

Michael had sent him a message.

Can you help with a job tonight? Should be done by 7. Too much for me + C.

C was Chris. Nick sighed. He was already behind with school, but he'd be able to study at Adam's, right? Michael wouldn't ask if he didn't need the help.

The exhaustion that had been clinging to Nick's back all day doubled in weight. For an instant, he was tempted to say no.

But Michael expected a yes. And Nick always did what his brothers expected.

Nick slid his fingers along the face of the phone.

Sure. I'll be there.

Quinn spent all day dodging Becca, but her best friend— *ahem*, former best friend—caught up to her next to her locker after last period.

Quinn didn't even look at her. Like she needed to see Becca's straight, shiny dark hair, her perfect little figure, or Chris Merrick's arm slung over her shoulder.

Well, Chris wasn't *really* there, but he might as well have been.

"I can't talk," said Quinn. "I need to catch the bus."

Becca was studying her. Quinn could *feel* it. But her voice was easy, casual. "Want a ride?"

"Nah."

"You *want* to ride the bus? What are you pissed at me about now?"

Quinn slammed her locker shut, making the metal crash echo down the hallway. She flung her trig textbook into her backpack. This was so like Becca. Acting like Quinn was *such* a drama queen, so let's laugh off all her problems and treat her like everything is trivial.

And of course all this slamming and flinging was probably driving that point home.

Quinn picked up her bag and started walking.

"Come on," said Becca, catching up with her. "Would you stop wasting time and tell me what's wrong?"

"Nothing is wrong."

"I thought you were all into doing the double-date thing with Nick and Chris. What happened?"

Nick is gay and you kept secrets.

"Forget it," said Quinn. "Just go back to your perfect life."

Becca stopped short. Quinn kept walking, but Becca called after her. "Oh, my perfect life? You mean with my father showing up out of nowhere? Or having the entire school know exactly what I did with Drew McKay? Or—"

Quinn whirled. "Shut up." The worst part was that she *did* feel badly about all of those things. She marched back to Becca. "If you're going to start listing your life difficulties, why don't you start with the truth?"

Now Becca looked exasperated. "Damn it, Quinn, I don't even know what you're talking about."

"I'm talking about how I learned all your secrets from the Last Airbender last night."

Becca looked almost incredulous. "A cartoon? What? You—wait—you—"

Quinn watched sudden realization dawn on Becca's face.

"Nick told you," Becca whispered.

"No shit he told me. Why didn't *you* tell me is what I want to know."

When Becca didn't have anything to say to that, Quinn started walking again.

Becca caught up to her in a hurry. Her voice was a whispered rush of words, hidden beneath the bustle in the hallway. "Quinn, I couldn't tell you. Did he tell you everything? About how they're marked for death? About how the Guides will come for them—"

"He told me all that."

"Did he tell you about my father? How both Hunter and I aren't supposed to exist, either?"

"Yes."

"Did he—"

Quinn shoved her away. "He told me all of it, Becca!" She glared at her, feeling fury pour out of her eyes. "Why didn't *you*?"

"I . . . couldn't."

I couldn't.

Quinn could hear the subtext.

Because I couldn't trust you.

And suddenly, that pinpointed the real problem here.

Becca hadn't trusted her with this secret. Maybe she thought Quinn was too volatile, maybe she didn't think Quinn was worthy of knowing. Maybe Becca was genuinely worried and she didn't want to put Quinn in danger—but that felt like a load of bullshit since her friend hadn't stopped her from dating Nick.

Quinn felt like such an idiot.

"He told me all about it," Quinn said, hating that her throat felt thick. "All of it, Bex."

Then she stood there waiting for Becca to re-categorize the last few weeks, the same way Quinn had done when she'd first learned everything from Nick.

The time Becca had totaled her car on the bridge, but Becca's father, the Guide, had really been behind it.

The fires in town, the destruction of the school library, the students who were killed at the carnival.

How the kidnapping of a dozen local teenagers had nothing to do with a local criminal, and everything to do with a Guide coming to town to destroy the Merricks. How Calla Dean wasn't a victim, but a murdering pyromaniac.

Becca knew all of it.

She'd never breathed a word to Quinn.

"You told me you miss your father," said Quinn. "You cried and told me how much you wished you could trust him. Why would you lie about that?"

Becca looked stricken. "I didn't lie about that. And now—now he won't even let me see him—"

"Oh, wait, you can tell the truth when you want something?" Quinn scoffed and walked away. "Need a shoulder to cry on? Forget it, Becca."

"Quinn, stop!"

"Why?" Quinn stopped and looked at her. "Why, Bex? You don't give a crap about me. Not really."

"I do—please, stop, talk to me."

Becca's voice was heavy with tears, and Quinn almost broke. She *did* know what her friend had gone through, and it hadn't all been sunshine and roses.

Quinn knew because she'd let Becca cry on her shoulder about some of it.

But clearly not all of it.

And Quinn's life wasn't exactly sunshine and roses, either. Not like Becca gave a crap.

"I don't want to talk," said Quinn. "I've got my own secrets to keep."

Then she burst through the double doors into the chilled air waiting for her.

CHAPTER 7

The job took too long. Good, in a way, because Nick barely had time to shower, much less think about what he was doing. He threw on jeans and a striped Henley before checking himself in the mirror. His hair was a mess of wet clumps, and he could probably stand to spend five minutes with a razor. Five minutes he didn't have.

Stellar. He was going to show up on Adam's doorstep looking like he didn't give a shit.

Gabriel appeared in his doorway. "I thought you had to study."

"Library. Helping Quinn with trig." Nick couldn't meet his eyes. It was easier keeping the secret from Chris and Michael, but Gabriel would see right through him. Now he definitely couldn't linger.

He grabbed a tube of hair stuff and squeezed some into his hand. He ran it through his hair as he went down the steps, hoping it would be enough. Then the car keys were in his hand and his messenger bag was over his shoulder.

"Nicky—" Gabriel started.

"Later, okay?" Nick said. "I told her I'd pick her up at eight."

"But—"

Nick shut the door in his face. Then he paused there on the porch, his hand on the doorknob. For an instant, he wanted to pull the door open. Gabriel knew he was hiding something, as clearly as Nick had known it when Gabriel was sneaking into burning houses with Hunter.

As clearly as Nick knew Gabriel was on the other side of this door, his hand on the same doorknob, deliberating whether to come after him.

For an instant, Nick wanted him to. He wanted Gabriel to throw open the door and demand something like *what the fuck is going on with you, Nicky?* Because then he could tell him, and he wouldn't have to carry this secret around anymore.

The door jerked open and the knob slipped from under his hand. Nick gasped and tried to hold on to his heartbeat before it bolted straight out of his body.

Gabriel studied him, his expression fierce.

Nick braced himself. *Tell him. Tell him tell him tell him.*

His lips froze. He couldn't speak. He couldn't breathe.

"Hey," said Gabriel. "You tell Quinn if Tyler messes with her again, I'll track him down and make him hurt for a month."

Right. Quinn. His girlfriend.

The air left Nick's lungs. He turned and stepped off the porch, willing the adrenaline to get the hell out of his body. "You don't even like Quinn."

"Yeah, but it's nice to have an excuse to go kick his ass."

Nick pushed the button to unlock the car and didn't say anything.

"Nicky," Gabriel called from the porch. His voice gained an edge. "Are you mad at me about something?"

No. Yes. Nick had no idea.

"No," he called back. "Just late."

He started the car so he didn't have to hear what else Gabriel said. But his brother's offer rolled around in his head, gaining traction while he drove. Quinn wasn't even his girlfriend, so it shouldn't have pissed him off.

But it did. Mostly because Gabriel was right: Nick hadn't done anything to protect her.

He knew being gay wasn't the equivalent of being weak, but right now, it sure felt like they went hand in hand.

He couldn't exactly dispute it, either, not while he was sneaking out to see a guy instead of avenging Quinn.

When he pulled into the parking lot, he killed the engine, then sat there. He'd been keyed up about seeing Adam all day, and now he wanted to crawl back into that proverbial closet and wedge the door closed.

This was like physics class, where he didn't know the right formulas. Adam would be expecting something from him tonight, and Nick had no idea what. Was *study here* just code for *come over and make out*? What if it was, and Nick missed the cues? Worse, what if it wasn't?

He looked at the clock on the dash. Ten past eight. He was already late. He could start the engine and peel out of here. Forget their kiss. Forget everything.

Coward. First he couldn't face Gabriel, and now he couldn't face Adam.

A hand knocked on the passenger window, and Nick jumped a *mile.*

Adam stood there in the dark, his eyes shadowed and his expression hidden.

Nick unlocked the car, and Adam climbed in without hesitation, bringing the scent of cloves and oranges with him.

He didn't say anything, and Nick peeked over at him. He'd expected loose dance clothes like last night, but Adam wore dark jeans and a red T-shirt under a charcoal gray pea coat. He had a messenger bag, too, beat-up brown leather that looked like it would explode from the weight of whatever was inside. His expression was easy, but his eyes were cautious.

When he spoke, his voice was gently teasing. "Do I pass muster?"

Nick jerked his eyes away. "You look great. Good. Yeah. Fine."

Jesus, was he going to sound like a raving idiot every time he saw this guy? *Me Nick. Me like boys. Me especially like how you look in that pea coat.*

Adam smiled, and it chased some of the tension from his eyes. "You look great, good, fine, too. Are you hungry?"

"Starving, actually." He hadn't eaten dinner before meeting his brothers, and there sure hadn't been time once he'd gotten home. Nick reached for the keys, but he couldn't start the car. His brain was screaming at him. *Public! Public! Public!* He didn't know whether that was better or worse than going down to Adam's apartment. He had to clear his throat. "Where do you want to go?"

"Little place up the road. Dirt cheap and always deserted because they don't have a liquor license."

Something loosened in Nick's chest. "Sounds great."

Adam reached out and stopped his hand before he could start the engine. "I thought maybe we could walk." He paused. "Unless you think the weather won't hold. It's windy. Might rain."

Nick looked at Adam's hand on his wrist. "It won't rain."

The wind welcomed him into the outdoors, kicking up to swirl around him. He could feel rain on the air, but a distant promise, nothing they'd have to worry about for hours yet. He was glad for the chance to walk. With a destination and a task and his element feeding him power, his brain relaxed a little.

Until Adam said, "You were sitting in your car for a while."

Wind rushed between darkened buildings to form tiny whirlwinds from the dead leaves along the sidewalk. Nick fed energy into the air, sending them spinning higher. Clouds blocked the starlight overhead, making their walk very dark between streetlamps. "I didn't realize you'd be waiting for me."

"I wasn't. Not really." Adam paused, and that hint of uncertain tension found his voice. "I figured I could use a walk either way."

Either way. Nick took a second to figure that out. Adam had thought Nick was standing him up. Then he'd seen him sitting in the car—quite obviously not getting out. Shame took Nick by the shoulders and shook him. He was disappointing everyone today.

"I'm sorry I was late," he said.

"Don't be. You're here." But Adam rubbed at the back of his neck, leaving Nick to wonder how much of that was true.

They fell into silence again. Nick let the air swirl around them, seeking answers about Adam's mood. Waiting for some signal of how to proceed.

"I didn't mean to ambush you," Adam finally said.

Nick looked over, confused.

"When you were sitting in your car. Were you thinking of leaving?"

Nick inhaled to lie, but then thought better of it. He nodded.

Adam took that at face value, but he kept walking. "When I saw you sitting there, I thought about doing the same thing."

Nick ran that scenario through his head. Finally getting the guts to walk down to Adam's apartment and finding no one home.

That—that would have stung. Given the thoughts he'd been having in the car, he probably would have deserved it.

"I'm glad you didn't," Nick said, his voice rough.

"Just because I'm *out* doesn't mean I don't *care*, Nick."

Nick. It was the first time he'd heard Adam say his name, and it sounded like an accusation.

"I know that," he said tightly.

"If you're not ready for this," Adam continued, his voice gaining momentum from anger, "I get it. Trust me, I get it. If you want to walk away, it's fine. But don't string me along while you—"

"Jesus," Nick snapped. "I'm *not*." He rounded on Adam, reaching to grab his arm, to stop him, to confront him.

But Adam was suddenly five feet away, his back to the darkened building, his shoulders tight, his hands curled into fists. Breath left his mouth in quickened bursts.

Nick held still for a moment. Then he closed the distance between them, stopping when he sensed Adam was going to back away again—or fight. His fists were up now, his expression resolved.

Nick kept his own hands low. "Did you think I was going to hit you?" he said carefully. "I wasn't. I wouldn't."

Adam studied him. His expression reminded Nick of last night, when Adam had almost flinched from his touch. Then the fear faded, quickly replaced by something closer to embarrassment. He turned and started walking again.

"Whoa." Nick caught his arm and hauled him to a stop.

Adam stopped, his eyes locked straight ahead. His arm was tense under Nick's hand.

Nick moved closer and dropped his voice. "I'm not trying to string you along," he said quietly. "I thought about leaving, but I wasn't going to. I couldn't stop thinking about you all day."

Adam turned his head to meet his eyes, and Nick felt his cheeks go warm.

"All day?" said Adam.

"I failed a physics test because of it."

A shadow of that easy confidence sneaked back into Adam's voice. "I blew a chem lab tonight because of you."

Nick's eyes widened. "A chem lab?"

"Yeah. I had class. I told you."

"I thought you meant dance."

"I wish. I suck at chemistry."

Nick loosened his grip on Adam's arm, but he didn't let go. "I'm great at chemistry."

Adam's eyes flicked to his lips. "I bet."

Nick hesitated, not wanting to damage the mood, which felt precariously balanced between flirtation and forgiveness. But it also felt like a big old heap of evasion. "Can we talk about what just happened?"

Adam pulled away and started walking. Nick fell into step beside him, expecting Adam to need to walk to talk. But then his companion remained silent.

Nick didn't press. He had enough experience from his brothers—to say nothing of Quinn—to know that people wouldn't talk until they were damn good and ready. By the time they made it to the tiny restaurant, he no longer expected an answer.

The place looked like it didn't know what it wanted to be. Red-checked tablecloths, cheap metal chairs, and all manner of food on the menu, from dim sum to stromboli. Soft lighting did nothing to hide the fact that they were the only patrons in the place.

After they were seated at a four top, with sodas in front of them, Nick was desperate for anything to lighten the mood.

"Fast service," he said wryly. "Do you want me to accuse you of dazzling the waitress?"

Adam choked on his soda. "Is that a *Twilight* reference? How is it possible your brothers don't know you're gay?"

Every time he said that, Nick wanted to flinch as hard as Adam had on the street. "I said a girlfriend was making me read it."

Adam lost the smile. "Quinn said you've had a lot of girl-friends."

Nick shrugged and wondered what the safe answer to that was. " 'A lot' is relative, I guess." He paused, wondering what else Quinn had said about him. "And you?"

"Girlfriends? None."

Nick smiled but wondered if they were going to play this game all night. The entire rhythm of the evening felt off, like they'd hit the wrong note right from the start, and they'd never really found the melody.

Adam unstrapped his bag and pulled out a chemistry text-book, followed by a spiral notebook. "Didn't you say you wanted to study?"

So they weren't going to talk about anything of substance at all. Nick pulled out his calculus textbook, glad he'd brought it along. He worked through the three homework questions he'd missed, hoping he could convince the teacher to give him half credit. Then he moved on to tonight's assignment.

Adam made for quiet company. Nick had worried it would be uncomfortable, but the restaurant was warm, the French dip sandwiches were exceptional, and an hour had passed before he realized it. He shoved his calculus textbook back into his bag and reached for physics.

The air whispered frustration, so Nick glanced across at his companion's notebook. Adam hadn't lied about hating chem-istry. It looked like it hated him back, from the amount of cross outs and eraser marks on the paper.

"Balancing equations?" Nick said.

Adam glanced up. "No. Murdering equations."

"No offense, but why are you taking chemistry if you hate it? I thought you were all gung ho about dance."

"I am, but I'd like something to fall back on. I need a science credit." He shrugged. "It was this or biology, and I didn't want to cut up dead animals."

Something to fall back on. Another thing Nick admired about him. "You want me to take a look?"

"Sure."

Nick expected him to turn the book around, like Gabriel would, but Adam didn't move. So Nick took his pencil and moved to the other side of the table.

The table wasn't tiny, but it was small enough that his thigh brushed Adam's when he sat, and he could feel the warmth of his body in the space between him and the wall.

Chemistry. Focus.

"Here," he said, writing the first formula on a new line. "I think you're trying to make it too complicated. I always find it easiest to start with the element that only shows up in one reactant and product. Like here, it's oxygen, so double the H-two-O on the right side of the arrow."

"Then I have too many hydrogens."

"So double it on the left." Adam did, and Nick said, "Now look at the carbon."

They worked through the rest of that problem and then started a new one. Nick walked him through that, too. By the third, he shut up and let Adam work through it alone.

"It seems so simple now." Adam glanced up. "You're a good teacher."

Nick flushed at the praise, but he shrugged it off. "Do you want to do another one?"

"Sure." Adam started writing. When he got to the end of the line, he hesitated, his pencil stopping on the paper. He kept his eyes down. "Do you remember how I told you that my parents wanted me to pretend to be straight, after I got out of the hospital?"

"Yeah."

"It sucked. I was determined to show them just how gay I

was. I started dating someone right away. It wouldn't have mattered who it was; I needed a guy so I could show my parents that I was in a relationship. At the studio where I danced then, they rented the space once a week to a martial arts school. One of the instructors was a guy named Matthew. Cute as hell, built like he was born on steroids—you know the type."

Adam set the pencil down and stopped there. His eyes were still on the chemistry paper. "I flirted with him," he said. "I flirt with everyone—gay, straight, whatever, I'm not shy."

Nick remembered. Adam had flirted with him the first night they met, before he even had a clue that Nick might be interested in boys.

"Was he straight?" Nick said.

"I thought he was. But he wasn't. He'd ignore me when I flirted in public, but once he caught me in the back room and asked me out. I didn't know anything about him, really, but he was hot, I was shallow, and that was that."

That wasn't that. Adam's voice had gained tension, and Nick waited, listening, glad for the privacy and the dim lighting.

"He wasn't out," Adam said, "but he was a few years older. He had his own place, so we only went there. The first time he kissed me, he was all hesitant and tentative. I thought it was charming. When he invited me back the next night, of course I went." He shook his head. "He kissed me again, but this time it went further—a lot further."

Adam stopped again, his jaw clenched now.

Nick wanted to touch him, to offer some comfort. He wasn't sure Adam would accept it. His brothers sure wouldn't, and he wasn't exactly rolling in experience with comforting other guys.

"So we're in his apartment," Adam said, his voice very low, "and he's practically naked, and he begs me to take care of him. He's hot and sweet and nice, and I'm into him, so I do. And we lie there for like thirty seconds, and I'm thinking I've finally found someone special. Instead, he tells me to get the fuck out of his apartment. I'm confused, right? Like, what the hell. But clearly I wasn't moving fast enough, because he punched me in the stomach and slammed me into the wall beside his door."

Nick's breath caught. He wasn't sure where he'd thought this story was going, but—that wasn't it.

Adam looked up. He met Nick's eyes and quickly looked away, ashamed. "This is insane. I can't believe I'm telling you this. I'm sorry. I'll shut up."

Nick reached out and touched his cheek, bringing his face back around. Adam's eyes closed and his breath shuddered, but he didn't pull away.

"Don't shut up," Nick said softly. "Talk. Tell me."

Adam pulled Nick's fingers away from his face, but then he kept a death grip on his hand. "It happened too fast. He was on his knees apologizing, comforting me before I even knew what hit me. He said he snapped, that nothing like that had ever happened before. And you know what's *really* insane? I believed him. I let him buy me dinner. I thought he was genuinely sorry. And when he asked me to come back the next night, I went. He was sweet, he was charming—it was fine. But a week later, the exact same thing happened.

"So here I'm dating a guy who's beating the shit out of me, the *exact thing my parents warned me about*, and I couldn't tell them because it would be one more thing to reinforce what they wanted. And the worst part is that I started to believe I deserved it. Or that it was normal. That it was something all gay relationships went through. Like aggression is just part of the package or something. Besides—what was I supposed to do? Complain that another guy was beating me up? Do you know what that sounds like?"

Nick knew exactly what that sounded like. "You're not weak," he said.

"Oh, I was. This went on for a long time. I never knew what would set him off. Some days he was wonderful, and I'd think it was all in my head. He would cry and tell me how he wanted so badly to be better. Other days he was . . . terrifying. I told him I didn't want to see him anymore, and he said he'd tell everyone that I was sexually harassing him, that I was some kind of deviant, that I shouldn't be allowed to work with kids. I loved my job. I didn't know what to do." Adam looked up. His eyes were shining, but he wasn't crying. "He was smart, too. He knew how to hit where it wouldn't show. I'd be too sore to dance, but there wouldn't be a mark on me. I remember once I threw up blood, and I wanted to go to the hospital. He said he'd tell them I had HIV. I don't—I've never—I . . . My dad would have found out, and I couldn't—"

He broke off. His hand was tight on Nick's. He took a long breath, steadying himself. "I couldn't go. After that, I was scared to tell anyone *anything*. For three months. Then he was offered a job somewhere else, and he moved. That was it. I didn't even solve my own problem. It just went away."

Nick moved closer, breathing along Adam's neck. "I'm sorry," he said. He touched Adam's face again. "I'm sorry."

"It was a long time ago. I've never told anyone." But his voice was still heavy. He brushed Nick's hand away and started to put some distance between them. "I can't believe I told you."

Nick caught him with a hand against his neck, but gently, so Adam could move if he really wanted to. "I won't hurt you." When Adam didn't resist, Nick stroked his thumb along his jaw and put his forehead against his temple. The waitress could probably see them, but he couldn't make himself care, not now. "I understand now. I won't hurt you."

Adam shook his head and gave a choked laugh. "You asked earlier about boyfriends? None, since him. I'll go out and have a good time, but I never go to anyone's place. I never bring anyone back to mine."

Nick drew back so he could look into Adam's eyes. "Except me."

"Except you." Adam paused. "You know when I first knew I was going to fall for you?"

Nick shook his head.

"On the beach, when we were rescuing Quinn. That one guy was going to hit me, and you got in front of him. You took the hit. I'd never seen anyone do anything so brave in my life. Especially not for me."

"I'm not brave," said Nick. "Not at all."

"You're letting me hang all over you in a restaurant. I'd say that's pretty brave."

Nick smiled. "A deserted restaurant. And you're not hanging all over me. I think you're the brave one, putting up with all that. I'm in . . . in *awe* of you." Nick felt heat crawl up his cheeks again, but he couldn't offer anything less than honesty now. Not after that. "You've got your whole life together. You know what you want, and you're even making a backup plan. I've got a drawer full of college letters that I'm afraid to open, and I'm living with four guys who don't know I'm . . . ah . . ."

"Say it," said Adam.

Nick shut his eyes and sighed. "Gay. I'm gay."

"See? Brave."

"I'm not—"

Adam kissed him. Gently, his mouth moving slowly against Nick's. He pulled away before too long.

"Thanks for listening," he said quietly.

"Thanks for telling me."

"You boys need anything else?"

Nick started. The older waitress was there beside the table. He hadn't heard her approach. Worse—he hadn't *felt* her approach. Would she say something? He should probably start disentangling himself from Adam. His voice wouldn't work and his face felt like his cheeks were going to burn clean off.

"No, thanks," Adam said. He sounded amused.

She ripped a piece of paper from her pad and set it on the table. "You two are just the cutest ever."

Nick froze. She didn't care. They'd been head to head at this table, and she hadn't batted an eye.

Adam winked at her. "Sounds like someone's looking for a tip."

"Here's a tip," she said. "Don't flirt with old married ladies when you've got a sure thing in your arms."

"Am I the sure thing in this scenario?" said Nick.

"I don't know," Adam said. "Are you?"

The waitress laughed and left them with the check.

"She didn't care," said Nick softly. "I know it's stupid, but I thought—"

"What, that people would come out with pitchforks? Flaming torches?"

"Maybe."

Adam kissed him on the cheek. "You're adorable. People surprise you sometimes. Especially when you give them the chance."

The words hit Nick hard, the way words you *need* to hear usually do. He held them in his head for examination later.

When they walked back to Adam's apartment, he reached out to hold the other boy's hand. And Nick didn't care one bit who saw.

CHAPTER 8

Quinn stretched her leg against a tree and shivered. She slid her fingers across the face of her iPod, looking for a playlist to suit her mood. The strip mall parking lot was tempting, but off limits thanks to that dickhead Tyler. The lot looked empty under the halogen lights, but that didn't mean anything. She'd stay right here at the edge of these woods, where she could see without being seen.

She didn't have any transportation, so it wasn't like she could go anywhere else. Her brother was out tonight—but her mom wasn't.

Quinn was waiting her out. She could sneak back into the house after midnight. Her mom usually wasn't conscious that long.

She'd hoped Nick would want to go out tonight, but he'd mentioned he was meeting Adam to "study"—*sure*—and Quinn didn't want to get in the middle of that.

She wondered if he was avoiding her after that stupid, *stupid* kiss. She blushed now, remembering. What had she been thinking?

You were thinking that he was really *your boyfriend, instead of a pretend one.*

Her phone chimed. She checked it. Becca.

Please. Talk to me. I'm sorry.

Quinn rolled her eyes and shoved the phone into her bag.

A branch snapped somewhere off to her right, and she froze, her eyes searching the darkness.

Nothing. Whatever.

She found Adam's audition song, melodic R&B with a driving beat.

Then she threw herself into the routine.

The ground was uneven here, and she had to watch out for branches, but she had sound in her ears and cold air on her skin. One of her favorite things about dance was that she could do it *anywhere*.

Her body was getting stronger from working with Adam, but she still had miles to go before she'd reach his level. Her turns needed more balance, and she still missed the beat in the more complicated moves. When Adam had first asked her to be his partner for his audition piece, she'd been ready to laugh it off. She had no real professional training, no expensive dance clothes or private instructors or anything to bring to the table other than raw talent. But even after he'd convinced her, she hadn't been ready for his work ethic. His intensity.

Adam wasn't fucking around. He *wanted* this scholarship.

And the stronger Quinn got, the more she realized she wanted him to get it, too. She didn't want to let him down.

She wanted to *accomplish* something, for once in her life.

She spun too fast and landed hard, stumbling. Damn. She used the slider on her iPod to back the song up a bit, then launched herself into motion.

The stars whirled above her, bearing witness to her dance. She wished Nick were here to feed power into the air. She could feel it when he did that now, driving energy into the music until she couldn't help leaping higher and moving with every beat. She tried to find that same energy now, without him, but the woods were empty, the wind's only power the ability to keep her cold.

Wham. Something slammed into her, and the music died instantly. Quinn hit the ground before she realized she was falling.

Then the earbuds were yanked free of her ears, something

snapped at her waistband, and footsteps were tearing away through the underbrush.

Wtf?

Then she got it.

"Come back here!" she screamed, running after the thief. She'd saved every penny for *months* to buy that iPod. "Stop! *Stop!*"

Her assailant had a pretty good head start. This had to be a guy, from the size and the way he moved. He bolted into the street without looking. Quinn followed.

A horn blared and she stumbled. Headlights filled her eyes, tires screeched, but the impact never came. Quinn made it to the curb and kept running, tearing across the parking lot of the strip mall.

"Thief!" she shouted. "Somebody stop him!"

Somebody. Like there was anyone out here.

He was getting away, gaining ground. The farthest part of the strip mall was pitch-black now, dark store fronts featuring a pediatric dentist's office and an eyewear shop. Beyond that, more woods. If he made it past the edge of the shops and into the trees, she'd never catch him.

"Stop, you asshole!"

Oh, who was she kidding? She was never going to catch this guy. He was twenty feet from the curb leading to the woods. She was at least fifty and her lungs were burning.

But then, as he neared the corner, a figure stepped out of the shadowed walkway and knocked him flat. Just *pow!* a solid strike and the thief hit the ground. Flat on his back. She could hear him moaning from here.

"Yeah!" Quinn cried. Mr. Big Fists was getting a *kiss* for this. With tongue.

But then her savior pulled out a gun. He pointed it at the thief and cocked the hammer.

Quinn skidded to a stop. "Holy shit."

A step forward brought the gunman into the light. Short blond hair, fierce expression. Tyler.

The guy on the ground was scrambling back. "You're crazy, man! It's a frigging iPod! You're—"

"Shut up." Tyler held a lit cigarette in his free hand. He put it to his lips and inhaled, but he didn't lower the weapon. "Give it back to her."

The thief—thin and filthy and not much older than she was—shoved her iPod across the concrete. He'd probably scraped the crap out of the case.

She didn't move to take it. She couldn't take her eyes off that gun. Her breathing felt too quick.

She should be running now, right? Saying thank you? What the hell was happening here?

Tyler jerked his head toward the road. "Get out of here, punk." When the thief didn't move fast enough, Tyler made a threatening move. The kid fought for his footing and ran, his feet scraping pavement.

Quinn kind of wished she could swipe the iPod and tiptoe away.

Tyler slid the gun into a holster at the small of his back and took a long drag from his cigarette. "You going to take that or what?"

Her iPod was on the ground right in front of his boots, and Quinn really didn't want to get that close. She remembered the burning pain of his palm on her forearm. She remembered Nick telling her that Tyler had roughed up Becca.

Then again, Becca sure hadn't thought he was scary enough to warrant telling Quinn about it.

"Come on," said Tyler, a dark smile on his lips. "If you don't have music, I can't enjoy the free show anymore."

"What does that mean?"

His eyes flicked at the woods across the street.

Screw him. She turned her back and started walking. "Go to hell."

"I think maybe a thank-you is in order."

"I think maybe a *fuck you* is in—"

"Would you take the stupid iPod?"

She whirled, hearing him right behind her. He was closer than she was ready for, and her breath rushed out of her chest.

In his hand was her beat-up iPod.

She hesitated, then took it. She wanted to fling it at him, but pride wilted in the face of practicality. It would take her forever to gather enough money to get another one. The case was scratched but unbroken, and the screen lit up when she pressed the button.

He didn't move back, and she finally had to, lest he think she *liked* being this close to him.

Tyler took another draw on his cigarette. The glow lit his cheeks and turned his eyes haunting. "Scared of me, baby girl?"

"Are you *aware* you sound like a douche bag?"

He laughed, blowing smoke through his nose. "Where's your boyfriend?"

"None of your business. Have another cigarette?"

His eyebrows went up. "You want one?"

No. She didn't. She'd only ever smoked once. But she had nowhere else to go and nothing else to do and she needed something to do with her hands before they started shaking.

She gave Tyler a look. "Yeah. You have one or not?"

He pulled a pack from his back pocket and shook one free. "Do you have a lighter?"

"No. Don't you?"

He gave her half a smile, then put the new cigarette to his lips. He inhaled slowly, and after a moment the end glowed red and burned. A fresh burst of nicotine hit the air. Then he pulled it out of his mouth and held it out to her.

Quinn stared despite herself. "Gross."

And somehow a little sexy, but she'd put his gun to her head before admitting that.

He cocked an eyebrow. "You were sitting next to a Dumpster last night, and now you're afraid of a little spit. Jesus. You want it or not?"

His voice was full of derision, but challenge, too. *Scared of me, baby girl?*

She took the cigarette out of his hand and put it to her lips.

For a second she was worried she'd do the moronic thing and explode with coughing, but she inhaled slowly, letting the warmth travel into her lungs. She expected it to taste nasty, but it didn't.

"Why are you out here with a gun?" she asked, easing the smoke out. "Isn't that against some law?"

He looked vaguely affronted. "I have a permit, and I'm protecting my property. No, it's not against *some law*."

"This strip mall is yours. Seriously. And you have all this money and nothing better to do than wander around dark parking lots pointing guns at petty thieves? Yeah, okay."

"This strip mall belongs to my parents," he said, taking another long inhale on his cigarette. Smoke curled away from him into the night sky. "And we've been having a problem with vandals, so I've been hanging out the last few nights."

"Gee, I'm so sorry for you."

"You've kinda got a chip on your shoulder, huh?"

Yeah, the size of Rhode Island. Quinn flicked ash from the end of her cigarette and didn't respond. She hadn't inhaled again, and it was just burning away between her fingers.

"What were you dancing to?" he asked.

The question took her by surprise, but his voice was challenging again, so she fired up the song on her iPod and held out an earbud.

He listened for a long moment, then nodded and handed the cord back. "Nice."

This was so bizarre. "Glad it meets with your approval."

"Why were you dancing in the woods?"

"I'm helping a friend get a scholarship."

"Oh, yeah? Why aren't you getting a scholarship?"

"I don't think that's really any of your business."

He shrugged and backed up to lean against the steel beam supporting a roof over the walkway. He took another drag and blew out smoke rings. "My sister was a dancer."

His sister. Nick had told her Tyler's sister had died in the rock quarry years ago.

"A singer, too," said Tyler. "She was always on my parents to let her move to New York after graduation."

Quinn wanted to snap at him, something like, *So she couldn't wait to get away from you, either?* But his voice held this odd note that she couldn't identify. Not quite sadness, but something close. Resignation, maybe. She didn't want to mock it.

"Full of piss and vinegar," Tyler said. "She'd probably laugh her ass off to hear you talk to me now."

"I'd probably like her."

"Maybe." He crushed out the end of his cigarette and glanced down at hers, hanging abandoned in her hand. "You going to let that burn away to nothing?"

She quickly took another draw. Too fast. Smoke flooded her lungs and she choked hard, fighting for air.

"Sit," said Tyler, plucking the cigarette from her fingers. "Breathe."

She sat and tried to inhale while tears streamed from her eyes. He dropped onto the curb beside her.

"All talk," he said. "Should've guessed." Then he took up her cigarette and smoked it himself.

Quinn stared at him, confused by this sudden intimacy.

"Seriously," he said suddenly. "What's with the lurking behind the 7-Eleven last night?"

She shrugged and looked out at the dark parking lot.

"Homeless?" he asked, his voice matter-of-fact.

"No," she snapped.

"Do those Merrick morons know you're out here?"

Those "Merrick morons" probably thought she was out with Nick. "What do you care?"

"So that's a no." He snorted, blowing smoke. "Not surprised that one of those idiots can't take care of a girlfriend."

Like Tyler could? "I bet they'll be disappointed they don't live up to your standards."

His voice turned dark. "They know what I think of them."

"No kidding." She held up her arm. "I got a firsthand demonstration, you asshole."

He rounded on her so fast that Quinn almost fell back on the step. He was right in her space. "You think you know what you're talking about? You don't know shit. You have no idea what they've done to me."

Quinn punched him in the chest, giving him a solid shove. "Maybe they did, but *I* never did anything to you. Back off." When he didn't move, she put her face almost against his and reinforced her voice with steel girders. "Back. Off."

He held her there, probably trying to use his size or his attitude to intimidate her. Like he had anything on her home life. She stared back at him, waiting.

He finally shifted forward and put the cigarette to his lips again.

"They killed my sister," he said quietly.

No way was he buying her pity from a sob story she'd already heard. "Nick told me you chased her and Michael into the quarry."

"He's a fucking Earth. How the hell do you think that rock-slide started?"

She stared into the face of his obvious fury and gave him the only answer she had. "I don't know. I wasn't there."

Tyler seemed to deflate. He crushed out the rest of his cigarette and looked out at the night, rubbing a hand across the back of his head.

Then he looked over. "You hungry?"

Yes. She was starving. "I'm not going anywhere with you."

"Why?"

"Because I think you're a psychopath."

He laughed softly. "I was going to get some taquitos from 7-Eleven. Want some?"

Quinn thought about it. If she said no, it might be hours before she'd get the chance to eat. And what was the difference between smoking with Tyler and eating with him? At least if she was with him, no one was trying to steal her stuff.

Sad that her life had devolved into choosing between lesser evils.

Her cell phone chimed again. Nick this time.

You ok?

She thought about it.

All OK. Have fun with your boyfriend. xoxo

"Taquitos sound great," said Quinn. She climbed to her feet. "I like mine extra spicy."

CHAPTER 9

Quinn had never sat on the roof of a strip mall before. She'd never really sat on the roof of any building before. But Tyler obviously had: a few nylon folding chairs sat by the edge of the roof, and there was even a little table between them.

She sprawled in one of the chairs and stretched her legs out in front of her. "So is this where the magic usually happens?"

Tyler cracked open a bottle of Mountain Dew and sprawled in the chair beside her. "The magic?"

"Is this where you bring girls? Promise to show them the world?"

He waved a hand at the trees, the suburban sprawl. "Oh, yeah. Check out the world of Arnold, Maryland." He let out a low whistle. "You can almost see the waste disposal plant from here. Want to take your pants off yet?"

"It's hard not to."

"I don't usually bring girls up here. I have an apartment for that."

An apartment. For about two seconds, Quinn wondered how old he was, then decided she didn't care. Nick had said he was younger than Michael, so he couldn't be older than twenty-two. He definitely wasn't in high school. "I feel so special."

He stood and walked to the edge. The lights from below

caught his features and made them glow. "It's easier to keep an eye on things from up here."

"What kind of vandals are you looking for?"

He came back to the chair. "Bored teenagers, mostly. It's quiet up here, too. I can get a lot of studying done."

Studying. College. Check.

"Two chairs," she said.

"I've got a friend who works at the Sunglass place. Sometimes he brings a six-pack and we shoot the shit." He paused. "You have a lot of questions about my rooftop habits."

Quinn shrugged. "Just trying to figure out how to avoid you."

He looked at her. "Yeah, you look like you're trying really hard. Let's cut the crap. What's really up with you and Merrick?"

"He's busy, that's all. What do you care?"

"Maybe I don't want to babysit his girlfriend."

"Fuck you." Quinn stood with enough force to make the chair scrape back a few inches.

Tyler caught her arm. "Stop. I'm messing with you."

She turned fierce eyes his way. "No one needs to *babysit* me."

"No kidding." His voice softened, just a little, just enough. "Sit down. Eat your taquito. I don't like them extra spicy."

She sat in the chair and unwrapped the paper, taking a small bite from the end. It was like a heart attack rolled up in a tortilla and fried, but she was starving. "What's really up with *you* and Merrick?"

His voice was bitter. "You already know."

"No," she said. "I don't think I do."

"I don't want to talk about them."

"Do you really want to kill them?"

"I don't *need* to kill them. That's what the Guides are for."

"Would you do it, if you could?"

"I don't really want to go to prison for doing someone else's job."

"Aren't you a big bad Fire Elemental? Couldn't you burn down their house or something?"

"No!" he snapped with sudden fury. "That wouldn't make

me any better than *them*. That's the whole reason they're supposed to be put to death. They are a *danger*. Don't you get that?"

She ignored his sudden vehemence, keeping her voice level. "Do you really think they deserve to die, for what they are?"

He didn't say anything for a long while, twisting the bottle of Mountain Dew in his hands, making the plastic crackle. He sat that way for so long that she didn't think he was going to say anything.

Finally, he said, "You were right. When my sister died, she was with that douche bag. My friends and I were going after them. But I didn't start that fucking rockslide. And even if Mike Merrick didn't *start* it, he sure as hell didn't stop it." His voice tightened. "That rock hit her, and he didn't even get her out of the water in time. He let her die, okay? So if someone wants to come to town and kill them, I'm sure as hell not going to get in their way. If that makes me a psychopath, fine. There's no secret about how I feel."

"No secret," she replied. "I like that."

He turned and looked at her, eyebrows raised.

Quinn shrugged. "My life is full of secrets. Sometimes I'm sick of keeping them." She paused, wondering if she was stupid to be here with Tyler. He hated the Merricks, that much was obvious. It was probably a violation of her friendship with Nick that she was even *sitting* here.

But she could hear every ounce of pain in Tyler's voice when he spoke about what had happened to his sister. Could she blame him for that? If someone contributed to the death of someone in her family, then wandered around town like they hadn't done anything wrong, how would she have dealt with it?

Well, if someone did something to *her* older brother, she'd probably send them a thank-you note.

She thought of Tyler's anger in the driveway, when he'd confronted Nick. Was some of that pain? Resentment? Tyler had been a dick, for sure. But then again, Nick had threatened to kill him.

Who was right? It didn't feel like either of them was.

"I'm really sorry about your sister," she said quietly.

Tyler looked up at the sky. "Me, too. I was a crap brother. I wish I could go back and fix it."

"Do you—"

"Hey." He looked over, and she could see emotion in his eyes. "Would it be okay if we talked about something else?"

"Yeah." She paused. "I'm sorry."

He shook his head. "Stop. Something else. Anything. Talk about dance. I was serious, earlier. Why aren't you trying for a scholarship?"

"You don't really care."

"I do, actually. When I was watching you, I was thinking—" He broke off.

Quinn straightened. "What were you thinking?"

His voice turned sheepish. "Nothing. Forget it."

She could only imagine what he'd been thinking. "Now you definitely need to tell me. Was it that you didn't realize a full grown hippo could do spins like that?"

His head snapped around. "What the hell are you talking about?"

"I know I'm not built like a typical dancer."

"What does that even mean? Are you another one of these girls who tries to live on carrots and hot water?"

She waved the taquito in his face. "No, but I probably should be."

"You're insane, baby girl." He paused and rubbed at his jaw. "I was thinking that Nick Merrick is one lucky bastard."

Quinn flushed, pleased.

At the same time, she felt a curl of anger. Sometimes she hated being Nick's pretend girlfriend.

"Yeah," Tyler continued, "I don't know a *whole* lot about dance—just what I remember from Emily—but if anyone is going for a scholarship, you should be."

Quinn swallowed. "There's an application fee, and it's extremely competitive, and I don't—it's just—"

"Afraid of competition?" His eyes were dark and shadowed, his voice rough. "You don't strike me as the type."

He did not sound sexy. He *did not*.

Yeah, she wasn't convincing herself. "I'm not the type to have a spare hundred bucks lying around, either."

Tyler winced. "Sorry."

She shrugged and scowled out at the night. "My whole life is full of *almosts*. I almost made it on the dance team, until the bitch teacher wanted to get rid of me because of my attitude and my body type. I almost made it as a cheerleader, but they all called me *Crisco* and acted like I was white trash. I almost had a great—"

She cut herself off. She'd almost said, *I almost had a great boyfriend, but then I caught Nick kissing another guy.*

"Almost what?" said Tyler.

Quinn shook her head, surprised to feel tears hiding somewhere behind her eyes. "Nothing. What I want always seems just out of reach, you know?"

Tyler sighed. "Yeah," he said. "Sometimes I know exactly what you mean."

Chapter 10

Nick's morning classes crawled by. He could barely stay awake for Dr. Cutter's physics lecture. He'd come home late again, dragged himself into bed, and replayed his evening with Adam. Their walk. Their studying.

Adam's secrets.

After learning about that, everything had felt somewhat raw, as if a scab had been scraped off too early. He'd felt the need to proceed slowly, to let trust grow in the space between them. So he'd come in when Adam invited him, but he'd sat on the couch and sipped coffee and talked, keeping his hands to himself.

Nick had been worried that some of his infatuation was because Adam was the first boy he had kissed, the first outlet for years of repressed attraction.

But Adam was *smart*. He read everything, from genre fiction to biographies to *The Economist* to a weekly sex advice column. He could talk about all of it. Nick might have had him beat in chemistry, but Adam had him by a mile in subjective analysis. He'd never met someone who would genuinely care about his opinion—but then expect him to defend it.

Nick loved it. He loved it so much it'd been hard to leave.

But then he'd leaned in to kiss Adam good night, and he'd seen the flash of vulnerability, reminding him to tread carefully.

That first night, his time with Adam had been like riding a

runaway train, having no idea of the destination, just hurtling into the darkness while clinging for dear life. Exciting and terrifying.

Now it felt like someone had pressed a map into his hands and explained how to ease off the throttle.

"Earth to Nicholas. Come in, Mr. Merrick."

Crap. Dr. Cutter was glaring at him. What were they talking about? Diagrams covered every inch of whiteboard, but Nick hadn't even cracked his textbook. His notebook was open, but he hadn't written anything down.

Nick cleared his throat. "I'm sorry. What?"

"I asked if you'd come up with an answer for the third question."

Nick took another desperate glance at his notebook, as if the answers would have magically appeared. He couldn't afford to piss off Dr. Cutter, who was already giving him a free pass by letting him retake the unit test he'd bombed yesterday.

Nick looked back at the board, at the third diagram, hoping it would be something he could work out in his head.

Yeah, right. This was AP Physics. He knew it had something to do with velocity and mass, maybe—

"Perhaps I can explain what you've missed when you stay after class."

Half the class sucked in a breath and looked at him.

Gabriel would fling his pencil down and level the teacher with some snarky comment. He'd probably get himself thrown out of class.

Nick could never do that. Shame was curling his stomach into knots. "I'm sorry. It won't happen again."

After class, Dr. Cutter was a lot less accommodating than he'd been the previous day.

"This is an advanced placement class," he said, a slight edge to his voice. "We move through the material quickly. Are you having difficulty keeping up?"

"No," said Nick. "I'm sorry. Really, it won't happen again."

The teacher's eyes narrowed. "I don't really have Gabriel Merrick sitting in front of me, do I?"

Nick flinched. It shouldn't have been an insult, but it felt like one. "No. I swear."

"I had to call your name three times."

Nick didn't know how many times he could apologize for the same thing. He rubbed at his eyes. "I'm having a rough week."

Dr. Cutter studied him. "Are you aware you're the student with the highest average in this class?" He frowned. "Or you were before yesterday's test."

Nick pulled his hands down. He'd thought he was better than average, but the highest? "No, I didn't know."

"And you're second in your class in AP Calc. I spoke with Mrs. Rafferty. In fact . . ." He reached behind him for a folder on his desk. He flipped the cover open. "Out of the entire senior class, based on a weighted GPA, you're ranked fourth overall."

Wow. He'd had no idea.

He should have been proud. He wasn't. The pressure clamp on his chest tightened by one notch. One more expectation he had to uphold. If he were like Gabriel, Dr. Cutter wouldn't have given a crap that he didn't know the answer in class.

"Have you started applying for colleges?" said Dr. Cutter.

Nick's mouth went dry. "Yeah—a few. I just—" *I just have their sealed responses hidden in a drawer.* "I haven't heard back."

"University of Maryland has a program that allows a few select students to take college level science and math classes for the spring semester. It's by teacher recommendation only. It's an opportunity to get a jump start on an already competitive program."

Nick stared at him, unsure where this was going.

"I'd like to recommend you. But I also need to know you're focused."

Reassure him. Say you're focused. Or thank you. Say thank you.

But he couldn't say anything. A jump start? He was terrified of the prospect of leaving his brothers to start college next fall, and this guy wanted to accelerate that by nine months.

Dr. Cutter grabbed a cardigan off the back of his desk chair and shivered. "It certainly got chilly in here. Do you have any thoughts?"

Nick grabbed his bag and stood up. "I need to think about it." He bolted for the door.

"Nick!"

The instinct to obey authority overrode his desire to get the hell out of the classroom. Nick stopped in the doorway, but he didn't turn all the way around.

"I don't know what's going on with you," said Dr. Cutter, "but make sure it doesn't damage your chances at a future."

His voice wasn't unkind, and Nick swallowed.

Then Dr. Cutter added, "I want to make sure I recommend the right student for this opportunity. Do I make myself clear?"

"Perfectly. Thank you."

He should have been excited.

He wasn't.

At lunch, he sat with his brothers and their girlfriends, but Hunter and Quinn didn't show up. He didn't care what his roommate was up to, but he did care about Quinn. Nick sent her a quick text.

She responded almost immediately.

I'm getting study help for US History. I'll see you later. Can you give me a ride to the studio tonight?

The studio. Adam.

He mentally calculated. He was supposed to help Michael on Wednesdays, but they'd be done by seven-ish.

Sure. 7:45?

"What's eating you?" said Chris.

"Nothing," said Nick. He set the phone next to his tray and drove his fork into the cafeteria meat loaf.

Becca leaned in against the table. "Is Quinn okay?" she asked quietly. "She's really upset about the Elemental stuff."

She hadn't said anything to Nick, but he knew Quinn didn't want Becca to know how rough her home life had turned. And maybe she was still smarting from the secrets Becca had kept. Nick didn't necessarily agree with either course of action, but Quinn wasn't exactly giving him all the details, either. He nodded. "I'll talk to her. I'm taking her to dance tonight."

Gabriel snorted. "Wow, playing chauffeur. Sounds like true love to me."

His girlfriend Layne hit him. "Leave him alone."

"Will you tell her I'm worried about her?" said Becca. "I don't—I didn't mean to hurt her."

Nick gave her a reassuring look. "I'll tell her."

His phone chimed while he was shoveling a bite of meat loaf into his mouth. Nick reached for it.

But then Gabriel said, "Who's Adam? And why is he asking if he's going to see you tonight?"

Nick choked on his food.

Stupid. Stupid, stupid, stupid.

His heart beat so quickly that he could swear all the blood rushed away from his head just to keep up with it. For a horrifying moment he wondered if he'd pass out from panic.

He needed to say something. He needed to say something *now* before they started guessing.

They were all staring at him. Because they suspected something?

No, moron, because you're choking on meat loaf.

Did Gabriel sound suspicious? Why would he be suspicious? What did he think?

"Quinn's dance partner," Nick said quickly, wheezing a little. He needed to calm down, but his brain wouldn't let him stop talking. "He's auditioning for a scholarship, and she's helping him."

"Why is he asking if he'll see you?"

"I don't know." Nick shoved the phone in his pocket. "I guess he's wondering if Quinn has a ride."

That was probably sufficient, but he couldn't look at any of them, couldn't meet their eyes to see if they'd already guessed his secrets. They hadn't, right? Or had they? He was going to need to look up.

If he'd been telling the truth, it would have felt like enough, and he wouldn't have felt compelled to keep going. But he was lying through his teeth, and he needed to make sure there was no question of his non-relationship with Adam.

"He's gay," he heard himself saying. "Quinn said he has a crush on me. She thought it would be funny to give him my cell number."

What the fuck was *wrong* with him? Did he really say that?

"That's not funny," said Layne. She looked vaguely disgusted.

"It's not like that," said Nick quickly. His shirt felt like it was sticking to the back of his neck. "He knows I'm not. It's like— it's a joke now."

God, he needed to *shut up*.

"It's creepy," said Gabriel.

Nick froze. "Creepy?"

"A dude hitting on you? Yes. Creepy."

Suddenly he wanted to punch his twin.

Do not pick a fight over this.

Do not.

Do. Not.

"He's not hitting on me," Nick said tightly. "He just asked if I'd be there tonight."

"No, he asked if he'd *see you*, which is *creepy*."

"Knock it off," said Becca. "He's Quinn's friend. Nick's trying to defend him, and you're being a royal—"

Chris wrapped an arm around her neck and put his hand over her mouth. "I love you, but please don't pick a fight I'm going to have to finish."

"Oh, I'll finish it," Becca said through his fingers.

"No, *I'll* finish it," Nick snapped. He stood, grabbing his tray so roughly that he almost dropped half his food on Chris. "An asshole," he said to Gabriel. His throat felt tight, and it hurt to talk. "You're being a royal asshole."

Then he stormed away from the table and slammed the tray onto one of the waiting carts.

"Hey, Nicky," Gabriel called after him, "remember what I said about drama?"

Fuck him. Nick slammed through the double doors leading out of the cafeteria, choking on emotion. He pinched his fingers over his eyes.

He wished he could take it all back. Adam had trusted him with a terrible secret, and now Nick had crapped all over it. Making what they'd shared into a *joke*.

He wanted to storm back into that cafeteria and shake some sense into his brother.

He wanted to call Adam and apologize.

He wanted to stop hearing the derision in his brother's voice. The way he'd said *creepy*.

Most of all, he wanted to stop crying.

Creepy. Creepy creepy creepy.

Like he was some kind of pervert. He'd known his twin's rejection would hurt, but he hadn't realized it would hurt like this, a subtle stabbing a hundred times over.

Nick ducked into the restroom. Empty. Finally, a break. He went into a stall anyway. He swiped at his eyes and dug his phone out of his pocket.

There was Adam's message.

Will I see you tonight?

Nick squeezed his eyes shut and had to swipe at them again. Then he typed back.

We'll be there at 8.

Adam's response appeared almost immediately.

Can't wait.

Then a second later, another message appeared.

U OK?

Nick sniffed. He started to type back, *Yeah, fine*, but they'd found this path of honesty, and he didn't want to veer into the unknown.

Gabriel said gay guys are creepy.

As soon as he hit SEND, he felt ridiculous. He might as well have typed, *My brother is a big meanie. Wah.*
But his phone buzzed almost immediately.

You told him???

Oh, shit. No. Nick shook his head, like an idiot.

No. Said in passing.

The phone didn't buzz with a new message. But the end-of-lunch bell rang. Nick sniffed again and got himself together. He spent a minute splashing cold water on his face, until some freshman guys came through the door.
His phone buzzed before he made it into his next class.

You are not creepy. You are great good fine. And brilliant and patient and gentle and kind.

Jesus, he was going to start crying again.
Before he could, the phone buzzed.

And frankly, you're kind of hot. Do you know how hard it was to keep my hands off you last night?

Nick laughed before he could help it.

He took a seat and hid the phone under his desk, then slid his fingers across the screen.

You, too, for what it's worth. And thank you.

His phone buzzed almost immediately.

NP. Been there. See you tonight. Don't be late this time. ;-P

Nick wouldn't be.

CHAPTER 11

Quinn stumbled into the truck and flung her bag on the floor between her feet. She could barely feel her toes, but somehow she was supposed to spend the next two hours dancing. Her hands slapped over the vents. "Can you turn the heat up?"

Nick obliged her, reaching over and turning the dial all the way to the right. "You okay?"

Her fingers hurt from the cold, and she flexed them a few times. "Yeah. I've just been outside for a while."

He reached over and took her hands, pressing them between his. He brought them to his lips and blew warm air along her fingers. "You should have texted me. What happened?"

Quinn looked up at him over their clasped hands. His face was close, his blue eyes gentle and intent on hers. His clothes were different from what he'd worn to school, and he looked like he'd shaved again, too.

He looked amazing.

A flicker of regret hit her between the eyes. This was so unfair.

She pulled her hands away. "Stop looking at me like that."

"Like what?"

"You're late."

"I'm not. It's seven forty. Did something happen?"

"My brother had his stupid pothead friends over." Quinn

grabbed the seat belt and jerked it across her chest. "I had to get out of there."

She'd been lucky to get her dance clothes without being groped. Then her mom had gotten in her face and demanded to know where she'd been last night.

Why, Mom? Were you conscious?

At the stop sign at the end of her lot, Nick turned to look at her. "You could have called me. I would have come to get you."

"You were working." She sounded petulant and she didn't care. She knew he would have come to get her, because that's what perfect boyfriends did. "Did you dress up for Adam?"

He gestured down at his clothes. "I wouldn't call this dressing up."

She would. Dark-washed jeans and a forest-green pullover that clung to the muscles of his chest. He'd probably told his brothers he was getting ready for a date with *her*.

Quinn looked out the window. She didn't know what was wrong with her tonight. This felt like jealousy, but that was *insane*. It had been her idea to keep pretend dating in the first place!

"Are you mad at me?" Nick sounded puzzled. Almost hurt.

"No, Nick. I'm not mad."

He put an arm out. "Come here. What's wrong?"

She was tempted to curl against him and let him stroke her hair or whisper assurances or whatever he was so good at. She didn't move. "Forget it. It's fine."

He sighed, then swore under his breath. When they came to a red light, she could feel his eyes on her.

"Please don't do this," he said, his voice quiet but intense. "You're the only friend I can talk to. If I've fucked something up, just tell me." He paused. "I know you're not talking to Becca. What happened?"

"How do you know that?"

"She asked me about you."

"Oh, she remembers me now? That's awfully sweet of her."

"She's concerned about you. When you said you were all right last night, I thought you were at her place."

"Well, I wasn't."

"Where were you? Did you go home?"

"No, I was waiting out my mom. I was dancing on the trail by the woods." Part of her didn't want to talk about this, about *any* of it. Another part of her wanted to throw everything in Nick's face.

God, this *sucked*. He was too good looking, too nice. Throw supernatural powers in the mix, and it was like fate was playing a cruel joke on her. Maybe next he'd tell her he had a winning lottery ticket in the glove box.

"You were dancing on the trail? Where?" said Nick.

"Where you picked me up the other night."

Nick blew a loud rush of air through his teeth and ran a hand through his hair. "For god's sake, Quinn, are you insane?"

"Probably. Some punk tried to steal my iPod."

"You're lucky that's all that happened. Tyler lives near there. He could have—"

"Tyler stopped him."

Nick's jaw tightened. The truck instantly went ten degrees colder. Quinn shivered.

"Stop it," she snapped. "I'm already freezing."

He turned the vent to high, but it didn't help much. "What do you mean, Tyler stopped him?"

It wasn't until he spoke that she realized this was what she wanted. Fury in his voice. A hint of anger and jealousy and protectiveness. "The kid who stole my iPod. Tyler stopped him before he could take off with it. Then he bought me taquitos and we drank sodas on the roof of his strip mall."

She flung the words at Nick like an attack. She didn't know what she expected from him. A reaction, for sure. But silence captured the interior of the truck cab, thick and hard to breathe. His disapproval hung in the air, pressing against her skin.

"Please tell me you're kidding," he finally said.

"I'm not kidding. It was fine. He was nice."

"He is not *nice*, Quinn."

"Maybe not to you, but he was nice to me."

"This isn't a game!" he snapped. "If he's being nice to you, it's so he can *use you* against me."

"Why?" she fired back. "Because I'm only good for guys to use me? That's working out really great for you, isn't it, Nick?"

The air in the cab moved, lifting a few strands of her hair. Nick's hands clutched the steering wheel like he wished it was Tyler's neck.

"Look," he said, his voice rough and low like gravel. "Tyler is cruel. Destructive. You *know* this. He hit you in the face and burned your arm and—"

"He didn't hit me in the face!"

Nick gave it right back to her. "Then who did, Quinn?"

She locked her eyes on the windshield, suddenly afraid she might cry. Air moved through the cab again, warmer now, a caress along her exposed skin.

It felt ridiculous, but she couldn't tell him. Like Becca, Nick knew some of what her home life was like, but not enough. They mostly knew what it had been like before: the screaming matches with her mother, the father who seemed to forget he had a family. But since the fire, things had changed. Money was tight, and it was like her parents clung to Jake and his scholarship as if that was the shining star in their lives. Like that put food on the table.

More likely, keeping her mom away from the liquor store would do a lot more for their family than Jake's stupid scholarship.

Not like Jake was making use of that scholarship, the way he kept frying his brain cells every night.

If Quinn told Nick about how her mother practically drank herself unconscious, or how her brother could barely string a sentence together, but didn't mind strong-arming her into the wall when he needed twenty bucks, Nick would step in. He'd be the white knight in shining armor. He'd rescue her.

And then he'd kiss her on her forehead and go off with a knight of his own.

"I can't help you if you won't talk to me," said Nick, his tone resigned. "I can't believe you think that asshole could be *nice*—"

"He was nice," she said icily. "You know, he still thinks your brother killed his sister. He actually seemed kind of upset about it."

"Upset. Yeah, okay." Nick looked disgusted. "Did he tell you about the time he tried to kill Chris? Or the time he and his friends pinned Michael down in a parking lot and took a butane lighter to his face? Or how about the time he cornered me in the gym and—"

Nick broke off, breathing fast.

"And what?" she said.

"You know what? Forget us. Think about *Becca*. Just ask her what she thinks of Tyler."

Quinn didn't want to think about Becca. Lately, any time thoughts of Becca entered her brain, a bunch of jealousy and resentment crowded in alongside. "Well, maybe if Becca had been honest all along, I'd already know her thoughts about Tyler."

Nick looked incredulous. "Maybe if you'd talk to her, she could be! Tyler's best friend was one of the guys who tried to *rape* Becca. Seth Ramsey. He and Drew McKay dragged her onto the soccer field at Homecoming. Remember that?"

Quinn flinched. She remembered Becca's torn, rain-soaked dress, the way her best friend had shivered in the backseat on the drive home. Chris Merrick had witnessed the attack, and Seth and Drew had been expelled from school. "I remember. But I'm not going to hold Tyler responsible for something Seth and Drew did—"

"Jesus, Quinn, *fine*. Maybe not then. But he tried to kill her at Drew's party a few weeks ago. She and Chris ran into the water, and Tyler tried to shoot them. With a *gun*."

Quinn didn't say anything to that. Her brain was roiling with two different emotions.

Fear. Tyler had a gun. She'd seen it. He'd played it off by saying he was protecting his property, but . . . he'd been shooting at *Becca*?

Then *anger*. Becca had never said anything about Tyler shooting at her that night.

She'd never said anything about *any* of this.

Becca acted like she wanted to kiss and make up, but what was the point? Quinn was so *tired* of all these secrets.

Nick kept going. "I can't believe you thought he was *nice*. Do you just find the most destructive people you can and latch on to them?"

She flinched. The words hurt more than anything her mom had said. Anything her brother had done. Quinn had to squish her eyes closed to keep the tears from planning an escape route.

When she was sure her voice would be steady, she looked at him. "I don't know, Nick. Do I?"

He jerked the wheel to turn into the parking lot of the dance studio, then flung the vehicle roughly into park.

He didn't look at her.

She wasn't going to wait around for him to make her feel worse, so she got out of the truck and slammed the door closed.

Then she pushed into the nearly empty studio and stomped across the wooden floor, throwing her bag on the ground beside where Adam was making notes on a clipboard.

He looked as good as Nick, despite the bare feet and cutoff sweatpants. He was all unruly hair and dark eyes and caramel skin. A maroon long-sleeved tee did little to hide his build.

Her hair was a windblown mess, and if she took her sweatshirt off, there was probably a roll of pudge hanging over the waistband of her spandex capris. God only knew what state her makeup was in, after nearly crying in the car.

Adam glanced up, but she wouldn't meet his eyes. One kind word and she'd go to pieces.

Nick hadn't followed her.

She wanted to cry for all the wrong reasons.

Adam set the clipboard down, and she could hear it in his indrawn breath, that he was going to pry. His hands were already reaching out to touch her.

Just what she needed. Another guy who had no interest in her.

Quinn swiped at her eyes and grabbed her bag. "I can't do it tonight, Adam. I'm sorry."

"You—wait. Stop, Quinn—what's wrong?"

"Not tonight," she called back. She walked through the back door to the studio, bursting into the cold night air.

Nick's truck was on the other side of the building—if he'd bothered to wait at all. Quinn hunched her shoulders and headed for the road.

What a dick. Everyone else got everything they wanted. Becca had Chris. Nick had Adam. Quinn had *nothing*. She had a fake boyfriend who gave her a raft of shit the first time someone else was nice to her.

The thought rang false inside her head, and she told her subconscious to stick it.

A metro bus was rolling up to the curb. The brakes squealed into the darkness and the door creaked open. Adam took the bus all the time, but Quinn had never tried. At least it was a surefire escape from Nick.

She climbed the steps and sniffed back the last of her tears. "How much?"

"One sixty, one way. Three fifty, ride all day."

All day. Quinn wondered who would spend the entire day on a bus. Then she realized it was warm in here, and empty aside from the driver. No one to bother her.

"Ride all night, too?" she asked.

"We stop running at two."

Well, there went that. She counted out a dollar sixty and crammed her money into the slot.

Once the vehicle started moving, she realized she had no idea where she was going.

Wasn't that always the case?

Her phone chimed. Nick.

Where did you go?

Quinn deleted it.

Then she started a new text.

Playing sentry again tonight?

The response text took less than three seconds.

Why? Need rescuing, baby girl?

Quinn smiled.

Now that you mention it, yeah. I do.

Her phone vibrated almost immediately.

What's up?

I'm on a bus, bound for nowhere.

Sweetheart, it's a TRAIN bound for nowhere.

Her heart gave a little *squee* at the endearment. It meant nothing and everything all at once. She smiled over her phone while she texted back.

Well, I'm on a bus with no destination in mind.

Want me to come get you?

Quinn stopped and stared at the phone. Was this dangerous? It didn't *feel* dangerous. Tyler had had ample opportunity to hurt her last night and he hadn't.

When Becca had first told her about finding Chris in the middle of a fight with Tyler and Seth in the parking lot, Quinn's first question had been, "Why?"

She'd never gotten a good answer.

She slid her thumbs across the face of her phone.

Are more taquitos in my future?

Play your cards right and there might be a soda, too.

His texts were teasing, so she wasn't sure if his offer to come get her was genuine. She didn't want to get off the bus until she knew for sure.

Then her phone lit up with a new message.

Don't make me ride the bus all night. Where should I pick you up?

"Excuse me," she called to the driver. "What's the next stop?"

"Annapolis Mall. West side."

Next stop is Annapolis Mall. West side.

Well look at that. You just got upgraded to a soft pretzel. See you in 10.

CHAPTER 12

Nick swore at his cell phone for the third time. Or maybe the tenth. He'd lost track.

"Enough." Adam reached across his tiny kitchen table and took the phone. He put it behind him on the counter, next to where the coffeemaker was choking out a pot.

"I'm sorry," Nick said.

"It's all right. I care about her, too."

"I'm sorry you didn't get to rehearse."

Adam shrugged. "I'll make do."

But it bothered him. Nick could tell. Adam had less than two weeks until his audition, and Quinn's temper tantrum might not be for tonight only. "I shouldn't have set her off in the truck."

Adam frowned. "That's not your fault."

Nick blew out a long rush of breath and ran a hand through his hair. He glanced at his phone on the counter. "I just wish she'd answer."

"She did answer."

Nick gave him a look—but he was right. Quinn *had* answered. She'd told him she was fine. Then she'd told him to fuck off.

"I'm worried she's going to hang out with Tyler, just to piss me off."

The coffeemaker beeped, signaling it was done, and Adam stood. "And would that piss you off?"

His tone was easy, but there was the tiniest bit of an edge hiding there. Nick blinked and realized he was being an idiot.

"Yeah," he said. "But not like that. I want Quinn to be happy. But Tyler is *not* a good guy."

"You think he'll hurt her?"

He'd hurt her once already—but Nick couldn't explain that without explaining everything. "I hope not. I don't know."

Adam fetched milk from the refrigerator and poured some into one mug, leaving the other coffee black. Nick watched this, bemused that Adam had remembered how he took his coffee.

Adam interrupted his thoughts. "How do you know him?"

Nick wondered how to answer that without spilling every secret he had. For the first time, he was tempted to tell Adam all of it. His shoulders felt tight with tension—from the fight with Quinn, from school, from his family, from living up to everyone's expectations.

"He used to go to school with my older brother. His family and my family—we don't get along."

Adam turned from the counter with mugs in hand. "Why?"

Because Tyler thinks we should be put to death for something we can't control.

Nick rubbed at his eyes. "It's a long story."

He heard the mugs slide onto the table, but jumped when Adam's hands landed on his shoulders.

"Relax," Adam said softly. "Relax." Then he pressed his thumbs into the muscle there.

The trapezius muscle, Nick's brain supplied helpfully.

God, he was such a nerd.

Adam's hands felt amazing. Warm and strong with just enough pressure behind his fingers. But instead of being relaxing, his touch had Nick ready to leap out of his chair. Was this a prelude to something? Obviously, right? But what if it—

"*Relax.*" Adam shook him gently. "Are you really this wound up over Quinn?"

"No. Yes. I don't know. I feel like I should go get her."

"Yeah, and how would that go?"

Tyler would want to fight. He'd win—Nick could hold his

own if he had to, but he didn't fight dirty. He had Gabriel for that. Tyler would get the upper hand and beat the shit out of him, if Nick didn't suffocate him first.

Neither option sounded all that appealing.

"It would suck," he said grudgingly.

"So your families hate each other. Are you guys the Montagues or the Capulets?"

Nick snorted. "Romeo and Juliet? I don't think so."

But his brain flashed on that day when he was twelve, when Tyler's sister had died. When Michael had come home soaking wet and terrified. When their parents had told them all to lock themselves in the master bedroom and not come out for anything. It was the first time he could remember seeing his mother frightened.

It wasn't the last.

Adam's hands brought him back to the present. "Do you ever think that maybe this Tyler guy thinks *you* are bad for *Quinn*? That maybe his intentions aren't evil at all?"

The thought brought Nick up short.

"I remember reading something once," Adam continued, "about divorce. It said that just because someone is a bad husband doesn't mean they're a bad father. I think about that a lot, how people have different capacities for failure. And even if you fail in one area doesn't mean you fail in *all* of them."

Nick ran that through his head a few times. What had Quinn said?

He still thinks your brother killed his sister. He seemed kinda upset about it.

Tyler had talked about his dead sister with Quinn? That didn't seem like something he'd do to get under Nick's skin.

Adam's hands moved lower, along his shoulder blades, his thumbs pressing into the area alongside Nick's spine.

"You have great hands," Nick said without thinking, then blushed.

Especially when Adam leaned in and breathed along his neck. "You have no idea."

Nick shivered.

Adam brushed a kiss against his neck. His hands eased lower, finding Nick's rib cage. "Still obsessing about Quinn?"

Obsessing. Was that what Adam was hearing? Nick had to clear his throat. "Quinn who?"

"That's better." Another slow breath against his skin. "What else has you so uptight?"

Your hands. My imagination.

"School," he murmured. "I'm fourth in my class, and my physics teacher wants to nominate me for some program that will let me take college classes next semester."

"You don't sound happy about it."

"I help my older brother run the landscaping business. Gabriel is taking a special course to be a firefighter in the spring, so if I stop helping, too . . ." He let that thought trail off.

"You told me you were applying to some schools anyway, right? Have you heard back from any?"

Nick hesitated.

Adam's hands went still. "What?"

"I've heard back from all of them."

"And?"

Nick wished they could get back to the sexy talk. That was loaded with pressure, too, but he didn't want to think about college. "And . . . I haven't opened any of the envelopes. Or the e-mails."

Adam smacked him on the side of the head.

"Ow." Nick sat up straight and looked over his shoulder. "What was that for?"

"That was for you being an idiot." Adam grabbed Nick's shoulders and pulled him straighter. "And for your posture, while I'm at it. I've been wanting to do *that* for three days."

"What's wrong with my posture?"

"What's wrong with your *head* is a better question. You probably have acceptance letters in there. Maybe even scholarship offers, if you're fourth in your class."

"I don't want to talk about school." His shoulders had tightened back up, and all of a sudden, he didn't want to be a part of this conversation.

Adam pulled him back in the chair, using a little more force than was absolutely necessary. "Do your brothers have any idea that you're sitting on a stack of unopened mail?"

"No."

Adam didn't say anything, but his hands were slower now, less suggestive.

"I can feel you judging me," Nick said.

"Not judging." He paused, thoughtful. "Did you work tonight?"

"Yeah. Nothing big—a little yard maintenance." He'd ridden the mower while Chris and Michael did the detail work. He'd been glad to have an excuse not to talk. Chris watched him the whole time, but never said a word about the cafeteria outburst.

Nick should have kept his stupid mouth shut.

Damn Gabriel.

"Do you work every night?"

"No—not really. Sometimes. But Mike's been busy this week, so he asked me to pick up a few extra nights."

"You still have homework to do?"

"Not a lot." A lie. But he could probably finish when he got home, if he didn't fall over from exhaustion. If he was desperate, he could get up early and finish. And he had yet to crack the book on the physics test he'd missed. He still had Thursday night for that.

"You still worried about Quinn?"

WTF. Nick shoved Adam's hands away and started to get up. "I thought the whole point was to be relaxing."

Adam grabbed him and jerked him back into the chair again. He held him there and put his lips against Nick's ear. "It is. But you're all jacked up worrying about everyone else. I'm starting to wonder who worries about Nicholas."

Nick flushed and relaxed back into his hands. "I like that," he murmured.

"That no one worries about you?"

His cheeks warmed further. Someday he'd be able to reconnect his mouth to his brain. "No. The way you said my name."

"So I have a thought," Adam said, leaning closer to run his

hands down the front of Nick's chest. He did it slowly, letting each part of his hand stroke its way down. Fingertips, then palm. Shoulders, then muscle, then nipples.

Nick hissed in a breath. He wanted him to stop. He wanted him to keep going.

"What's your thought?" he said quickly.

"Why don't you let me worry for an hour." Adam's hands moved lower, finding the hem of Nick's shirt and skirting below it. Warm fingers brushed bare stomach. Nick jumped and fought for breath.

Then those fingers slid inside the waistband of his jeans.

Nick froze and captured his hands. Then he couldn't move. He couldn't breathe.

Adam's voice was low and soft, his face against Nick's neck. "Talk to me."

Nick clenched his eyes closed. His thoughts were spinning like a tornado, completely out of control. "I don't know what you want."

Low laughter against his neck. "I don't think that's true."

Nick thought his cheeks would never cool. That emotional tornado left him scattered and scrambling to pick up the pieces. He couldn't decide if he was angry or turned on or both. "Don't tease me."

The amusement left Adam's voice. "No teasing. No judgment. You're safe here, remember?"

"I remember." Nick warred with his thoughts.

"Talk to me," Adam whispered.

"I don't want to do the wrong thing. I don't want you to—"

Adam pulled a hand free and put it over Nick's mouth. His other arm went across Nick's chest, making it more of an embrace. "No more worrying. What do you want? Does anyone ever ask you that? What do *you* want, Nick?"

No. No one ever asked him that. Nick put a hand over Adam's, where it rested on his chest. He drew a shuddering breath and shook his head. "I don't know. I don't know what I want."

Adam put a hand against his cheek and turned him, kissing him lightly, sweetly. No pressure, just a brush of lips before drawing back.

"Well," said Adam, and Nick could hear the smile in his voice. "Maybe I could give you a few ideas."

CHAPTER 13

Quinn giggled and looked up at the starry night sky, accented by bits of flying ash from the fire. "I didn't realize you'd make a whole bonfire."

Tyler lay next to her on a fleece beach blanket he'd fetched from the truck. "Well, you said you were cold."

The fire stretched over six feet high, whipping in the breeze. Tiny gas lamps glowed across the bay; this probably looked like a distress beacon. "Won't someone see it?"

Tyler snorted. "You say that like I'd care." He held out a paper bag. "You want the other pretzel?"

Quinn hugged her hands to her stomach. She was still hungry, but she should probably be chewing on a lettuce leaf. "Nah."

"Come on. Don't make me throw it out for the gulls."

"If you insist." She took the bag and tore off a stretch of pretzel. Butter and salt and heaven.

They'd been out here on this deserted stretch of beach for fifteen minutes, and she'd been sure the beach-fire-blanket combo was nothing more than a play to get into her pants. Nick's words about Tyler using her to get at him kept bouncing around in her head.

But Tyler hadn't made a move toward her. Even now, he left a clear five feet of space between them, just like last night on the roof of his shopping center.

Take that, Nick.

He'd bought her pretzels as promised, then walked a few laps of the mall at her side, only asking if she wanted to go for a drive when stores began unrolling their security gates. His anger from yesterday seemed to have faded, his violence from the first night completely gone.

But fury and aggression hid there, just below the surface.

He is not nice, Quinn.

She knew that. Tyler was like an attack dog who'd failed out of doggie school. He might eat treats out of your hand and wag his tail, but if you made the wrong move, he'd bite your hand off and come back for the other one.

It was kinda terrifying.

And kinda sexy.

"What?" he said.

Quinn didn't look away. Why bother? He'd already caught her staring. "I was thinking you're kind of hot when you're not being a total dickhead."

He let out a low whistle and looked back at the sky. "Turn a guy's head with talk like that."

She expected him to see that as some kind of invitation, but he didn't move.

After a moment, his voice dropped and he said, "Thanks." He paused. "You're not breaking any mirrors yourself."

But he still didn't move.

It thrilled her and exasperated her at the same time. Like last night, when he'd dropped that line about Nick being one lucky bastard.

Either he's not using me or he's not interested.

It made her want to provoke him. "I thought I was enough to turn you off from sex forever."

Now he turned his head and looked over. The fire turned his blond hair gold and bounced off his eyes. "That had more to do with Merrick than with you."

"I don't know what that means."

"It means I said that to get under *his* skin. You could look like a supermodel and I would have said you were a total turnoff."

"Hmph. Nick would say any girl was a turnoff."

As soon as the words were out, she wished she could suck them back into her mouth.

Tyler went still.

Oh, crap.

Oh, crap.

Take it back take it back take it back.

But she didn't know what to say. She needed to undo this. She needed to undo this *right now*. She'd kept this secret from everyone who was important to Nick, and now she'd practically told his mortal enemy.

She had no idea what to say to change the course of this conversation.

Haha, just a joke. Look! A bird!

Sure.

"That's interesting," Tyler finally said. He sat up and pulled a cigarette from the pack in his back pocket. "Very interesting."

She needed a rewind button. A time machine. Something. She'd give anything to be back at the dance studio, falling on her face in front of Adam's perfection. *Anything.*

She sat up on her heels. Could she beg him to keep it a secret? Would that be better or worse than pretending it wasn't a secret at all?

"So you're not really his girlfriend," said Tyler.

And what was she supposed to say to *that*? Here she was sitting with a guy she was attracted to, and she was going to have to pretend to be madly in love with Nick, just to keep a stupid secret.

But Tyler looked over, and she could read it on his face. He knew.

Her voice was soft, almost lost in the sound of the surf. "No. Not really."

He started to move the cigarette to his lips, but then he flung it into the fire, unlit. His expression was fierce, all angles lit by the flames. He shifted on the blanket like he was going to leave.

Was he going after Nick? Was he going to take this information and pick a fight, or use it against his brothers somehow? Or was he—

Tyler took her face in his hands and pressed his lips against hers.

Quinn stiffened in surprise—then yielded. He was rough and forceful, but in all the right ways. She'd kissed a lot of boys, but Tyler kissed like a man. No hesitation, no fumbling. First, his mouth, hot and searing and making her feel things low in her belly. Then his hands, finding her waist, pushing her down on the blanket. Then his tongue, pulling at hers.

His body felt secure against her, and his arms caged her there on the blanket. When he drew back to look at her, she wanted to grab his shirt and drag him back down.

But then she remembered what she'd just said.

"Please don't tell anyone," she whispered.

"Tell anyone what?"

"About Nick."

He straightened his arms, pushing himself up until she missed his weight. "Nice," he said with clear derision. The fire whipped higher behind him. "I kiss you, and you're still thinking about that stupid f—"

Quinn slapped him. Hard, with all the passion of their kiss and her panic behind it. "Don't you *dare* call him that."

Tyler caught her arm and pinned it to the blanket. He got in her face. "Don't *you* dare hit me. I was going to call him a *stupid fuck*."

Oh. It wasn't *better*, but somehow, it was.

She looked up at him. "I'm sorry."

"For what." He said it flatly, not even a question. He didn't even wait for an answer, just moved off her to sit back on the blanket and stare at the fire.

She sat up next to him.

Talking about Nick seemed like a minefield, but all she could think about was how badly she'd derailed this entire evening. For everyone.

She wanted to touch Tyler—but she didn't.

"Why did you kiss me?" she whispered.

He had another cigarette between his fingers, twirling it across his knuckles like a miniature baton. He mused for so long that she wanted to throw it into the fire after the first one.

Then he said, "Because I wanted to."

"No," she said. "Why did you kiss me *now*? After you knew about Nick?"

He looked at her. "Because I could."

She licked her lips, tasting smoke from the fire. "I don't understand."

He looked back at the flames. "I could have screwed with you to mess with him. I thought about it. Last night." He shrugged it off and looked at her. "I didn't want to do that."

Quinn couldn't decide if she'd destroyed everything, or if she'd cleared a path for something to grow.

Tyler looked at her. "Why were you sitting behind the 7-Eleven Monday night?" She opened her mouth, and he gave her a hard look. "The *truth*."

She hadn't even told Nick the truth.

When it got right down to it, she didn't even want to admit it to herself.

Quinn stared right back into his eyes and made her voice as challenging as his was. "Because my mom drinks like a fish and it turns her into a crazy bitch."

He studied her for a long second. "Is that all?"

He didn't say it like it wasn't enough of a reason to be upset. He said it like he knew that it wasn't a complete answer, like he knew there was more behind it.

Quinn shook her head. "I have to wait until she passes out or falls asleep if I want to go home. Otherwise she'll start screaming at me."

"She hit you, too?"

Quinn shook her head.

Tyler didn't believe her. "So she wasn't the one to knock you around the other night?"

Quinn looked at the sand. "She's slapped me before, but she's never left a mark."

"I know you said Nick didn't hit you. Who did?"

"Would you just smoke another cigarette or something—"

"Jesus, you're hardheaded. Answer the question."

"My brother."

She felt Tyler draw himself up, and she peeked over at him. The look of fury on his face was almost terrifying, and she was glad she wasn't the target.

"What happened?" he said.

"It's nothing—"

"Shut the fuck up about *it's nothing*. What happened?"

Her mother had defended Jake for so long that Quinn was shocked to hear someone act like her brother's actions were *not* okay. "He's home from college. He keeps smoking pot in my room. He has his friends there all the time. The other night, he slammed my face into the wall because he thought I stole his money or his stash." Her voice started to break, and she kept talking fast, as if fractured words would hold off tears. "I can't even get my clothes out of there to crash somewhere else, because his friends think I'm fresh meat. They keep touching me, and I can't—I can't even—"

She stopped short. Tyler was standing, pulling her to her feet, picking up the blanket to shake it free of sand.

"What are you doing?" she asked.

"I'm driving you home to get your stuff."

"You're—what? Why?"

"Because I can. Because I have an apartment, and you look like you could do with eight hours of sleep. Because—"

"You expect me to *stay* with you? But—"

"But what? You have a dozen better offers? Get in the truck."

She got in the truck. They were a mile down the road and he hadn't said anything else when she finally turned to him. "Because what else?"

He looked at her like she was nuts. "What?"

"You said *because*, and I cut you off. Why are you doing this?"

His voice dropped. "You don't have to stay with me. I didn't mean to make it sound like I was kidnapping you."

"Shut up. You're not making me do *anything*."

He snorted and rubbed his cheek. "No kidding."

"*Shut up!* Because what else?"

He looked away from the road long enough to meet her eyes. "Because I like you."

"No one has ever done anything like that for me," she said.

Not Becca. Not Nick.

You didn't tell them, her brain whispered.

But they'd never pushed as hard as Tyler.

"Well," said Tyler, "maybe it's time someone should."

CHAPTER 14

Quinn stopped Tyler in front of her apartment door. Her older brother's car was in the parking lot—*of course*—so she slid her key into the deadbolt carefully.

"Worried you're going to wake someone up?" said Tyler.

"No," she said, too forcefully. She was worried someone would hear her and make this worse than it needed to be.

She'd never brought anyone home to this apartment. She and Becca had hardly seen each other since the fire, and when they did, it was always at Becca's place or the Merrick house. When Nick drove her home, she never let him get farther than the apartment landing. She didn't want anyone to smell the pot or the alcohol. Even now, outside the door, embarrassment sent heat coursing up her neck. What if Tyler saw her mother stumbling around in a nightgown? What if the shrieking started and Quinn couldn't get her to shut up?

She looked at Tyler and put a hand up. "Just wait here."

For an instant, she was ready for Tyler to refuse.

But then he shrugged and said, "Okay," and she realized she'd been *hoping* he would refuse.

The lock gave and she was through the door. She closed it gently, quietly, leaving it unlocked to spare her one extra second if she needed to get out fast.

This was ridiculous, creeping into her own house. Back before the fire, when she'd lived around the corner from Becca, everything had been on the ground level, and she hadn't needed to pass anyone to get in and out of her room. The window had worked fine for that. And while their house had never been large, everyone had their own room.

This bullshit with Jake was infuriating.

Even now, the living room was empty and dim. Her mother must have been in the bedroom, or hell, maybe she'd gone out, too. But Quinn could see light beneath her own bedroom door. She could hear them in there—but barely, with the racket her heart was kicking up.

She wanted to turn and run through the door and tell Tyler all her clothes had been stolen.

And then what would she do? Go back to his place with her dance shorts and her worn fleece pullover? Wear that to school?

She hated that her life had devolved to the point where she had to choose the lesser of two evils.

But . . . maybe Tyler wasn't evil at all. She still couldn't tell. The kiss, the admission that he'd wanted to ensure she was free before making a move . . . she couldn't wrap her head around it.

God, she was stalling. Ridiculous. She needed her stuff and she was going to walk in there and get it. She straightened her spine, stalked over to her bedroom door, and threw it open.

The room smelled acrid and foul. She stumbled back. Jake sat on the floor with three of his friends. They all looked up when she entered.

Two guys looked dazed and confused. She'd never seen them before. Heavy-lidded and slack-jawed, they were leaning up against her bed like they had no intention of moving. Ever.

The other guy, sitting next to Jake, looked interested, and not in a good way. In a don't-touch-me-you-creep way. He also looked filthy, like he hadn't showered in three days. Lank dark hair clung to his forehead, and he wore a tank top and shorts despite the fact that it was getting below freezing at night. A glass pipe sat in his hands.

Nice.

Jake got to his feet, a little unsteadily. He was tall and lanky and muscled, befitting a star basketball player. But whereas he'd once been quite a looker with blue eyes and that shock of blond hair, now he looked drawn and washed out. His eyes were bloodshot. And paranoid. "Get the fuck out of here, Quinn."

"I just want my stuff," she said.

Greasy tank top snorted. "She's cute, J, where've you been hiding her?"

She expected his voice to be lazy and drawling, to match the boys who could barely hold themselves upright, but it wasn't. His tone was too interested. Too alert. It made her skin crawl.

Quinn wanted to step past them, to grab clothes from her dresser, but she remembered the last time she'd run into one of Jake's friends, and she kept her distance.

"Get out of here," said Jake. He took a step toward her and grabbed her arm. "You hear me? Quit messing with me."

She jerked free. "I'm not *messing* with you!" she snapped. "I haven't even *been* here!"

He came after her. "Look, you—"

She ducked under his arm and slid through the doorway into her room. Jake grunted, and she half expected him to grab her, but judging by the racket he made, he must have stumbled into the doorjamb. She made it past his friends and flung open a dresser drawer. "Just let me get my stuff. Then you can keep smoking pot until your lungs burn out."

"That's not pot."

Tyler's voice. Quinn spun.

He'd caught Jake's arm and twisted it behind him, and just now had him pinned up against the wall.

Her brother was struggling, but though he was tall, Tyler had the advantage in mass.

Tyler gave her a look. "Hurry up, huh?"

Quinn hustled.

Greasy boy took all this in stride, his sharp eyes watching everything. "Is that Tyler Morgan?" he said. "Dude, I didn't know this was your scene."

"It's not," said Tyler. His voice was even, as if Jake wasn't trying to buck his hold.

Quinn flung clothes into her backpack without looking. Her heart was in her throat. Jake was cursing at Tyler now. Tall-dark-and-sinister was flicking a lighter, but he couldn't seem to get it to spark.

She had no idea whether this was going better or worse than if Tyler hadn't intervened.

The bag wouldn't hold any more, and she jerked at the zipper.

"Get the keys out of my pocket," said Tyler. "Go down and start the truck."

The dark-haired boy flicked the lighter again. Still no flame. "Sure you don't want to stay, sweet thing?"

"I'm worried I might puke on you," said Quinn. It took everything she had not to kick him in the face.

Especially since he grabbed her ass when she skittered by him.

She whirled, her hand balled into a fist.

"*Go*," said Tyler. "Ignore him."

"I'm going to fuck you up," Jake wheezed. "You think you're so—"

"Yeah, yeah," said Tyler. "Quinn. The keys."

His body was tighter than a bow string, taut and rigid as he held her brother against the wall. Quinn had to get close to fish the keys from his pocket. This felt too intimate, sliding her hand along the front of his hip, searching for a metal ring.

Then the keys were in her fingers.

"Go," said Tyler. "I'll be down in a second."

"The hell you will," Jake snapped.

Quinn hesitated. That lighter kept flicking, never finding a flame.

Tyler glanced over his shoulder. "Go on," he said, and for the first time, she heard a breath of strain in his voice. She saw the warning in his eyes. This could unravel in a real hurry. "Don't stop. Start the truck."

She ran. Halfway down the stairs, she heard them start to fight. Someone was yelling. Then a woman was shrieking.

Her mother.

Quinn hesitated at the turn in the steps. A gun fired. Glass shattered. The shrieking stopped.

Suddenly, she couldn't breathe. There was no love lost between Quinn and her family, but had Tyler shot—had he—?

And then he was just *there*, grabbing her hand, yanking the keys out of her fingers, physically picking her up when she couldn't run with him.

He shoved her into the cab of his truck and she scrambled across the seat to get away from him. He started the ignition and rolled out of the parking place, but not with any great burst of speed.

Quinn couldn't catch her breath, couldn't stop shaking, and she wondered if she should be diving out of the vehicle right now, running for her life.

"Are you okay?" he said. "Hey, look at me. Are you all right?"

She realized she was making hysterical little keening noises.

Tyler rolled to a stop at the stop sign. A siren kicked up somewhere in the distance.

He looked at her, and she grabbed the door handle, still contemplating leaping out of the vehicle. Her breath shook with panic. "Did you—did you kill them?"

"Are you insane? No!"

"But a gun—a gun—"

"It wasn't mine. It was Anthony Spinnetti's."

She must have looked blank, because he rolled his eyes. "The douche bag with the crack pipe."

That was a *crack pipe*?

She stared at him. Her eyes felt too wide. She still couldn't get a handle on her breathing. "Who got shot?"

"No one. Well, your door frame. I got it out of his hands and threw it through your bedroom window."

The glass breaking.

But Tyler had wrestled someone with a gun?

He was on Ritchie Highway now, but he glanced over at her. "He was about to come after you. Your brother told him you stole his money. Is that true?"

She put her hands on her cheeks. "No."

"Maybe a little warning that you were leading me into a dealer's den would have been in order."

"I didn't—I had no idea."

"Jesus Christ, girl, how long have you been living like that?"

"I don't—I didn't know what they were doing." She felt naïve and stupid, which was ridiculous. She couldn't wrap her head around this. "You really didn't shoot them?"

"Sweetheart, I don't walk around armed. My gun is locked up. I'll prove it to you when we get to my place." He paused and ran a hand back through his hair. "Unless . . . do you want to go to the cops? Your neighbors are already calling them, but . . ."

Her life had to be pretty shitty to have *two* guys offering to take her to the police in the span of one week.

And this time, at first, she did want Tyler to take her to the police station. She'd tell them everything she'd seen, and she'd have him there to back it up.

But then they'd arrest her brother. And possibly her parents. Quinn was only seventeen. Where would they send her? A foster home or something? Or would she be arrested, too?

And what would they do to Jordan? At least her little brother was practically living at his friends' houses. She hadn't seen him in over a week. She didn't have to worry about him coming around.

"No," she whispered. "No cops."

"You all right?"

She shook her head. "How do you know that Anthony guy?"

"We went to school together. I didn't know your brother was Jake Briscoe. Talk about how the mighty have fallen."

Quinn blinked at him. They'd come to a red light, and it reflected off Tyler's fair skin and hair, making him look a little softer. "What does that mean?"

"Didn't he win a scholarship to Duke or something?"

"Yeah. He's home on a break."

Tyler looked over. The expression on his face said, *Come on, don't be stupid.*

But she must have been, because she didn't get it. "What?"

"What break? It's the middle of October. I'm not on break. Why would he be?"

"You think—you think he left school?"

Tyler snorted. "He's smoking crack with a high school dropout. I'd bet my truck your brother got kicked out of school."

Kicked out of school. The golden boy.

Quinn wondered if this added a new intensity to her parents' problems.

And it wasn't like things were great before.

"Was my mother okay?" she whispered.

"She was lit," said Tyler. "Where's your dad?"

Quinn shook her head. "I never know anymore. Sometimes he works nights, but sometimes . . . I try to stay out of there as much as I can."

And now she'd burned her bridges with Becca and Nick.

She had nowhere to go.

Tyler was silent for a long while, and she watched the lights zip by outside his truck.

"You want me to take you somewhere else?" he finally said. "You have a friend you want to stay with or something?"

Quinn shook her head. "You can just—" She had to clear her throat. "I'm all right. You can let me out at the next street corner. I'll call someone."

"You think I'm buying that?"

She had no idea what to say. She had no idea what Tyler expected. Just like before, she felt trapped by circumstance. She could get out of this truck and . . . and, what? Sleep on the street? But if she went home with Tyler, would he be looking to hook up?

She kept thinking of the way Anthony had grabbed her ass. He certainly wasn't the first of her brother's friends to lay a hand on her. She swallowed.

At least Tyler's apartment would mean a place to sleep. At least he wasn't a *total* stranger.

"Your place is fine," she said. "If the offer is still open."

"It is," he said. He shut up and drove.

* * *

Tyler's apartment was a *lot* nicer than she was expecting. Hell, it was nicer than her family's apartment.

Lush wine-colored carpeting stretched everywhere. Two bedrooms were at the back, each massive. One had a king-size bed, the other had two queens. A huge kitchen sported granite countertops. Plush furniture sat everywhere and a huge flat-screen television hung on the wall. It wasn't immaculately clean or anything—enough comfortable clutter was scattered around that it looked *lived in*—but Tyler wasn't a slob.

"Wait," she said, taking a second look around. "Is this your parents' place?"

"Yes," he said. "Sort of. My grandmother used to live here, and they inherited it when she died. They were going to fix it up to sell it, but then they told me I could live here if I did the work."

She looked around again. "You did all this yourself?"

"Mostly. I had a few friends help me. Mom had the counters installed, but I tore down the old wallpaper and did all the painting. Hung the new cabinets, too." He shrugged. "It beats a dorm."

No kidding. Then she had another thought.

"Do you live alone?"

"Yeah." He hesitated. "My friend Seth was going to move in after he graduated, but . . ." His voice trailed off.

Seth. Seth Ramsey. Quinn knew all about him. "But *your* friend tried to rape *my* friend and now he's in a ton of trouble," she finished.

Tyler frowned. "He's not really my friend anymore."

"Don't like rapists?" she quipped.

"You going to hold me accountable for something Seth did?"

It was almost the same thing she'd said to Nick. She didn't know why she was even picking at this. Maybe because she needed to pick at *something* before her brain exploded.

A crack pipe. In her *bedroom.* God.

She dropped her backpack on the floor and swung into one

of his dining room chairs. "So why isn't Seth your friend anymore?"

Tyler leaned on the back of a chair and looked at her. "You know I don't like the Merricks, yeah?"

"It's come up once or twice."

"Fucking with them is one thing. They aren't supposed to exist. They aren't supposed to *be here*. But that's not—it's different. What Seth did . . . I could never do . . . *that*."

"So it would have been okay if he'd shot her, but raping her is *wrong*."

Tyler just stared back at her.

"What?" she said. "I'm trying to figure out your bizarre morality. You're the one who lit my arm on fire. Didn't you rough Becca up yourself?"

He didn't even look ashamed, reminding her that Tyler was no white knight, either. "It's not my morality," he said. "I'm not a Guide. Full Elementals are identified and put to death. Period. Who cares if they get a little *roughed up* on the way?"

"You're an Elemental," she said. "Why are you allowed to live?"

His eyes hardened, and she realized she'd struck a nerve. "Because I can't accidentally destroy an entire town if I have a temper tantrum. You've seen the damage they can do. I know you have."

"You aren't the only person who lost someone," she said quietly. "Their parents died in a fire, didn't they?"

"Yeah, so did Seth's."

She hadn't heard *that*. Quinn thought about the carnival fire that had killed seven other students. Or the earthquake that had destroyed the bridge near school—and almost killed Becca. Or the arson attacks that had destroyed half a dozen homes—including hers—and killed people in the community. Whole families devastated because of a *temper tantrum*, as he called it.

She didn't want Tyler to be right. But a tiny part of her agreed with him. Maybe Gabriel had been saving people, but she knew enough about Nick's twin brother to know he had a cruel streak every inch as wide as Tyler's.

"Nick is my friend," she said quietly. "I don't care what he is."

"You should."

"I *don't*. He's never hurt anyone."

"How do you know? Have you asked him?"

That question drew her up short. She thought of Nick in the woods behind his house, showing her what he could do. *Relax. It's only wind.*

But then he'd told her about the accidental tornado on the soccer field. The storm that had shattered his leg. His abilities had let him heal in record time. What if a normal kid had been caught up in that storm?

What else could Nick do by accident?

"I trust him." She hesitated. "He warned me to stay away from *you*."

Tyler snorted. "Wait, let me put on my surprised face. You want to stay away from me? There's the door."

Quinn didn't move.

Tyler's eyes didn't leave hers. "Where was friendly ol' Nick Merrick when your brother was smacking you around? I don't see him putting those powers to good use to protect you."

"He didn't know," she whispered.

"Why not? Too busy with another guy?"

She flinched. It was just a little too close to the truth. "Just because Nick didn't know about my brother doesn't mean he should be killed."

"If a lion escapes from the zoo, do you think they should let it run loose, or do you think they should shoot it before it hurts someone?"

"They can shoot a lion with a tranquilizer dart."

Tyler circled the table, leaning down over her. His voice was intense, but his words were soft. "Or that could piss it off so it causes more damage."

Her eyes flicked to his lips. She had no idea why he was sexier while he was arguing, but there it was.

"In fact," he said, "I have a theory."

"What's that?" she said.

"If a Guide comes to town to kill them, he's going to have to be good. Really good. He's going to have to figure out a way to take them all out at once."

Quinn swallowed. She didn't like that he sounded happy about that. He was so hard to classify in her brain: protecting her, kissing her, defending her.

All while wanting her friends dead.

"Why?" she whispered.

Tyler smiled. "Otherwise, he'll learn what I learned. You just have to mess with one to piss the rest off."

CHAPTER 15

Nick didn't make it home until one a.m. He expected to find the house dark and quiet, but Michael was half asleep on the couch, some late-night news program throwing light against the back wall.

He'd hoped to sneak up to his bedroom unnoticed, but Michael sat up and rubbed his eyes when Nick slid the deadbolt on the front door.

"It's late," he said quietly.

"Sorry," Nick said, wondering if he was going to catch any crap about coming home after midnight every night this week.

"How's Quinn?" Michael said.

Nick shrugged, feeling like the question was a trap. "She's all right."

"You okay? You look a little scattered."

"Just tired. You know."

"Anything going on?"

Nick's heart kicked into triple time from all the questions. Michael wasn't one for small talk. "No. Why?"

Michael picked up the remote and turned off the TV. "What did you do tonight?"

This was starting to look like a round of *Let's Talk*, and Nick really didn't want to play.

He shrugged again. "Nothing really."

I pissed off Quinn, and probably chased her into the arms of a psychopath.

Yeah, Tyler. Remember him? He used to make our lives hell.

Oh, and I made out with another guy. It's a miracle our clothes stayed on.

He suspected the latter half was Adam trying not to push him further than he was ready to go. Amazing and excruciating, all slow hands and fierce kissing, broken only when Nick would hesitate. Adam never pushed.

Nick wondered if some of that was for Adam's own benefit, too.

Knowing what he knew, Nick never pushed, either. It left them tangled in a careful dance of caresses and stronger touches.

He hadn't wanted to leave.

Michael was studying him. "Gabriel said you and Quinn seem to be getting pretty close."

Great. Nick dropped into the armchair and wondered how much he could say without incriminating himself. What else had Gabriel said? Did Michael already suspect something?

"She's going through a lot," he offered, keeping his eyes on the end table. "At home. You know."

"You want to talk about it?"

Yes. He did. Emotions wrapped around his neck and jerked tight, and he wanted to tell Michael everything. About Quinn. About Tyler.

But if he talked about them, he'd have to talk about Adam.

For an instant, he hated Quinn for putting him in this position. Then he hated himself for putting *her* in this position.

This sucked.

He met his older brother's eyes. "Not really." He rubbed at the back of his neck. "She'll be all right."

Like Michael would leave it at that.

His brother inhaled—a loaded breath. Nick braced himself for an interrogation.

Why'd you get all jumpy when Gabriel said gay guys are creepy? Are you gay, Nick? Of course it's creepy. God, and we've been living under the same roof. Jesus, what would Mom and Dad say? Maybe you should sleep in the basement.

But Michael didn't say any of that. "I need to ask you a favor."

Nick coughed. He needed to turn his brain off. "What?"

"I feel bad asking, because I know you worked two extra nights this week—"

"It's fine. What is it?"

His tone was rougher than usual, and Michael looked a bit unsettled. "Tomorrow is Hannah's birthday. Her parents are taking her out to dinner, and they asked if I'd like to join them."

Nick went still. So this had nothing to do with him at all. "What's the favor?"

At this point, he'd do pretty much anything if it took the focus off of him. *Paint a replica of Van Gogh's* Starry Night *on the ceiling? Sure, Mike. Let me get my brush.*

"You can say no if you want," said Michael.

Now all the uncomfortable small talk made sense. Nick's subconscious let out a sigh. "Why don't you get around to what it is before I start saying no?"

"Would you babysit?"

"You mean for James?"

"No, Hannah's *other* five-year-old. Yeah, I mean James."

"Do I have to go there?"

"No, she can bring him over here."

Nick smiled. "Okay."

Michael's eyebrows went up. "Really? I was worried you'd have plans. Everyone else does."

It would probably be good to let Quinn have a night off from his presence. At least she wouldn't have a reason to bail on Adam again. "Nah. I have a big physics exam on Friday. I can study after he goes to bed." His insides relaxed. "What's everyone else doing?"

"Gabriel and Layne are watching Simon's basketball game, then going to a movie; Chris said he and Becca are doing *something*, which sounds suspiciously like *taking advantage of the fact that her mom won't be home;* and Hunter said he and his mom were going to catch a late dinner to talk things out."

"No landscaping jobs?" said Nick.

"No jobs. I was actually planning to watch James so she could go out with her folks. We could take him with us, but I thought maybe I could get one of you to watch him . . ."

The air was practically trembling with anxiety. "You're nervous," said Nick.

"I've met her dad, but it wasn't on the best terms."

Meaning, the night Gabriel had been arrested for arson. Hannah's father was the county fire marshal.

"They asked *you,* right? I think that's a good sign."

"Maybe."

"You don't sound happy."

"I've never done the *parent* thing."

"Pretend they're new clients."

Michael looked at him. "Yeah, okay."

"No. Seriously. That's what I do." Nick never had any idea how to treat his *girlfriends'* parents. He always worried they'd see right through him, and it wasn't like he wanted to pretend to stare at his date's boobs right in front of Mom and Dad, just to prove a point. He knew how to deal with teachers, and how to deal with landscaping customers. He treated parents the same way. They always liked him. Then again, maybe they could sense he wasn't a threat to anyone's virginity.

Whatever. He shrugged. "It's worked so far."

Michael smiled and hit him on the shoulder. "Thanks, Nick." He headed for the stairs. Nick watched him go, bemused. And relieved.

And a little disappointed.

"Hey," Nick called after him.

"What?"

"I'd lose the long hair."

Michael made a face. "If I cut my hair, that means I have to *keep* cutting it."

Typical Michael. Not making a statement with his looks. Just not taking five minutes to care what he looked like. "You're the one who wants to make a good impression. Just saying."

Michael gestured. "I can't do what you guys do."

"So cut it short."

"It won't look stupid?"

"Right now you look like you're trying to bring back the grunge era, so you tell me."

Michael rolled his eyes and started up the stairs. "All right, all right."

Nick watched him go. The camaraderie felt good. He'd missed this. So much that he wanted to call Michael back down, to take him up on that option to *talk*.

Then again, his older brother hadn't really *meant* it. That had been BS conversation until he could get around to asking a favor.

And really, if he'd said a word about Adam, that camaraderie probably would have vanished into thin air.

Quinn woke to the sounds of a guitar strumming.

She lay in bed and listened, trying to orient herself. Darkness cloaked the room, barely letting any light through the blinds. A light was on somewhere down the hallway.

Right, Tyler's apartment.

The guitar was muffled, probably a neighbor or something.

She was alone in bed, which wasn't a surprise. She was in the room with the double beds, curled up under the quilt.

The whole night had been bizarre, from her fight with Nick, to the kiss from Tyler, to the drug addicts in her bedroom.

It hadn't gotten any better.

Tyler had asked if she wanted to take a shower to clean up a bit, which she'd assumed was an implication that it was time for her to earn a place to sleep for the night. Kind of like when boys took you out to dinner and a movie and then expected a little somethin'-somethin' in the car before they took you home, but on a whole new level.

But no, she'd climbed in the steaming hot shower alone and

stayed that way. She took her time, too, not knowing when she'd get another chance to spend more than five minutes in a shower before someone started screaming at her.

And later, when she'd emerged with pinned up damp hair and yoga sweats, Tyler had been killing the lights in the apartment. "Stay up and watch TV if you want," he'd said. "I'm going to bed. I've got an eight a.m. class." Then he'd taken a quick look in the second bedroom and said, "Do you want an extra blanket?"

Pretty clear where he'd expected her to sleep.

Thinking about it now, she wondered if she'd messed something up.

You going to judge me for something Seth did?

She had no idea how to read him. He'd said terrible things to her in Nick's driveway—though he'd talked his way out of those. But then that night behind the 7-Eleven, when he'd burned her . . . was that a cruel side of Tyler, the way boys would yank the wings off flies, or was that a panicked side trying to figure out what dangers were affecting the Elementals in town, using the only leverage he could find?

And here she was, sleeping in his spare room. After he'd helped her get her things and protected her from an addict and a dealer. That had to count for something.

No, a *lot*. That had to count for a lot.

The guitar music kept up, and she listened, thinking of Nick, of the night he'd told her his family secret, the way the air had carried her.

She thought of how much he *hated* Tyler, and wished she knew how to reconcile all these facets of the same guy.

The guitar music changed, becoming something more lively. Still muffled, still at a distance, but enough that she could pick out the rhythm and melody. Was someone outside? But they were on the third floor.

She swung her legs onto the velvet softness of the carpeting, padding into the doorway. Definitely outside.

She peeked through Tyler's doorway, expecting to either find him asleep, or sitting up in bed, as confused about the music as she was.

His bed was empty.

The light over the sink was on, casting a soft glow across half the apartment. Quinn approached the glass door that led to the porch, seeing that someone was indeed out there, sprawled on one of the porch chairs, a guitar in his lap.

Tyler.

Quinn slid the glass door open. "What happened to your eight o'clock class?"

"Nothing. I couldn't sleep." He was good enough that he didn't lose the rhythm or the melody. "Did I wake you?"

"You're probably waking half the building."

"Doubt it." She opened her mouth to fire back, but he nodded at the opposite chair. "Want to join me?"

Like she had anything better to do. She dragged the door closed behind her and eased into the vinyl chair. It was way too cold for a tank top and stretch pants, but she was used to being underdressed for the weather. She caught a whiff of smoke in the air, then saw the lit cigarette perched on an ashtray on the table beside him. A beer sat there with it.

Definitely way too old for her. She didn't give a crap.

"You're very good," she said quietly.

"Thanks," he said equably.

"Do you sing, too?"

She'd been kidding, but he nodded. He didn't demonstrate, however.

"I don't get a show?" she mocked, thinking of his comments when she was dancing in the woods.

He pressed a hand against the strings, stopping the music abruptly. "Do you want one?"

Was his voice suggestive? She couldn't tell.

"Sure." A breeze slid through the railing and she shivered, running her hands up and down her arms.

He picked up his beer. "Cold?"

"No, it's a tic."

He laughed softly, then moved the guitar off his lap. He wasn't quite holding his arms open for a hug, but the invitation was there. He clinched it when he said, "Want to sit with me?"

Quinn studied him in the near darkness for a long moment. She remembered their conversation about the lion earlier. Right now she felt like she was climbing into a lion's cage. Or rather, his lap.

Another gust of wind gave her all the urging she needed. She eased into Tyler, finding him warm and solid. He smelled like cigarettes and beer and something warmer, more inviting, like cinnamon or vanilla or both. His arms came around her, dragging the guitar into *her* lap. He shifted, moving her slightly. It put her face almost against his neck, his breath against her hairline.

She suddenly wasn't cold at all.

"I don't think there's room in this chair for the three of us," she said softly.

"Please," he scoffed. "As tiny as you are? Plenty of room."

Tiny. Tiny! Quinn almost fell off his lap. Maybe he couldn't feel her crushing his femurs.

But then he started to play, his fingers spilling across the strings, picking out a quick-yet-slow rhythm. His arms were warm and strong, caging her in his lap, and Quinn closed her eyes.

When he began to sing, it took her by surprise. His voice was low, rough and raspy, carrying a tune effortlessly. She didn't know the song, but it felt vaguely country, with lyrics about pretty girls and apple trees. Her cynical mind wanted to mock it, to mock *him*, because he was being gentle and kind and it threw her off balance more effectively than when he'd physically dragged her out of her apartment building.

But damn, he had a sexy voice. Quinn felt drunk on the sound, like he was playing her body instead of the strings.

His fingers eventually went still, and he dropped a kiss against her temple.

She shifted in his lap, turning, rising up to kiss him.

For an instant, she almost panicked and drew back, thinking of the night she'd spent with Nick, when she'd kissed him and made an absolute fool of herself.

But Tyler was kissing her back, setting the guitar against the wall, using both hands to catch her waist and slide under the tank top. She was suddenly straddling him, and even though she'd gone all the way with boys before, this felt like *more*, like she'd been playing Little League all her life, and all of a sudden she'd been dropped in the middle of a Major League game. It was exhilarating and terrifying at the same time.

He grabbed her hips and pulled her against him, and Quinn gave a little gasp.

Then his mouth was on her neck and his hand was under her shirt. When his fingers discovered that she wasn't wearing a bra, he made a low sound in his throat. His thumb stroked over her breast again, and Quinn felt the touch all the way through her body.

"God, you're good at this," she gasped.

He laughed, and she felt the sound roll through his body. His hands pulled free of her shirt to stroke up the lengths of her arms. "Are you still cold?"

She shook her head.

He brushed blond hair out of her eyes, tracing a finger down the side of her face. It was the first time she'd ever known him to be gentle. "You know I didn't invite you here for this," he said softly.

"Careful," she whispered back. "I might start to think you're nice." She reached down and grabbed his beer, then took a long sip.

She watched his eyes follow her movement, and she had a pretty good idea what he was thinking when she put the bottle to her lips.

Then his eyes narrowed, just a fraction. "How old are you?" he said.

She shifted against him, leaning closer, beginning to stroke a hand against his neck. "Does it matter?"

He caught her hand. "Yes."

Quinn froze and looked at him. "Eighteen," she said. "Too young for you?"

He visibly relaxed. "For a second I was worried you were going to tell me you were sixteen or something."

A month ago, she *had been* sixteen. "Yeah, that would've been crazy." She laughed and took another long sip of beer.

Tyler watched this, then snatched the bottle out of her hands. He took a long drink and finished it off. "Jesus," he muttered. "You *are* sixteen."

"Seventeen," she whispered.

He closed his eyes and banged his head back against the chair. Several times.

"Trying to get the blood flow back to the head that matters?" she said.

"Trying to figure out if I'm committing a *felony*."

"You're not. How old are *you*?"

"Twenty-one."

"Four years. We could have been in high school together." That seemed to settle him. "So you're a senior?"

"Junior. And what, you're a junior in college? It's totally like the same thing."

That made him smile.

"Is this more of your freaky honor code?" she said. "Murdering an innocent family is okay, but a slight gap in age—"

"They're not innocent," Tyler snapped.

"Quick, bang your other head against the chair. Too much thinking is going on."

Tyler sighed. He put his hands on her waist, almost a caress. But then he tightened his grip as if he was going to set her on her feet.

"Wait," Quinn said, putting her hands over his. "Don't stop it. Please."

"Why?"

A genuine question. So she gave him a genuine answer. "Because I like you," she said.

His thumbs stroked over her abdomen. "I like you, too."

"Maybe we should go back to Little League," she said.

"What?"

"Or at least the minors."

His eyebrows went up. "Are you telling me to slow down?"

"Not for my benefit. For yours, old man."

Now he definitely looked like he was going to put her on her feet. So she rotated in his hands to sit against him again. She pressed her face into his neck. "Sing me another song?"

He hesitated just long enough that she thought he'd refuse.

But then he picked up the guitar, set it across her lap, and started to play.

Chapter 16

While he slept, Nick forgot about the lunch table argument with his brothers. Or rather, his *brother*. Maybe it was Quinn's drama, maybe it was the peace and quiet of Adam's apartment, but *creepy* didn't come crashing back into his brain until Gabriel opened the bathroom door the next morning, while Nick was brushing his teeth.

Every muscle in his body tensed. He wanted to shove Gabriel back out and slam the door in his face.

Instead, he spit toothpaste into the sink and wiped his mouth without looking at him.

"What is up with you?" said Gabriel.

"Nothing is *up with me*." Nick moved to edge past him.

Gabriel caught him around the neck and roughed up his hair. "I know how to make you talk, Nicky."

The motion was good-natured, the kind of thing that would usually make him laugh.

But Nick twisted free and shoved Gabriel into the wall so hard it rattled the towel rack. He pinned him there and forced his voice to stay low. "Leave me alone. Okay?"

Gabriel stared at him, identical blue eyes searching his. He could have fought back, but he didn't. "Sure, Nick. Whatever you want."

Whatever you want. Yeah, right.

Nick let him go and stepped into the hallway, jerking the door shut behind him. His throat felt tight, and he had no idea what expression was on his face, but it must not have been good. Chris stood there in the hallway, and when Nick met his eyes, Chris put his hands up and took a step back.

Damn it. He couldn't find the right rhythm with anyone lately.

Nick went into his bedroom and closed the door. Hunter was already downstairs, his air mattress made like a military bunk. Nick sat on the edge of his bed and put his head in his hands.

Part of him wished Gabriel had fought back, had pushed and needled and forced the truth out of him.

Part of him wanted to go back in the bathroom and punch his twin brother.

A knock sounded at his door.

Nick stared at the six-foot panel of wood and wondered if fate was going to deliver those options on a silver platter.

Then the door cracked open, just enough to let his younger brother peek through. "It's Chris." A pause. "Can I come in?"

Nick sighed. "Sure."

Chris opened the door, but he didn't come inside. He leaned against the doorjamb and looked hesitant. "I don't want to get in the middle of something, here."

Please. Pry. Tell me you've figured everything out.

"It's fine," Nick said. It wasn't even seven a.m. and he was already exhausted. "What's up?"

"Are you and Quinn all right?"

Nick let out a frustrated breath. "Why does everyone keep *asking* me that?"

"Because you look like you want to kill someone, and that's usually Michael's gig."

"I don't want to kill anyone."

Except Tyler. And maybe Gabriel.

Chris came all the way into the room and dropped onto the side of the bed. "Becca told me to ask if you guys wanted to come over to her place tonight. We're going to get a pizza, rent a movie. Hang out." He waggled his eyebrows. "Et cetera."

There was a time when Nick would have jumped at the chance, just to force other things out of his brain. And, he admitted to himself, to keep up appearances. He and Gabriel used to take girls out together, just because they could. But since he and Chris had been dating Quinn and Becca, they'd done the double date thing a few times.

Now, however, he was glad to have a reason to refuse. "I can't. I told Mike I would babysit."

Chris smiled. "Sucker. I knew you'd say yes."

Of course he did. Nick always did what his brothers needed.

Maybe Chris read his darkening mood, because he lost the smile before Nick could say anything. "Well, I said I would ask." He paused and looked at the wall like something interesting was happening there. He didn't say anything for a long time, but the air felt heavy, and Nick waited. Chris wasn't a talker, and when he had something to say, it took him a while to get around to it.

When he finally spoke, his voice was low. "If something is going on, you can tell me. I know you always tell Gabriel everything, but—I'll keep your secret, too."

Nick looked at him. He didn't know what to say.

When Becca's father had come to town to kill them all, he'd trapped Chris and Nick in a walk-in freezer. Nick's leg had been broken, and he'd barely been able to move. Just another instance where he wasn't strong enough to save anyone. Michael and Gabriel had rescued them.

For the first time, Nick realized that Chris hadn't been able to save himself, either. And Chris might have been a year younger, but he sure as hell wasn't *weak*.

Nick had been quiet too long. Chris finally turned away from the wall and met his eyes.

There were too many variables here. Nick worried the tension in his body might rattle it to pieces.

His cell phone buzzed on his nightstand. Nick jumped. He could see the screen lit up with a text message, but he couldn't see the sender.

Chris was closer. If he looked over, he'd see it.

He didn't look.

Nick ran a hand through his hair, putting some order to the mess Gabriel had made. "I need to finish getting ready for school."

Chris nodded. "Me, too." He hesitated in the doorway. "If you see Quinn, please tell her Becca's really worried about her. She's not responding to her texts or anything."

Join the club. But at least Nick could offer an explanation for this. "I told Quinn the truth. About us. I think she's upset that she didn't learn about it from Becca."

Chris winced. "That's not Bec's fault."

Nick smiled. "Girls."

Chris didn't smile back. "I'll tell her. See you in the car."

He was barely out the door before Nick grabbed his phone.

Not Adam. Quinn.

Still alive. I've got a ride to school.

Nick sighed and wished he knew how to fix this. He shoved the phone in his pocket and grabbed his backpack.

He was halfway down the steps when he realized what Chris had said.

If you see Quinn.

If. Not *when.*

I'll keep your secret, too.

His secret. Not Quinn's.

It wasn't enough to be absolutely certain, but Nick could connect the dots. Chris might not know for sure.

But he'd guessed.

The homeroom bell hadn't rung yet, but it was close. Quinn shoved a notebook in her bag and swung her locker shut.

Only to find Becca standing there.

Perfect, pretty Becca, with all those special secrets she didn't think to share.

Quinn shouldered her backpack and started walking.

"Come on," said Becca. "Would you at least *tell me* what you're so pissed about?"

"Why don't you ask your boyfriend? Maybe he could write a message in steam or something."

Well, that shut Becca up.

But only for a second. "Please—would you stop walking? I wanted to tell you, Quinn." She hesitated. "You had so much going on, and I—"

"Don't you dare make this about me. You don't know anything about me."

"Because you won't say anything! I've been trying to talk to you all week!"

Like Becca would be able to relate to Quinn's problems. "Forget it. You're right. I have too much going on."

"It wasn't only my secret to tell," Becca said quietly. "If Nick told you everything, then you know they're in danger."

Quinn stopped and looked at her. She made her voice equally low. "And so are you. Didn't feel like sharing that? Didn't feel like mentioning how some guys came after you with a gun? Maybe if I'd known that, I wouldn't have spent the night making out with—"

She cut herself off. What was *wrong* with her? She'd almost sold Nick out *again*. And while Tyler didn't have any reason to tell the Merricks, Becca would *definitely* tell Chris something was up.

But all of a sudden, she hated denying the night she'd spent with Tyler. The kissing in the darkness, surrounded by his arms, her ears full of his raspy voice and the strum of his guitar.

Becca was staring at her.

"With Nick," Quinn finished.

And of course, thinking of kissing Nick felt . . . *wrong*. She remembered what a fool she'd made of herself that night he'd let her sleep in his bed. She turned away from Becca again. "I need to get to class."

Becca didn't say anything for the longest time, until Quinn didn't think she was going to bother.

And that, more than anything, made Quinn's throat tighten.

Then Becca called, "I miss you."

Quinn hesitated. She wondered what would happen if she turned around, walked back to Becca, and told her everything.

She thought of the cops coming to her apartment, and wondered if she even had a home to return to. She had no illusions that she could keep sleeping in Tyler's second bedroom. She didn't even know if she *wanted* to.

But Becca wouldn't understand this. There were too many variables, too many *what-ifs*. Too many secrets.

Quinn looked at her. "I miss you, too." Then she turned around and kept walking.

Becca didn't come after her.

And the worst part was, Quinn really wished she would.

CHAPTER 17

Nick had had no idea babysitting would be so exhausting. He and James played hide-and-seek in the woods until dark. Not much of a challenge for Nick, who merely had to ask the air to locate the boy, but he could *pretend* to seek. Then tag. Then football in the lengthening shadows of twilight. Nick made a good show of falling down when sixty pounds of kindergartner tackled him.

Just when the edge of the sun dropped below the horizon, something foreign brushed Nick's senses.

It didn't feel malicious, but Nick grabbed James, tossing the boy in the air while he laughed and shrieked.

Nick ignored that and cast his senses wide.

Nothing.

He dragged James inside anyway. The kid promptly dumped a massive plastic tub of Legos in the middle of the living room floor.

Then he grinned up at Nick. "Can we build a whole city?"

So they built a whole city.

His phone buzzed around eight, just when he was telling James that *yes*, his mother *did* want him to brush his teeth. Nick slid the phone out of his pocket with his heart in his throat, hoping for a message from Adam.

He hadn't heard from him all day.
Not Adam. Michael.

Hannah's folks are going to come pick up James so he can sleep in his own bed.

And that was it. Typical.
Nick texted back.

How was dinner??

Terrifying.

A pause, then another message appeared.

Good call on the haircut.

Nick smiled.
"Can I play Angry Birds?" James asked through a mouthful of toothpaste.
Nick slid his fingers across the keys. "In a minute."

Are you coming home?

Going out for a while. Don't wait up.

When Hannah's parents showed up, they didn't look like they wanted to kill anyone, so Nick figured the dinner had gone pretty well. Hannah's mother was a petite blond woman in a sweater set, and she tried to give Nick sixty dollars for babysitting. He turned it down.

The fire marshal looked at him long and hard, reminding Nick that this guy had interrogated his twin brother a few weeks ago.

But Hannah's mother stepped between them to kiss him on the cheek and say thank you. The fire marshal shook his hand. James gave him a hug.

Then Nick had the house to himself.

He couldn't remember the last time that had happened.

He grabbed a can of soda from the refrigerator and dragged his physics textbook out of his backpack.

As soon as he looked at the page, he realized he didn't want to be doing this.

His cell phone rang.

Nick looked at the display and smiled. He pushed the button to answer. "You are my hero."

"I like the sound of that." Adam's voice was rich and warm in his ear, and Nick realized this was the first time they'd talked on the phone.

He wanted him to keep talking.

"How was dance?"

"Could've been better." Adam sighed, and his voice was tired. "Quinn didn't show up."

Nick ran a hand down his face, feeling his emotions vacillate between worry and exasperation. "Man, I'm sorry."

"She texted me that she couldn't make it. It's all right . . . *man.*"

Nick could hear the smile in his voice. "What are you going to do?"

"Would you think less of me if I said I had a backup routine?"

"I wouldn't think less of you if you had a backup *partner.*"

"Good. I've got one of those, too."

Nick blinked. "Really?"

"Nothing official, but I could get one of the girls from the studio to dance with me. I liked Quinn for this piece because it's raw and edgy and passionate, and she fit the part." He sighed. "Enough about dance. How's your night?"

"The height of awesome. I'm sitting in an empty house with my physics textbook."

"Want to come over?"

Nick's heart bounced around in his chest. "Can't. I don't have the car."

"How long are you alone?"

"I don't know. Three hours, maybe?"

Adam hesitated. "Want some company?"

Just the words sent a curl of desire winding through Nick's thoughts. He told his thoughts to get real. "God, I wish."

"How far do you live from a bus stop?"

Nick straightened. Adam could not come here. Could *not*. "I have no idea."

"How far do you live from Ritchie Highway?"

Nick wet his lips and hesitated. He should be telling Adam that there was no way this could work. But when he opened his mouth, he found himself saying, "Three blocks. We're on Chautauga. Just south of the community college."

"Near the firehouse, right?"

Of course Adam would know the area. "Ah . . . yeah."

"I can be there in fifteen minutes. Twenty, tops." Adam's voice dropped. "So let me ask you again. Want some company?"

Quinn sat in Tyler's truck and stared at her apartment building. Her mom's car was in the lot. So was Jake's. That didn't mean much other than that their cars hadn't been towed. If her brother had been arrested, his car could still be here, right? What about her mom?

She'd been waiting for a call to the guidance office all day, expecting to find a social worker sitting in the waiting room or something. She was prepared for hushed voices to say things like, "We didn't realize how bad things had gotten. We have a few options, but we're going to take care of you . . ."

But that call never came. Quinn slogged through her classes, making her way toward the end of the day, hating the thought of going home.

She'd been ready to ride the bus all night, but Tyler texted to ask if she wanted to be his rooftop companion for the evening.

Without Nick, she didn't have a ride to the dance studio.

Without Tyler, she didn't have a place to sleep for the night.

Rooftop taquitos it was.

It had been nice to sit in the nighttime quiet, to eat and drink and not worry that someone was going to hassle her. She'd told Tyler about school, about waiting for the call that never came. She'd confided her fears that her brother might have done something to her mother. That maybe Jordan had come home and Jake had hurt *him*. That maybe the cops hadn't come at all. That maybe Quinn had walked out of one mess, only to leave a bigger disaster in her wake.

"You don't have to go up there," said Tyler. "I can check on them if you want."

Quinn shook her head. Sit down here and wonder if her brother was going to answer the door with a gun in his hand? "I'll go. Wait here."

"You're insane if you think I'm letting you go up there alone."

"You're insane if you think I'm letting you—"

"Jesus, do you need to be balls-to-the-wall about everything? If you want to go up, go up. I won't get in your way."

She thought that meant he was going to wait in the truck after all, but when she climbed the stairs, he was right behind her.

Halfway up, she stopped short at the tiny landing. "Am I being an idiot?"

"Of everyone I've met in your family, you seem like the least idiotic."

Well, that wasn't really saying all that much. "My mom and I—we've never gotten along."

"I kind of assumed that when you told me she was knocking you around."

"She's not—she's under a lot of stress—"

"So are you. So am I. I don't give a shit, Quinn. Your mom is *messed up*. So is your brother. And what the fuck is your dad—"

"Okay, okay. Forget it." She spun away from him.

"No. Stop." Tyler caught her shoulders, gently, securely. "She's your mother. I understand."

Quinn hated tears. *Hated them.* Especially hated that they were flocking to her eyes right this very second.

"We don't have to go inside," said Tyler. "Knock on the door, make sure she's okay, and we'll leave."

"And then what?"

Tyler sighed. "We'll go back to my place. You can figure out what to do."

She shrugged his hands off. "Try not to sound so enthusiastic—"

He spun her around and seized her arms. "Stop it. Do you just need someone to call your bluff? Fine. Called. Get your ass up there so we can get out of here. You don't need to be afraid. I'm right here."

Quinn stared up at him and gritted her teeth. She wanted to jerk away from him.

Sort of.

Okay, not at all.

She took a long breath. "I'm worried he's still here," she said, her voice small.

"Tony?"

The dark-haired creeper. She shook her head, then nodded. "Or my brother."

His expression softened. "Do you want to call your mom again?"

Quinn had been trying all day. Her mom's mobile phone had been ringing straight to voice mail every time. She routinely let the battery die, so it wasn't really a sign of anything.

But it bought her another thirty seconds, so Quinn tried again.

Voice mail. Quinn checked her texts to see if her little brother had written back yet, but he hadn't. A phone call to him had gone unanswered, too.

Wind swirled through the open staircase and Quinn shivered and thought of Nick. She should have been dancing tonight, stretching her muscles in a warm studio, leaping and twirling through Adam's routine.

Not trembling on her apartment building's staircase, wondering if her mom was lying dead in her apartment.

She steeled her nerve and turned for the steps again. "Come on."

Quinn pulled her key ring out of her pocket, but when she slid the key into the deadbolt and turned, she discovered that the lock was already thrown. Feeling her heart in her throat, she reached out and twisted the knob.

As always, the foyer was a well of quiet stillness. Quinn stepped lightly anyway, moving slowly along the carpeting. Tyler was a shadow at her back, mirroring her movements, creeping into the apartment as if they didn't have a right to be here.

Everything felt wrong. The air carried tension. She expected to step on a dead body.

Stop thinking of dead people, she told herself.

Her cell phone blared into the silence. Quinn almost broke an ankle from jumping so hard.

She fought for the correct button to stop the call, but then she realized the display was lit up with *Jordan.*

She pressed the button to answer. "Hey," she said quickly, her voice a whispered rush. He was fourteen and jaded, but he wasn't an addict or an alcoholic. If she could help anyone in her family, it was Jordan. "Where are you? You okay?"

"Yeah. Fine."

He didn't sound fine.

"Have you heard from Mom?" Quinn said.

"Yeah."

That was all he said. Quinn could hear him breathing, heavy and rough on the other end of the phone.

"Where are you?" she said.

"At Kurt Culpeper's. Mom said—she said—" His voice broke. She heard snuffling.

"Jordan," she said. "Jordan, what happened? Where's Mom?"

"Hold on." His breaths were jagged now, and she heard a door close. "She said I can't come back there." Another shaky breath. "She said she couldn't—she couldn't—"

And then he was crying.

Quinn sank onto the couch, distantly aware of Tyler sitting beside her, probably close enough to hear half of what Jordan was saying.

Her younger brother barely talked to her except to ask when she'd be done with the television so he could play with his PlayStation. It was unthinkable he would be crying to her on the phone, and Quinn didn't know how to deal with this.

And where the hell was her mother?

"Are you okay?" she said. "Jordan, are you safe where you are?"

"Yeah." He sniffled loudly and got it together. "Kurt's mom said I could stay through the weekend. I told her Mom and Dad were going out of town. I was going to stay at Jeremy's, but his mom always wants to call."

"What happened with Mom?"

"I came home for clothes and she—she—" Crying again.

Tyler leaned into her and caught her eye. "Tell him we'll come get him," he said. "See if he can get you an address."

"Do you want us to come get you?" said Quinn. "I'm with a friend."

Jordan's voice tightened right up. "Gross. I don't want to hang out with you and your boyfriend."

Fear and tension caught up with Quinn. "Damn it, Jordan, I'm trying to—"

"Stop screaming at me, Quinn! I'm sick of people screaming at me!"

She so didn't need this. Quinn inhaled to lay into him, but Tyler plucked the phone out of her hand. "Hey, man, this is Quinn's friend Tyler. Are you all right where you are, or do you want us to come get you?"

His voice was level, easy, very we're-all-bros-in-this-together. And Jordan was responding, from the bits she could hear. Quinn stared at Tyler, wondering if she should grab the phone or kiss him.

Then Tyler said, "No, you're right. It sucks, kid. It does. Look, see if you can get a pen. I'll give you my number. If you change your mind, call me. We'll come get you. All right?"

Then he gave his number, got her brother to promise to use it, and pushed the button to end the call.

Quinn couldn't stop staring at him. She'd never met anyone

like him, so self-assured and confident yet not completely into himself.

"What?" said Tyler.

She shook herself. "Nothing. Let's get out—"

She froze. Her mother stood by the corner leading to the galley kitchen. A threadbare bathrobe clung to her frame, and Quinn was glad the belt seemed securely knotted, because the drooping shoulder showed that her mom wasn't wearing anything beneath the terry cloth. She'd showered at some point, because her hair had dried into unbrushed clumps, but from the waves of alcohol emanating from her, she'd been hitting the bottle since then.

The expression in her eyes was terrifying. A trophy was clutched in one hand. A basketball trophy. One of Jake's.

Quinn wasn't sure whether to be relieved her mom was still alive, or disgusted that she was obviously still obsessed with Jake's *success*.

Then her mother spoke.

"How could you do that?" she said, her voice cracked and raw. And slurring. She took a few steps toward the couch. "How could you, Quinn?"

Quinn swallowed. "I didn't—I didn't do—"

"Shut up! Shut up! You're out whoring around and now you—"

"I'm not whoring around!" Quinn was on her feet, ready to get in her mother's face.

"Take it easy." Tyler had a hand on her arm, and his voice was quiet. "Let's just walk out."

"Shut up!" Quinn's mom shrieked. "You were here, too! You did this! He had a future, you bitch! You screw up everything! Everything!"

"I didn't do anything!" Now Quinn was crying, and she didn't care. "He was—"

"Shut up!" The words were practically unintelligible with rage. "Shut the fuck up! You did this! You!"

And then, without warning, her mom crumpled to the carpet, sobbing, the trophy pressed to her face.

Quinn stood there, shaking. She couldn't breathe. She didn't know what to do.

Tyler's voice was low. "Let's get out of here, Quinn."

But she couldn't leave, not like this. Some part of her couldn't leave her mother a weeping mess on the floor. The drooping side of the bathrobe gaped now, revealing a sagging breast. Hair was sticking to her mother's saliva. She wailed.

Quinn went to her, dropping to her knees. "Mom. Mom, stop. Please, let me help you." She put a hand on a shaky shoulder. "Mom, it's okay—"

"Don't *touch* me! You ruin *everything!*"

Then her mom swung at her with the trophy.

Quinn didn't even see it coming. The marble base caught her square in the face. She saw stars. Constellations. Whole frigging galaxies. Then blackness.

She wasn't out for long. She came to in Tyler's arms, still in her apartment foyer. Her mother was shrieking at them to get out, to get the fuck out, to get that *whore* out of her apartment. Quinn couldn't seem to get her eyes to focus on anything, from Tyler's face, to the doorway, to the dashboard in front of her when Tyler buckled her into the seat.

"Fuck this," he said, starting his ignition, but not shifting into gear. He pulled his phone out of his pocket.

Quinn struggled to get her limbs to respond. "No," she said. "No police."

Tyler sucked in a long breath and touched her face. "Sweetheart, I think you need an *ambulance.*"

"No. Please. No. They'll call—they'll call—"

She couldn't get her voice to work, and she realized she was crying.

"Shh," said Tyler. "It's all right. I'll just drive you to the hospital. Okay?" He shifted into gear.

"No. No. They'll make me go to a foster home or something. Please, Tyler. Please." She was hiccupping now, ugly crying, full out. "Please. No."

He stopped at the end of the parking lot and looked at her.

"You need help. She might have broken your cheekbone." He winced. "Your face is already swelling."

She knew it was. She could feel it all the way into her eye. "Can't you heal it?"

He looked back at the road. His voice was suddenly hollow. "I don't know. I don't know if I could."

"Nick healed me once. Please, Tyler. Please, I can't—I can't—"

"Okay," he said softly. "Okay." He rubbed at his temples, then pulled out of the parking lot.

"No hospital," she said. Her words were slurring, and it reminded her of her mother. That made fresh tears well.

You ruin everything.

Her breath caught and stuttered.

"Easy," said Tyler. "No hospital, okay?"

"Then where?" He hit a bump and a wave of pain swept through her face, and she almost reconsidered.

"The beach," he said. "I need fire."

Quinn felt like time somehow vanished.

Stars scattered overhead, spinning wildly every time she moved her eyes. She lay in the sand, beside a roaring bonfire that seemed to stretch a mile high. The heat was intense, forcing sweat from her skin. Her head pounded like her mother kept swinging that trophy over and over again.

Tyler crouched over her, stroking his finger along her cheek, so lightly that Quinn barely felt it. "She broke the skin, too."

Quinn sniffed and put a hand to her eyes, but she felt the edge of the swelling and dropped her hand. "I don't—I don't know why she hates me."

"I don't think she hates you, baby girl," he said. "I think she hates herself."

She gave half a choked sob. "I feel ridiculous when you call me that."

"Do you want me to stop?"

She shook her head. The motion hurt. She wanted to throw up. Nausea meant broken bones, didn't it? She was terrified to touch her cheek, to feel whether anything would shift.

"Heal it," she said. "Please."

"Quinn—" His voice was tight. Distressed. "Maybe I should just take you to the hospital. This was a bad idea."

"No. No, I'm okay." She struggled to get her arm underneath her.

Wrong idea. The horizon shifted. So did the contents of her stomach. She gagged and almost threw up.

"Whoa," said Tyler. He gently eased her back down. The fire seemed to blaze brighter, or maybe her eyes were playing tricks.

"Are you worried?" she said.

"Worried?" He leaned close, his eyes picking up the glow from the fire.

"That you can't do it?"

He grimaced and looked at the fire. "No."

She wanted to punch him, but she'd probably end up puking all over him instead. "Then what—why won't you help me?" A thought occurred to her and she started crying again, shaking sobs that made her head pulse with pain. "Do you hate me, too? Did I fuck it up with you, too? Did I—"

"No! No, Quinn. No." He leaned close again, pressing a hand to her cheek. His palm was fire-hot, but it didn't hurt. Instead, she wanted to lean into it.

Then heat surged through her veins, fire swirling through every blood vessel, making her gasp.

"I'm not worried because I don't think I can help you," Tyler said quietly, his eyes afraid, his expression intense. His voice dropped until she could barely hear him over the flames. "I'm worried because I know I *can*."

CHAPTER 18

When Adam knocked on the front door, eagerness and panic were waging a full-on wrestling match in Nick's stomach. What was he supposed to do, text everyone something like, *Just want to make sure you'll all be out past eleven. Nothing to see here. Just me and my textbook.*

He'd taken the fastest shower in the history of time and changed clothes, but it left him feeling more on edge. The whole five minutes he'd been in the shower, he worried Adam would show up at the same time as one of his brothers.

But now Adam was here, knocking, and Nick couldn't seem to get the door open fast enough.

Somehow Adam managed to look better every time he saw him. The porch light threaded his hair with gold and painted shadows under his cheekbones.

"You look nervous," said Adam.

"I am nervous," Nick breathed. *But you're here. You're on my doorstep. You're in my space, and I don't want you to go.*

Adam didn't wait for an invitation. He moved across the threshold and pushed the door closed quietly behind him. "Are we still alone?"

"Yeah."

Adam stepped forward and kissed him. Nothing hesitant, nothing unsure. Simply the soft pressure of his lips against

Nick's mouth. Then the first brush of tongue, lighting sparks in Nick's body, sending his thoughts reeling. The room felt warmer, the air soft and welcoming, eager for the way his mood lightened in Adam's presence.

Adam shifted closer, until Nick could feel the heat of his chest and the brush of his hips. Then closer, his hands finding Nick's face and winding in his hair.

Nick made a low sound and slid his hands under Adam's coat, finding the warm muscled span of his waist.

Adam drew back and smiled. His voice was soft in the space between them. "Keep going like that and we'll never leave the foyer."

"Is it wrong that I don't care?"

Adam laughed. "I want to see where you live."

"It's very exciting. Here, give me your coat." *And your shirt, and your—*

"It *is* exciting." Adam shrugged out of his coat. "And I might not get another chance."

Well, that was sobering. But Nick took his coat and stashed it in the front closet.

Adam followed him through the lower level without much comment, until they came full circle to the staircase.

"No pictures," said Adam.

"What?"

"There aren't any pictures anywhere. Of your family. Or—" He hesitated, as if realizing he'd made a misstep. "Of your brothers."

Nick shrugged, but his shoulders felt tense again. "We used to have some. They were destroyed."

"Fire?"

Nick shook his head. "It's—it's a long story."

A lie. It was a pretty short story, really. He didn't want to re-live it, but his brain was more than happy to supply the memories. While Nick and his brothers were at their parents' funeral, Tyler and his best friend Seth had broken into the house. They'd destroyed every picture they could find.

Nick remembered coming home, still shaken from watching

glossy wooden boxes lowered into the ground, and finding shattered glass everywhere. Michael had called the cops. Chris had holed up in his room to cry. Gabriel had stormed out—probably on a mission of vengeance.

Nick had cleaned up the mess.

Five years, and the memory still had the power to knock the breath out of him. "I don't really want to talk about this."

"I'm sorry," Adam said softly. "I didn't mean—"

"It's fine." Nick tried to shake off the emotion, but it wouldn't loosen. "It's a stupid thing to be upset about—I mean, we still have old memory cards and stuff. We just—we never reprinted anything. And then after they were gone, no one really felt like taking pictures of anything meaningful."

"Your brothers weren't into trips to Sears wearing identical sweaters?"

Nick half smiled. "No."

Adam pulled his phone out of his pocket and held it up. "Say cheese."

"Don't take my—"

"Too late." He turned it around so Nick could see.

Adam had snapped the picture before Nick had started talking, so the photo captured his mouth in a thin line. His shoulders were hunched and his eyes dark.

"Delete it," he said.

"No way." Adam leaned close to whisper along his jaw. "I felt like taking a picture of something meaningful."

Nick blushed. There was a good chance he might melt right down these steps.

Adam grinned and said, "Wait, now I need another picture."

This time, Nick let him, but then he snatched the phone out of Adam's fingers.

"If you delete them, I'll just have to take more."

"I'm not deleting them." Nick turned the phone around and took a picture of Adam. Unruly hair, crooked smile, solid grip on Nick's heart.

He texted it to himself.

Adam took his hand and tugged. "Come on. Show me the upstairs."

At the top of the stairs, Nick pointed at each room in turn. "Chris, Michael, Gabriel, me. And the bathroom. I told you: thrilling."

But there *was* something thrilling about Adam's being here, in the upstairs hallway, breathing the same air. Anxiety had faded, leaving only longing and contentment.

Adam started forward, and Nick expected him to head for his bedroom. But Adam went to Gabriel's door.

Nick didn't follow him, but he crossed his arms to lean against the wall. He didn't want to think about Gabriel now.

"I expected your brother to be a slob," Adam said, leaning around the door frame to peer in.

Gabriel kind of *was* a slob, but they'd all learned pretty quickly that if they left the place a mess, there wasn't anyone around to pick up after them. Nick frowned. "Why?"

"Because he's careless."

"He's not—"

"He is. He's hurting you and he doesn't even realize it."

Nick couldn't exactly deny that.

Adam abandoned Gabriel's room and moved to Nick's doorway. "Can I go in?"

Nick nodded and followed.

But Adam stopped short. Nick knew what he'd spotted without even seeing around him. "What's with the air mattress?"

"Hunter sleeps there. He's my temporary roommate."

"You didn't say you had a roommate."

Nick shrugged. "I don't really think about it." He smiled. "Jealous?"

"Maybe."

"Don't be. He's going through some stuff with his mom." Nick paused and stepped around him to turn on the light. "He's also Gabriel's best friend."

Adam pulled out the desk chair and straddled it backward, leaning his arms on the back. "Then why doesn't he room with Gabriel?"

Nick shrugged and dropped onto the end of his bed. "I have more floor space. Gabriel and I used to share this room, until . . . well, until we didn't have to anymore."

Until his parents had died, and Michael finally got around to cleaning out the master bedroom. It hadn't happened right away. Two years had passed before any of them felt like changing around the sleeping arrangements.

Gabriel had been eager for his own space. Nick hadn't wanted him to go.

And now the tables were turned, with a drawer full of college letters offering him a way out of this house. Maybe out of this town.

"So serious," said Adam quietly. "What's rolling around in your head?"

Nothing he wanted to talk about. "I'm glad you're here."

"Me, too." Adam paused, then unwound himself from the chair to join Nick on the end of the bed. He found Nick's hand and threaded their fingers together.

Then he said, "Are you still hoarding a stack of unopened mail?"

"Yeah."

"Why haven't you opened them? What are you afraid of?"

Nick shook his head. "I don't know."

Adam hesitated. "I don't think that's true. You know."

He was right. Nick *did* know. Opening those letters would force him to make a choice. A decision about where his life was going.

A decision about staying or leaving.

"It's so different for you," Nick said. "You *know* you want to be a dancer. You know you're good at it. I want—I—I don't know."

"I don't think it has anything to do with what you *want,* and more about what you don't want. You don't want to disappoint your brothers." A pause. "Isn't that the same reason you don't want to tell them about you and me?"

Nick looked away, but Adam kept a firm grip on his hand. "I'm not chastising you. I understand it. I know I'm disappointing my parents every day. But you know what? I can't live my life for them. I have to live my life for *me*."

"You're disappointing your parents?"

Adam scoffed and rolled his eyes at the ceiling. "Please. You think they want their only child to be a dancer? My dad is always asking if I'm sure I don't want to take a few pre-med classes. Me. Pre-med. I can't even slice into frogs in biology."

"What does he do?"

"He *is* a doctor." Adam smiled. "Wait, ready for some irony? He's a gynecologist. Mom tells him that he's looked at so many vaginas that I came out predisposed to avoid them."

Nick burst out laughing.

"There." Adam whipped out his phone and snapped a picture. "I needed one with your smile."

"You're incorrigible." But Nick snatched the phone and took another picture—of Adam trying to get it back.

They wrestled for it, laughing, rolling, a tangle of limbs and mock fierceness. Then Adam's lips found his, his body trapping Nick on the bed, the hand that had just been grappling for the phone stroking down the length of his chest, finding the hem of his shirt and sliding underneath.

For the first time, Nick didn't hesitate at his touch. Maybe it was Adam's admission about his own insecurities, maybe it was the fact that they were *here*, in his room, in his space. Maybe it was the time limit, knowing this could be cut short at any moment if his brothers came home.

Maybe it was Adam's tongue drawing at his.

A thumb brushed his nipple and Nick gasped, feeling it all the way through his body. He grabbed the hem of his own shirt and broke the kiss long enough to yank it over his head.

Adam grinned. "Someone's feeling more comfortable."

"Someone's liking the feel of your hands."

"Just my hands?" Adam's mouth descended on his neck, trailing lips and breath and teeth along Nick's skin.

Nick sucked in a breath—then held it when Adam kissed a line down his chest.

Brown eyes flicked up to meet his. "What do you want?" Adam whispered.

You.

But he couldn't say it.

Adam brushed a kiss against his lips, then shifted off the bed. Nick caught his arm. "Don't. Don't go."

Low laughter. "I'm not going anywhere." Adam stretched to turn off the light, sending the room into near darkness.

When he reached for the door, Nick sat up on his elbows. "Leave it open so I can hear if anyone comes home."

Adam closed it halfway. Nick was going to protest even that, but then Adam pulled his shirt over his head, and Nick forgot his own last name.

"Whoa," he breathed. "I think you need to turn the light back on."

Adam crawled back on the bed, his dusky skin rolling with shadows as he moved. "You sweet-talker."

Nick wanted to reach out, to let his fingers drift across the muscled planes of Adam's chest, but he couldn't move. He'd spent so long denying any kind of attraction to a boy that having one shirtless in his bed was making every nerve ending hypersensitive. He felt like a land mine. One touch and he'd explode. "Why did you turn the light off?"

Adam eased in close to him, until their chests were touching. He put a hand against Nick's cheek and kissed him. "Because it's easier to turn off worries in the dark."

Nick met his eyes in the darkness. "Yours or mine?"

"Both." Then Adam kissed him again, a broad hand exploring Nick's chest. Nick touched his face, his shoulder, letting his hands roam. His teeth nipped at Adam's lip, then his jaw.

Adam made a soft sound, a good sound. Nick did it again, biting a little harder. The room felt ten degrees warmer. Maybe twenty. He had to be doing it, but he didn't care.

Adam trapped one of Nick's legs under his and shifted closer, pressing into him until there was no doubt he was happy to be there. Now Nick couldn't help the low moan that escaped his throat. His breathing quickened, thrusting his chest into Adam's with every inhale.

Adam's hand drifted lower, finding Nick's stomach, slow fingers sliding along the waistband of his jeans.

Adam's hands, his mouth—Nick couldn't think. His body was acting on instinct, and he couldn't process every emotion.

Especially when Adam stopped teasing and stroked his hand over the front of Nick's jeans. No hesitation, no gentleness, but enough grip to steal every thought from Nick's head. He sucked in a breath. The room spun.

"Too much?" whispered Adam.

"Not enough."

Deft fingers flipped the button loose. Before Nick could contemplate exactly what that meant, Adam was touching him.

Nick cried out. Adam captured the sound with a kiss.

He never wanted this moment to end.

And then it did.

Someone called his name and the overhead light flipped on. Suddenly Nick was scrambling to right himself.

Then Hunter was swiftly backing out of the room, saying, "Oh. Oh, shit. I am—I'm going—I'm sorry—"

He slammed the door. Nick heard his footsteps on the stairs as he jogged down.

"Fuck," said Nick. He sat up and pressed his hands into his eyes. He was shaking and he couldn't stop. His emotions couldn't handle the abrupt one-eighty. Part of him wanted to cry and another part wanted to punch something. "*Fuck.*"

Adam's hands touched his shoulders. "It's okay," he said softly. "It's okay."

"It's not okay. He'll tell—I can't—" His voice broke.

Hunter would tell Gabriel. He might be telling him *right now*. Nick could imagine the text messages. *Dude. Just found your brother with another guy. No, seriously.*

Nick choked on his breath. The heat in the room was turning into a bitter chill. He shivered.

Adam's arms came around him from behind, holding him.

"It'll be okay." He brushed a kiss against Nick's hair. "I promise. It'll be—"

Nick jerked free and hit him in the chest, shoving him away with a force driven by rage and fear. "It is *not okay!*"

As soon as he did it, he regretted it. With the light on, he could see every ounce of hurt in Adam's eyes. Every ounce of disappointment.

Every ounce of anger.

Nick took a breath. "I'm sorry. Adam—wait."

But Adam was already pulling his shirt on, shoving his phone into his pocket, heading for the door.

Nick went after him, catching his arm. "Please," he said. "I'm sorry."

Adam stopped, but he didn't look at him. "Let me go, Nick."

"I don't want to." He paused and moved closer. "I'm sorry. I didn't—I wasn't ready for that—"

"You know what?" Adam looked at him now. "I've heard it before, okay?"

Nick jerked back. "I would never hurt you."

"Too late." Adam pulled the door open and kept his voice low. "Let me go. Now."

Nick couldn't take the pain in his voice. He'd build a rainbow banner in the front hall announcing his sexuality if it would fix this. "Please. Adam, stay. Please."

Now Adam turned and shoved him away, dislodging Nick's grip. "I told you to let me go." He didn't wait for a response, just walked out the door.

Nick followed, buttoning his pants as he jogged down the steps after him. He had no shoes, no shirt, but he was ready to follow Adam down the street barefoot if he had to.

"Stop," he pleaded. "Wait—wait. At least let me walk you to the bus stop."

"I'm not a girl, Nick." Adam didn't even hesitate at the front door.

"Please wait. Please—I'm sorry."

Adam rounded on him on the porch. His eyes were shining in the light. "You know what sucks about *sorry*? It's the worst word in the world. Because it always happens *after* you fuck up something good."

Then he turned and started walking. Nick went after him again. Wind whipped between them, whispering of Adam's fury.

Adam whirled. "Don't you follow me. I don't want you near me right now. Do you understand? You're so worried about what everyone else will think? I'll make it real easy for you."

"Stop it. Let's talk about this."

"What's to talk about? You care more about what people *think* than you care about me. Crystal clear. Message received." He started walking again.

Nick took a step, but Adam called over his shoulder. "You follow me, and I'm calling the cops."

He was serious. Nick could feel it in the air between them.

He could also tell that Adam was crying.

It broke his heart and almost sent him running down the driveway.

Instead, he dropped onto the wooden steps and watched Adam walk, casting his senses far and wide, feeling Adam's presence even after he disappeared from view. He stayed there, holding on to that tiny connection, until Adam stepped out of range or got on a bus.

Nick lost the sense. Adam was gone.

CHAPTER 19

Nick eventually had to go back in the house.

Hunter was messing around in the kitchen. Nick had no idea what he was doing. He didn't want to face him, but his stomach was in knots wondering if Hunter had texted anything to his brothers. Sitting in his room waiting for them to come home was a little too much like sitting on death row.

He found his shirt on his bedroom floor and went back downstairs.

But once he was there, he couldn't walk down the hallway. He sat at the bottom of the steps and put his head in his hands.

He didn't want to cry, but apparently his emotions didn't give a crap about what he *wanted*.

He'd fucked this up with Adam. He didn't even know how to fix it.

He didn't even know if he *could*.

You're going to break my heart. I can feel it.

Yeah, he'd sure lived up to that.

He wished he could talk to Quinn, but he'd fucked that up, too.

The air told him Hunter was in the hallway before he heard him.

Nice. Why couldn't the air have told him Hunter was coming into his frigging bedroom?

You might've been distracted by Adam's hand down your pants.

Nick couldn't look at Hunter. He swiped the last tears off his cheeks. This was so humiliating. All he needed now was for Gabriel to walk through the door.

Hunter stopped beside the staircase bannister. He didn't say anything for a long moment.

Nick stared at his shoes and waited, ready for mockery. Derision. Anger. Disgust. Something.

"I made you a cup of coffee," said Hunter.

Surprised, Nick looked up, but only halfway, to see that Hunter carried two mugs.

Coffee. So unexpected that it hit Nick like a fist to the face. Honestly, a real fist to the face would have been *less* surprising. He was so on edge that he was ready for Hunter to say *Just kidding* and dump it in his lap.

"If you want," Hunter said. "I thought you might need some."

No malice in his voice, but Nick still couldn't look at him. He reached out and wrapped his hands around the mug, inhaling the steam. "Thanks."

"Can I sit down?"

Nick nodded.

Hunter eased onto the step beside him. "That—that sucked."

Nick stared at his coffee. Was Hunter looking for an apology? Or offering one? Tension crawled across his shoulders and dug in its claws.

"I'm really sorry," Hunter said quietly. He was staring at his own mug. "I am really, really—"

"It's not your fault." He should have closed the door. Or hung a sign.

Or really, he should have turned Adam down to begin with.

Hunter rubbed at the back of his neck. "I didn't think anyone was home, but then I came in and it was like ninety degrees in here. Your light was off, so I thought maybe you were having a nightmare, especially when . . ." Hunter winced. "Um, when you cried out—"

He broke off, and Nick could feel his embarrassment.

But that was it. Just embarrassment. None of those other things.

Nick cut a glance to the side. He had to clear his throat. "I left the door open so I could hear if someone came home."

"I let Casper run for a while. I came in the back door."

And, really, Nick had been so wrapped up in Adam that a marching band could have come through the front door and he wouldn't have noticed.

The suspense was killing him. His voice was rough. "What did you tell my brothers?"

"Are you crazy? Nothing." Hunter hesitated, and his voice turned careful. "They don't know?"

Nick shook his head.

Hunter let out a sigh. "That's kind of a relief. I thought maybe I was the only one who wasn't in on the secret." Another pause, and his voice held the slightest bit of fascination. "Didn't you sneak Quinn into your bed, like, two nights ago?"

Nick twisted the mug in his hands. He still hadn't taken a sip. "I'm not sleeping with Quinn. She needed a place to get away from her family."

"So your room is kind of like a haven for the lost and misdirected."

Nick looked at him. Hunter's voice was vaguely teasing. He had no idea how to read this. He'd been so ready for an attack that a simple conversation felt like a trap.

"Quinn knows. About me. She's a friend."

"Does anyone else know?"

Nick thought about Chris, and his promise to keep a secret. "I don't think so."

"Who's the guy? Does he go to our school?"

"Adam." Nick swallowed. "No, he's in college. He's a dancer. A friend of Quinn's."

"How long has this been going on?"

"Not long." He paused. "A few weeks. I met him that week school was closed." He felt like they were side-stepping around something important, and it was killing him. "Look, if you want to change where you sleep, I get it. I can sleep on the couch, or—"

"Why would I want to change where I sleep?" Hunter looked at him like he was nuts.

"Aren't you bothered?"

Hunter rubbed at his jaw and gave a short laugh. He was blushing. "Okay, I'm not going to lie. That totally wasn't what I expected to find when I hit the light switch. But I'm just—I'm *surprised*. I had no idea. But I'm not upset about it."

Nick studied him. He wasn't sure what to say.

Hunter studied him back. "For what it's worth, I think you should tell your brothers. Gabriel thinks Quinn is jerking you around. I had to talk him out of going off on her today."

Nick made a disgusted noise. "That would've been spectacular."

"He's worried about you."

"Yeah, okay." He paused and picked up his coffee mug, taking a sip so he didn't have to say anything else. Hunter sat there quietly and didn't say anything, either.

But it was nice, Nick realized, to sit with someone who *knew* yet wasn't openly judging him.

Adam hadn't judged him, either. Nick felt fresh tears come to his eyes, and he tried to pinch them away.

"Did you guys have a fight?" said Hunter. "You and Adam?" He hesitated, and sounded embarrassed again. "I heard a little, when you came down the stairs."

Nick nodded. "When you walked in—I panicked. I didn't exactly take it well."

"Man, I am so sorry."

"No, it's not your fault. It was mine. He left." He swiped at his eyes again. "Jesus, I wish I could stop fucking *crying*. So gay, right?"

Hunter put a hand on his shoulder. "Don't do that to yourself, Nick."

Nick froze. Until Hunter touched him, he hadn't realized how much he'd expected this revelation to bring about nothing but revulsion.

In a flash, a memory came to him. He was standing at the stove with his mother, learning how to make macaroni and cheese. He had to be eleven or so. She'd put an arm around him and kissed him on the top of the head.

He'd leaned into the contact, and she'd said, "You're the only one who still lets me do that. My gentle boy."

He'd let her do it still, if he could. He missed her touch more than anything.

She wouldn't have judged him. He knew. He could have told her.

He rubbed his hands down his face before his eyes could get ready for a fresh round.

"Are you going to tell Gabriel?" he asked.

"No," said Hunter. His voice changed and he looked over. "Do you want me to?"

Well, that was a loaded question.

Nick finally shook his head. "No. You'd seriously keep it a secret?" he said skeptically. "He's your best friend."

"I know a lot about keeping secrets," Hunter said. "And this one isn't mine to tell. But I know it's going to tear you up until you let it go."

Nick knew that. This secret already *was* tearing him up.

A key pressed into the front door, and Nick jumped. He knew—*knew*—it was his twin brother. He quickly wiped his eyes on his sleeve and took a quick gulp of coffee. He'd run for his room, but he'd never make it up the stairs before Gabriel came in the house.

With a quick flash of fury, he wanted to tell him. He wanted to fling the truth in Gabriel's face. He wanted to pick a fight, to let this rage and fear and pain pour into something.

Then Gabriel was in the foyer and Nick couldn't breathe.

Gabriel took one look at them and shook his head before pushing between them to head upstairs. He smacked Hunter on the back of the head. "Leave my brother alone, jackass. He's already got enough freaks pining after him."

It was a miracle Nick didn't shatter the mug between his hands.

Hunter didn't move until Gabriel disappeared into the bathroom. Then he said softly, "Look, I get it. Why you don't want to tell him."

Nick had to put the mug down or he was going to spill coffee everywhere. "Really? You sure? He's so *subtle*."

"He doesn't understand—"

"No, but I do. He thinks gay guys are creepy freaks. Got it." Nick didn't want to stay here. He was almost shaking with rage. He couldn't imagine sleeping under the same roof as his brother.

But he had nowhere to go.

Hunter took a breath. "He doesn't think *you* are a creepy freak, Nick. I think you should give him a chance."

"Fuck him. He doesn't deserve a chance."

"Wow." Hunter pushed the hair back from his face. "All right. Your secret, your call." He stood.

"Hey," Nick said, losing some of the rage. "Thanks. It—it means a lot."

"No problem." Hunter paused and leaned against the bannister. "You're wrong, by the way."

"I'm *wrong*?"

"I'm not his best friend, Nick. You are."

CHAPTER 20

Quinn studied herself in Tyler's bathroom mirror. Steam clouded the glass, but she could make out her face, her neck, and the edge of the towel wrapped around her body. A shadowed bruise remained across her cheek, but the swelling was gone, along with her headache.

She was glad for the lingering bruise. She didn't want to forget her mother's voice or the way she'd swung that trophy.

Or the things she'd said.

Whore. You ruin everything.

The worst part was, Quinn believed her mother. Hell, she had proof. She dated guy after guy who was perfectly content to sleep with her and shell out the bucks for a movie or a dinner, but when she needed a friend? Yeah, busy. Or the dance team at school, who'd kicked her to the curb for a bad attitude. Well, who could blame her, with those bitchy girls. Attitude was just a way to endure it all.

Maybe that was her fault, after all. Maybe she had ruined it.

But then Nick. And Becca. No one wanted her. No one *needed* her. Even when she *was* needed—like for Adam's dance audition—she couldn't get it together to show up with any regularity. Clearly her fault.

Besides, it wasn't like Adam had asked what was wrong when she'd texted him earlier. He'd almost brushed her off like he'd *expected* her to space out. Suddenly furious, Quinn picked up her phone to read the text again.

No worries, he'd said. *Let me know when you can meet again.*

Okay, maybe she was reading negativity into that. He didn't know what was going on. Maybe she should have texted something like, *Sorry. My room was turned into a crack den. Catch you tomorrow maybe?*

Yeah, and then what would have happened? He probably wouldn't have believed her.

Quinn remembered this one time her mom had thrown a knife at her head. Two years ago, the first week of freshman year. They'd been screaming about something inconsequential—as usual—and her mother had grabbed a steak knife from the block on the counter and flung it at her.

Quinn had run to Becca's, using the key her best friend's mom had provided, sitting shaking in a kitchen chair until Becca came home.

Becca had thought she was being overdramatic. "A knife," she'd said, her voice ringing with skepticism. "Come on, Quinn."

And Quinn had been worried she'd alienate the only friend she had, so she'd recanted her story.

Becca never brought it up again.

Admittedly, it was rarely that bad back in those days. Her mom had been normal enough, coming to Quinn's school events on occasion, mingling with other parents like she didn't come home and knock back a bottle of Jack Daniel's every other night.

Then their lives had started a downward spiral.

Or continued down it, depending on your perspective.

A knock sounded on the bathroom door, and Quinn jumped. Tyler spoke from the other side. "You okay in there?"

"I'm a girl. Takes a while." But Quinn hurriedly started pulling her hair into a messy knot at the back of her head. She untied the towel wrapped around her body and threw it over the shower rod.

"I'm not trying to rush you," he said. "Just checking."

Quinn glanced at her folded clothes waiting by the sink: the old dance sweats she usually slept in, plus a flimsy T-shirt that would leave a few inches of midriff bare.

She glanced at her naked body in the mirror. The other dance girls were full of angles. Graceful angles, but angles nonetheless: a hip bone here, a sharp edge of shoulder there, a jawline practically cut from marble.

Quinn's body was all sloping lines and curves.

She squeezed her eyes shut. She had a new worry: keeping Tyler interested so she had a place to sleep.

He'd been quiet in the truck, but it was an anxious sort of quiet. A nervous tension had clung to the vehicle, worrying her that any minute he'd pull over and demand that she get out.

"You're like them," she'd whispered finally, terrified that he'd snap and demand that she keep his secret.

"Like them?" he'd said flatly.

She'd had to lick her lips. "A full Elemental."

But he hadn't snapped. He'd just nodded.

That same tension was hanging around his apartment now. What would he do, now that she knew? It seemed like enough of a reason to put her out. Quinn pulled on the T-shirt and a pair of lace panties, then slapped a coy smile on her face and strolled out the door.

It sounded like all the air left Tyler's lungs at once. Quinn kept walking, picked up a copy of *Maxim* magazine on her way to the couch, then sprawled suggestively against the cushions. She flipped open to the middle and didn't look at him.

She could practically hear his brain cells reorganizing to head south.

But then her sweatpants hit her in the chest, landing on the magazine. "Put some pants on," he said.

She glanced at him. "You don't really want me to."

He came and sat in the chair in front of her. He kept his eyes level with hers. "If I hadn't just watched your mom lose her shit, you're right. I wouldn't want you to. I don't know what you think you're doing, but I'm not going to play. Put some pants on."

She pouted. "Make me."

He sighed. "Fine. The hell with it. Sit around half naked."

She pushed the magazine and the pants to the side and crawled into the chair with him, straddling his lap like she'd done the night before.

Tonight, however, his jaw was set, and he didn't make a move to touch her.

But when she leaned in, pressing her chest against his, he caught her waist, holding her at a slight distance.

"What do you think?" he said. "That if you don't sleep with me, I'm going to put you out on the street?"

Well, that was honest. Anger flared, and Quinn started to climb off his lap.

Tyler's hands tightened on her waist. She struggled, but he held fast. "Why is it that you get to screw with me, but when I call you on it, you get all indignant?"

Honestly, because arguing was easier than *thinking.*

"Let me go," she said.

"No way. Not until you tell me what's rolling around in that head of yours."

She met his eyes and made her expression hard. "Let me go or I'll tell Nick and his brothers what you can do."

Well, that broke his control. His face turned furious and he shoved her onto the couch roughly, leaving her there and storming into the kitchen. The refrigerator door opened with a creak, and he slammed it shut hard enough to make the contents rattle.

"You don't know what the fuck you're talking about," he snapped, using an opener to jerk the cap off a bottle of beer. "Don't you get it? This isn't a game."

"Yeah, I get it," she fired back. "You're all gung ho for someone to kill my friends, when you're guilty of the same thing."

"I'm not guilty of anything!" he yelled. "I never hurt anyone with this! *They did.*"

Quinn sucked back into the couch, holding her breath. His anger was frightening, reminding her of that first night behind the 7-Eleven, when he'd burned her arm and demanded answers.

He wasn't done yelling. "I risk myself for *you*, and you're going to turn it around and threaten me? Are you fucking *kidding me*? Do you understand that the Guide could be watching? That what I did was enough to earn a bullet to the head?" He took a long drink and slammed his beer onto the counter. "God *damn* it."

Quinn wished she could make herself invisible. She hugged her knees to her chest and wished she'd put the pants on. She felt too exposed. Too vulnerable.

She was ready for him to stride across the apartment and shake her or slug her or physically shove her out the door. But he just stood there and took another long drink.

After a minute, he looked back at her. His voice was rough, but not aggressive. "Nice job, getting the conversation off of you." He paused, and his expression turned resigned. "Tell the Merricks whatever you want. I know what I did—what I *am*. I can't undo it."

Quinn kept her breathing shallow, scared to move.

As usual with Tyler, she wasn't sure whether he was a good guy or a bad guy. He'd helped her—more than once, and at risk to himself. What was she going to do—tell Nick about Tyler's secret so these mysterious killers could kill *more* people? Turn Tyler in for saving her life?

But he was sitting here judging the Merricks for something he struggled with *himself*. That was the worst kind of hypocrisy, right? Hating someone for something you hated about yourself?

I never hurt anyone with this.

Did he really believe that? He'd burned her arm. He'd brutalized the Merricks—she knew that from Nick. Hell, he'd gone after Becca more than once.

Or did he think that was okay because his sister had died? That because he hadn't *killed* anyone, he somehow got a free pass?

Quinn pulled the sweatpants up her legs and walked into the kitchen.

"I'll keep your secret," she said quietly. "You were right. I was angry—I didn't want—I don't—"

Then her mother's anger and violence overtook her, and Quinn started crying.

Tyler folded her into his arms and sighed against her hair. "What a crazy, fucked-up night."

She laughed through her tears, sniffling against his shoulder. "Tell me about it." She hesitated. "Do you really think there's a Guide in town?"

He took a long breath. "There have been a lot of fires. I'd be more surprised if there's *not* a Guide in town."

"And they'd kill you for *saving* me?"

"I don't know. I don't know." He paused. "Did Merrick ever tell you what really happened at that carnival last week?"

She nodded against his chest. "Some of it. A girl named Calla Dean was trying to bring the Guides here. She wanted to start a war."

Tyler drew back to look at her. "Calla Dean? I don't know her. Her family wasn't part of the original deal with the Merricks."

Quinn swiped remnants of tears from her eyes. "You might not ever know her. She disappeared after the carnival. Nick said they don't know if she was killed or if she ran. But there haven't been any further arson attacks, so . . ."

She drifted into silence, letting the rest remain unsaid. Calla might not be dead, but she hadn't made a reappearance in town. Maybe she'd moved on to start her war somewhere else.

Tyler held her for the longest time, but when he finally spoke, his voice was careful. "I know you don't want to talk about it, but your mother—"

Quinn started to pull away. "You're right. I don't want to talk about it."

"Are you going to hide here forever?"

His voice was gentle, but it made her cry again. "I don't know what to do. Would they arrest her? What would happen to me and Jordan?"

"I don't know. But . . ." He paused. "She could have really hurt you, Quinn. Jesus, she *did* really hurt you. If she'd hit you a second time—"

"I'm *not* calling the cops. I'm not. If you want me to leave, fine. But I'm not—"

"Shh, take it easy. I'm not telling you to leave."

"I just need a few days, okay? Let it blow over."

Tyler stiffened. "You want to go *back* there?"

"She's not always like that. If Jake is gone, maybe it won't be so bad."

Tyler sighed.

"Please?" she begged. Then she winced. This reminded her of the night she'd been in Nick's truck, begging him for a place to sleep, too.

"Okay," Tyler finally said. "We can give it a few days."

She turned her face up and kissed him.

Tyler pulled back. "Quinn. Stop."

She froze, then jerked away from him. "Forget it," she cried, feeling fresh tears on her cheeks. She punched him in the chest. "Forget it. I don't need charity from—"

He caught her wrists and pinned them behind her back. The motion was so quick, so rough, that she almost cried out. It put her right against his chest, staring up into his eyes. "What do you want?" he said. "Is this how every guy treats you, like you have to pay to play? Tell me, Quinn."

"Didn't you hear her?" she said. "This is all I'm good for."

"It's not," he whispered. "I promise you, it's not."

"No one wants me. I can't even *make* someone want me."

He closed his eyes and pressed his forehead against hers. "You poor, mixed-up girl."

"Fuck you. If you don't want me, then let me go."

"You're funny. You have no idea how hard it was to act honorably when you were parading around here in your underwear."

She snorted. "Like you know how to act honorably."

He froze, then released her. He grabbed the beer from the counter and headed back to the living room. "Come on," he said. "Let's watch a movie. Grab some snacks if you want."

Quinn stared at his retreating back. "A movie? That's it?"

"That's it."

She couldn't keep up with his rapidly shifting emotions, but maybe he felt exactly the same about her. He was already flipping on the television, searching through the pay-per-view listings.

"What do you feel like?" he said.

"Slasher flick," she said.

He rolled his eyes and settled on a romantic comedy.

Quinn groaned. "These are cheesy."

"Sweetheart, I think you're overdue for something cheesy."

She hesitated by the couch, but he opened his arms like he'd done on the porch, and she snuggled into the warmth of his body, inhaling the scent of him.

Later, when she was almost asleep on his chest, she murmured, "I'll keep your secret."

"You don't need to." He stroked a hand through her hair—the most intimate thing he'd done all night. "You keep enough secrets. I'm definitely not asking you to keep mine."

CHAPTER 21

Nick had thought his physics test was bad on Tuesday. He probably should have stuck with that score. This was impossible. He couldn't think straight. He had no idea what he was writing on the paper.

And he didn't care.

His pencil moved, but his mind was elsewhere. Adam wasn't responding to his texts. Well, he'd responded to one this morning, when Nick finally begged him to confirm he'd got home all right.

I'm home.

And that was it. Nick almost would have preferred the silence. Now he knew Adam was getting his texts and choosing not to respond.

Quinn was no better. He'd tracked her down in the hall this morning, but she'd turned her back on him and said she'd talk to him later.

But not before he'd caught a glimpse of the new bruise on her cheek.

What. The. Hell.

He'd tried to catch up to her, but she'd disappeared into a

classroom, and the teacher had all but closed the door in his face.

And of course texts demanding to know what had happened had been hopeless. *No one* would respond to him, it seemed.

He didn't want to be around his brothers, with Chris suspecting something and Gabriel being an *asshole* and Hunter knowing everything but keeping quiet. At least Michael was swamped with work, and he hadn't resumed the prying.

Nick turned to the last physics test question and sighed. He didn't have a chance.

He gave it his best shot anyway, hoping for partial credit.

Yeah, right.

Luckily, Dr. Cutter was speaking with another student when Nick brought the test up to his desk. He turned it over, placing it facedown on the desk blotter.

Then he walked out of the room, feeling the pinch of guilt between his shoulder blades.

He had *never* failed a test. Ever.

And now he'd done it twice.

He couldn't go to the cafeteria—not like he wanted to eat anything anyway. He shifted his backpack and headed for the library.

While he walked, he scrolled through the texts from Adam until he found the picture he'd sent himself.

His eyes blurred, and he blinked moisture away. God, he'd been such an *idiot*.

His phone vibrated in his hand, making his heart leap.

Not Adam. Michael.

I hate to ask, but can you help with a job tonight?

Nick sighed.

But what else did he have to do? He texted back quickly.

Sure.

By the end of the day, he was regretting it. Tension was making him surly and snappish. Janette Morrits asked for a pencil in seventh period and he just about flung it in her face. Teachers responded to his attitude with lectures to pay attention, to focus, that they expected more.

Every snicker, every giggle, every stupid use of the word *gay* or *fag* had his head whipping around.

Maybe Hunter changed his mind and told everyone. Maybe they're all talking about me.

He found himself wishing he sat in the back of every room, instead of the front.

No, he found himself wishing he'd cut school.

At the final bell, he stormed out the side door. He didn't want to ride home with his brothers. He didn't want to work a job with Michael.

Cars were lined up illegally in the fire lane, parents who couldn't be bothered to sit through the heavier traffic on the other side of school. But trees lined the grounds beyond those vehicles, dense woods that led the way home. Nick headed for the crosswalk. He'd cut through the woods and clear his head. Maybe after three miles of fresh air, he could get it together to spend a few hours slinging pavestone or planting bushes or whatever Michael needed help with.

Heavy clouds swarmed the sky, trapping cold air near the ground. Or maybe he was doing that. He cast his senses far, feeding power into his element. Reckless and dangerous, but he didn't care. Wind whipped through his hair, feeding on his temper to blow loose debris along the curb. A notebook flipped open to spill papers across the quad. Girls shrieked and scurried to catch them.

Rain spit at his face, and Nick pulled up the hood of his sweatshirt. It kept out the cold and his classmates, especially since not too many students came out this side of the building.

The hoodie didn't keep out sound, however. A car door slammed; then a voice called out as he slid between two sedans.

"Windy out, huh, douche bag?"

The air brought the words right to him. Nick stopped and

lowered the hood. Tyler stood by the curb, two cars up, leaning against his truck.

What was he doing here? Nick gritted his teeth and balled his hands into fists.

He *hated* that his first thought was to wish Gabriel was here.

Especially when Tyler moved away from his truck to approach him.

Thunder rumbled through the sky overhead. Wind blasted Nick in the face and pulled at his clothes. He called for more, asking his element to rip Tyler's face clean off.

Nick knew better than to fight him physically. Tyler fought dirty enough to give Gabriel a run for his money. Nick couldn't suffocate him, either, not with his senses so scattered. The wind pulled his power in too many directions. Thunder cracked and rolled again.

He begged for cold, and the next blast of wind was downright arctic.

"Go away, Tyler," he said, keeping his voice low. "You're not supposed to be here."

Tyler laughed in his face. "I'm not allowed to pick up a girl?"

Nick froze. Was Tyler here for *Quinn?*

Then Nick thought of that second bruise on Quinn's cheek, and he started forward. Quinn was exactly the type of girl to fall in with someone like Tyler, someone who'd make promises to take care of her, but would then turn around and backhand her across the face. He thought of Adam's history, and fury made his voice tight. "You leave her alone. She has enough problems without you screwing around with her."

Tyler shoved him back. "Yeah, and what do you know about it?"

"I've seen enough. You keep your hands off her."

"Jealous?" sneered Tyler. "That's funny." Then he hit Nick in the chest again, hard enough to knock him back, toward the woods.

Nick shoved him back, feeling his wind pick up fistfuls of twigs and rocks to pelt them at Tyler.

Bonus: twigs and rocks pelted Tyler's truck, too.

Nick had the satisfaction of seeing Tyler fall back a step, an arm raised to protect his eyes. A rock hit his face and drew blood. Then a small branch hit his upraised arm with enough force to tear his shirt—and the skin below it. Nick caught the scent of blood on the wind.

Tyler surged forward to grab Nick's arm. "Cold out. Maybe I should light something on fire."

Nick swung a fist and called for stronger wind, but Tyler ducked and caught his wrist. They struggled, but Tyler had him by a good thirty pounds. He twisted Nick's arm until Nick thought his elbow might give out.

More thunder, more wind. Trees began to sway.

Tyler applied more pressure. "Aw," he said. "Is that painful?"

Yeah. It was.

"Fuck you," Nick gasped. He remembered a time when he was younger, when Tyler had trapped him after gym class, when he'd pinned him much like this to let Seth Ramsey beat the shit out of him.

God, he *hated* this guy. He hated his own fear more.

Wind tore between them, stinging Nick's cheeks, pelting him with the same debris he was using to attack Tyler. But then his gusts began to pull into a spiral, almost against his will. The clouds overhead shifted. In a minute, he'd have a tornado. His power was always like this—no middle ground. Lively breeze one moment, massively destructive weather event the next.

At least Gabriel's fire needed something to burn. Air was *everywhere.*

He needed to rein this in before he leveled the school.

Tyler smiled. "Guess what, douchebag? You don't get to play like that anymore." He tightened his grip on Nick's wrist.

And then flame curled from under his hand.

Fire bit through fabric to find skin, and Nick yelled, fighting like mad. His sweatshirt was on fire, a flame trapped beneath Tyler's fingers. Nothing anyone else could see. The burn clouded his senses, eating into his arm like something alive.

He redoubled his struggles, wishing someone would see and help. But while a few kids were out here, they glanced at the fight and kept walking. No one said anything. No one took any action.

Hell, they probably thought he was Gabriel. And Gabriel *never* needed help.

The wind swirled harder. Nick tried to bite back the pain, focusing all his energy into keeping a tornado from forming. The atmosphere fought him, trying to form a funnel. His element enjoyed the rage in the air, pulling power from his pain and anger.

Tyler shook him a little, sending agony shooting through his elbow. It looked like it was snowing. Or maybe those were stars shooting through his vision.

"Turning you on?" said Tyler, his voice low and sinister. "Quinn said you were into guys."

If *anything* could have broken through the pain in his arm, that was it.

Nick couldn't think, unsure which hurt more: the searing heat in his forearm or the raging dismay of betrayal.

Quinn. Had. Told. Tyler.

He couldn't fight. He couldn't focus. A tornado was going to whip through here and leave a wide path of destruction, probably taking him with it. Then again, Tyler was about to burn him to ash, right here beside the fire lane.

But then someone hooked a hand around Tyler's throat, jerking him back *hard*. Tyler went down harder. Nick stumbled back, losing his footing from the sudden freedom.

His first thought had been Hunter. Or Gabriel.

But Tyler was on the ground and Michael stood over him. He looked down at Tyler like he wanted to kick him in the face, but he cut a quick glance at Nick. "You all right?"

No. He was breathing through his teeth and the wind wouldn't settle. His arm hurt like a *bitch*. He could smell burning fabric, on top of something sickly sweet that he didn't want to identify. Nick fought his way out of his sweatshirt.

Mistake. He did it fast, and it took skin with it. The wound wasn't big, but Nick felt the skin separate and peel away. Every nerve went with it. He thought he might pass out. Or throw up. Or both.

But the air was charged with his power, and it surged into the exposed skin, healing him without thought, stealing some of the pain immediately. Nick sucked a breath through his teeth and shivered. The weather no longer seemed centered on destruction, but trees creaked and groaned as the wind battered them.

Michael looked back at Tyler. "Keep your hands off my brothers."

Tyler got to his feet and spit at him. "Fuck you, Merrick. He started it."

"Nick." Michael glanced at him. "Get in the truck."

Nick looked at the fire lane. There was Michael's truck, about six cars back. Had Michael been here the whole time? Had he heard what Tyler said?

"Go," said Michael. "He won't follow you."

Like Nick was six years old being chased down by a bully. But what could he do? He clutched his aching arm to his chest and walked.

Tyler didn't help matters by calling after him. "Yeah, it's a good thing big brother showed up, huh, Nicky?"

Nicky. He somehow made it an insult.

Nick slammed the cab door and ran a hand through his hair. The frigid wind had cleared the quad, whipping between vehicles to make the truck rock. The open wounds on his arm had closed, turning to nothing more than soft scabs.

Michael was five seconds behind him. He slammed the door, then shoved a key into the ignition and got the heat running.

Nick hadn't realized his breath was fogging up all the glass. He couldn't even see what had happened to Tyler. But Michael hadn't been out there long enough to have done any damage.

"You didn't fight him?" Nick said.

"He won't fight me." Without any more explanation than that, Michael put the truck in gear, but kept his foot on the brake. "Let me see your arm."

"It's okay. I'm okay." Nick held it up, but he didn't care

about his arm now. His thoughts felt like the debris scattered all over the quad from the wind. Had Michael heard? *Had he heard?*

But Michael said, "What made him come after you?"

Nick had no idea. He wished he could get his thoughts to focus. What had Quinn told Tyler? Why? How could she—why would she—?

"Nick?"

He shook his head. "I don't know—Tyler's never done that before. With the fire." He wished Gabriel weren't being such a dick—Nick could ask him how much power that would take. Tyler wasn't supposed to be very strong, but something so focused would require a lot of control, right?

You don't get to play like that anymore.

What was Tyler telling him? What had he said?

She has enough problems without you screwing with her.

Then Tyler's sneering, *What do you know about it?*

What did Tyler know? What was Quinn telling him?

She'd clearly given up his secret. What did that mean?

The windshield cleared in patches. Michael pulled out of his space. "Has he been hassling you?"

"No. Not really." Nick paused. "Why won't he fight you?"

"Because he genuinely believes I killed his sister, and he's afraid I'll do the same to him." Michael glanced over. "I'm serious, Nick. What's going on?"

His older brother sounded pissed—but only at Tyler. Not like he'd learned anything new and shocking. In a way, it was disappointing. Nick shook his head and looked out the window. "Nothing. What were you doing there?"

"I came to pick you up. I saw the guys getting into the car and you weren't with them. Gabriel said you were PMS-ing, which I took to mean you were walking home."

Nick clenched his jaw and glared out the window. Trees along Old Mill Road flew by. Wind was still blowing leaves in every direction, matching his mood.

Then he whipped his head back around. "Why were you picking me up?"

"What's with all the suspicion? Because I'd like to get this job done before the rain starts."

Oh. Of course. Nick settled back into the seat. His sweatshirt was destroyed, and he could do with a change of clothes, but the last thing he wanted to do was face his brothers. "Do you have an extra pullover in here?"

"You don't want me to swing by the house?"

"No."

Michael reached between the seats and flung a fleece half-zip at him. It smelled vaguely of topsoil and mulch, but not in a bad way. Nick pulled it over his head.

"Hungry?" said Michael.

Nick shook his head. He hadn't eaten lunch, either, but the last thing he wanted was food.

They drove in silence for the longest time. Nick leaned his head against the window and wondered what it would be like to lie down and sleep forever.

When Michael spoke, his voice was quiet. "You want to talk about what's up at school?"

That familiar tension dug its teeth into Nick's neck. "Nothing is going on at school."

"Your physics teacher called and said you failed a test."

Nick swore. "Great."

"He said you were distracted. He asked if something was going on at home. Asked if he could help."

"You don't have to do this, Mike. I'm fine. Things at home are fine. It's one test. He shouldn't have called you."

Michael glanced over. "He said he'd told you about a precollege program he'd like to nominate you for, but you brushed it off. I thought you were all gung ho for college."

"I don't—I don't know what I want. Can you just leave it? It's one test. I don't know why he's blowing it out of proportion."

"I don't think he's worried about the test, Nick. And I'm pretty sure you know I'm not, either." He paused. "You've been on edge at home, too. I know you said things are fine with Quinn. Are they really?"

Nick stared out the window and set his jaw. "Yeah."

"I know you've been covering for your brothers a lot. I didn't mean to load more on you. You should have said something. You know you can say *no*, right?"

Sure. And then Mike would lose a job and money would be tighter than it already was. "I'm *fine*. Really."

"All right. If you're sure."

"I'm sure."

Then Michael shut up and they drove. Nick kept his eyes on the windshield.

That just gave him time to think.

After a minute, he yanked his phone out of his pocket and shot off a text to Quinn.

wtf. Why did you tell Tyler?

He didn't expect a response, so he was shocked to get one almost immediately.

Wtf. Why did you ATTACK Tyler? Are you crazy???!!!

She thought he'd *attacked* Tyler? Was *she* crazy?

Nick wanted to punch something. Hell, it worked for Gabriel. And Tyler, clearly.

It made him think of how he'd treated Adam last night.

Or of Adam's words: *Do you ever think that this Tyler guy thinks maybe you are bad for Quinn?*

What had Tyler just said? *He started this.*

Had Nick started this? He didn't think he had. He'd choked Tyler in his driveway, but that was after Tyler swung a fist.

Right? He couldn't remember. Maybe not, but what had Tyler done to him over the last five years? What was he doing to Quinn?

Nick's thoughts kept veering back to Adam. To Matt, the guy who'd used Adam like a punching bag. How hard had Nick hit him? He couldn't remember.

It felt like something he should remember.

When you wake up hating yourself, I don't want you taking it out on me.

Nick had panicked. Adam had to know that. He would *never* do what that other guy had done.

But . . . had he already? Just on a smaller scale?

Michael hit the turn signal, and Nick looked up. They were turning off Generals Highway and pulling into the nearly empty parking lot of Famous Dave's.

"Did you miss a turn?" he said.

"No." Michael parked the truck. "In case you hadn't noticed, Nick, it's like thirty degrees in here, and I'm blasting the heater."

His breath was fogging. "Oh. Sorry. I'll stop. Just—drive. It's fine."

But Michael unbuckled his seat belt and climbed down from the cab.

Nick stared at him.

"Come on," said Michael. "You want to get some ribs?"

"You don't have to do this."

"Wrong. If I don't eat something, I'm going to kill someone."

"What about the job?"

Michael looked at the sky. "Looks like I won't be able to get there before the storm." His eyes snapped back to Nick. "It's called a breather, little brother. Take it."

CHAPTER 22

Once they were sitting there with menus, Nick didn't even bother reading his. When the waitress came around, he ordered a soda and handed her the folded cardboard.

Michael ordered enough food to feed an army.

"You're so fidgety," Michael said.

"I don't know what we're doing here. We can't afford to blow off a job."

"First of all, I'm not blowing it off. I'll pick it up over the weekend. Second, what do you know about what we can afford?"

Nick gave him a look. "I do the bookkeeping."

"For the business. Not for the family."

"What's the difference?"

Michael laughed. "A lot. If we only had the business to live on, I'd be worried."

"We don't?"

"No." His brother frowned. "Have you been worried about that?"

"About how we were going to get through the winter? Yeah."

Michael winced. "Look, we'll be okay through the winter. Mom and Dad had life insurance, and there's not a lot left, but there's *some*. I try not to touch it, because I never know when we'll have a real emergency, but it's more than enough to fill in the cracks. Besides, Dad always said to have three months in savings as a reserve, so I've got that, too."

Nick stared at him.

"What?" said Michael.

"Nothing." Nick rubbed at the back of his neck. For months, he'd worried about the finances, had felt a personal obligation to make sure the business brought in as much cash as possible. He'd seen the bottom line of the business creep closer and closer toward the red as they took bigger jobs and needed more supplies. He'd worried about college and leaving his brothers without help.

He'd had no idea that Michael had a safety net.

"I wish you'd said something," said Michael.

"I didn't want to stress you out."

"Please. That's like a constant state of being."

The waitress brought their drinks, followed by the basket of onion rings and the steamed shrimp that Michael had ordered for appetizers.

Nick stared at the food and realized he was starving.

"Go ahead," said Michael. "I knew you'd change your mind once it was in front of you."

Nick grabbed a shrimp and started peeling. It felt better to have something to do with his hands. At least he couldn't check his phone every ten seconds.

"Sometimes I forget," Michael said slowly while peeling his own shrimp, "that you're the same age as Gabriel, and not the same age as *me*."

"You mean, aside from the fact that we're identical and all?"

Michael gave him a rueful look. "No, I mean sometimes I forget that you're still just as much a kid as he is."

Nick peeled another shrimp and didn't say anything to that.

"That's not an insult," said Michael.

"Oh. Okay."

"Actually . . ." began Michael—but he stopped there. He ran a hand across his newly short hair. Gabriel had asked him when he was shipping out, but Nick liked it. It made Michael look older, more serious and less angry.

Nick hadn't said so. Stupidly, he felt like any acknowledgment of a guy's looks would show his hand.

He kept his eyes on his food. "Actually what?"

"Sometimes I forget to pay attention."

"Attention to what?"

"To *you*. I think I've got a pretty good handle on Chris and Gabriel. I know when they're veering off the rails. You're a little more challenging."

Nick met his eyes. "I'm all right, Michael. I'll work it out."

Michael picked up an onion ring. "See, that's why you're tough to crack. Even keeled, nothing wrong. I'd almost buy it if I hadn't frozen my ass off on the drive here."

"I was just pissed at Tyler."

"Yeah, and who else?"

"I really don't feel like sitting through an interrogation."

Michael shrugged. "I'm not interrogating you. Talk or not."

"Not."

So they ate in silence. When the waitress brought platters of ribs, Michael thanked her, but Nick remained silent.

He wished Michael had pushed. Did everyone think he had it all together? He felt like his life was a hot mess of lies and secrets and betrayals.

Quinn.

His fury had faded, but now he felt bewildered. Why had she told Tyler? *Why?* Why was she spending *time* with him? Was he the one who'd hit her in the face?

Or was Nick misreading everything?

He used his fork to pull a new section of ribs apart and kept his eyes on his plate. "Will you tell me what really happened with Tyler and Emily, that day at the quarry?"

They'd been silent for at least fifteen minutes, and Michael set his food down and wiped his hands. His voice was soft, but not empty. "You know what happened, Nick."

"I know she—" He stopped and cleared his throat. He knew she'd died. He knew what had happened after. Not the details of *before*. Suddenly this felt cruel, making his brother relive it. "Never mind."

"No, I'll tell you." Michael hesitated. "She worked the counter at that sports place on Mountain Road. I always used the batting cages. Remember, I used to take you guys there?"

Nick did remember. He hadn't thought about it for years, but he remembered learning how to hold a bat, how to swing. It was one of the few sports he'd played better than Gabriel. He didn't like playing baseball, not really, but he'd liked swinging the bat in those cages. He didn't recognize it then, but he knew now: the air had told him everything. The speed of the ball, when to swing.

"She hated me," Michael continued. "At least at first. She tried to chase me out of there—even had her parents call Mom and Dad and threaten them. I just wanted to play ball. I was pissed. Split a crack down the middle of the parking lot, right in front of her. The deal was brand new. I thought she'd turn me in for sure."

"She didn't?"

Michael shook his head, then smiled a little sadly. "She didn't. It started . . . something."

Nick didn't smile, because he knew how this story ended. "Something."

"We never went out or anything. It never got that far. Just . . . there was something there. But then there was her family, too. Tyler was young, but he had a lot of friends. They hid in the back of the truck and jumped me. Tyler put a butane lighter against my face and I couldn't control myself. I almost killed them."

"But you didn't."

Michael's expression tightened. "No, I didn't, and I've wondered a thousand times how that day would have ended differently if I'd killed them right then."

The waitress appeared beside their table. "Can I bring you anything else?"

Michael cleared his throat. "I would really, really like a beer. Anything on tap."

She hustled off.

"First time I haven't gotten carded," said Michael.

"Haircut," said Nick.

"I owe you." Michael paused and his voice resumed its former gravity. "We ran. Emily and me. We took a trail down to the back side of the quarry. Tyler and his friends chased us. We jumped in the water and swam like hell. She wasn't a strong swimmer, but I knew if we could get near the other kids who were swimming on the far side, they'd have to back off."

He shook his head. "They didn't. We made it, but they were right there. I could feel the rocks overhead were loose, but I thought we were okay."

He stopped and took a breath. Nick studied him. "Mike— you don't have to tell me this."

"It's all right. She—she went back to them. We were there in the water, near the wall, facing off. There were six of them, and Emily was a tiny girl. I think—I think she thought they'd go away and leave me alone if she went with them. She swam toward them before I could stop her, going to Tyler. I remember him looking at me, all victorious, like she'd *run* from me. I know that wasn't it. She was trying to *protect* me."

He went quiet for so long that Nick wasn't sure he was going to keep talking.

"So what happened?"

Michael glanced up. "She never got a chance to say anything. The rocks fell. I tried to stop it, but I wasn't strong enough—or maybe I just wasn't fast enough. They hit her and two of the other kids. I went down to get her, and came up with one of them. Same thing again. By the third time I went under, I only found her body. I knew it looked like I'd killed her." He paused. "I ran home. You remember."

Nick did remember. "Wow."

"Yeah, no kidding."

The waitress returned with a glass and set it in front of Michael before rushing off again.

Nick had no idea where she was going so fast. The restaurant was deserted. It was barely four. Maybe she'd picked up on the tension.

"Tyler blames me," Michael said. "I don't fight him, because I get it. I blame me, too." His eyes narrowed. "But that doesn't mean I'm going to let him beat the crap out of you guys. Seriously, Nick. What's going on with Tyler? Why did you want to know about Emily?"

Nick clasped his hands under the table and shook his head. He couldn't talk about Tyler without talking about all of it. "Quinn asked me," he offered. "I didn't know all the details."

"Oh, right. Quinn. Your girlfriend."

Nick couldn't figure out the note in his voice. Talking didn't seem safe now. He took a sip of his soda.

Had Michael heard what Tyler said? Maybe Chris had said something? Hunter?

Michael leaned in. "I wish you'd talk to me, Nick." He hesitated, as if choosing his words carefully. "I'm not going to judge you."

Nick's eyes snapped to his. His heart pulsed against his rib cage. "What does that mean?"

"It means you don't have to go through this alone."

He knew. He had to know. How did he know? Nick rubbed his hands over his face, worried his dinner might make a reappearance if he couldn't calm down. The restaurant simultaneously felt too cold and too hot.

The waitress came by the table to remove their plates, then left a tiny folder with the check.

Michael didn't reach for it. "Look," he said quietly, "I'm not going to say I know what it's like to be in your position."

"Lucky you."

"You have a choice, Nick, about—"

"You think there's a *choice* here?" Nick almost couldn't speak through the sudden rage in his throat. "You think I would *choose* this?"

"Calm down. I'm trying to talk to you."

Nick could barely keep his voice level. He'd been ready for anger and disappointment, but he hadn't expected closed-mindedness. He shoved out of the booth. "Fuck you, Michael. I don't want to talk to you."

Michael grabbed his wrist. His voice was low and equally angry. "Damn it, Nick, grow up. There's a time limit here. If

Quinn is pregnant, you need to get your shit together and talk to someone."

Wait.

Wait.

Wait.

Nick turned around, his eyes wide. "You think Quinn is *pregnant?*"

Michael stared back at him. "She's not?"

"No. She's not." Nick sat back down.

Michael blew out a long breath. "Thank god. That—I just—wow."

"Crisis averted, right?" Nick could barely keep the bitterness out of his voice. Of *course* Michael hadn't guessed right.

"Something like that." Michael pulled a credit card out of his wallet and slid it into the folder.

Nick couldn't stop the disappointment tightening his chest. As much as he'd hated thinking Michael would be such an idiot as to believe sexuality was a *choice*, there'd been a measure of relief in not having to tell him.

Now they were back to square one. And they were leaving. In half an hour, he'd be at home, feeling more alone than ever.

The waitress took the leather folder and zipped away.

And Michael just seemed relieved. Quinn wasn't pregnant, nothing else could be wrong. Reliable Nick always had a handle on everything, and wasn't an unplanned pregnancy like the worst thing he could possibly face?

Nick didn't want to look at his brother anymore. Being wrong wasn't Michael's fault—but it felt like it. "Why would you think that?" he asked, his voice quiet.

"Actually, it was Hannah's guess."

"Hmm."

Michael centered on him. "It wouldn't have been a bad thing. I just—I didn't want you to think you couldn't tell me."

Nick didn't say anything to that.

Then the waitress was back and Michael was signing his name, and this little moment was ending.

Nick didn't move. He couldn't. He felt like he was standing

on the edge of a cliff, looking down at water far below. A short flight through air, with an impact that might kill him.

Michael hesitated at the edge of his booth. "You ready?"

"No."

Say it. Tell him.

Two words. He couldn't even get two words out of his mouth.

You care more about what other people think than you care about me.

Adam had faced a lot worse than this.

Nick looked at his older brother, then shoved the empty beer glass toward him. He felt dizzy, like the air was too thin to breathe. His voice came out wispy. "You might want another one."

"Why?"

"Because you guessed wrong." He laughed shortly. "Way wrong."

Michael studied him but didn't say anything.

Nick took a breath and forced himself to look up. "Michael. I'm gay."

CHAPTER 23

Three feet of wooden table stretched between them, but it might as well have been three miles. This moment between words and reaction seemed to stretch into infinity.

Nick had leapt off that cliff, and now he was waiting to see what he'd hit at the bottom.

Michael eased back into the booth and leaned his forearms on the table. He edged Nick's half-empty soda glass toward him. "Here. You look like you're going to pass out."

Nick couldn't move. He worried he *would* pass out if Michael didn't say something more substantial than that.

The waitress came to the table again, obviously noting that they hadn't left. She fidgeted, clearly unsettled by the tension.

Or maybe she was cold. Nick tried to get a handle on the temperature in the room.

She picked up the folder with the signed receipt. "Did you boys need anything else?"

"Coffee," said Michael. "Please."

She disappeared, leaving them in silence.

Michael cleared his throat. "I don't know how to say this, Nick . . ."

It was like his older brother had picked up a spear and begun to shove it through Nick's back. He felt the pain that acutely.

But then Michael winced and looked at him. "Would it be weird if I said that's not surprising?"

What?

What?

Nick came out of his seat to reach across the table and punch Michael in the shoulder as hard as he could. "You dick. I thought you were about to throw me out of the house."

Now Michael looked like Nick had checked his brain at the door. "Why on earth would I throw you out of the house?"

"I don't know! I had no idea how you'd react!"

"You want me to punch you? Cause a scene? We could totally put on a show."

However Nick had imagined this conversation going, this . . . this wasn't it.

Some of the tension slipped from his shoulders. Nick took a long breath and blew it out through his teeth.

"How long have you been carrying that around?" said Michael.

"I don't know." Now Nick felt dizzy for an entirely different reason. He gave a choked laugh. "I don't—a long time." Then he stopped reeling and looked at his brother. "Why not surprising?"

The waitress chose that exact moment to bring their coffee. Nick was glad for the distraction, though. It gave him something else to look at, something new to do with his hands.

When she was gone, Michael said, "It's difficult to explain. Nothing I would have put my finger on, you know?" He paused, then stirred his coffee. Pointless, since he drank it black—but maybe he needed a minor distraction, too.

"Little things," he said. "Meaningless things. You'd go out with girls, but you never really *talked* about them. You're not aggressive. You're not . . . Jesus, Nick, I don't know. I've never thought, *gee, Nick might be gay*, but when you said it, it was like the last piece of a puzzle, if that makes any sense."

"It makes sense," Nick said. He couldn't quite believe that Michael was sitting here dropping a phrase like *Nick might be gay* without batting an eye.

"Am I the last to know, as usual?" Michael said.

"No. The first. Sort of."

"The first! I should be celebrating." Then he raised an eyebrow. "Sort of?"

"Hunter knows."

"How'd he take it?"

Nick shrugged and wondered if there was a safe answer to that question. *Well, you know. Last night, he caught me in bed . . .* "Hunter was okay."

"Yeah, I can't see him having a problem." Michael paused. "Not Gabriel?"

Nick stared into his mug and shook his head.

"So that's why you two are fighting."

"We're not fighting."

"Could've fooled me."

Nick gritted his teeth and looked away. "I don't want to talk about him."

"Are you afraid of how he'll take it?"

"No. Yes. I don't know."

Michael didn't say anything for the longest time. After a while, he drained his mug of coffee, then set it back in the saucer.

"I remember," Michael said, "when you were babies, Gabriel used to scream his fool head off. All the time. He wouldn't fall asleep at night unless Mom put you in his crib." He smiled. "It got so that any time he'd fuss, I'd just pick you up and put you next to him." His smile turned a little sad. "I still remember the one time Mom caught me doing it. She was fit to be tied. *Michael! Do not pick up the babies!*"

Nick held still. It was *rare* that Michael would talk about Mom and Dad.

He kept talking. "But even when you grew older and got your own beds, we'd always find you in there with him in the morning. Curled up on top of his covers, just sleeping next to him. Mom used to say that you always knew when your brother needed you." He paused. "I used to find you like that after they died."

Emotion balled up a fist and struck Nick square in the chest.

He tried to breathe around it. He remembered that. He *remembered* it.

"She was wrong," he said, his voice husky. "That was when I needed him."

"I don't think so, Nick," Michael said quietly. "If that were true, he'd know your secret."

Nick rolled that around in his head for a moment.

Michael kept going. "And look, I can't pretend to understand this twin thing you two have. But I know Gabriel *knows* you. And right now, he knows you're keeping something from him. It's probably tearing him up."

Nick wanted to scoff, but he couldn't. He felt it every time he was in the house.

Too bad he was such a creepy freak, or he'd do something about it.

"Do you think maybe you resent him for not figuring it out on his own?" Michael said. "Or for not pushing you to tell him?"

Nick snapped his eyes up. "No."

But he'd answered without thinking about it. Now the thought was lodged in his brain and he couldn't *stop* thinking about it.

He could picture Gabriel right now. Sitting with Layne, working through math problems, trying to get his grades up so he could take the firefighter course in the spring.

But he was thinking about Nick. Nick could *feel* it.

His cell phone chimed.

A message from Gabriel.

How long do I have to leave you alone?

Nick turned the phone around to show Michael, who rolled his eyes and said, *"See?"*

Nick slid his fingers across the screen to respond.

But then he changed his mind, deleted what he'd typed, and shoved the phone back in his pocket.

He took a gulp of his rapidly cooling coffee. "I don't want to talk about him anymore."

"All right. Another question then." Now Michael looked the slightest bit flustered. "Is there . . . you know . . . a guy in the picture?"

Nick couldn't keep the blush from his cheeks. "Ah . . . yeah."

"Aha. I was wondering why you told me *now*. Does he go to your school?"

"No."

Michael stopped with the mug halfway to his mouth. "Please tell me he's not thirty-five and you met him on craigslist."

Nick glared at him. "No. Jesus, Michael. He's nineteen. He dances with Quinn."

"So all this time you've been spending with Quinn . . ."

"I've been spending with Adam." His jaw tightened. "And Quinn has been spending with Tyler."

"Whoa!" Michael's eyebrows went way up. "Now we're building a new puzzle."

"Yeah, it's fantastic."

"Can I revel in this first-to-know status and get the whole story? Or do I have to drag that out of you during another dinner?"

"No," said Nick, feeling something like relief for the first time in a week. "I'll tell you everything."

Michael had always made for a good audience, and he kept his mouth shut while Nick talked.

Until he started laying it out, Nick hadn't realized how much he'd been carrying around. He felt like sandbags had been strapped to his back for weeks, and now someone had stabbed a hole in one of them: it all poured out. He told Michael about the first night he'd met Adam, the way Quinn had gotten in trouble with some bikers on the beach. He talked about Adam's audition, and Quinn's role, and—hesitantly at first—about the first night at Adam's apartment.

When Michael's expression didn't change to disgust, Nick gained momentum, revealing Adam's past experience and Quinn's home situation. He talked about the way Tyler had burned her arm, how she'd called Nick to pick her up in the woods, and how he'd snuck her into the house because she didn't want to go home.

Michael was pissed about that. "Nick, if your friends need help, you need to *tell* me. Don't sneak them inside."

"No girls spending the night, remember?"

"That's not the same and you know it. Are you aware that when people dump their problems on you, you don't actually have to solve them by yourself?"

Nick didn't have an answer for that.

Michael kept going. "I'm actually more concerned with how you describe her home situation than I am about her spending time with Tyler."

Nick flinched. "She won't tell me all the details. I don't know what's going on at home half the time."

"If she's hiding in the woods, it can't be good."

Right now, after what she'd done, Nick didn't really give a shit if Quinn was *sleeping* in the woods.

No. That wasn't true. He did care. A lot.

She sure didn't make it easy. "She says she's waiting for her brother to go back to school. Her family is under a lot of stress since the fire."

Michael sighed and ran a hand down his face. "Will she talk to anyone? What about Becca?"

"She won't speak to her because Becca never told her about the Elemental stuff. Then she got all pissed at me because I told her Tyler was a dickhead who'd just hurt her. Now she's avoiding everyone *except* Tyler." Nick's voice turned thick with disgust. "I think he was at school to pick her up. She said she has a new ride to school."

"What about Adam? Will she talk to him?"

Nick looked down at the table. "Maybe, but she hasn't been showing up to dance."

"Could you ask him to reach out to her?"

Nick picked at the edge of his place mat and didn't say anything.

"Come on," said Michael. "Don't leave out part of the story."

So Nick told him about the previous night. About Adam. And Hunter. His cheeks were on fire, and he didn't go to any great detail, but he talked.

"Wow," said Michael, dragging the word into three syllables. "No wonder you're so keyed up."

Nick shrugged. His mood darkened as his brain replayed shoving Adam *again*. "Guess I'm aggressive *sometimes*, huh?"

Michael hesitated. "I didn't mean that as an insult, Nick."

He didn't need to. Nick got it. He couldn't help Quinn, he couldn't fix things with Adam, and hell, he couldn't even stand up to frigging *Tyler*.

"I'm going to talk to Becca's mom," Michael said finally. "She knows Quinn's family."

"You don't need to get involved," Nick said.

"Wrong. I think I should have gotten involved a long time ago." He paused and drained the last of his coffee. "I also have a few thoughts about Tyler."

Nick looked at him in surprise. "You're going to confront him?"

"No. I'm going to leave him alone, and I think you should, too." When Nick started to protest, Michael held up a hand. "I don't think he's hurting Quinn." He paused, and his voice took on a shadow of the pain he'd expressed when he'd talked about that night at the quarry. "He hates me. He hates our whole family. He hates what we are and he hates what we can do. We see the dark side of Tyler because that's all he lets us see."

"Maybe that's all there is to see," Nick said bitterly.

"I don't think so," said Michael.

"Why not?"

"Because he loved his sister," Michael said. "Very much."

"How do you know?"

"Because he was the first kid I pulled out of the water that night. He was bleeding all over the place and his shoulder was dislocated, but once I brought him around, he coughed up a gallon of water and fought like hell to go back under to find her." He paused. "I understand why he hates us, Nick. I do. But I think part of him hates himself, too."

Nick thought of the burn on Quinn's wrist. Of the way Tyler

had grabbed him two hours ago. Of the years of abuse he'd suf-
fered at the hands of Tyler and Seth and their friends. He kept
flashing on that gym class freshman year, when Tyler had cornered Nick in the locker room and beaten the crap out of him.

Nick could still remember feeling powerless, clenching his
fists so he wouldn't call elements by accident, afraid to swing
because he didn't want Tyler to hit him harder.

He'd switched places with Gabriel the next day. His twin
wasn't afraid to hit back.

What had Quinn said? *Tyler still thinks your brother killed
his sister.*

Tyler had confided in Quinn. About something that had happened five years ago.

Quinn had confided in Tyler. What else had she told him?

Nick's head couldn't handle all these emotions. "Can we
go?" he asked abruptly.

Michael took it in stride. "Sure. If you're ready."

The drive home was quiet aside from the steady rain smacking the windshield. This time, the temperature in the cab remained steady. No tension hung between Nick and his brother.

"Thanks," Nick finally said. "For being okay."

"You don't have to thank me for that." Michael paused. "I
won't say anything to the guys."

Nick nodded. "Thanks."

Michael was silent for a while. "Can I tell Hannah?"

Nick thought about it. "Yeah. I think that'd be okay."

Michael nodded and didn't say anything else.

Nick wanted to put everyone's troubles out of his head, to let
the sound of rain on the windshield steal his thoughts and let
him relax. Instead, he kept analyzing his conversation with
Michael. About Quinn, about Adam.

About Tyler.

They were almost home when Nick figured out what Michael
had meant about Tyler.

He was the first kid Michael had pulled out of the water.

*Covered in blood with a dislocated shoulder, but when I
brought him around . . .*

Tyler had been hit by a rock, too. Michael hadn't just lost Emily that night.

He'd saved Tyler's life.

Quinn blotted at the cut on Tyler's cheek, being a little rougher than she needed to be. "Why did you pick a fight with him?"

"I didn't pick a fight."

"You're telling me you were only standing there and Nick Merrick walked up and started bringing down a tornado on your ass? Yeah, okay."

Tyler looked at her, not flinching as she pressed a cotton ball full of antiseptic against his face. She honestly didn't know why she was bothering—the cut was an hour old, and he could probably light a candle and heal himself. Or something.

When he spoke, his voice was rough and angry. "I hated them before, but now—" He gritted his teeth. "I hate that he's using you, Quinn."

"He's not using me," she said quietly. "It's—it's an illusion. I'm not *doing* anything for him. And he's my friend. I hate that you got into it with him."

"If he's your friend, he should be protecting you."

She flung the cotton in the trash. "I can take care of myself."

"How? By clinging to any guy who will give you a second glance?"

"Fuck you." She swung a fist to punch him in the chest.

He caught her wrist and, when she fought, wrestled her back against the wall. She glared up at him, breathing heavy, seething with anger.

He got right in her face. "Get as mad as you want, baby girl. You know it's true."

She hated him. *Hated him.*

She would not cry. *Would not.*

He held her there. "You sure do make it tough to help you. I'm almost inclined to give Merrick a free pass."

"At least he doesn't treat me like *this.*"

"Like what? It's okay for you to punch me, but when I stop you, I'm the asshole? Is that part of *your* screwed-up morality?"

Quinn didn't have anything to say to that.

Tyler kept going. "You keep acting like I'm hurting you because I don't want to sleep with you. Guess what, sweetheart. I don't want to sleep with someone who keeps acting like it's a form of *payment*."

She flinched hard, unable to swallow past the sudden lump in her throat.

"Do you even like me?" he said. "Or did I just show up at the right time?"

That made her sag under the tension of his hands. She looked away from him, clenching her jaw against tears and speech. Her hair fell across her face, and she studied the bathroom tile.

"I've never lied to you," said Tyler. "I'm not going to start now, okay?"

She had no idea where this was going. It sounded like a prelude to him kicking her ass out of his apartment.

But then he said, "I've liked you since the day you went off on me in Merrick's driveway. I like that you aren't afraid of me. I like that you don't seem to be afraid of *anything*. I like that you're driven, that you dance in the middle of the woods when you have nowhere else. I like that you've been through hell with your family, and you're still willing to come up kicking."

Quinn peeked at him through the fall of hair.

"You know what I hate?" he said evenly. "I hate that you're too stubborn to ask anyone for help, even though you damn sure need it. I hate when someone *tries* to help and you do everything you can to make them wash their hands of you. But the absolute worst thing, the thing that I can't fucking stand, is how you're this beautiful, talented girl, but for some reason you act like you need to buy a guy's favor."

Tears were running down her cheeks now. "I don't do that. I don't."

"You do, Quinn." His hands softened on her wrists. "You do it with me, and you did it with Merrick."

"I never did *anything* with Nick."

"Are you kidding me? You pretended to be his girlfriend! You were so desperate to be attached to a guy that you latched on to one who *doesn't even like girls*."

"I was *helping* him," she cried. "Because he was my *friend*."

"No, you were afraid to let him go," said Tyler. "Because you were afraid to give someone a chance to like you for *real*."

She needed him to stop talking. She needed to stop crying. She needed out. To get out. Of here. Right now.

But her limbs felt too weak, like she couldn't hold herself up.

"I get it," said Tyler. "I've seen your family. The people who should love you, *don't*. I just—you're worth more than that. I wish you could see that."

"Have you been studying for your Psych one-oh-one final or something?" she said, trying for anger, but her voice came out defeated. "Why don't you leave me alone."

He sighed and let her go. Quinn didn't move.

Tyler ran a hand through his blond hair. "Are you hungry?"

Quinn glanced up at him. After a long minute, she nodded.

"Feel like Chinese?"

"Okay." Her voice sounded broken.

His cell phone chimed, and he pulled it out of his pocket to glance at the display. He sighed again, heavily. "Damn it. One of the alarms is going off at the strip mall. I need to go check it out." He hesitated. "Are you going to be okay for half an hour? I'll bring food back with me."

No. She wouldn't be okay.

But Quinn nodded. What else could she do?

"Come on," he said. "I can't just leave you collapsed on the floor of the bathroom."

She wiped the tears off her face and flopped on the couch instead.

He hesitated at the door. "I'm not going to come home and find you gone, am I?"

She shook her head. Where else would she go?

Then he was gone, and it took everything she had not to call him back.

His voice reverberated through her head.

You're this beautiful, talented girl, but for some reason you act like you need to buy a guy's favor.

Did she do that?

She thought of all the boys she'd dated, the way she treated them, the way they treated her. Rafe Gutierrez, the boy who'd acted surprised when she told him that *no*, they didn't have an open relationship. Or Andy Kauffman, who said she was boring when she didn't want to get naked in his basement night after night. Or Lev Spartara, the boy she'd strung along with promises of heavy make-out sessions in the backseat of his mom's Toyota.

Had she been using them the same way they'd been using her?

She remembered sitting in Nick's front seat, climbing into his lap, practically unbuttoning his pants after he'd told her she couldn't spend the night at his house.

And then offering to continue being his girlfriend—under the pretense of keeping his *secret*.

Tyler was right. She and Nick might have been friends, but there was dishonesty on both sides of that relationship.

She fought her phone out of her pocket, scrolling through all the text messages she'd ignored.

With shaking fingers, she dialed. The line was answered almost immediately.

"Quinn? Are you okay?"

What did it say about her life that she got a greeting like that?

"Becca," she said, and suddenly she almost couldn't speak through her tears. "Becca, I really need to talk to you."

CHAPTER 24

Nick found Gabriel in his bedroom, sitting cross-legged on his bed, surrounded by textbooks. Headphones trailed from his ears, and his pencil tapped in time with whatever he was listening to. He either didn't notice Nick standing at the door, or he deliberately wasn't looking up.

Nick wanted to shove him off the bed and kick him in the face.

Not aggressive, my ass.

Gabriel finally looked up and yanked the headphones free. "So I have to leave you alone, but you get to stand there like a freaky stalker?"

Oh, good. New adjectives. Nick told his heartbeat to chill out. He pushed Gabriel's door open. "I need to talk to you about something."

Gabriel stared at him. Nick could read the debate on his face: screw with Nick or just play it easy.

He went with the latter. His pencil dropped into the spine of his trig textbook. "Okay. Talk."

"If you grabbed someone by the wrist, could you set their skin on fire without anyone knowing you were doing it?"

Gabriel's eyebrows went up. "Not exactly what I thought you'd want to talk about."

Nick didn't have an answer for that. He kept his gaze steady and waited.

"Look, Nicky . . ." Gabriel hesitated. "Whatever I did to piss you off, just—"

"Forget it." Nick was halfway out his door before Gabriel slid off the bed to grab his arm.

"Stop," said his twin. "I'll answer your question, all right?"

Nick stopped, but he didn't look at him.

Michael was so right. Nick did resent Gabriel. For not figuring it out. For not understanding.

For making it impossible to come out to him.

Gabriel drew a ragged breath, and it took Nick a second to even remember his question about burning. "I don't know. I'd have to try it. It would take a lot of control. A lot of focus."

"Fine." Nick held out his wrist, the good one. "Try it."

"Okay."

Nick braced himself, but Gabriel turned his head. "Hey, Chris. Come here. I want to try something."

Chris came out of his room, took one look at them, and turned around. "No way. I know that look."

But Gabriel was too quick. He rushed around Nick and caught Chris's door before it latched. He forced his way through.

And five seconds later, Chris was yelling and punching him and shoving past Nick to get to the bathroom. He was clutching his wrist. "What the *fuck*, Gabriel?"

Then the door slammed and the water was running.

Gabriel turned to Nick and smiled. "So, yeah. I can do it."

Nick didn't smile. "So can Tyler."

Gabriel sobered. "Tyler Morgan? No way."

Nick held up his arm and pulled back the sleeve, showing his scabs. "Way."

His brother's face darkened. "I'm going to kill him."

Nick couldn't help it. All his rage boiled up and he shoved Gabriel. Hard. "You don't need to defend me all the time!"

Gabriel fell back a step and put his hands up. "Jesus, Nick. Fine! *You* kill him. Whatever."

God, none of his conversations were going the way he expected. Nick took a second to get it together. "I don't know if I could. I think he might be a full Elemental."

"Well," said Gabriel. He glanced behind him and dropped his voice. "You want to go find out?"

Gabriel had an idea already. Nick could sense it. It would probably be half cocked and downright crazy. The kind of plan Nick would usually talk him out of.

The kind of plan Nick was *expected* to talk him out of.

"Sure." Nick met his eyes. "Let me get my coat."

Common sense would have dictated that they bring Hunter along. He was a Fifth, and a powerful one, and they were literally playing with fire.

But Nick was already on edge, and he wasn't sure he could handle the pressure of being with two people on opposite ends of a spectrum: one knowing his secret, one not.

So he and Gabriel went out alone.

Nick drove. Gabriel usually claimed the driver's seat, but Nick needed to be in control of *something* or he was going to go to pieces. He'd snatched the keys out from under his brother's hand in the front hall, ready for Gabriel to protest.

But his twin had just shrugged and said, "Fine. You drive."

Thick clouds hung overhead, blocking the stars, cloaking the road in darkness. The rain had stopped, but those clouds would only need a little *push* to start dumping water again.

Rain could've been a safety net. Maybe they should have brought Chris.

If nothing else, for conversation. Gabriel wasn't saying a word. He'd been silent for *miles*. Nick could feel the tension like a vibration in the air, mixing with the cool humidity, as if his brother's uncertainty created a whole new level of energy.

Gabriel was waiting for Nick to spill, to pour out his problems the way he usually did. Nick was the thinker. The talker. The analyzer. Gabriel was all about action. If Nick presented a problem, Gabriel provided a solution—even if his idea of a *solution* was a fistfight.

Not having a way to solve this problem, this *distance*, was making Gabriel nuts. Nick could tell.

And a petty, vindictive part of Nick reveled in it.

That lasted about twenty seconds. Then he felt like crap.

He glanced over. "Hey. What's your plan?"

"To set him on fire."

"Seriously."

Gabriel's eyes were on the windshield, his voice dark and full of anger. "I am serious. I'm sick of him fucking with you, Nicky. I don't know what he's doing to you and Quinn, but I know something is up."

So all that silence had left Gabriel with time to draw the wrong conclusions.

"We're not setting him on fire," Nick said.

"Fine. What do you want to do?"

The words were a challenge. Nick wasn't sure how to respond. Honestly, he wished they could simply walk up to Tyler and ask what the deal was. He was so tired of *fighting*.

"I don't know yet," he said.

A bolt of lightning cracked the sky in front of them, followed by a roll of thunder. Gabriel's power flared in the air. He wasn't tired of fighting. If the eager tension in the atmosphere was any indication, he was ready for a *battle*.

Suddenly, Nick didn't want to be out tonight. He didn't want to be picking a fight. Maybe he'd used up all his emotion earlier in the evening. Maybe Michael's talk about Emily and Quinn had softened the edge of his anger against Tyler.

Or maybe he was afraid.

Nick swallowed that back. If he admitted fear now, he'd lose more ground with his twin. He'd be the creepy freak who couldn't solve his own problems. The weak one.

"Where are we *going*?" said Gabriel.

"Tyler's parents' shopping center," Nick said. "Quinn said he's been guarding the place every night. From vandals or something."

Just as he said it, they crested the hill, and the lights from the

7-Eleven sign broke through the darkness. Nick could see the big SUV in the parking lot and knew Tyler was there.

He wanted to keep on driving.

Instead, he hit the turn signal and pulled off the road just past the shopping center, killing the lights as the car drifted to a stop along Ritchie Highway.

Then he turned off the engine and sat there.

He didn't want to do this. Everything felt wrong.

"How does Quinn know?" said Gabriel.

"What?"

"How does Quinn know what Tyler is doing at night?"

"Apparently she walks over here sometimes. That's her apartment building." Nick pointed.

Gabriel was quiet for a minute. "So do you think she and Tyler—?"

"Come on," Nick said. He didn't want his brother to finish that thought. He climbed out of the cab.

Nick wished he'd chosen more concealing clothing than a white T-shirt under a jacket. Gabriel was a shadow in a dark hoodie and charcoal-gray jeans. They stepped over the guard rail to slink through the trees beside the road.

The 7-Eleven sign grew larger with each step. Nick could hear his own breathing, faster than Gabriel's. When they came to the tree line, Nick hesitated, not wanting to lose the cover. To cross the street, they'd pass directly below half a dozen street-lamps.

He expected his brother to move on without him, leading the way to disaster.

But Gabriel stopped, too, and looked at him.

"What?"

"You tell me, Nicky." Gabriel's voice made small clouds of steam in the air.

Nick froze. Those words seemed loaded with more than just an inquiry about what to do next.

He had to look away from his brother, so he put his eyes on the strip mall. "I don't want to cause damage to someone else's property. There have been enough fires."

"Let's go back in the woods. Burn some leaves." Gabriel fished a lighter out of his pocket and tossed it.

Nick caught it. "Why?"

"It'll lure him out. If he's a pure Elemental, he'll sense it."

"Even from here?" They were at least a hundred feet from the parking lot.

Gabriel nodded and started walking back into the dense darkness of the woods.

Nick followed, sliding the lighter between his fingers. "What if he ignores it?"

"Then he's not a full Elemental and I can go punch that mofo in the face." He stopped once they were out of sight and pointed to the ground. "Here's good. The leaves are dry underneath and they'll smoke more. I don't want anyone to see it from the road yet."

Nick held up the lighter. "You still need these?"

"No, but you do. I don't want him to sense my power." He paused and glanced around, surveying the area. "It might be better if he thinks you're alone."

"So we're setting a trap."

"Yeah. See if he'll come after you again."

"Lucky me."

Gabriel studied him again, as if trying to figure him out. "Do you not want to do this? We can say screw it and get coffee or whatever."

Yes. Let's.

Wait. No. Talking would be a bad idea.

Nick cocked an eyebrow. "You want to run from a fight?"

"No, Nick!" Gabriel snapped, closing the distance between them. "I want you to tell me what the fuck is going on."

Nick ignored him. He flipped open the lighter and struck the igniter. Then he dropped and touched the flame to the dead leaves trapped under the damp ones. The fire caught immediately, sending smoke curling between them, turning the air hazy.

"Go," Nick said. "Hide."

Gabriel swore, but he turned his back and walked. He didn't go far. Nick could still sense his presence nearby—like he could still sense his agitation. No, his fury.

It was probably a good thing Nick had the car keys.

He fed oxygen to the fire, and thicker smoke bloomed from the smoldering leaves. Nick called for a gentle breeze to push the smoke toward the strip mall, despite Gabriel's assurance that Tyler would sense the presence of his element.

It wasn't necessary—or maybe it worked too well. In less than a minute, Nick sensed another presence in the woods. He pulled wind through the trees, asking the air for information.

Nicotine and male sweat. Curiosity and irritation. Tyler.

Nick thought of the way his skin had practically melted off his wrist, but he held his ground.

"Starting a little fire?" said Tyler.

"Something like that," said Nick. He kept his attention on the burning leaves. Tyler hadn't reacted to the fire, and Nick sensed no power in the space between them. Maybe he was wrong.

"Don't tell me," said Tyler. "You think you owe me one for messing with your brother."

What? Who else had Tyler—

Oh. *Oh.* The lighter in his hand, the fire on the ground— Tyler thought he was Gabriel.

Infuriating. Even *Tyler* knew he couldn't stand up for himself.

Sudden wind whipped through the trees, responding to Nick's anger. It swirled around them, buffeting the flames, pulling the smoke into the beginning of a spiral.

"Wrong," said Nick. "I think I owe you one for messing with *me*."

He had the satisfaction of seeing Tyler look startled, but then his expression settled into something closer to determination. He started forward, heedless of the wind and the flames.

Nick instinctively took a step back—but he didn't need to. His wind grabbed the flames and pulled them high, feeding oxygen to the fire, creating a barrier between him and Tyler.

Tyler stopped, but his eyes narrowed. "You think a little wind and fire are going to scare me?"

"Looks like it's scaring you now." Nick held his ground, but his heart was in his throat. He remembered the pain of his wrist under Tyler's grip. The smell of his skin burning. He fed power into the wind, letting it draw the fire higher, until the flames began to pull sideways, spreading to surround Tyler.

This was like the leaves with Quinn. Only terrifying, as he realized that leaves wouldn't hurt anyone, and a spinning plume of fire could have very real consequences.

Focus.

"Think you're something?" said Tyler. "You want to call elements against me? Fuck you, Merrick."

And then he sent the fire driving outward.

Nick felt it—maybe the air warned him, or maybe Tyler was stronger than Nick had imagined. But the circle of fire flared outward, reaching for him, full of murderous rage.

Nick sent the wind a flare of power himself, full of vengeful rage about every single thing Tyler had ever done to him. The circle paused, hesitating in a vibrant red glow that encircled Tyler.

Then it snapped, collapsing inward, attacking Tyler with fire. The other boy's clothes lit up like he'd been doused in kerosene. Then the tight coil of wind caught his body and flipped him in the air. He came down in the leaves, a pile of burning clothes and rage.

Holy shit. Gabriel really had set him on fire.

Or maybe Nick had.

The leaves caught, sending black smoke to swarm around them. Between the smoke and the fire, Nick was going to lose sight of Tyler in a moment.

And if Tyler wasn't a full Elemental, he was going to die in minutes.

From the way Tyler's face contorted, it might only be seconds. He looked like he was screaming, but he wasn't making a sound. His hands scrabbled at his throat.

Shit. Shit, shit, *shit.* Nick hadn't come here to *kill* someone.

Where the hell was Gabriel?

Nick was torn between sucking the oxygen out of the air and forcing it into Tyler's lungs. Was he burning to death or suffocating? It didn't matter. The atmosphere was too focused on destruction now. Thunder rolled overhead. Lightning hit a tree. Ozone charged the air and flaming branches rained around them.

Tyler's eyes rolled back in his head. Another lightning strike somewhere off to Nick's left.

"Damn it, Gabriel," Nick called. "Stop! Help me!"

Tyler's cheeks were red and raw. His eyes fell closed. Nick reached forward and grabbed the other boy's jacket. The zipper was hot from the flames and burned his palms. Nick flung all of his power into the space between them. He did this with Gabriel all the time—stopped fires before they caused too much damage. He could do it now.

Stop this, he pleaded with his element. *Heal him.*

It took a moment, but the wind listened. The fire died down to nothing more than a few spirals of flame dancing in the breeze. Wind licked between them, settling, stealing the redness from Tyler's cheeks.

For an instant, Tyler didn't move. Then he sucked in a rough breath of air. Then another.

"Jesus," said Nick, feeling a bit breathless himself. "You're not dead."

Tyler's eyes opened. Nick let him go, expecting to see pain, confusion, fear.

He saw derision.

"Not dead yet," said Tyler. He grabbed Nick's jacket with fistfuls of flame and *shoved*, true power in the motion. Nick's back hit a tree.

But that didn't hurt half as much as the bolt of lightning that hit him next.

CHAPTER 25

"Nick. *Nick.*"

Gabriel's voice. He sounded almost panicked. Hands gripped Nick's shoulders, shaking him. "Come on, Nicky. Please. Come on."

Nick couldn't remember how to open his eyes. It felt like he'd been hit by a truck.

"No, you idiot," Gabriel said, that panic giving way to choked relief. "You were hit by lightning."

Were his eyes open? He couldn't see anything. Was he talking?

"You're talking," said Gabriel. "Open your eyes."

He didn't want to open his eyes. The air was dancing on his skin and it felt wonderful.

Dancing. Adam.

Nick wished he could apologize. He wished he could fix it.

"Come on, Nick," said Gabriel. "You're scaring me."

He was kind of scaring himself. He felt disconnected, like his body ached, but he couldn't feel it yet.

Next time, he was *so* making Gabriel play bait.

Gabriel choked out a sound, half laugh, half sob. "I will, Nick. I promise." It felt like he was patting Nick's cheek. "Come on. Wake up."

Nick opened his eyes and looked at his brother.

Gabriel was kneeling there in the charred leaves and undergrowth, holding him up against a tree, his eyes tense and worried.

Nick was struck with déjà vu. They'd been eight or nine, riding bikes through the woods, jumping the creek the way they'd done a thousand times. A storm had washed away part of the creek walls, leaving the ground soft and muddy. Gabriel, in the lead as usual, made the jump with little difficulty.

But his bike had made a rut. Nick's bike caught it and sank into the mud, stuck. It had stopped. Nick hadn't. His head had cracked into a tree.

He'd woken up just like this, staring into his twin brother's panicked eyes.

"My bike broke," he mumbled now.

"Not this time." Gabriel smiled, but there was still a shadow of worry behind it.

Of course he'd share the exact same memory at the exact same moment.

"How do you feel?" said Gabriel.

"Oh. Stellar."

"No—I mean, can you walk?"

Nick thought about it. "Not yet."

Gabriel sighed, but he didn't let him go.

"Tyler?" said Nick.

"He ran," said Gabriel. His voice grew dark. "As soon as you collapsed. If you think you can stay upright, I'm going to find him and kill him."

Nick struggled to find his hands, and he grabbed Gabriel's wrist. "No—no." He paused, trying to make his addled brain sort out the evening's events. But one thing was clear—they'd come here with the intent to out Tyler's abilities. Nick remembered the power in the air, the way his fear had manifested itself in damaging winds that attacked Tyler until fire consumed him.

He'd been the bully tonight. Not Tyler.

It should have been satisfying. It wasn't.

"Our fault," he said.

Gabriel shook his head. "My fault." He paused. "I should have helped you."

Now Nick remembered. His thoughts were straightening out, finding true clarity. "You let him burn! You called lightning! You let him—"

"I didn't call that lightning, Nick. He did." Gabriel looked away. "I should have helped you before it got to that point."

Nick shoved his hands away. "Yeah, thanks. Thanks for making me play *bait*, and forgetting to snap the trap."

"An hour ago you got all shitty because I wanted to defend you! What the hell do you *want from me*, Nick? What?"

I want you to know what I want.

Nick put a hand against the ground and pushed himself to his feet. He wavered for a second, but Gabriel didn't grab him.

He looked down at himself. Pieces of leaves clung to his jeans, and his jacket was smudged with bits of soot where Tyler had grabbed him, but really, he didn't look any the worse for wear.

The air was happy he was awake. He felt better with every breath, as if he inhaled pure power.

He started walking toward the car.

After a moment, Gabriel jogged to catch up with him.

"Give me the keys," he said. "You're in no shape to drive."

Nick wanted to protest, but his twin was probably right. He pulled them out of his pocket and handed them over. He didn't look at Gabriel when they climbed in to the car.

This whole evening hadn't solved anything. So Tyler was a full Elemental. So what? When the next round of Guides came to town, they could add him to the list. When Tyler came after him again, he could mess with Nick all that much more effectively.

This sucked.

Nick pulled his cell phone out of his pocket to see if fate had inspired Adam to send him a message.

Fate told him to go to hell. The phone was completely dead. Either the lightning had killed the battery, or it had killed the phone completely.

Great. Nick slammed it into the center console.

The tension in the car was thicker now than when they'd first left the house. Nick's skin *crawled* with it.

After a few minutes, Gabriel pulled his phone out of his pocket and held it out. "Here. Use mine."

Yeah, right. Nick shook his head.

His brother sighed and shoved it back in his pocket.

Silence again. This time, more strained than before, if that was possible. The temperature in the car dropped ten degrees. Nick was almost shaking with the effort of sitting here calmly.

"Fuck this," said Gabriel. He yanked the wheel abruptly, sending them careening into a parking lot along Ritchie Highway. By some miracle, they avoided striking a parked car.

"Are you insane?" Nick grabbed the handle over the door. "What the hell are you doing?"

"Parking." Gabriel jerked the car into a parking place in front of a coffee shop. It wasn't Starbucks, but instead a huge café with leather couches and oak tables and hot sandwiches.

Nick had brought a girl here once. After a movie or something. He couldn't remember her name. Tonight, it was packed.

"What are we doing here?" Nick said.

Gabriel kept his eyes on the windshield. He didn't say anything for a long moment. "I can't do this, Nick. I know—" His voice caught, and he took a second to get it together before continuing. "I know I deserve it. After keeping the fires from you. But this—this doesn't feel like something you're *doing*." He peeked over at Nick.

Nick couldn't move. He couldn't even look at his brother.

"What happened last night?" Gabriel said. "When you were talking to Hunter?"

Nick's head snapped to the side. Gabriel was referring to whatever had led to Nick looking like a hot mess on the stairs, but all Nick heard were Gabriel's words. *My brother has enough freaks pining after him.*

He must have looked fierce because Gabriel put his hands up. "I don't want to fight with you," Gabriel said. "Christ—I don't even know why we *are* fighting."

Nick swallowed and looked at the windshield.

"You don't have to tell me," Gabriel said after a minute. "I—I wish I knew why you won't."

It sounded like it cost him something to say that.

"I want to tell you," said Nick.

The words fell out of his mouth almost against his will.

And as soon as he said them, he realized how true they were. He wanted to tell Gabriel about Adam. He told his brother *everything*, and now he felt more strongly about another human being than he ever had, and he couldn't breathe a word about it. The mental strife was choking him.

No, the terror of losing his brother was choking him.

But wasn't he doing that anyway?

I can't do this, Nick.

Nick couldn't, either. He cleared his throat and nodded at the front of the café. "I probably should have picked coffee when you suggested it earlier."

"Pick coffee now."

Sit. Talk to me. That's what his brother was saying.

Nick took a breath. He nodded. "Okay."

The café had looked crowded from the parking lot, and getting up close to the front door confirmed it. Every table seemed occupied, but the line for the register wasn't too long.

Still, someplace this packed wouldn't exactly be conducive to the kind of discussion Nick had in mind.

Then again, Gabriel probably wouldn't flip out in the middle of a crowd of people.

"We can come back out here to sit," said Gabriel. "Plenty of room."

Nick looked at him. It was barely forty-five degrees, so all the tables were deserted. But sitting in the fresh air would help—Gabriel knew that. This was an olive branch.

"It's not too cold?"

Gabriel dropped into one of the wire chairs in front of the restaurant. "Nah. I'll hold the table so we don't have to play the twin game."

Meaning the thirty-eight thousand questions they encountered when seen in public together. Nick smiled, though it felt uncertain. "All right."

He waited in line inside the warm bustle of the restaurant, wondering if this was an olive branch, too: Gabriel giving him time to think.

And he *needed* time to think.

Nerves made him jittery. What if his brother walked away? What if he said he wasn't okay with it?

Creepy. Freak.

Nick ran a hand through his hair and told himself to calm down.

Maybe he should lead off with Adam. *So . . . I've met someone. It's new, and it's special, but . . . it's a guy.*

Maybe not.

I know you're worried about Quinn, but we're not really together. No, not since she caught me kissing a guy.

Ugh. This was horrible.

I've been lying to you for years.

Sure.

The line inched along. An older couple came in and got in line behind him.

Nick took another slow breath. Maybe this would be like it had been with Michael. Maybe it would be okay. Awkward at first, but . . . okay.

No, Gabriel was nothing like Michael. Gabriel would have a reaction.

Who do you think the hottest person in the restaurant is? Then Gabriel would pick some girl, and Nick could pick the busboy who looked a little like Adam.

Jesus, he sounded like a frigging *moron*. These were the best ideas his brain could come up with? No wonder he was failing physics.

Some girls came in, giggling and jostling each other as they moved to the end of the line. He could smell their perfume from here, bubblegum sweet. Nick ignored them, shifting forward one place when the line moved.

But then he caught the tail end of what one girl was saying. ". . . out front look like they're gonna fight."

Fight. A word practically synonymous with Gabriel.

Nick turned. The lights inside made it difficult to make out what was going on behind the glass, but he could see his brother's form. He looked like he was talking to someone.

Then Nick saw the shove, hard enough to make the other person fall back.

Nick swore and gave up his place in line. Had Tyler followed them here somehow?

But then he got close enough to the glass storefront to make out Gabriel's opponent.

Adam.

Nick's heart tripped and stalled in his chest. He couldn't remember how to breathe. He couldn't remember how to *move.*

How had this happened?

Adam had his hands up. He looked agitated, but he didn't want to fight.

Gabriel shoved him anyway. Adam fell back another step.

That forced Nick's feet into motion. He needed to stop this. *Now.*

Cold air hit him in the face, carrying Gabriel's voice, low and angry. "What the fuck do you mean, you're sorry about last night? What are you doing to my brother?"

"Stop!" Nick said. Neither paid attention to him.

"It's a misunderstanding," said Adam, his voice careful.

Gabriel shoved him again, harder. "A misunderstanding?"

Adam fell back, but he kept his hands up. "Yeah." Now his voice was edged with anger. "Just calm down."

"Calm down? You want me to *calm down*?" Gabriel shoved him *again.*

Adam gave up the surrender position and shoved him back.

Gabriel drew back an arm to hit him.

Nick didn't even remember moving. He had a hold of Gabriel's arm and he was driving him back, until his twin hit the cinder block wall of the shopping center.

"Don't you *touch* him," he said fiercely. He might have been

yelling. He gave Gabriel a shove against the wall for good measure. "You hear me? You keep your hands *off him*."

Gabriel's eyes were wide. Their breathing was loud, putting
twin puffs of steam between them. Time seemed to hold still.

Nick kept seeing Gabriel's fist drawn back, ready to smash
into Adam's jaw. Nick wanted to slam him into the wall again.

For the first time in his life, he wouldn't back down from his
brother for *anything*.

Gabriel's eyes went from Nick to Adam and back.

Then he coiled all his strength to throw Nick off.

Nick had leverage—and while he couldn't fight like Gabriel,
he was every bit as strong. He slammed him back into the wall.
Harder this time. Gabriel's head hit the cinder block.

"Hey. *Hey*." Adam put a hand on Nick's arm. "Take it easy,"
he said quietly. "Let him go. It's a misunderstanding."

Nick looked across into his brother's eyes. He saw the exact
moment when Gabriel put two and two together.

And Nick waited for his brother to swallow the aggression,
to be decent, to take this horrible moment and make everything
okay.

But Gabriel's expression turned dark and furious. "So is this
part of your big secret, Nicky?"

If he'd just said the words, Nick wouldn't have cared.

But Gabriel said it in a high-pitched mocking lisp.

Nick couldn't see through the rage. He lifted a fist to swing.

And that was all Gabriel needed. He twisted free of Nick's
grip and ducked under the flying fist.

Nick's hand cracked into the cinder block wall.

Then Gabriel's hand cracked into his face.

For the second time in one night, Nick went down.

And suddenly, they had a crowd. An older man was in front
of Gabriel, blocking him, his hands up. "Take a walk, son. Take
a walk. Cool off."

Nick saw stars and tasted blood. He couldn't feel his fingers
yet. He started to get to his feet, but Adam grabbed his arm and
held him there.

"Don't get up," he said. "Let him walk away."

Gabriel watched this, clear derision in his expression. "You don't have to hold him," he snapped. "Nick will stay down."

"*Walk*," ordered the older man. "Or we're calling the cops." He paused. "*Now*."

For an instant, Nick thought Gabriel would shove past the guy. The air held so much violent potential.

But then his twin brother turned and walked away. No parting words, no final epithets. Just measured steps along the sidewalk, across the stretch of road, before giving way to a car door slamming.

And then the rumble of an engine. He was leaving.

Nick was distantly aware that his breath was shaking. And now he could feel pain roaring into his fingers. Not to mention his face.

What just happened?

Adam was pulling at his arm now, gently. "Come on. Can you stand?"

He could stand. They tried to get him to go back in the restaurant, but Nick didn't want all those eyes on him.

But Adam insisted on sitting down, so Nick dropped into one of the metal chairs out front, the one closest to the shadows of the next storefront.

The man who'd gotten in front of Gabriel turned out to be the café owner. He brought them each a cup of coffee and a bag of ice for Nick.

Nick was shocked this guy wasn't calling the cops anyway. Nick had been the one to shove Gabriel into the wall.

"I'm sorry for disrupting your night," Adam said to him.

"You didn't do anything," the man said. "The girls inside said that other boy started it." He *tsked*. "Shame there are still such closed-minded people picking fights about this kind of thing. You're lucky your . . . friend was here to stop him."

"I know I am," said Adam.

"You sure you boys won't come inside? I'm worried he'll come back."

Had the man not noticed they were twins? That this wasn't

some random hate crime? Maybe it was too dark. Maybe it had happened too fast.

Nick cleared his throat. "He's my brother. He won't come back."

Those words hung in the air for a moment.

"We'll be all right," said Adam.

And then they were alone.

Nick hadn't touched the ice, but Adam sat in the opposite metal chair and reached for it. Then he put the bag against Nick's face.

And Nick was struck with an entirely different sort of déjà vu. A different night, a different fight, but Adam's hand holding an ice bag just like this.

Back then, Nick had leapt out of his chair to kiss him. Now, he wasn't sure what to do. About any of it.

"Would you rather put this on your hand?" Adam said.

Nick tried to categorize his injuries and came up with nothing. He couldn't think past his brother's angry eyes and the fight and the way he'd walked off.

And what he'd *said*.

It hurt. It hurt more than anything physical.

Nick swallowed and shook his head.

They sat there for the longest time in the darkness, breathing the same air. The pain began to fade from Nick's hand as his element worked its magic.

Nick almost wished it wouldn't. *This* he wanted to remember for a while.

When he finally spoke, his voice was rough. "Did he hurt you?"

"No." Adam looked chagrined. "And I shouldn't have shoved him. But he kept pushing me, and there's only so much of that big-dumb-straight-boy crap that I can put up with. Especially since . . . you know."

Nick did know. And if Gabriel had hurt Adam . . . Nick wasn't sure what he would have done.

But he'd felt a glimmer of it when he was slamming Gabriel into that wall.

He pulled the ice bag away from his face and set it on the table. "I'm sorry that he—that he—"

"It's not your fault." Adam touched his cheek, and his hand was warm. Nick shut his eyes and leaned into the contact. He felt the pain, but it was worth it.

He opened his eyes. "Then I'm sorry for what *I* did. Last night."

Adam nodded and withdrew his hand, reaching for the ice pack again. "I am, too." He glanced up, and the slightest bit of rueful humor slid into his voice. "In fact, I was trying to apologize to you fifteen minutes ago. I didn't realize that when you said identical twin, you weren't kidding about the *identical* part."

Nick frowned. "Only on the outside." Then he remembered the whole reason for the apology, and he looked away, ashamed. "Usually."

"No, what you did was nothing like what *he* did." Adam caught his eye and held it. "Don't get me wrong. What you did was not okay."

"I know."

"I know you know. That's why I'm sitting here."

"How did you know I'd be here?"

Adam picked up Nick's hand and held the ice against his knuckles. He looked sheepish. "I didn't. I came here to *avoid* you. I figured you usually go to the Starbucks down the road." He paused, then rubbed at the back of his neck. "I needed to grab a cup of coffee on the way to my parents', because I told them I'd stop by tonight. Then I saw you—well, your brother—sitting there, and I . . . ah, well, I couldn't go another minute without talking to you."

Nick studied him. The lighting was dim, but . . . "You're blushing!"

Adam looked away. "Yeah, yeah."

"But you wouldn't respond to my texts!"

"Well, I couldn't let you think you got off that easy."

"Oh, I get it. So you've been torturing me." But Nick smiled.

"Absolutely. And torturing myself at the same time." Adam slid his phone out of his pocket and snapped a picture.

"Oh, good," said Nick. "This is a moment I want a record of."

"You don't smile enough. That makes them meaningful." He paused, then turned the phone around so Nick could see. His voice lost any humor. "I should send this to your brother."

Nick glanced at it. A bruise was already forming on his cheek, more obvious because of the flash in the darkness.

He reached out and pushed the button to make the phone go dark. Gabriel's mocking voice was a never-ending echo in his head; he didn't need to see the evidence of physical aggression on top of it. Such a contrast to that moment in the car, when Nick had realized how badly he wanted to share this with his brother.

Or that moment in the woods. Gabriel's voice, tight with panic. *Come on, Nicky. Please. You're scaring me.*

Or the thousand moments before that. A lifetime of memories with his twin brother, undone in an instant.

You don't have to hold him. Nick will stay down.

"Okay," said Adam softly. "Okay. Come on."

It was only then that Nick realized his breath was shaking and his eyes had filled. Adam's fingers wrapped around his good hand and tugged. Nick allowed himself to be led.

When he was sure his voice wouldn't break, he said, "Where are we going?"

"Bus stop. My place?"

Nick nodded. He certainly couldn't go home.

If he was being strictly honest with himself, he was *afraid* to go home.

God, he was such a *wuss*.

But when they were on the near-empty bus, sharing a bench at the back of the vehicle, Adam leaned into him and spoke quietly. "When you pushed him away from me—that was the bravest thing I've ever seen."

Nick scoffed, but Adam put a finger over his lips. "It was. For me, it was. Take it or leave it."

Nick took it.

CHAPTER 26

Quinn hadn't told Becca everything.

She'd left out Nick's secret.

She'd left out Tyler.

She'd left out the trophy and the bruise and the fire on the beach.

But she'd cried and talked about how much she missed her best friend, about how much it hurt when Becca treated her like she was overdramatic, how she needed to figure out how to trust her again.

How much Quinn needed Becca to be there when she was ready to tell her everything.

She'd expected Becca to brush her off. If she was being strictly honest with herself, she'd expected Becca to sigh and huff and start talking about Chris.

But Becca had cried with her and told her how much she missed her, too, and Quinn realized that some of her worries about her best friend were exaggerations she'd created in her mind.

Another example of pushing someone away before they had the opportunity to help her.

Becca had begged her to come stay with her, but Quinn had refused. She needed more time to untangle the snarled mess of her thoughts. To decide how much trust she was willing to share.

Now, Quinn was ready for Tyler to come home with Chinese food, to sit across from him and have a real conversation.

She'd mocked him about honor, but really, he'd been incredibly honorable toward her. He'd never lied. He'd never taken her up on her offer to "repay" him.

She was ready to stop pushing him away.

Nick, too. Quinn reassessed the way she'd treated him. He'd been trying to protect her from Tyler, and she'd all but told him to fuck off.

Not *all but*. She had. She still had the text in her phone history.

She'd pushed Adam away, too, that night she'd blown him off, the night she'd jumped on a bus and texted Tyler.

When she really thought about it, she had a lot of people looking out for her, and she'd treated them all like crap.

Then Tyler strolled through the door looking like he'd been in a fight. His jacket was filthy, his jeans looking somewhat charred around the seams. He dropped a leaking bag of Chinese food on the table.

"Sorry I'm late," he said flatly. "The place was packed. I had to wait."

Quinn stared at him. "What the hell happened to you?"

"Your boyfriend happened," he said flatly. "He and his brother just renewed my desire to kill them."

Nick needed to call home.

He didn't want to, but if he didn't show up, Michael would worry.

He sat on the end of Adam's bed, staring at Adam's cell phone, while his host banged around in the kitchen, making something he claimed would be *better than coffee*.

Nick almost hoped it would be something better than hard liquor, because he wouldn't mind turning off his thoughts for a while.

It was close to ten. He only knew two numbers by heart: the house phone and Gabriel's cell.

No contest.

The house phone rang four times. With each ring, Nick's heart staggered as he prepared for Gabriel to pick up.

Fate smiled on him this time. Chris answered.

"It's me," said Nick. "Is Mike around?"

"He's out with Hannah." Chris hesitated. "Where are you calling from? Are you okay?"

"Did Gabriel get home yet?"

"No, why? Where are you?"

Nick absolutely *hated* that his twin brother had been such a dick, but he still felt a flicker of worry about where Gabriel had gone—or what he was doing. "Look—Chris, it's nothing. Can you tell Michael something for me?"

"Sure. Whatever you need." Chris hesitated. "Are you sure you're all right?"

No. Nick rubbed at his eyes. He wanted to crawl into a bed and sleep for a month. "Will you tell him—" Tell him *what*? That his twin brother had broken his heart? That he couldn't come home for . . . ever? Nick cleared his throat. "Tell him I'm spending the night with a friend. I accidentally left my phone in the car."

Another pause. A weighted one. Chris's voice was low. "Would this friend be Adam?"

Nick froze.

Chris continued, "That's who sent you the text message at school, right?"

At lunch. When he'd flipped out.

"Yeah." Nick swallowed. He couldn't read his brother's voice, and after the fight with Gabriel, this uncertainty left him on edge.

Chris was silent for a moment, and Nick could imagine him standing there, choosing his words carefully.

Nick couldn't handle the silence. "Say something, Chris," he said, more sharply than he intended. "You've obviously figured it out. So say what you want to say."

Adam had stopped whatever he was doing in the kitchen, and was now watching Nick from across the apartment.

You okay? he mouthed.

Nick nodded.

And Chris was still silent.

"Forget it," said Nick bitterly. "Just tell Michael where I am and that I'm okay."

"Wait," said Chris.

Nick waited.

Chris took a breath. "I'm sorry you thought you had to keep this a secret."

The words hit with every bit as much impact as Gabriel's had—but these didn't hurt. In fact, they seemed to absorb some of the earlier blow. Nick didn't know what to say.

"It's okay," Chris added. "I mean—with me. You're my brother, and—I want you to be happy, all right?"

Nick drew a shaky breath. He was nodding until he realized that was ridiculous and Chris couldn't see him. "All right."

"Seriously. You okay?"

"Yeah."

"What happened to Gabriel? Didn't you go out together?"

Nick drew a hand down his face. "I don't really want to talk about it. I only wanted to make sure someone knew where I was."

Chris didn't say anything for a moment. "I'll tell Michael."

"Thanks." Nick paused. "Hey. How did you know?"

"I didn't know for sure. But that day in the cafeteria. When Gabriel was giving you shit about the text message." Chris hesitated. "When you left, you were crying."

Damn. "Did anyone else see?"

"No one saw. I felt it." Another pause. "It's okay, though. I didn't say anything."

He felt it. The tears.

Nick almost smiled. "You're a good little brother."

"Nah, you caught me on a good day."

Now Nick did smile. "I'm glad you were home." He looked up and saw Adam standing by the stove. It looked like he was stirring something. Nick inhaled chocolate and cinnamon. "I should go."

"Okay." He paused. "I'm here all night if you need to call back."

If Gabriel's actions had shredded his heart, Chris was doing wonders to stitch it back together. "Thanks, Chris."

"No problem. I love you, brother." And before Nick could say anything to that, Chris hung up.

Nick stared at the phone, touched and bemused. Then he walked out to join Adam in the kitchen.

He hesitated at the juncture between carpet and linoleum. This felt like the first night they'd come here, when he wasn't sure what Adam expected. They'd apologized, and Adam had invited him here, but did that mean everything was fine?

Adam glanced back over his shoulder, but he didn't stop stirring whatever was in the saucepan on the stove. "Everything okay?"

Nick wanted to touch him, to feel some contact that wasn't full of violence and anger. "Yeah. What are you making?"

"Hot chocolate with Nutella."

"It smells amazing."

"It's my guilty pleasure. My mom used to make it when I had a bad day." He tossed another glance over his shoulder. "Don't tell anyone at the studio. I'm supposed to live on lettuce and carrot sticks."

"You're worse than Quinn." But now his eyes were on Adam's body, the breadth of his shoulders, the slow movement of his arms as he stirred the pot. The way dark hair curled at the nape of his neck. The softness of his skin, the hardness of the muscles underneath.

Touch him. Touch him. Touch him.

"I doubt that," said Adam. "Hey, can you pull down some mugs?"

Nick couldn't even remember what they were talking about. But Adam's request broke the spell and spurred him into motion. He found the mugs on the second guess, reaching to pull them down from the highest shelf.

When Adam's hands came around him from behind, he gasped and almost dropped both mugs.

Adam laughed and slid his hands up Nick's chest, moving close until they were almost pressed together. He kissed the back of Nick's neck, breathing along the skin there. "You were making me crazy, standing there like that."

He was making Nick crazy, standing there like *that*. When Adam's hand slid under his shirt, tracing the skin below his rib cage, Nick shivered.

"I wasn't sure what you wanted," Nick admitted.

Adam froze. The mood in the air changed.

Then his hand tightened on Nick's waist roughly, jerking him close. *Very* close. "Any question now?"

Nick blushed so hard he was glad he was looking away. He shook his head.

Adam let him go abruptly and took the mugs out of his hands, slamming them onto the counter beside the stove. Any playful banter was gone from his voice. "I think that's part of the problem," he said, killing the heat on the stove. "You're so damn worried about what everyone *else* wants. Well, you know what, Nick? You're going to disappoint people sometimes. You just are. And you know what else? They're either going to get over it or they're *not*. If they don't, it sucks. But it's not going to kill them, and it's sure not going to kill you." He poured the hot chocolate into the mugs, then slammed the saucepan back onto a cool burner. "In fact, if you ask me, Gabriel is long overdue for some disappointment."

Nick flinched.

Adam pulled a can of whipped cream out of the refrigerator and shook it like he meant it harm. "You can't live your whole life waiting around to make sure people approve of the choices you make. That's why you've got a drawer full of unopened college letters. That's why you've got a house full of brothers who didn't have a clue about what *you* wanted. That's why—"

Nick shoved him up against the refrigerator and kissed him. Hard.

Adam's breath caught, but he kissed him back, matching

Nick's intensity. The can of whipped cream hit the floor. Fingers tangled in Nick's hair.

Nick caught his wrists and broke the kiss, pinning Adam against the refrigerator with hands and body. He could feel everything, but he wasn't blushing now.

Adam's eyes were heavy with desire, but maybe a little fear hid there, too. His breathing came fast, too fast.

"I didn't mean to frighten you," Nick said, his voice low. Despite Adam's lecture about *doing what he wanted*, there were real stakes here. He softened his hold on Adam's wrists and backed off a bit, leaning in to kiss his cheek, the edge of his jaw, using his teeth to nip at the sensitive skin below his ear.

Adam's breath shuddered. "I like it," he whispered, so softly that Nick might not have heard him if not for the air carrying the sound to his ears.

Nick hesitated, the warm skin of Adam's neck under his lips. "What was that?"

When he didn't get an answer, he drew back.

The first night Adam brought him here, Nick had followed instincts and pressed Adam down on the couch. Adam had called a stop to it—for understandable reasons—but what had he said?

You're strong. I'm not complaining.

Nick searched his face. He took a chance. He seized Adam's wrist and dragged him. "Come on."

When they made it to the shadowed cavern of Adam's bedroom, Nick didn't hesitate. He shut the door, closing the darkness in around them. Then he grabbed the hem of Adam's shirt and pulled, dragging it over his head.

Then he shoved Adam up against the wall and kissed him again, holding nothing back. He let his hands explore, pinning Adam's wrists when he tried to do the same. Letting Adam's breath guide him.

When the air whispered of fear again, Nick gentled his touch and leaned close to whisper. "You'll tell me to stop if we get too rough?"

"You promise to stop if I say so?"

Nick caught his face in his hands and kissed him. "Yes. Yes, I promise. I will never hurt you. I promise."

Again, his brain whispered. *I will never hurt you again.*

"Then keep going," said Adam.

Nick kept going.

And Adam never said stop.

CHAPTER 27

Nick woke to sunlight peeking through the blinds and Adam's breath on his neck. A muscled arm lay across his bare chest. The air was full of warmth and comfort and satisfaction.

He didn't want to move.

But he was going to have to.

He eased out from under that arm, sliding across the sheets as silently as he was able. He grabbed his jeans from the floor and closed himself in the bathroom, begging the air to trap any noise in here with him.

Nick wished for a toothbrush and a razor, but made do with a capful of Scope, splashing cold water on his face for good measure.

Then he studied himself in the mirror. His hair stood up in tufts, and he ran a hand through it, trying to make it less of a mess. Useless. His cheek sported the bare remnants of a bruise that would probably disappear altogether by tomorrow.

Looking at his face made him think of his twin brother. He needed to get the hell out of this bathroom.

Nick eased the door open and found Adam still asleep, in exactly the same position he'd left him. Soft, even breathing, unruly hair drifting across his forehead. Nick wanted to curl up

next to him and watch him sleep, but he didn't want to live up
to the creepy freak moniker *that* closely.

Nick snatched his T-shirt from the corner and padded out of
the room, pulling the door almost closed behind him.

The clock on Adam's microwave revealed that it was barely
past seven—still early, especially on a Saturday. And now that
he was out here, he wasn't sure what to do. No phone, no car—
not that he had anywhere to go. No television, even.

He made himself useful and poured out the abandoned mugs
from last night, filling them with water to soak in the sink along
with the saucepan. Then he poked around long enough to find
coffee filters and a bag of grounds. He worried that his banging
around would wake Adam, but the air still felt heavy with sleep.

And now that the brewer was dripping, Nick felt awkward,
like maybe he shouldn't be out here alone. What if Adam didn't
want him rifling through his things? What if he didn't want coffee? What if he didn't—

Nick mentally smacked himself. He needed to turn his brain off.

But he couldn't shake the uncertainty, so he stepped through
the sliding door onto Adam's back patio. The air was just this
side of too cool, but Nick didn't mind the bite against his skin.
The rear of Adam's apartment building faced a drainage pond
surrounded by a split rail fence, backed by a row of pine trees. A
fine mist clung to the grass, hanging over the pond and offering
an ethereal quality to the morning. A road ran along the other
side of those trees, but it must have been too early for much
traffic.

Nick dropped onto the edge of the concrete porch, putting
his feet in the grass. Dew grabbed his feet immediately. He inhaled, letting the air draw threads of power to make the fog
drift and sway.

And of course, memories snuck up to sucker-punch him.

Gabriel standing in front of the café, fierce and terrifying, his
eyes dark and his hands in fists. *You don't have to hold him.
Nick will stay down.*

Such a contrast to what had happened before: Gabriel's eyes, tense and worried when Nick woke up in the woods. *Come on, Nicky. You're scaring me.*

Or two weeks ago, when Nick had found his twin crouched in the woods behind the house, dry-heaving against a tree and clutching a broken hand. Gabriel had thought his abilities had started a fire. He'd worried he'd killed his girlfriend. He'd been desperate and broken and sobbing, unable to carry the weight of his secrets any longer.

Nick had brought him into the house and cleaned him up.

And this was how Gabriel acted in return. With mockery. And anger.

And violence.

Nick expected to feel fury, or maybe sadness. All he felt was the gaping cold emptiness of resignation.

Because really, wasn't this what he'd expected all along?

He knew he couldn't stay here forever, but he wasn't exactly sure how he could go home, either. What if Gabriel apologized? Could Nick forgive him? Would he *believe* him?

What if he *didn't* apologize? That seemed more likely. And Nick was supposed to live with that? Sleep in the same house with someone who'd gone from love to hate in less time than it would take him to change clothes?

Nick rubbed at his eyes. He folded his arms across his knees and rested his forehead against them, breathing in the power the air offered.

You're safe here.

The door slid open. Maybe the air simply reacted to Nick's emotion, but the atmosphere practically cheered when Adam stepped onto the patio.

Yay, Adam!

Nick couldn't keep the smile off his face, so he didn't turn around. He peeked over his shoulder. "Hey."

Adam dropped onto the concrete beside him, close enough that Nick could feel the warmth from his body—but far enough that they weren't touching.

"Hey, yourself," said Adam. "Thanks for starting coffee." He held out a mug.

Nick took it, wrapping his hands around the ceramic. He suddenly felt shy, but somehow more self-assured at the same time. "I didn't mean to wake you."

"Yes, you were very loud sitting out here with your feet in the grass. You do realize I have chairs . . . ?"

Nick nodded. "I know." Adam's legs stretched out in the grass, too, one hand holding his own mug of coffee, the other resting on his thigh.

Nick hesitated. Then he reached out, threaded their fingers together, and lifted their joined hands to kiss Adam's knuckles.

Nick's eyes met Adam's brown ones. He'd never felt this way before, like he'd found something precious and fragile that could be taken away. It left him giddy and anxious. Fiercely protective.

Adam smiled. "That look is worth waking up alone."

Nick blushed and looked away. "I'm sorry. I was trying to let you sleep."

"Sleep is overrated." Now Adam shifted closer, eliminating any space between them. He pressed his lips to Nick's neck, abandoning his cup of coffee to stroke his free hand up Nick's chest.

Nick sighed and closed his eyes. He totally should have stayed in bed.

He left his own mug on the concrete to stroke his hand through Adam's silky dark hair, tracing a finger down the length of his dusky chin.

"Where are you from?" he asked without thinking.

Adam laughed softly and straightened. He reclaimed his coffee, but he remained sitting just as close. "Annapolis."

Nick winced and shook his head. "No—I meant—"

"I know what you meant." He hesitated. "My father is from Morocco, and my mother is from Brazil."

There was a lot of weight in that hesitation, and Nick proceeded carefully. "I'm thinking there's a story there."

"Hmm. Not really. He came here because he couldn't find paying work as a doctor in Morocco. Their economy was crap. She was a student at Johns Hopkins. They met three weeks before her visa expired." He gave Nick a wry look. "She tells everyone she married him for the green card."

Nick smiled. "I have a feeling I'd like your mother."

And as soon as he said the words, he realized he was wondering about *meeting* Adam's parents, and the thought struck a bolt of nerves into his chest.

Now he understood how Michael had felt Thursday night.

"She's very opinionated," said Adam. "Likes to rant in Portuguese because it makes my father nuts."

Nick's eyebrows went up. Just when he thought Adam couldn't get *hotter.* "Do *you* speak Portuguese?"

"More than I'll admit. Less than I should. My father grew up speaking Berber—it's like Arabic—but I barely know any of that. He wanted to lose his accent because he thought he'd get better work that way, so he hardly speaks it at all now. Most people can't even tell he wasn't born here."

A new note, something close to bitterness, had crept into Adam's voice. Nick frowned and wondered if he'd made a misstep by opening this line of conversation.

Adam shrugged a little. "He totally bought into the American dream of capitalism and baseball and apple pie—only to end up with a Brazilian wife and a gay dancer for a son."

Adam's father hid who he was. Then he'd asked Adam to hide who *he* was.

Nick wondered what his own father would have thought. While he felt certain his mother would have understood him— would have *supported* him, even—he had no idea how his father would have reacted. Michael had gotten into it with their father more than once, but never over something like this.

Nick stroked a hand across Adam's face. "Do they ever come to watch you dance?"

"Nah. Not really anymore. Honestly, I think my dad secretly hopes I'll outgrow it one day."

"I think your dad should take a second look at how lucky he is."

Adam laughed, but not like it was funny. "You know, if I wanted to do pretty much anything else with my life, I wouldn't need a scholarship. If I called him up and said I wanted to be an accountant, he'd be drafting a check to the college of my choice."

Nick thought of all those college letters sitting in his desk at home and felt a flash of guilt. "I'm sorry."

"Don't be sorry." Adam almost gave him a smile. "It'll mean more if I do it myself." He pressed his face into the curve of Nick's neck again. "Your turn."

"My turn?"

"Tell me something uncomfortable about *your* family."

"I'm pretty sure you witnessed something uncomfortable last night." Nick paused, tracing a finger along the stretch of Adam's forearm.

"Tell me something good then. Tell me something good about your brother."

The words summoned too many memories. Nick couldn't sort through them all. Setting fires on the beach, Gabriel using his power to send the flames coursing high into the air, Nick leeching oxygen from the atmosphere to help him maintain control. Hiding from Michael after putting spiders in his bed or peanut butter in his backpack or paint in his shampoo bottle. Gabriel knowing every single time Nick was worried or hurting or just plain *needed* him.

"We used to trade places all the time. He loves sports, and I . . . well, I really looked for any reason to stay the hell out of a locker room, so he pretended to be me so he could play *more* sports. The school limits you to two, so . . ." Nick shrugged.

"Hmm. And what did you do while you were pretending to be him?"

Nick snorted. "His math homework." As soon as he said it, he realized Adam was going to misunderstand. "Not like you think. When our parents died, he couldn't keep up. I started doing it to help him, just so he wouldn't be held back. It became . . . like . . . a *thing*. He believed he couldn't do it, and I wanted to do that for him. To be there for him. To—" He made a disgusted noise. "This is stupid."

"No. It's not." Adam leaned into him again. "What does he do for you?"

"I don't—it's not—" Nick pressed his fingers into his eyes. "Everything."

He kept hearing Hunter's words on the steps. *I'm not his best friend, Nick. You are.*

Nick realized he didn't even know if his brother had made it home okay.

He hated that Gabriel had monumentally fucked up, but he was still sitting here worried about him. "Can I use your phone again?"

Adam sat up and shifted to pull it out of his pocket. He held it out without a word.

Nick called the house phone. The line rang half a dozen times.

Maybe Gabriel had been hurt. Maybe they were all out looking for him. Nick remembered sensing someone in the woods near the house the other night—had he mentioned that to Michael? He couldn't remember. He'd been stupid to go out of touch for so long. His world could be crumbling right this very second, while he was sitting on Adam's back porch, completely out of reach.

Nick felt his heart pound against his rib cage, chastising him with each beat. He'd let his brother drive off in a fury. God only knew what he could have gotten into.

Tyler. Had Gabriel gone after Tyler? If something had happened, would Chris have thought to find Adam's number on the caller ID last night?

Maybe—

The phone clicked as someone picked up. "Merrick Landscaping."

Gabriel. Nick almost dropped the phone.

He didn't know what to say.

The line filled with silence for the longest time.

Then Gabriel said, "Nicky."

Not a question. He knew. Nick couldn't read anything from his voice. He still didn't know what to say.

And his brother wasn't filling the silence, either.

Finally Nick cleared his throat. "I just wanted to be sure you made it home."

Then, before Gabriel could say anything to that, Nick pushed the button to disconnect the call. He all but shoved the phone back at Adam.

They sat there in silence for a few beats.

Then Adam held the phone out. The display was lit up with an incoming call.

Gabriel was calling back.

"Do you want to talk to him?" said Adam.

"No." His heart was still working double time.

He expected Adam to press the button to refuse the call, but he answered it, putting the phone to his ear and saying "Hello?" before Nick fully comprehended what he was doing.

Nick sat there and stared, torn between grabbing the phone to disconnect the call, and sitting in morbid fascination about what Adam would say.

Adam drew his knees up and rested an arm against them. His voice was low, quiet and confident. "He doesn't want to talk to you right now." A long pause, then he said evenly, "I told you, he doesn't want to talk to you. Maybe you didn't understand me since I wasn't thpeaking in thtereotypes."

Nick snorted with laughter before he could help it, and had to slap a hand over his mouth. It was nervous laughter more than anything. His eyes were wide. No one *ever* talked to Gabriel like that.

Then Adam sighed and spoke into the phone. "Guess what, sunshine? It's not about what you want. I'll tell him you called, okay?"

He didn't wait for an answer. He disconnected the call.

This time, the phone stayed silent.

Adam looked at him. "He wants to talk to you. That's all he said."

Not *I'm sorry*.

Nick's emotions weren't sure how to process that information.

Adam set the phone on the concrete. "Why did you want to call him?"

"I just wanted to make sure he got home." Nick stared out at the dissipating fog. "I was going to tell him. Last night. That's why we were at the coffee shop." He glanced over at Adam. "I keep wondering if it would have turned out any differently."

"You mean, if he would have hit you either way?"

Nick nodded.

Adam shifted across the concrete to sit beside him again. "Look, I'm not going to defend your brother. I know he hurt you." His voice softened. "I know he hurt you a *lot*. But when he came after me, I don't think it had anything to do with me being gay, and everything to do with protecting you. On the phone just now, he wasn't an asshole, either. And he could have been."

"Do you think I should call him back?"

"Do you want to?"

Nick thought about it. He imagined his twin brother standing in the kitchen, deliberating whether to call a third time. Nick wished he could put everything back the way it had been.

Then he glanced at Adam and realized that wasn't true.

He shook his head. "No, I don't want to talk to him. Not yet."

"Okay." Adam took another sip of coffee. He laced the fingers of his free hand through Nick's again, and they sat there for the longest time, watching the mist thin and swirl.

Nick hadn't realized how easy this could be, sitting with someone who wasn't *judging* him. Who wasn't piling expectations on him.

Adam's phone chimed again, and Nick's pulse jumped. He should have known it wouldn't last for long.

But Adam smiled. "Well, look at that," he said. "Quinn wants to know if we're still on for dance this afternoon."

Nick hadn't realized how worried he'd been about Quinn until that very moment. She was okay. She had to be okay if she was sending a text about dance.

Adam was texting back, talking while his fingers slid across the face of the phone. "Studio classes end at one, so I can meet her after lunch. Want to join me?"

Nick looked away. "She probably doesn't want to see me."

Adam poked him. "What do *you* want?"

"I want . . ." Nick paused, feeling weight in the words. His brothers were probably cursing him this morning, because Saturdays meant large landscaping jobs, and Nick knew Michael had blown one off last night. Quinn definitely didn't want to see him at practice.

But his words were hanging out there. *I want.*

Such a stupid, simple phrase, but it felt so foreign.

"You want . . . ?" prompted Adam.

"I want to go with you," he said, the words a jumbled rush that came out too quiet, completely uncertain.

Adam poked him again, harder. He was smiling. "What was that?"

Nick leaned into him and said, "I want to go with you."

Another poke. "I can't *hear* y—"

Nick trapped those words with a kiss. "I want to go with you." Another kiss. "And if you'd shut up a second, maybe I could tell you what else I want."

CHAPTER 28

Quinn leaned against the window of Tyler's truck and closed her eyes, content.

She'd slept all night.

She'd taken a shower unimpeded.

No social workers or cops had shown up to break down the door or whatever they did in real life.

Her younger brother had responded to texts that yes, he was fine.

And Tyler was driving her to dance.

It had been his idea for her to go.

Actually, he'd narrowed his eyes at her over toast and orange juice and said, "Aren't you supposed to be rehearsing for some scholarship thing?"

And she'd mumbled and made excuses until he'd all but sent the text to Adam himself.

Tyler was having none of her self-pity. He kept whispering to her, seeming to know every time self-doubts crept into her head to set up camp. "You're not worthless," he'd murmur, when she started thinking that maybe it *was* her fault that her brother had started smoking crack on her bedroom floor. Or, "You are brave," when thoughts snuck up to talk her out of ever leaving his apartment.

But her favorite was "You are special," whispered while

dropping a chaste kiss on the back of her neck, stroking her hair down her back before moving away.

After going to sleep on a declaration of wanting to kill Nick Merrick, she hadn't realized Tyler would wake up with a mouth full of Hallmark platitudes.

She loved this side of him, this gentle, thoughtful side. She suspected he didn't reveal it often, or to many people.

The funny thing was, if Tyler and Nick weren't mortal enemies, she could see them becoming friends.

"What time are you going to pick me up?" she asked.

"Are you kidding?" He glanced over. "I'm planning on staying."

"Come on," she said. "You don't have to do that. It's not like you're getting any action from m—"

Tyler put a hand over her mouth. "I'm going to pretend you didn't just say that. I told you before: I thought your dance was pretty good, from what I saw on the trail. I'd like to see it all put together."

"Come on. You want to spend a few hours at a dance studio?"

"It's been a dream of mine." He glanced over and offered a wicked smile. "All right, brutal honesty: I brought my laptop. I have a paper due in history."

The dance studio parking lot didn't sport many cars; no surprise on a Saturday afternoon. This was Quinn's favorite time to dance: when the sunlight would be warm through the windows, and energy from the morning classes would still cling to the air in the room, and she'd move as if a thousand dancers accompanied her.

Her home life seemed miles away. Right where she wanted it.

At the door she stopped and faced Tyler. "Hey," she said quietly. "Thanks for bringing me here."

"You're welcome."

She pressed her lips together for a second. "No," she said. "All of it. Thanks for all of it."

He winced and looked away. "Not all of it." He paused and let his eyes find hers. "I'm sorry for some of it. For a lot of it."

The sunlight glinted off his hair. Tall and blond and strong— he looked like the proverbial white knight. All he needed was a suit of armor.

She kept her voice low, and stood on tiptoe to kiss his cheek. "You're special, too, Tyler. And brave. And definitely not worthless."

His eyes widened fractionally, enough that Quinn knew she'd affected him.

"Don't worry," she whispered. "I'll keep all that a secret."

He rolled his eyes and reached for the door handle.

Then they were through the door and face to face with Nick Merrick.

Quinn sat on the polished wood floor, stretching beside the mirror, watching Adam to follow his warm-up. They didn't have the studio to themselves yet, so they'd have to wait to use the main area of floor. She didn't mind the extra time—two days off had left her muscles tight. She folded low, reaching for her ankle, catching sight of Nick and Tyler in the mirror. They sat across the room on the wood risers, a good six feet apart, not speaking.

Waves of hatred radiated from them both.

When they'd first walked in, Nick had told Tyler to leave.

Tyler had told Nick to go to hell.

Adam had told them both to grow up or get out. He'd done it in the same voice she'd heard him use on the six-year-olds when they got rowdy in the beginner class. Half teasing, half serious.

Nick had backed off and found a spot on the risers. He hadn't looked happy about it then, and he looked downright furious now.

But to her surprise, Tyler had apologized to Adam, shaking his hand before finding his own place to sit and watch.

Adam switched legs and Quinn snapped back to the task at hand. She moved to mirror his motion.

"How long do you think we have before they kill each other?" Adam said under his breath.

His voice was easy, casual. She was glad—a small part of her had worried that he'd hold her recent no-shows against her.

"Nick hates him," Quinn said. She hadn't realized Nick would be here at all or she would've told Tyler to go elsewhere. She felt like she was straddling this ravine between taking joy in Nick's discomfort and hating that she'd caused it.

"I can see that." Adam paused. "He was really worried that you were dating him."

"We're not—" She faltered. Were she and Tyler dating? Were they friends? "I don't know *what* we're doing."

Adam put the soles of his feet together and folded low. "Is he being good to you?"

True concern was behind those words, another reminder that Quinn had spent too much time pushing away people who could have helped her. She nodded, thinking of Tyler's whispered comments all morning. Then she gave Adam a wicked smile. "Is Nick being good to *you*?"

Adam blushed. For real.

Quinn grinned and realized there might be a reason behind Nick's being here. "Holy *crap*. Did you guys spend the *night* together?"

"Shh!" Adam reached out and smacked her on the top of the head.

"Did you?!"

He turned it right back around on her. "Did you spend the night with Tyler?"

"Yeah, in his *guest room*." She hesitated, thinking of how Tyler's evening had gone. "He's being a gentleman. And he didn't have the greatest night."

"Neither did Nick. He came out to his brother and got punched in the face."

Quinn sat up straight. She glanced at Nick and lost every ounce of vindictive joy. Now she wanted to kill his twin brother. "Gabriel hit him?" she whispered. "Are you serious?"

"Yeah. He didn't want to go home."

Quinn couldn't blame him. "I wish I'd known," she said. "I wish he'd called me."

Then the irony of her own words smacked her in the face. Nick would probably be saying the same thing about her problems, if he knew.

She glanced across at where Nick and Tyler were sitting. They didn't seem to be speaking. Had Tyler moved closer? She couldn't tell. Nick almost vibrated with angry tension.

"I think I saw the last text you sent him," said Adam, his voice easy, his words not. "I'm pretty sure it said *fuck off.*"

Quinn flushed as guilt punched her in the back. "Yeah—I'm not—I didn't—"

New stretch, hands overhead, then lowering to reach for outstretched toes. "You don't have to explain it to me."

She didn't follow this stretch. "I was jealous," she said quietly.

Adam straightened and looked at her. "Of what?"

She looked away. "Of you. I guess." She swallowed and felt tears gathering behind her eyes. "And then Nick was telling me to stay away from Tyler, and I thought it was so unfair, how he got everything and I had to just sit there and pretend to be his girlfriend, and—"

"Quinn." Adam's voice was low, quiet. He moved close. "Quinn, he shouldn't have asked you to—"

"He didn't! That's the pathetic thing. He never asked me to. He even encouraged me to find someone else. But I didn't want someone else. I wanted . . ."

"Him."

Quinn nodded and looked up. "I'm sorry."

"Don't be sorry." He gave her half a smile. "I mean, I kinda get it."

"Are you mad at me?"

"No." He paused. "I wish you'd told me. Is that why you didn't come to dance?"

She bit her lip. "That's part of it."

"What's the other part?"

She took a deep breath until she was sure her voice wouldn't shake. "My mother—she threw me out."

His face fell. "I wish you'd told me that, too. You could have stayed with me."

She wagged her eyebrows at him. "Sounds like your apartment is kind of crowded."

"Don't do that. Don't joke. Are you okay? Do you have a place to stay?"

She hedged, worrying that if the wrong person overheard her, they'd call social services or something. This paranoia was ridiculous, but she'd rather sleep on a street corner than be forced into a group home or wherever they'd shove her. "I'm staying with Tyler right now. I'm just waiting out my mother." She made her voice casual, easy. "She needs a few days to dry out is all, and she'll forget what happened."

Or maybe she'd throw out Jake's trophies.

Adam was still studying her.

Quinn moved into another stretch, hoping he'd take this as a cue to change the subject. "I'm fine," she said. "Really. I'm fine." Motion in the mirror caught her eye. Tyler had definitely moved closer to Nick.

She'd taken Tyler at his word when he'd said Nick had picked a fight Friday night, but now, watching them, it made her wonder. Tyler had compared Nick's abilities to a rogue lion. Had he poked the lion with a stick, just to watch it break out the fangs?

With a flash of guilt, she remembered Nick's fear in his driveway. He'd hidden it under a layer of self-defense and aggression, but she'd seen it.

She was seeing it now.

Adam glanced over. "Nick said their families are fighting."

"He told you that?"

A nod. "That's why he didn't want you seeing Tyler."

"That's not all of it," she said. "I think Tyler used to beat the shit out of him when he was younger."

Adam froze. "He didn't tell me that."

"He barely told me. I had to drag it out of him. I almost didn't believe him. I mean, you look at Nick and you'd think anyone would be an *idiot* to pick a fight with him, but—"

"It doesn't matter what it *looks like*," Adam snapped. "All that matters is what it really *is*."

"I know," she said quietly. She hesitated. "Tyler isn't a bad guy, either, Adam."

Adam glanced at where Nick and Tyler were sitting. "I hope you're right, Quinn. I really hope you're right."

Nick wondered if he could suffocate Tyler right here and get away with it.

At least it would make this douche bag *shut up*.

"Your boyfriend looks pissed," Tyler whispered, his voice so low that Nick wouldn't have heard him if the air weren't so willing to carry the words to his ears. "Think he's jealous?"

Nick didn't respond. The rest of the studio had cleared out, and they had the risers to themselves. Adam and Quinn were dancing now, their movements full of passion and strength. But Tyler was right: Adam *did* look pissed every time he glanced at where they were sitting.

He couldn't possibly be jealous of Tyler. Right?

But why else would he be pissed off? Had Quinn said something? What?

Nick hated that this dickhead was sitting here putting thoughts in his head.

Part of him wanted to leave. He could sit outside, or even take the bus back to Adam's. Hell, he could take the bus *home* if he needed to—Adam had explained the line and given him a bus schedule, telling him which spot would drop him off closest to Chautauga if he really needed to help his brothers with a job.

But he'd finally broken and called home before coming here, hoping he'd get someone other than Gabriel.

By luck—or his twin's calculated avoidance, he wasn't sure which—Michael had answered the phone. Chris had agreed to work for Nick today. Hunter had already been planning on going with Becca to visit her father. Gabriel would be home alone with a pile of textbooks.

Pretty much a guarantee that Nick wouldn't be getting on a bus anytime soon.

Then again, sitting next to Tyler was quite possibly the only thing worse than facing his twin again.

Tyler shifted closer. "No wonder you could never fight back. I didn't realize Gabriel Merrick had a twin *sister*—"

"Shut up," Nick said.

"Or what? You'll huff and you'll puff and you'll blow this place down? Or do you only know how to blow—"

"Shut *up*." Nick glared at him and didn't bother keeping his voice down. "Fuck you, Tyler. You might have Quinn fooled, but I know what you've done. Michael might give you a free pass because you lost your sister and he feels some shred of responsibility for it, but—"

"Don't you dare talk about my sister."

"You think losing someone gives you a free pass to be a raging asshole? It *doesn't*. You're not the only person who knows loss."

He'd hit a nerve. Tyler was breathing heavily now, his fists clenched. "Shut up, Merrick."

"No, *you* shut up. You want to hate us because of *what we are*? Fine. Hate us. Punch me, burn me, call the Guides, whatever. But I know the truth. I know what you are. I know what you can do."

"You don't know *anything*."

Nick knew Tyler was a breath away from snapping, but he couldn't stop. Standing up to Gabriel had changed something in him. For the better, for the worse, he had no idea. But just like Adam poking him in the side this morning, demanding to know what Nick wanted, Tyler's presence was like a constant jab, over and over again.

And Nick wanted. It. To stop.

He leaned forward, holding Tyler's gaze. "I know you're probably scared to *death* that the wrong person is going to find out you're just as cursed as the big, bad Merricks. Guess it'd be pretty hard to cry to Mommy and Daddy, then, huh? Or do you think they'd pull the trigger themselves? God knows they've been dying to do it to *us* for years."

"I've never *killed* anyone," Tyler hissed.

"How do we know?" said Nick. "It's not like you don't spend every waking moment consumed by *hate*. God, for all we know, you could have been behind the fire at Seth Ramsey's—" Nick broke off and stopped short. "Holy shit."

The fire at Seth Ramsey's. Five years ago. It had killed Seth's parents.

And Nick's.

"Shut up!" Tyler yelled. His eyes were wide and panicked, his expression fierce. "Shut the fuck up, Merrick. I didn't start that fire."

Nick almost couldn't breathe. He couldn't even identify this emotion. Rage. Bewilderment. Shock. Sorrow, all over again. "It was you. You started it. Not Gabriel."

"Wrong," said Tyler. He was shaking his head fiercely. "Wrong."

"I'm not wrong. It was you."

"It was *both of us*," he cried. "Don't you get it? Just like last night. It was *both*."

Nick stared at him.

Tyler climbed down from the risers. He headed for the door.

Quinn and Adam had gone still in the middle of the dance floor. Nick had no idea how long they'd been watching.

Quinn glanced between Nick and Tyler, and finally ran after Tyler. The front door to the studio slammed.

It left Nick reeling, unsure where his emotions wanted to settle.

He was very aware of Adam's eyes still on him.

Nick looked at him. He couldn't speak. He wasn't sure what he would say.

"So," Adam said. His expression was some amalgamation of curiosity, pity, and resignation. "More secrets, huh?"

CHAPTER 29

Quinn caught up to Tyler in the parking lot. There were only two vehicles left: his truck, and a black sedan across the lot that some parent must have left here to come back for later. She grabbed Tyler's arm before he could jump in his truck and take off.

She expected him to spin in a rage and shove her away, but he didn't. He just stopped. He didn't look at her.

"Are you okay?" she said softly.

"No." His voice sounded thick.

"Is what he said true?" she said. "The fire that killed his parents—did you—"

"I don't know." He turned to look at her, and where she expected to find rage and fury, his expression only offered torment. "I don't know, Quinn. I was sixteen years old. My sister was dead. I hated Michael Merrick with everything. I don't—" His voice broke, but he caught it. "Gabriel Merrick hated us, too. They all did. I don't know for sure which one of us started it. But I know I wasn't the only one. I didn't have that kind of power, the way the whole house went up in a flash. Not then."

"But . . . but you've called the Guides against the Merricks. You've tried to have them killed. You stood in your kitchen and told me you've never hurt anyone with your power. What was that about?"

Now she got the fury. "What was I supposed to do?" he snapped. "My parents wanted to kill them for what they'd done to Emily. Was I supposed to stand up and say, 'Guess what, guys. I'm one, too! Let's get cake.' Do you have any idea what it was like for me, knowing what I was, knowing my parents were calling the Guides to come to town to kill off the true Elementals? Knowing I might have played a part in killing my best friend's parents? Do you have *any idea?*"

"No." She wet her lips. "I don't." She paused. "But you kept hurting them. You kept going after them. You went after Becca! You kept—"

"Because I had to!" he exploded. "Because that's what everyone expected! Don't you get it? They killed *my* sister. Everyone thought they killed Seth's parents. I had to hate them."

"Or else everyone would have hated *you.*"

A cool wind whipped through the parking lot, reminding her of Nick. Tyler's breathing was heavy.

"Yeah," he finally said.

She couldn't reconcile this in her head. The sweet things he'd whispered to her this morning, the way he'd helped her with her own insane family, the way he'd gotten in her face and made her confront her own fears about herself.

And then this . . . this *hate* borne of nothing but selfish fear.

"You could stop it," she said. "You could just . . . *stop.*"

"I can't. Quinn, you don't—"

"Didn't you pin me against your bathroom wall and tell me to stop pushing people away? That people would help me if I'd give them the chance? The sad, sorry truth is that the Merricks would probably *help* you if you weren't so determined to be an asshole."

"I don't *want* their help, Quinn."

"So you're just going to keep on being ignorant . . . why, exactly?"

The sarcasm was out before she could stop it. Tyler's face shut down, chasing away any emotion. "You don't understand. This isn't me being ignorant. This is me trying to stay alive."

"Just like they are."

"I can't argue this with you, Quinn." His breathing staggered. "Not now. Not—not now."

She took a step back. "Then go."

He stared down at her.

Then he turned and climbed into his vehicle. He started the engine, but didn't shut the door. He inhaled like he was going to ask her for another chance.

She took another step back. "Go. I'm not coming with you. Go."

A muscle in his jaw twitched. Quinn looked away.

She expected him to beg her to climb in with him, to make more excuses, to apologize, to break down and give in.

He didn't.

"Fine," he said.

Tyler slammed the door and backed out of his parking place, spraying gravel when he turned onto the main road.

Quinn was still standing there, watching the dust settle, when a dark-haired man climbed out of the black sedan and approached her. He was young, mid to late twenties, maybe, with dark eyes and very average features. He wore a sport coat and khakis. If she saw him on the street, she probably wouldn't give him a second glance. He looked like every other daddy of a three-year-old in a tutu.

Maybe he'd seen their argument and he wanted to make sure she was all right.

He said, "Quinn Briscoe?"

She frowned. "Yes?"

Then she kicked herself. What if this guy was a social worker? Or a cop? Wasn't this how it happened? They cornered you somewhere and made you give your name—

"I was wondering if you could help me for a moment," he said.

Sure. Maybe he was legit, or maybe he was a crazy rapist who would take her back to his commune.

But at least that didn't sound like the way a social worker would lead off. "Yeah, what kind of help do you need?"

"My name is Gareth." He pulled out a gun and put it right in her face. "And you're going to help me kill Nick Merrick."

Nick felt Quinn's flare of panic in the air like a bright starburst in his senses, amplified when the door to the studio swung open, sending the chimes ringing through the near empty space.

He grabbed Adam's arm and dragged him to the opposite side of the risers.

Adam inhaled to speak, but Nick got an arm around his neck and slapped a hand over his mouth.

"Be still," Nick said, his mouth right against Adam's ear. "Please. Be still."

Adam went still.

Nick hadn't had time to tell him much about his family, and he definitely hadn't gotten to the part where someone might be trying to kill them.

Quinn was silent, but her fear was a beacon, her shaking breath giving him information with every passing second. Footsteps approached, slow and steady on the wooden floors.

He could also feel whoever was frightening her. Even breaths, pure confidence. There had to be a weapon of some sort, for Quinn to be this pliant.

"See?" she said loudly. "They're gone already."

Please, Quinn, Nick thought. *Please don't be stupid.* He tried not to think of Michael's stories of what Silver had done to Hunter's girlfriend Kate. The torture, the final bullet to the head.

Was this Silver? Had he escaped from prison?

He begged the air for answers, stretching his senses far.

"They're here," said a male voice.

Adam went very still. He held his breath.

"Come on out," said the man. No British accent. Not Silver. But definitely a Guide.

Nick didn't move. There had to be a way out of this.

Had to be.

He tried not to think of his brothers. Had this guy gone after them first? Were his brothers dead and he didn't know it?

Not likely, if they were all together.

Then he remembered his conversation with Michael. They were scattered. That could mean anything.

And not just scattered. Scattered *remotely*. Gabriel would be home alone—with no Nick to warn of danger approaching. Chris and Michael were working a job, and if they were finishing the one Nick and Michael had skipped last night, it was a massive yard away from any other houses. Sitting ducks.

Hell, if the Guide took out Nick and Gabriel, he wouldn't even have to go looking for Chris and Michael. He could just wait for them to come home.

"You've already given me proof," said the man. "I know this girl is innocent. There is no need for her to die."

Think, Nick. God, what the hell use was his GPA if he couldn't think of a way out of here?

"Come out *now*," said the man. "Three seconds and she dies." He didn't hesitate. "Three . . . Two . . ."

"Nick!" Quinn's voice, high and panicked.

"Okay!" Nick shoved Adam down and stood, revealing himself. He didn't recognize this guy at all.

But he recognized the danger of a gun pointed at Quinn's head.

Nick put his hands up to show he was unarmed. "Okay. I'm here. Let her go."

Adam. Stay hidden. Please, Adam.

"That was easy," said the Guide.

Then he pointed the gun straight at Nick's head and pulled the trigger.

CHAPTER 30

The gun fired, and Quinn flew back and hit the wooden floor like someone had given her a hard *shove*. The studio windows exploded outward, but the sound only came to her distantly, as though she were underwater. The overhead lights burst and glass rained down.

Time stopped. She felt as if she lay there for a minute. An hour. A day.

After a while, she realized she could open her eyes. She turned her head.

Glass everywhere, sparkling in the light.

She couldn't see Nick.

She couldn't breathe.

Her ears were ringing and full, and she couldn't seem to move right yet.

Where was the man?

He'd shot Nick. She'd seen the flash, had seen Nick jerk and fall.

She had to run.

She had to get to her phone.

Her brain was racing, but everything else seemed to be moving in slow motion.

Move!

She still couldn't breathe. The pressure was intense, as if an elephant had set up shop right on top of her chest. Her vision was turning spotty.

Had she been shot? She felt like she'd been dropped into liquid amber, and her world was slowly coming to a crystalline stop.

What was *happening*?

And then, without warning, reality snapped back into place. Wind rushed into the studio, chilling her face and making the glass tinkle and drag across the wood.

She could move. She could breathe. She could crawl.

But no. When she rolled over, trying to get to her hands and knees, her body shook and protested the motion. Every joint hurt. Her head swam. Her skin pricked like she'd been sliced open by a hundred tiny knives.

Oh, look. Her arms were bleeding.

The lightbulbs. Glass under her palms.

Nick.

Nick was crumpled on the floor. Not moving.

His eyes were closed. Blood had pooled on the hardwood floor, glistening where glass had collected in it.

She realized she was screaming his name. Glass sliced into her hands and knees as she scrambled toward him.

Then she caught movement from the corner of her eye and flinched, remembering the man.

Hide. Hide, Quinn.

Her brain wasn't working. Hide where? In the open?

But no. It wasn't the man. She didn't see Gareth anywhere.

It was Adam. He was making the same slow crawl across the glass-strewn floor that she was. Blood streaked his forearms. His head was bleeding from the temple—what had happened?

His face was wet. He was crying.

She was yelling. She couldn't move fast enough.

Nick.

Nick.

Nick.

He didn't move at all.

No. No no no no no no.

Adam got to him first. Rolled him onto his back. Nick's arm cracked onto the hardwood floor, lifeless.

Adam was crying his name, too. He was pressing his fingers to Nick's neck, struggling to find a pulse. Adam's words came to her in slow motion, and her brain didn't want to process them.

He doesn't have a pulse.

He's not breathing.

Damn it, Nick.

The side of Nick's face was soaked in blood. It was already caking in his hair.

Oh, Nick. Quinn choked on her sobs.

Adam breathed into Nick's mouth.

And again.

Nothing happened.

Nick's voice was echoing in her head, from the night he'd told her their secrets.

A gun to the head is a surefire way to kill us.

God, now it sounded like a premonition.

She'd done this. She should have fought Gareth in the parking lot. She should have screamed a warning. She should have begged Tyler to stay she should have should have should have—

"Damn it, Quinn!" shouted Adam. "Snap out of it! Can you get to your phone? He's got a pulse. We need an ambulance."

Nick had a headache.

He couldn't open his eyes. He kept flashing on waking up in the woods, Gabriel leaning over him.

Come on, Nicky, you're scaring me.

Air swirled around him, fluttering at his skin, full of pride, seeking his attention.

Yes, yes, he thought. *I'm alive. Good job. This just really fucking hurts.*

He knew he'd been shot in the head, but only kind of distantly. Like maybe one day he'd be able to look back on this and say, "Well, the one time I took a bullet to the cerebral cortex . . ."

No. That was stupid. If the bullet had gone into his brain, he wouldn't be lying here thinking about it, would he?

He felt drunk. He wished he could open his eyes.

He wished he could move.

He smelled oranges and cloves.

Adam.

Oh, and Adam was kissing him. This was nice. Breath rushed across his tongue and filled his lungs. Power flared in his chest, finding his blood and sparking through his body.

Another breath and he could move.

Another breath and he could hear. Quinn's voice. "Come on, Nick. Come on. Please, Nick."

She sounded so worried. Didn't she remember their whole conversation about air pressure?

Another breath. Wait, this kissing was all wrong. Nick brought his hands up and captured Adam's cheeks.

Adam jerked back and swore.

Nick opened his eyes and found wide, panicked brown ones gazing down at him.

" 'Sup?" said Nick.

"Holy shit," Adam whispered.

"Holy *shit*," Quinn echoed. Her bright blue eyes appeared next to Adam's.

"It's . . . it's impossible," said Adam.

"Nuh-uh," said Nick. He shook his head and the ceiling tilted and spun. "It's physics."

"He still needs an ambulance." Adam turned his head to look at Quinn. "Try your phone again. Can you get a signal yet?"

"I can't even get the stupid thing to turn *on*."

Nick sucked in a deep breath, buying himself further clarity. It wasn't working. His brain couldn't seem to organize.

Adam was still staring down at him. "He shot you. I saw—I saw—there's blood—"

"Nothing works," said Quinn. "Whatever that guy did, there's no cell signal, no electricity, no cars on the road—"

"Me," said Nick. He winced as reality started to reform, bringing more pain with it. "I did it."

"What?" said Adam.

"The end of *Twilight* would have been so much cooler if this had happened in the dance studio, wouldn't it?"

"Are you seriously joking right now?"

Nick struggled to shift so he could sit up, and his arms found shards of glass. The pain helped his thoughts focus.

God, his head hurt.

"Easy," said Adam. His voice was still full of mixed emotion, as if panic and wonder battled for space. "Just lie still. Wait for help."

"I can't wait," said Nick, more sure now. "I need to tell— need to warn—"

"We can't warn anyone. Nothing *works*," said Quinn. "It's like a bomb went off or something."

"A bomb did go off," said Nick. "But without the explosion part. Help me up."

He took Adam's outstretched hand and pulled himself to sit up.

It wasn't the best idea. He had to grip hard just to stay upright. His stomach rolled and he worried he'd throw up all over the floor.

He had no idea how much damage his pressure wave had caused, or at what distance. Had he knocked out power to more than this building? What had Quinn said? No cars on the road?

God, he needed his brain to *work*.

"You're bleeding," he said, blinking at Adam.

"Most of it's yours."

Nick reached toward his temple. "No, there."

"Whatever happened knocked me into the wall." Adam glanced left. "Quinn hit the risers." He paused. "You were . . . you were out for a *long* time."

"It didn't hurt that asshole," she said. "He was gone when I woke up."

Of course. "Does he know I'm still alive?" said Nick.

"We didn't know you were still alive until about two seconds ago," said Quinn. "You had no pulse, Nick. You were . . ."

"I'm all right," he said. "I'm okay."

But no pulse. If the guy had checked, he would have thought Nick was dead.

Hell, looking at the pool of blood on the floor, Nick might not have checked himself.

Adam touched his face again, as if trying to reassure himself that Nick was really sitting here talking. His breathing was shaking, just the slightest bit, but his expression was full of resolve. "Why didn't he kill us all?"

"He's only after us. Me and my brothers."

Damn it, he *needed to call home.*

"The office," he said. "Is there a phone?"

"Dead," said Quinn. "We already tried."

Dead.

Chris and Michael were together, but Gabriel was home alone.

Did the Guide know that?

Had he gone there first?

Nick thought of his connection to his twin brother, the way he always seemed to know what Gabriel was thinking, almost before it happened. When Gabriel had rescued Layne from the barn fire, then run home with a broken hand, Nick had *known.* His twin brother's panic had woken him from a sound sleep.

God, he needed his head to *stop hurting.*

Nick pressed his hands to his temples. One came away sticky and wet. He looked at his palm and found a hand covered in blood.

Was he still bleeding?

What had happened to the bullet?

"Help me up," he said again. "I need—we need—"

"You still need an ambulance," Adam said, his voice finding that quiet confidence. "Quinn, I'll run up the road and see if I can find a place with a phone. Keep him still—"

"No," said Nick. If there was any chance the Guide was out there, he didn't want them to separate, too. "No."

"*Yes.*" Adam put his hands on Nick's shoulders. "I don't care what you want this time. You were—you were—" Now his voice faltered, and he visibly struggled to keep it together. "You're hurt. We'll call the cops, and—"

"No." Nick caught his wrists. "We need to get out of here. We need to warn my brothers. He'll shoot them next and they won't—they won't—" Now Nick's voice broke. Gabriel had been able to stop a gun from firing once. Nick had no idea whether he could do it again, especially without Hunter's power helping him focus. Chris and Michael would be on a job, oblivious to a threat sneaking up on them.

Nick thought of Chris's voice, the last thing his little brother had said to him.

I love you, brother.

It sounded so much like a good-bye.

Stop it. Stop it, stop it, stop it. This wasn't helping anything.

"*Help me*, Adam." Nick squeezed his hands and heard his voice break again. "Please. Help me."

"Okay," he said. "Okay. I'll help you."

"Me, too, Nick," said Quinn. "Me, too."

"Me, three," said a voice, and a shoe crunched on broken glass.

They all jumped and scrambled, ready to face a new enemy.

But there in the frame of the broken window, looking shaken and frightened himself, stood Tyler.

CHAPTER 31

Nick swayed with the motion of Tyler's truck. He leaned against Adam and wished his head would stop aching. At Quinn's insistence that they couldn't drive around town covered in blood, he'd washed his face in the studio bathroom—at least the water worked—but now he was damp and cold and shivering. Shock, probably.

Or maybe it had something to do with the agonizing pain he'd felt when he'd pried a bullet fragment out of his own forehead.

Adam had found him on the tile floor, and he'd been ready to drag Nick to a hospital *again.*

But now they were in the truck.

He didn't trust Tyler. At all.

But what choice did he have?

Tyler's cell phone didn't work, either. The Guide's car was still in front of the studio, windows blasted out. The trees along the road had been ripped out of the ground and lay across the parking lot, except for a few taller ones that lay across power lines.

The Guide was on foot, then. Good, in a way, because it would buy them some time.

Tyler had to veer around fallen trees, and every swerve made Nick clench his teeth and grip Adam's hand. The smaller trees and branches, Tyler drove straight over. That was worse. A few cars had run off the road here and there, and sirens wailed in every direction, but they kept driving. Once they got a mile away, trees were standing and they encountered more vehicles, but traffic lights were still nonfunctional.

No one was talking.

In the silence, Nick could only think of his brothers, and he was going to freak the fuck out if he kept doing that.

"What made you come back?" Nick finally asked, making no effort to keep the distrust from his voice.

"Quinn," said Tyler. He glanced over at her, sitting curled in the passenger seat. "I realized you were doing it again, pushing me away to see if I'd snap back."

"No," she said, "I was pushing you away because you were an asshole."

"That, then."

And they lapsed back into silence.

Gabriel, Nick thought. He wished his brother was with them now. He'd know what to do. He'd take charge and organize a plan. He'd figure out a way to find Michael and Chris, or at least a way to warn them.

"They'll be okay," Adam murmured. "We'll find them."

Nick looked up to find his eyes, warm and worried and intent on his. "You're taking this well."

"Don't worry, I'm sure my brain will explode with wtf any minute."

"I'm sorry," Nick said. "I should have—"

"Told me?" Adam gave a small laugh, but there wasn't much humor behind it. "You can fill in the blanks later." He paused. "Well, maybe you can fill in one now. How exactly *did* you do . . . whatever?"

"A pressure wave," said Nick. "You ever see an explosion on television, where it blows people back?"

"Yeah?"

Nick nodded. "Like that. All air pressure. It didn't stop the bullet, but it stopped it *enough*."

Quinn twisted in her seat. "And that blew out the windows?"

Nick winced. "Honestly, we're lucky it didn't bring the building down on top of us."

"You're lucky you didn't wreck my truck," said Tyler, meeting Nick's eyes in the rearview mirror. "The shock wave ran me off the road."

"Yeah, too bad," Nick snapped.

"Hey, dickhead, I'm *helping* you—"

"Shut up," said Quinn. Nick shut up, but she was really glaring at Tyler. She was twisted on the seat and jabbing at him. "You don't get to be nasty to him. You don't get to say *anything* to him. Do you understand me? If you want to talk to Nick, if you want to talk to *my friend*, the first word out of your mouth better be *I* and the next words better be *am sorry*. Otherwise, shut the fuck up and drive."

"Don't waste your breath," said Nick bitterly, though he appreciated the sentiment. "He's not sorry."

Tyler met his eyes in the rearview mirror again, and Nick expected him to snap back with something vicious, but he held the eye contact for a second, then looked away.

He cleared his throat, and when he spoke, his voice was rough. "Can you do that again?" he said. "The pressure wave?"

Nick hesitated, wondering if there was a trap in the question. "I don't know." He paused and glanced down at Adam's fingers linked with his. "I didn't know I could do it in the first place. It wasn't on purpose—sometimes power takes over when we're in danger, and we can't fully control it." His voice turned sharp and mocking. "Know anything about that, Tyler?"

"You covered a lot of ground," Tyler said, ignoring his tone. "At least two miles. Could you do something smaller scale to warn your brothers somehow?"

Nick wasn't sure. He thought of his connection to Gabriel again, tried to focus on it, to imagine what his brother was doing *right now*.

Was this a typical twin connection? Or did it have something to do with his element? Did the air *know* Gabriel, know their bond? All this time, was it just a matter of feeding power into the atmosphere?

He had no idea.

"Open the windows," he said.

Tyler pushed the button, and wind streamed through the truck's cab. Nick listened to the air, threading his power among the currents.

Danger, the wind whispered.

No kidding, he thought back. But then he paid more attention, focusing on the source of that danger. The clouds overhead were shifting, darkening in the south, promising a storm sometime in the future.

A storm. Rain.

Chris.

But Nick didn't sense Chris's power in the storm. Feeding energy into the wind might get them nowhere.

Tyler came to a stop sign at the end of Magothy Beach Road. "Still going to your house?" he said.

"Wait," said Nick. "Just wait."

They were half a mile from the house now. The air here was calmer: the storm was a few miles off yet.

Gabriel, he thought, sending power into the sky.

For an instant, nothing.

Then he felt it, his brother's presence, like a blazing beacon in his mind.

"Fire," said Tyler.

"Where?" asked Quinn. Nick didn't sense it, either—but then again, he wasn't a Fire Elemental.

And then he felt it, the reason danger rode the wind. It had nothing to do with the storm in the east.

And everything to do with the smoke to the west.

Quinn spent each moment vacillating between wanting to kill Tyler and wanting to hug him.

"Stay in the truck," he snapped, when he parked alongside the woods. She could smell the smoke now, a primal scent that warned her to stay away.

But she glared at Tyler and climbed out anyway.

"Stay in the truck," Nick agreed. But he wasn't focused on

her. He was focused on the woods. She wondered how much he could sense, whether Gabriel was in immediate danger. "This guy isn't messing around. You *saw* that."

"He didn't shoot me in the dance studio," she said. "Didn't you tell me that they don't kill normal people?"

"They kill anyone," said Tyler, "if it leads to the greater good. He didn't kill you in the dance studio because you weren't a threat."

"Well, I'm not exactly a *threat* now—"

A gun fired in the woods, and Nick and Tyler both jerked her down and against the truck. Adam crouched beside them.

"I am not helpless!" she snapped. But her heartbeat was in her ears, blocking other sounds.

Nick was practically breathless. Too pale. He'd healed his head wound, but she wondered how much damage he'd really taken. "Can you get to the house?" he said. "Everyone's number is on the wall. Call Michael. Tell him—tell him—"

"I'm not leaving you," she said.

"Damn it, Quinn, I can't help them all! I need—I want—"

Another gunshot. Everyone froze.

The wind kicked up, a sudden gust that lifted her hair. The air temperature dropped ten degrees. Nick went paler, if that was possible. "He's hurt. He's hurt. He's—"

Another shot.

"Go," said Tyler. "If you can get to a phone, call nine-one-one."

"We'll go," said Adam. "Come on, Quinn."

Then he grabbed her hand and dragged her, not leaving any room for argument.

CHAPTER 32

The woods blazed with fire, consuming dead leaves and trees and anything it could find to burn. Nick moved beside Tyler, hating that his mortal enemy was going to be at his side when he found his brother's body.

Stop thinking like that.

But he couldn't sense Gabriel now. The flames were too thick, and smoke clouded the sky, blocking what sunlight crept through.

More fire was good, right?

Or did it mean that Gabriel had lost all control, and the fire was raging of its own accord?

Nick stumbled and lost his footing.

Tyler caught his arm and hauled him to his feet.

Nick struggled and wrenched his arm away from him. His head still wasn't ready for this much movement, and he hit the ground anyway, landing in burning leaves.

"Fine," said Tyler. He took a step closer to Nick and the fire moved away from him, leaving Nick alone, too. "Do it your way. Face this guy while you can barely stand up."

"Fuck you," said Nick, despising that he wasn't even strong enough to find his brother on his own. "I don't want your help."

Gabriel. Gabriel, Gabriel, Gabriel. Where are you?

"He's not dead," said Tyler.

"You don't know that."

"I do." Tyler reached down and scooped up a handful of fire, letting it burn from nothing, a rolling ball of flame suspended over his palm.

Nick stared. He'd seen Gabriel do this hundreds of times. It was unsettling to see the same show of power from Tyler.

"Fire likes him," said Tyler. "It likes me, too. He's still alive out here. He's just hiding." He glanced up at Nick. "If I can follow the flames to find him, so can the Guide. He's being smart. Not using his power. Letting the smoke cover him."

It was covering him and Tyler, too, and Nick could keep the smoke dense around them. But Gabriel was hurt—the air or their twin connection or *whatever* had told Nick that much.

In a flash, Nick realized that all this panic he was feeling wasn't just his own. Fear bled through the smoke, riding the very air to find Nick's senses.

I'll find you, he thought. *I'll save you.*

He remembered playing hide-and-seek with James, and Nick threw power to the wind, opening his senses fully.

Seek.

In his mind, he saw the land as a grid, the atmosphere stretching around him in a circle, locating people like flashing pinpoints on a map. Him and Tyler. Quinn and Adam, running like hell.

The Guide, a flare of power so bright that Nick wondered how the guy had snuck up on them at the dance studio.

And Gabriel, a fading light. Not far. Maybe fifty feet straight ahead.

Nick's temper flared and the air responded, shifting, moving the smoke. Wind whipped through the trees, bringing debris and flaming sparks to sting his skin.

"This way," he said to Tyler, and started walking.

Tyler caught his arm. "He has a gun."

More wind, blowing harder. It ruffled Nick's hair and fed him power, sending smoke spiraling. "He shot my brother." Then he jerked free.

Nick kept his mind focused on the Guide, letting his wind swoop and whirl, remembering his demonstration for Quinn, the way he'd surrounded her with leaves.

This time, he did it with fire.

He did it carefully, the way he'd done for Quinn, slowly at first, enough power that it wouldn't be noticed right away. But then he sent it spiraling high enough to block forward motion, sending it faster and faster, until he could *see* it, a near tornado of fire, trapping the Guide inside. At the same time, he drew oxygen into the flames from the inside, choking the man where he stood. Tyler helped, feeding power to the fire, until it was a spinning web of energy and destruction.

For an instant, Nick felt a rush of victory. He'd close this knot, collapse the flames. The Guide might not die, but he'd lose consciousness.

Then he could die from other things.

But then power flared back at him. The tornado began to expand. Nick's tight cone of power loosened, like a skein of yarn being shaken free.

"Oh, shit," said Tyler. Nick could feel his struggle to keep the fire where it needed to be—but the air pressure was too strong.

In that instant, Nick knew what was happening. The Guide was gathering power, building the same thing Nick had done in the dance studio: a blast of air pressure that would radiate outward.

This blast would flatten the woods. It would knock out Nick and Tyler, and possibly kill Gabriel, all in one wave of power.

Worse, the outside of this pressure wave would be a wall of fire. Nick had compared the dance studio to a bomb going off—this really *would* be like a bomb going off. From the strength behind the force, this would be enough to level the neighborhood.

Reverse it.

Nick's element kicked in before he'd completed the thought, using every ounce of power he had to collapse the air pressure around the Guide. It pulled the spiraling flames in toward his quarry, and he felt the Guide fighting it, scrambling to send power outward.

Nick wasn't going to be strong enough. The fire glowed brighter, fed by the oxygen in the air. The circling flames accelerated, ready to pull free of his control.

His knees landed in the underbrush as he struggled. His eyes clenched closed. He begged his element for the upper hand, feeling as though he grasped for nothing more than empty fistfuls of air. The spiral loosened further.

He was going to lose it.

Tyler grabbed his forearms, and his hands were full of burning pain.

Nick gasped, and his eyes snapped open.

"Do it," Tyler said. "Do it, Nick. You think of every goddamn thing I've ever done to you, and you *make this happen*."

Nick thought of it. He couldn't *not* think of it, the way Tyler's fingers burned into his skin.

Tyler's voice grew louder. "You think of how much you hate me. You think of how I know you're the weakest, most pathetic Merrick."

Nick gritted his teeth. Tyler's hands were scalding hot, but the pain didn't steal Nick's clarity, it enhanced his focus. Nick swallowed. He gained an inch with the air. Lightning cracked among the spinning flames.

"You know what I thought when Quinn told me you were gay?" said Tyler, his voice low and insidious. "I thought, *well, doesn't that fucking figure.*"

Another inch. As soon as he killed this Guide, he was going to kill Tyler.

"At least I got to meet your boyfriend," Tyler said. "Now I have someone to mess with when I'm waiting for Quinn. He won't be able to fight me off, but—"

With a scream of rage, Nick threw him back. He felt a *snap* in the air. Anything not tied down went surging forward, toward the Guide. Fire, leaves, underbrush.

That included him and Tyler. They hit a tree.

Reverse pressure. Nick couldn't breathe. All the fire died as oxygen was sucked from the air. For an instant, he couldn't *think*, as if time were suspended.

Then the pressure gave. Wind exploded from the middle of the woods, blowing leaves and underbrush back out. Twigs and branches caught exposed skin.

Nick hit the ground. Then something wet hit him on the cheek.

And on the arm.

For an instant he couldn't move. Then his limbs decided to work. Nick swiped at his cheek and came away with fingers full of blood. And something thicker.

Oh, god.

"Holy shit," said Tyler. "You—you blew him up."

His voice held the same awed fascination that Nick would expect from his twin.

"We," said Nick. He needed to find his brother.

Nick ignored the pain in his arms, the speckles of blood decorating his shirt. "Gabriel!" He staggered toward where he'd sensed his brother the first time. "Gabriel!"

Nothing.

But then Nick saw him, lying motionless among charred leaves. He'd been shot, more than once, from the amount of blood soaking his clothes. His face was darkened with soot. Nick could smell the blood once he got close.

But his brother was breathing. He could *feel* that.

Nick got down close to him. "Gabriel." His voice was shaking and he didn't care. "Come on. Gabriel. Open your eyes."

Then, to his wonder, Gabriel did. "Nicky." His eyes fell closed again.

"Come on. Open your eyes again." Nick patted his brother's pockets, looking for his phone.

Dead. Damn it.

"Guides," said Gabriel. "I have to find you."

"You found me," said Nick. "We got him. You're okay."

"Both?" asked Gabriel.

Nick frowned. "What?"

"Hey, douche bag," Tyler called from twenty feet away. "Didn't you say you were shot by a guy?"

Nick froze. "Yeah?"

"Well, there's a hand here, still wrapped around a gun, if you can believe that. And either the dude who shot you liked a nice French manicure, or the Guide you just killed was a woman."

Quinn's lungs were burning by the time they made it up the hill to Nick's house. She'd been inhaling smoke the whole way, but adrenaline was kicking her ass and keeping her going.

So was Adam's presence beside her.

With every step, she kept seeing Gareth pulling the gun and shooting Nick in the head. It made her want to turn back.

Phone, she thought. *Get to a phone.*

The landscaping truck was in the driveway.

Quinn almost screamed in relief. Nick's brothers were here! They could help!

She didn't even bother knocking, just grabbed the front doorknob and pushed through to the foyer.

Her eyes registered everything at once.

That Gareth guy wasn't in the woods with Nick and Gabriel. He was here, *right here*, in the Merrick living room.

Michael and Chris were on their knees. Chris was shaking. She could hear his breathing from here.

She didn't blame him. Gareth held a gun barrel three inches from his forehead.

"Oh, god," she whispered.

"Come on in," Gareth said. "If you've come to warn them, you'll see you're too late."

Quinn couldn't move. She wished she could tell Adam to get the hell away from the house, before he was seen.

"Your friend, too," said the Guide. His voice sharpened. "Now. Or this one dies. Three . . . two—"

Adam shoved her through the door, keeping a hand on her shoulder. "We're inside," he said, his voice very careful. "We'll do what you want."

"I want you both to sit down," Gareth said evenly. "We won't be here long."

"Please," said Quinn. She couldn't look away from Chris's terrified eyes. His breathing had kicked up during Gareth's countdown. The gun didn't waver.

All she could think was, *Becca, I'm going to watch your boyfriend die.*

"Please let them go," she said. "They haven't hurt anyone."

"Sit," said Gareth.

Adam took her hand and dragged her toward the couch. She started to speak again, but he squeezed her hand so tightly that she gasped.

Then they sat in silence, listening to nothing but Chris's fractured breathing. So long that she wondered what they were waiting for. So long that Chris's fear began to capture her, too, until tears slipped down her cheeks.

"Hey," said Adam softly, talking to the Guide. "He's a kid. Why don't you let him go and put the gun on someone else?"

"You think he's just a child? He's a Water Elemental. I let him go, and suddenly I have blood boiling in my veins or frozen eyeballs or anything else he can come up with. Isn't that right, Christopher Merrick?"

Chris didn't speak.

"He doesn't do that," said Michael.

"He should do it now," said Quinn. Her voice was thick with tears, but strong. "If you're going to go out, Chris, you should do it with a bang."

Chris shook his head, just a fraction, just enough.

"He knows," Gareth said, "I'm supposed to witness evidence of destructive abilities before I kill him. Nicholas and Gabriel demonstrated that last night. You two, however . . ."

"Then let us go," said Michael. "We're not going to demonstrate anything."

"I bet I can make you show a little something," said Gareth. He cocked the hammer and pointed the gun lower.

"No!" she screamed.

She didn't know what she expected. Maybe some kind of Elemental show. But Michael moved, shoving Chris hard, pushing him to the ground, shielding him with his body. The gun fired.

The bullet missed Chris, but Michael cried out. Blood bloomed on his shirt. A lot.

But at least it wasn't his head.

The Guide aimed again.

Quinn didn't think. She flew off the couch. Her hands slammed into Gareth.

For the first time, she was glad she wasn't one of those stick-thin twigs who lived on lettuce and water. He wasn't a big guy, and she had the element of surprise. She hit him with the full force of her rage, and he went down.

But *damn* he was strong. She tried to go for his gun, but he was faster.

Then Adam was there, adding his strength to hers, pinning Gareth's arm, trying to pry the gun from his fingers.

They were going to get the gun. And she was going to shoot this fucker in the forehead and see how he felt about it.

But she'd forgotten Gareth wasn't an ordinary human, limited to finite things like strength and leverage.

Suddenly, she couldn't breathe. At first she kept fighting, trying to get the gun anyway. But black spots danced in her vision. Her muscles started to cramp. Her fingers couldn't grasp at the steel.

Adam was suffering the same thing.

She had to let go of the gun. The Guide shoved her to the side. He freed himself from their weight and stood. He aimed at Michael.

Quinn needed to move.

She needed to stop this. She needed to *stop this*.

She couldn't.

She was going to see two people get shot in the head on the same day.

Only she didn't think Michael was going to be able to stop this one.

The gun was in Gareth's hand.

He cocked the hammer.

The sound of the gunfire made her jump. Tears sprang to her eyes again.

But Michael was still staring, still bleeding, still covering his younger brother.

The Guide was on the ground.

Quinn stared. Her brain couldn't make sense of it.

Gareth was quickly creating his own blossom of red on the beige carpeting of the Merrick living room. He'd been shot in the head.

And Tyler was standing in the doorway, a gun in his hand.

"There," he said, sounding like he was panting. "Now I don't owe you anything anymore."

CHAPTER 33

For the second time that day, Nick sat with Adam on the concrete step of his patio.

Now, the sun was nearing the horizon, and Quinn was in Adam's bathroom, taking a shower.

Six inches of space separated Nick from Adam.

It felt like a mile. They'd been sitting in silence for a while.

"Are you okay with everything?" Nick finally asked.

"I'm not sure *okay* is the right word." He rubbed at his jaw. "It's a lot. I watched someone *die* today." He paused. "More than once. And very . . ." He shook his head. "Very *violently*."

Nick nodded.

"Your brothers. They'll all heal?" Adam said. "Just like—like you did?"

Another nod.

Adam's eyes flicked over, dark and shadowed in the moonlight. "Your brother Michael can . . . get rid of the bodies?"

"Yeah." Nick didn't correct him to *body*, singular. He hadn't told Adam exactly what had happened to the Guide in the woods. He wasn't quite ready to deal with that himself. Nick still had no idea who she was or where she'd come from.

Or if there were more out there.

Hunter and Becca had brought her dad, Bill Chandler, back to the house when they'd called to tell them what had happened.

Bill had looked at Gareth's body and had said to Michael, "You all killed Gareth Brody. You might not have wanted a war, kid, but I think you just started one."

Adam studied Nick in the darkness, his eyes full of wary uncertainty. Nick wondered if this was the *wtf* coming home to set up shop.

Adam frowned. "And the studio . . . if the police come knocking, you expect me to tell them we left before anything happened? That we had no idea?" His voice was level, even.

Nick shifted on the step to look at him. "I don't expect you to do anything, Adam. You don't need to keep my secrets." He sighed, resigned. "I know what I am. I know what happened. If you want to tell the cops everything, I can't stop you."

Adam nodded.

And that could mean anything.

"Okay," Nick said softly. "I don't want—" He hesitated. "I'll leave."

He waited for Adam to protest. Adam didn't.

Nick stood and opened the sliding door. His voice was rough now. This was a thousand times worse than when they'd been caught by Hunter. "Thanks for taking care of Quinn," he said.

Then he didn't wait for a response. He slid the door closed and walked through the apartment to the front door.

Follow me. Please. Follow me.

Adam didn't. Nick made it up the steps of the apartment building, through the locked front door, and across the parking lot.

But when he pressed the button on the car door clicker, Adam's voice stopped him.

"Nick. Stop. Wait."

Nick turned. Adam was jogging across the stretch of pavement to catch up with him.

Nick wasn't sure what he expected. A kiss, a plea to stay, a *hug*, for god's sake.

But Adam stopped and said, "Why didn't you tell me the truth about Tyler?"

Nick frowned. "I don't know what you mean."

"Quinn told me that when you were younger, Tyler used to beat the crap out of you. That Gabriel used to stop him."

Oh.

Nick leaned against the car and memorized the asphalt. "I didn't lie to you. Tyler *is* an asshole." But he couldn't say it with the vitriol he usually saved for Tyler Morgan.

Adam didn't say anything.

Nick glanced up, then quickly away, feeling the weight of Adam's eyes, knowing he needed to offer more of an answer. "I never told you because I was embarrassed." Another hesitation. "And because I didn't want to diminish what had happened to you."

"I wish I'd known." Adam hesitated. "And what happens to you doesn't *diminish* anything that happens to me."

"It's fine. It's not a big deal."

Adam moved closer, and Nick froze. "It *is* a big deal. All of this is a big deal. If you're in danger—if someone is threatening you—" He broke off and swore. "Damn it, Nick. If this is going to work, you have to trust me to care about you *back*."

If this is going to work. Nick stared at him.

But Adam still looked agitated. "You made it sound like—I thought it was some stupid family rivalry. I yelled at you at the studio, and I would have—I *should have* told him to get the hell out of there." He put his hands on Nick's face, warm and strong and secure.

But then he shook his head. "I'm so pissed that you thought you had to sit there with him."

Nick put his hands over Adam's and held them there. "No. I'm glad I had to sit there with him. Because I finally got the chance to tell him off."

Honestly, now that they'd come to this point, Nick wondered why he hadn't said something to Tyler *years* ago.

No, he knew why. Because he'd never met anyone who made him feel like he had a right to what he wanted, not just what everyone else *expected*.

"Besides," Nick said. "You were right. People *do* have different capacities for failure."

"And triumph," said Adam. Then he leaned forward and kissed him.

He drew back before too long, but not far. His voice was soft. "Can you stay?"

Nick wanted nothing more.

But he shook his head. "Michael will have a panic attack if I'm not home soon. Too much is up in the air."

"Are you in danger?"

"We're always in danger."

Adam stroked a finger along Nick's cheek. "Can danger wait five minutes?"

Nick smiled. "Danger can wait ten."

Darkness had claimed the sky by the time Nick made it home. Michael was waiting for him in the living room, re-arranging the furniture to cover a large cut-out portion of carpeting. Nick could hear Chris and Becca and Hunter having a hushed conversation in the kitchen.

"I was about ready to send out a search party," Michael said.

Nick flung his keys on the side table. The day had been long and terrifying. But now that his family was safe, old worries forced their way back into his head. "I'm fine. They're fine." Michael looked like he was going to start picking, and Nick wanted to head that off at the pass. "What happened to Tyler?"

"He helped make sure the woods were clear, offered to help re-carpet the living room, and then he left."

Nick scowled. He'd hoped Tyler would be the usual selfish prick he knew him to be. "Wow, that was generous of him."

"Sometimes," said Michael, "when a fight has been going on for a long time, it stops being about who's right and who's wrong, and it starts being about who can bury the hatchet first."

Nick was too tired for this. "Thanks, Yoda. Wise words, you say." He headed for the stairs.

"Hey," Michael called after him. "I'm not just talking about Tyler."

Nick didn't pause. "Caught the subtext, Mike. Really understated."

Nick expected Michael to say something else, but his older brother moved away from the bottom of the stairs.

When Nick made it to the top, Gabriel was leaning against his bedroom door frame. Waiting.

Nick had known he would be. He'd known it almost since he'd walked through the front door.

His twin looked worn. Tired and drawn. Nick knew the feeling. But Gabriel's bullet wounds had healed. A good night's sleep and some sunlight and he'd probably be good as new.

"Hey," Gabriel said. Hesitant, probably for the first time ever.

Nick was tempted to blow right past him and slam his door in Gabriel's face. But he stopped. "Hey."

"Will you come in? Will you talk to me?"

Nick glanced at his own door. "I'm tired."

"Nicky." Gabriel's voice was rough. "Nicky, I just—"

"Stop," said Nick. He realized he didn't want to listen to this. He didn't want to *hear* it. He wished he *had* stayed with Adam, and Michael's worry be damned. He wanted to run to his room and slam the door and never face his twin brother again.

No. That wasn't true.

Nick stepped up to Gabriel and kept his voice very low. "Save it. Don't apologize. I might have saved your life, but that doesn't mean we're okay. You said in the car that you wished you knew why I was keeping something from you. I guess you got your answer, didn't you?"

Gabriel visibly flinched. "Nicky—"

"Stop calling me that. Stop talking to me. You can't undo what you did. Ever. Do you understand that?"

He didn't wait for an answer but turned for his bedroom. He didn't bother with slamming his door. He just pushed it closed.

For half a second, he wished Gabriel would push it open.

He didn't.

Nick stared at the paneled wood and wondered if what he'd said was true.

You can't undo what you did. Ever.

He thought of Tyler coming back for Quinn. Or in the woods, grabbing Nick's arms and reminding him of past wrongs, feeding him enough power to stop the Guide.

Or later, Tyler with a gun, pulling a trigger to save Michael. Risking his life. Tying himself to their fate.

Had that undone the years of torment?

Nick wasn't sure.

He thought of everyone around him, what they wanted, what they needed. It felt so natural, so comfortable, rearranging what he wanted to fit what he thought they needed.

He almost went back into the hallway to listen to his twin brother.

But then he stopped. He thought about what *he* wanted. What he needed.

Without hesitation, he went to his desk and pulled out the stack of college envelopes he'd hidden.

Then he slid his finger under the first flap and started ripping.

CHAPTER 34

Quinn was in French class Wednesday morning when the call from the guidance office came.

And just like that, she *knew*.

She'd been living with Adam, and she'd told him it would only be a few days, until her mom dried out. He'd told her she could stay as long as she needed. And the longer she went with a quiet home, a clean shower, and eight hours of sleep, the less she wanted to leave.

But she knew that was unrealistic. Adam had one bedroom and one bathroom. He was dating Nick, and she felt like more of a third wheel with them than she had with Chris and Becca.

She hadn't heard from Tyler since she'd seen him kill the Guide.

She wasn't sure she wanted to talk to him, either, but it hurt that he hadn't reached out to her.

And now, walking down empty school hallways, terror settled into her muscles, slowing her pace.

They couldn't make her go somewhere, could they? Brittany Asher had been in foster care, and she'd told horror stories around the lunch table about gross foster fathers sneaking into her room in the middle of the night. Or foster mothers whose tempers would rival Quinn's mom's.

Quinn stopped in front of the door to the office.

She couldn't breathe. Her eyes blurred.

She had to run. She could hide.

"Quinn?"

Quinn swiped a sleeve over her eyes. Becca's mother stood there, signing in for a visit to the office. Quinn almost didn't recognize her in street clothes—the woman practically lived in nursing scrubs.

And Quinn was standing here with a running nose and heaving shoulders.

Mrs. Chandler abandoned the sign-in book and put her hands on Quinn's shoulders, rubbing gently. "Are you okay, sweetie?"

Quinn shook her head. "I don't—I don't—they're going to take me—"

Then she couldn't hold it in anymore, and she was crying on Mrs. Chandler's shoulder, clutching at her sturdy form. *This* was what a mother was supposed to be like: all soft curves and gentle hands and quiet support.

"Please don't let them take me somewhere," Quinn said, clinging to any possibility that an adult could fix this. She knew she wasn't making sense, but she couldn't stop *begging*. "I want to go home. Will you tell them it's okay? Tell them to let me go home. Please—"

"You can't go home," Mrs. Chandler said gently. "Not now, Quinn."

Quinn cried harder. She couldn't stop shaking. "Please. Please help me."

"Oh, I'm going to do that. Calm down now." She stroked Quinn's back. "Let's go inside and talk about it. We're supposed to be doing this with your guidance counselor."

Quinn lifted her head. "What?"

Mrs. Chandler pulled tissues out of her pocket. "I called to set up the meeting. I just found out about your mother, and your brothers, and what's been going on in that house of yours."

Quinn sniffed and swiped at her eyes. "But I didn't—Becca doesn't know—"

"Well, she will soon. If I get my way in here, you and your younger brother are going to stay with me until your mother can get into a treatment program."

"But—but—"

"But nothing, Quinn." Her voice was gentle, but stern. "I've always told you that my door is open to you. We've never had any secrets between us. I wish you'd told me what you were going through."

"I'm sorry." Fresh tears welled. "It got—it got out of control so fast—"

"I know. I know. Come on, let's go inside and see if we can work something out."

Quinn nodded and wiped at her eyes again, scared to let herself feel something like hope.

But when Mrs. Chandler pushed at the door to the office, Quinn said, "Wait. If Becca didn't tell you, then how did you know?"

"Your friend called me this morning. He said he got my number from Michael Merrick. He wanted to help you, but he wasn't sure how. He sounded pretty upset about what was going on, but he didn't want something bad to happen to you."

Quinn's heart was pounding. "My friend? Who?"

"Nice young man. Said he knows Becca, too. Tyler Morgan."

By Wednesday night, Nick and Gabriel had settled into an uneasy truce.

Well, Nick had settled into one. He lived in the house and went through the motions of living with four other guys, but where his twin was concerned, he went out of his way to avoid him. He caught a ride to school from Michael or Hunter. He went to the studio at night to watch Adam and Quinn dance. He studied in his room with the door closed.

At first, Gabriel had dogged him, begging for a chance to apologize. Nick had ignored that.

Then, true to form, Gabriel had turned antagonistic, mocking his silence. That was even easier to ignore.

But tonight, Adam had class and Quinn had texted that she was busy, so Nick was home. He'd been ready for more hassling from his twin, but Gabriel was the one staying out late.

Nick wondered if his twin was avoiding *him*, now, if he'd made it so uncomfortable that Gabriel didn't even want to be in the same house with him.

Good.

Actually, tonight, Nick was glad for his twin's absence. He found Michael sitting in a dim kitchen, hunched over his laptop. A stack of invoices sat next to him.

Nick stopped short. "I can do that."

"I know you can," said Michael. "So can I." He looked at Nick, then nodded at the pile of papers in his hands. "What do you have? Something for school?"

"Sort of." Nick hesitated. "I need to tell you something. Ask you something. Whatever."

Michael uncapped a bottle of water and took a sip. "Shoot."

Nick pulled a chair free and eased into it. "My physics teacher said he needs a decision about that semester of math and science at Maryland this spring." The words were rushing out, and he couldn't figure out Michael's expression, so he kept talking. "It's college credit, and they only accept a few students from each high school, but it's also a lot of work. I don't want to take time away from the business, because I know spring is our busiest season."

His brother frowned. "Are you asking me if you can do it, or trying to get me to tell you not to?"

Nick took a breath. "I have no idea."

Michael closed the laptop and pushed it to the side. He leaned in against the table. "Forget the business. What do you want to do?

"I can't *forget* the business, Michael. It's—it's not like it's your side job or something. I'm not going to cut back on my hours if that means the family needs to live on ramen noodles for the entire year." He rolled his eyes. "We might not even *make* it to spring anyway, so I don't know why I'm even considering this."

"The same could be true of anyone on earth, Nick. When the Guides come, they come. We keep doing what we've always done. *Not revealing our true abilities.*"

Nick didn't say anything to that. There was a warning there.

Michael studied him for a long minute. "Stay here. I want to show you something."

He wasn't gone long. When he returned, he had a beat-up white Teflon envelope stuffed with papers. He tossed it on the table in front of Nick.

Nick glanced at it, then back up at Michael.

"Go ahead. Open it."

Nick slid the contents out of the envelope. The papers were wrinkly and a little worn. On top was a college letter addressed to Michael. From five years ago.

Welcoming him to LSU.

Nick read the next line and snapped his head up. "They offered you a baseball scholarship."

Michael shrugged. "I had two offers, actually. Money from a lot of other places, too. The letters are all in there."

"But why didn't you . . . why . . ." He didn't even know how to finish that sentence.

He *knew* why.

He met Michael's eyes. "Does anyone else know?"

"Nope."

"I won't tell."

"It's not a secret, Nick." Michael paused. "Mom and Dad knew. I'm surprised they didn't have banners made. You'd have thought I won the lottery or something. But when they died, there wasn't any question of what I needed to do."

Nick's throat felt tight. He couldn't meet his brother's eyes.

Michael put a hand on his arm. "Stop. Look, I didn't show you this to make you feel *bad*, Nick. I could never have gone off to school and left you guys. This isn't a guilt trip."

Nick nodded. But he felt the guilt all the same.

"You're a smart kid, and you work your ass off." Michael squeezed his arm. "Mom and Dad wouldn't have wanted you to throw away an opportunity. They would have been proud of you, too."

Nick made a sound that was half laugh, half sob. "Would they have been proud of all of it?"

"Yeah, Nick." No hesitation. "They would have been proud of everything you are."

Nick swiped at his eyes and looked back at Michael's letters. "Do you regret it?"

"Regret? No. Do I think about what ifs?" He shrugged again, then smiled a little ruefully. "Yes. Every spring when I watch Chris play."

"What are you going to do with the business, though? If Gabriel and Hunter are going to take the EMT course, and—"

"Nick, it's fine. I'll hire some people."

He dropped the words so simply that Nick felt like an idiot for not even thinking about it. "You'll—wait. What? You can do that?"

Michael leaned back in his chair. "Sure. I'd probably like it. I could do a job with someone who won't give me a load of crap at the dinner table or sneak out of the house."

Nick studied him. "You sound like you've been thinking about that for a while."

Michael paused, and now he looked a little hesitant. "At dinner, Hannah's father had some thoughts about how I could expand the business . . . maybe do more with it . . . I don't know. It's something to think about. Maybe this college course is a sign." He grimaced. "And honestly, Nick, you'll need all the help you can get. You know we don't have a lot of money for college."

"Well," said Nick, "maybe I can help with that." He shoved his original stack of letters across the table.

Michael read the first. Then the second.

He didn't even get to the third.

He was too busy pulling Nick out of his chair to hug him.

CHAPTER 35

Nick sat in the darkened auditorium, watching auditions, feeling the music as it rolled through the theater. Adam and Quinn had been sitting with him, offering running commentary on every dancer to take the stage. He'd nodded along and pretended to understand half the stuff they gossiped about, but now they were due on stage themselves, and they'd left him out here to watch.

He could feel their nerves from here.

Nick tried to feed positive energy into the air.

A hand grabbed the seat-back next to him, then someone swung into the seat beside him.

Nick almost did a double take. Gabriel.

It was enough to shock him out of silence. "What the hell are you doing here?"

"Shh. People are performing."

"You shouldn't be here." Nick's chest felt tight with rage. "This is important. This isn't a *joke*, Gabriel."

"No kidding. Would you calm down?"

"Get out. Now." His breath was shaking and the air had dropped a few degrees. That his brother would *use* this—that Gabriel would show up here—this was—this was—

Nick swallowed and tried to keep it together. "If you mess with him—if you screw this up—I swear to god—"

"I'm not messing with him. And I know it's important."
Gabriel turned away from the stage and met Nick's eyes. "I came
here to support my brother's boyfriend. That okay with you?"

Silence hung between them for the longest moment.

It poked the tiniest hole in Nick's anger. He quickly plugged it
up. "I'm not falling for this."

Gabriel sighed. "All right. Don't, then." He got up, shifted
into the aisle, and started walking toward the exit.

No, he moved down a few rows, easing into a new seat.

Nick sat there and watched him. He could feel his twin's disappointment, his anguish. He felt it himself.

Damn you, Gabriel.

He finally sighed and moved down a few rows to sit beside
his twin brother.

Gabriel offered a wicked smile. "I knew this would get you."

"I hate you."

The smile vanished. "No. You don't."

"I do. A little." Nick faced forward and rubbed at the back of
his neck. A girl in pointe shoes was twirling across the stage.
"You really hurt me. A lot—a lot more than I thought was possible."

"I know. I'm sorry."

Nick didn't say anything. He didn't know if he wanted this
apology.

"I wish I could take it back," Gabriel said. "You have no
idea—"

"Don't. Don't do this here."

Gabriel shut up as if Nick had smacked him. They watched
the next routine in tense silence.

Then Gabriel leaned in. "I read your text messages."

"You *what*?"

Half a dozen people turned around and hushed him.

Nick clenched his fists and glared at Gabriel. "What are you
talking about? When?"

"When you left the phone in the car. At first I just plugged it
in to make sure it wasn't busted. But when it powered up, I saw
it was on the text chat with Adam, so—"

"So you read them?"

Gabriel met his eyes and didn't recoil from his anger. "Those things I said—I didn't mean them. I didn't know, Nicky." He winced. "Nick. I didn't know. I never meant to hurt you."

Nick didn't say anything to that. Was this enough? It didn't feel like enough.

He turned his head and asked the question that had reverberated through his head since the instant he'd felt his twin's fist slam into his face. "How could you, Gabriel?" His whispered voice almost broke. "How could you do what you did?"

"I didn't know what was wrong," Gabriel said, his words rushed, as if he worried Nick would cut him off again. "I didn't know your secret. And then—then this complete stranger was apologizing to me, and I knew you were so upset. It was—that night, it was all wrong. I was keyed up from the fight with Tyler. It was a misunderstanding. And then you were fighting me, and I figured out that you had been keeping this huge monumental secret, and I just—I snapped."

"That's not good enough." Nick gritted his teeth. "You shouldn't have been fighting him. You shouldn't have put your *hands* on him."

"I know. And I apologized to him."

Nick's head was reeling. "What? When?"

"This morning, when I called him and asked what time his audition was."

Nick stared at him.

"I told him not to tell you," Gabriel added. He hesitated. "I didn't think you'd let me come."

Nick wouldn't have. He had to clear his throat. "What else did you talk about?"

"I asked him why you thought you had to keep this a secret from me."

Nick glared at him. "You *know* why. You showed why."

"No." And on this, Gabriel's voice was firm. "I acted like a total shit that night. I apologized for it, and I'll do it a hundred more times if I have to. But you went to a lot of trouble to keep this secret, way before we went to that coffee shop. Jesus, Nick, two weeks ago you and Quinn were making out on the floor of your bedroom."

Nick looked away.

Gabriel leaned close, and his voice was very quiet. "Please. Please, talk to me."

Nick had to swallow. He felt his brother's pain in those words, how much this imposed distance had hurt him. If Nick was being strictly honest with himself, it had hurt him, too. He missed his brother.

He kept his voice very low. "What did Adam say?"

Gabriel grimaced. "He said I needed to ask you."

"I knew you already thought of me as . . . as something *lesser.* I didn't—"

"Nick, you are *not*—"

"Don't. Gabriel, don't."

"I have never thought you were *lesser*, Nick. Never. Do you understand me? Sometimes—sometimes I envy you. Your control—you're stronger than the rest of us."

Nick looked at him. "I am not."

Gabriel nodded. "You are. Look at what happened in the woods."

Nick didn't say anything to that. His eyes fixed on the seat in front of him again.

"Nicky—" Gabriel made a frustrated noise. "*Nick.* If you think you're *lesser* because of the whole gay thing, that's just insane—"

"Is it?" Nick snapped his head around, suddenly furious again. "You made it *so easy* to tell you all about it."

Gabriel flinched. He swallowed. "You're right." He paused. "I was wrong. *So* wrong."

They sat there in silence for the longest time, the air full of music and unspoken thoughts.

Finally Nick cut a glance sideways. "I didn't—I didn't trust you not to let me down. That's why I didn't tell you."

"And when you took a chance, I blew it." He paused. "You needed me. For the first time, you really *needed* me."

Nick looked at him. "Yeah, Gabriel. I did."

Gabriel didn't look away. "I'm sorry." He paused. "Will you give me a chance to make it up to you?"

Nick nodded. "Okay."

He expected Gabriel to hug him, but his brother whipped out his phone and started texting.

Nick watched his fingers fly across the screen. "What are you doing?"

"Telling Hunter to get everyone down here. Aren't Adam and Quinn up soon?"

"Yes—but they'll never get here in time—"

"Sure they will. They're waiting in the back of the auditorium."

"Waiting—what?"

Gabriel finished his message and looked up. "Oh, you didn't think I was coming alone to support your new boyfriend, did you?"

Quinn stood beside Adam and peeked around the corner of the curtain, looking for Nick.

She saw the crowd of people and went rigid. "Holy crap," she whispered. "He brought everyone."

Adam was taking long, slow breaths, watching the dancers before them. "Everyone?"

"Everyone," she breathed. "I told Becca and her mom not to come. But this . . . this is *everyone*."

All of Nick's brothers. Michael's girlfriend. Layne, and her little brother, Simon. Becca and Hunter. Becca's mother, who'd even brought Quinn's little brother.

But not Tyler.

Well, of course not. He and the Merricks hadn't magically become friends. Firing a gun didn't erase years of hatred.

And it wasn't like Tyler had reached out to her, even after Mrs. Chandler had told Quinn about his phone call.

Maybe he saw it as just finishing a good deed and stepping aside.

Adam was fidgeting, smoothing the adhesive number against his shirt for the zillionth time.

Quinn put her hands over his. "You're amazing. You've got this."

"You're amazing," he said back. "Thank you for doing this for me."

She lost her smile. "Thank you for believing in me."

Then the emcee called his number and their music began.

Once the beat caught her, Quinn felt like her world exploded into color. She knew this routine; her muscles had memorized each leap, each turn, each step, but today everything felt new and fresh, as if the music and the crowd added power to their dance.

Adam's hands were strong, catching her perfectly each time, and she matched his height, leap for leap. For the first time, she appreciated the power in her body, reveled in the muscles and the curves and the lines. When Adam did the complicated twist where she went airborne before twirling into his arms, the crowd whooped and whistled. When the music and drums reached a crescendo and he spun her so fast she thought she'd take flight, Adam caught her in midair, right on the beat, and froze.

Silence, for a second. Then the auditorium erupted in applause.

The center judge leaned into her microphone and said, "Thank you."

Adam set her on her feet and kissed her on her cheek. "You were amazing."

The judge leaned forward again and spoke into the mic. "Excuse me. Miss. One moment, please. Young lady."

Adam grabbed her arm. "Quinn. She means you."

Quinn stared out into the lights. "Yes?"

"Please be sure to have your number on for the solo portion."

"Oh! I'm not—I'm not—"

"Here it is!" called a male voice from the edge of the stage. A white sticker was in his hand, and he was holding it up to her. "You left it with me, baby girl."

"Tyler," she whispered. What had he—what—

"Please clear the stage for the next participants," the judge said.

Adam grabbed her hand and dragged her down the steps.

And sure enough, Tyler was standing there, his hair and eyes glinting from the stage lights. Quinn stared up at him, completely at a loss for what to say.

Tyler snorted and dragged her away from Adam, into the darkness of the side aisle. "You with no words," he whispered. "There's a first." He peeled the backing off the adhesive number.

"How did you—what did you—"

"Well," he said, moving close, pressing the number over her abdomen, letting his fingers linger along her waist. "Remember when you said you weren't the type to have a spare hundred dollars lying around?"

She wet her lips. "Yeah."

"Well, maybe I am."

"You signed me up."

"Someone had to." He leaned in, finding her face with his hands, coming close enough to share breath. "And this, I'll let you kiss me for."

"This, I don't *mind* kissing you—"

"Shut up," he said.

Then he leaned in and pressed his mouth to hers.

CHAPTER 36

Nick leaned against his back porch railing, holding Adam's hand, keeping him close. A few boxes of pizza and salad were open on the picnic table and candles were lit everywhere.

It had been a hastily thrown together celebration party.

One full-time scholarship for Adam.

One evening-school scholarship for Quinn.

It was late, and everyone was tired, so conversation was dying and couples were pairing off.

Adam leaned close, until Nick could feel his breath on his neck. "Your family has been nothing but kind to me."

"I know. I love them for it." And he did. But this was still new, and fresh, and he was worried that the instant he let go of Adam's hand, it would all unravel. "Honestly, I don't know if it's more surreal that you're on the deck, or that Tyler is."

Tyler had kept himself at a distance, as if he felt as uncertain about being here in the open as Nick did.

But he treated Quinn with a gentleness that Nick hadn't expected. So when Tyler met Nick's eye and gave him a nod, Nick nodded back.

Again, surreal. And not *nice*, exactly, but . . . okay. Better.

Nick shifted closer to Adam, inhaling his scent, grateful for quiet company and a peaceful evening.

"Is everything okay with your brother?" Adam asked.

Nick nodded. "I think so." He paused, then smiled. "He offered to make out with Hunter if it would prove that he's okay with me being gay."

"Hmm," said Adam. "Yeah. I think I need to see proof."

"Shut up."

"Tell him it has to be shirtless. Wait, let me get my phone out—"

Nick shut him up with a kiss.

A good kiss. A slow kiss. A long one, because they were in the shadows—but really, he didn't care who caught a glimpse.

But then someone did see them, because a wolf whistle split the night. Then another, and Nick broke away, blushing fiercely.

"Okay, okay," he said.

"Not just okay," Adam whispered, his lips close to Nick's ear. "Great, good, fine."

Nick turned his head to pick up where they'd left off. But then something brushed his senses, and the candles suddenly blazed hotter.

He straightened, moving to the middle of the porch with his brothers, their eyes searching the darkness for the threat.

They didn't have to look far. Calla Dean came walking out of the woods, pink and blond hair glinting in the firelight.

"Hello, Merricks," she called, smiling broadly. "I hear you're starting a war."

No one moved.

She stopped in the grass, looking up at the porch.

"Guess what," she said, losing the smile. "I want in."

BEYOND
THE
STORY

AFTERWORD

In *Secret*, Nick deals with the fear and isolation surrounding coming out to his family, while Quinn deals with a dangerous and abusive family environment. Though their stories are fictional, young adults all over the world are living with these same issues—and worse. I want all of my readers to be happy and comfortable and safe, but I know that's not always the case. I know sometimes it feels like it may *never* be the case. Being a teenager means living with people who have control over your life: financially, emotionally, and sometimes physically. Many families are amazing and supportive. Unfortunately, many families are not.

I'm going to plagiarize Dan Savage here, but *it gets better*. I promise you, it gets better. Middle school and high school are full of your peers—but they can also be the most isolating years of your life. You're not alone. I promise. There are many amazing people you have yet to meet, and they will change your life in the most amazing and unexpected ways. I don't ever want a child or young adult or *anyone* to feel that no one cares, or that ending his or her life is easier than continuing to live it. Life is worth waiting for. Trust me. Even though it might not feel like it right now, the world is a huge place, and it's waiting for you. You're so important. Life gets better—a lot better.

If you're distressed, if you're in trouble, if you just need someone to talk to, here are some resources.

The It Gets Better Project—www.itgetsbetter.org

The Trevor Project—www.trevorproject.org
  24/7 free confidential support: 866-488-7386

National Suicide Prevention Hotline—
www.suicidepreventionlifeline.org
  24/7 free confidential support: 1-800-273-TALK(8255)

PFLAG: Parents, Families, and Friends of Lesbians and Gays—
www.pflag.org

SECRET PLAYLIST

"Demons" by Imagine Dragons

While I had many songs that fired up my imagination for Adam and Quinn's dance routine, this one seems to have stuck in my head. It's so perfect for all the relationships explored in the book.

"Hey Pretty Girl" by Kip Moore

The first time I heard this song on the radio, I took a snapshot of my XM display so I could remember to buy it on iTunes. I *knew* it was going to be in this playlist, right from the first listen. Rough, raspy, sexy voice? Swoon-worthy lyrics? I mean, come on. This is the song I imagine Tyler playing for Quinn on his porch, the first night they spend together.

"Same Love" by Macklemore feat. Ryan Lewis

Many, many people suggested that I listen to this song when they found out what I was writing about. I loved it from the first listen. What a fantastic message. What a fantastic melody. I love every word.

"Cough Syrup" by Young the Giant

This song is simply . . . amazing. If you're a *Glee* fan, it's the song that Blaine sings while Karofsky is contemplating suicide after he's unfortunately outed at school. It's a powerful song, and I listened to it on repeat a dozen times while writing some of the more intense scenes with Nick and Adam.

"Get Your Shine On" by Florida Georgia Line

How can anyone not like this song? It's so summertime-good-feeling. "Slide that little sugar-shaker over here . . ." Totally reminds me of Tyler and Quinn.

"Follow Your Arrow" by Kacey Musgraves

This song is all about being who you are and not letting other people's expectations draw your life map. I should have had Adam play it on repeat for Nick.

"#thatPOWER" by will.i.am feat. Justin Bieber

This song really doesn't have much to do with the book. I just listened to it about three bazillion times while writing. There were many times I wanted to get up and start dancing at Starbucks, just listening to this song.

"Bruises" by Train, feat. Ashley Monroe

I loved this song the first time I heard it. When Adam is teaching dance class, this is the song I imagine him using.

"Brave" by Sara Bareilles

If you haven't heard this song, you need to go listen to it immediately. Go on. I'll wait. It's all about standing up to bullying, and it's amazing.

"Stubborn Love" by The Lumineers

This song completely reminds me of Tyler and Quinn. You need to listen to understand.

"All This Time" by OneRepublic

I actually first heard this song on a YouTube video for a girl who owned a horse that everyone said was a complete waste of time, but she ended up training him and riding him all the way through to her B rating in Pony Club. (That's a big deal. Really.) It's a moving song that really makes me think of Nick and Adam, first, but also of Nick's relationship with Gabriel.